Praise for BRUJO, EYE OF THE RAVEN

Pour yourself a glass of Champagne, put a "Do not Disturb" sign on the door and throw your cell phone into the nearest arroyo. Then, open Jann Arrington-Wolcott's fast-paced novel, BRUJO, Eye of the Raven, *and be caught up in a world of obsession, seduction, danger and magic. This tightly plotted, carefully researched, well-written thriller is so riveting you won't be able to move until you've finished the very last page.*—Peggy van Hulsteyn, award-winning author and lecturer

His power as a man enticed her. His power as a sorcerer possessed her. Now only her power as a woman can save her. —Peter Saurberey, USA Network

This masterfully plotted thriller hooked me on page one and took me on an unforgettable journey. The minute I finished it, I was on the phone optioning the movie rights. —Martin Markinson, Producer/Theatre Owner, Helen Hayes Theatre, New York

SENSATIONAL! Once BRUJO *gets hold of you, it doesn't let go! A first-rate thriller!*—It's A Wrap, New Mexico Entertainment Industry Quarterly

Jann Arrington-Wolcott extracts new lifeblood from the Gothic thriller genre in this steamy page-turner! She combines a deep-rooted knowledge of New Mexico with a passion for the exotic and a flair for the dramatic. —Jon Bowman, Editor, *New Mexico Magazine*

I loved this story so much that I cancelled a European vacation to star in the movie version!—Suzanne Somers

This book grabs you by the throat and won't let go, even after the last page is turned. Arrington-Wolcott expertly explores the unbelievable in this authentically researched tale of witchcraft in the American Southwest. —Bobette Perrone, Award-Winning author of *Medicine Women, Curandaras and Women Doctors*

I was totally seduced by BRUJO! Jann Arrington-Wolcott has done an extraordinary job of examining the shadow side of human nature in this engrossing novel. —Christine Hazard, Ph.D, Clinical Psychologist

Jann Arrington-Wolcott's New Mexico-based thrillers are well-researched, brilliantly crafted, and compulsively readable. I'm delighted to recommend BRUJO, Eye of the Raven, *and eagerly awaiting the next one!* —Emmaly Wiederholt, Editor, *Fine Lifestyles Magazine* Santa Fe

For Wonderful, beyond ~ beautiful, Talented Susan!

xoxo

BRUJO

EYE OF THE RAVEN

[signature]

JANN ARRINGTON — WOLCOTT

Cover Design: Antelope Design

This is a work of fiction. Any references to places, events or
people living or dead are intended to add to a sense of
authenticity and to give life to the story. Names, characters
and incidents are products of the author's imagination and
their resemblance to any real-life counterparts
is entirely coincidental.

Pronghorn Press
pronghornpress.org

*This book is dedicated
to my loving and ever-supportive husband
Dr. John H. Wolcott
who for forty-one years has done his best
to keep his fire-walking, vision-questing,
sweat lodge-participating,
adventurous wife grounded.*

SANTA FE, NEW MEXICO

1996

1

She climbed through the darkness along a narrow path that wound close to the cliff's edge. At the top of the mesa, she rested, leaning on her walking stick and gazing out across the moonlit canyon far below. Her heart felt heavy. There was much to do and time was short.

Something small dashed through the thick brush off to her left. A rabbit. They were fat and plentiful that year. Tomorrow she would set her trap and make a stew, using sweet roots and herbs that grew around the Sacred Cave of the Grandmothers. The thought made her mouth water. She was tired from the long climb and had not eaten since early morning.

A familiar boulder stood near the cliff's edge a short distance ahead. Shaped like a crouching bear, it was carved with symbols sacred to the Grandmothers. The cave lay just beyond.

Suddenly, a tall figure stepped from the shadows to block her path. He moved swiftly toward her, the night wind lifting his long black hair. Cold fury radiated from his body. Perched on his shoulder was an enormous raven.

She froze, her throat constricting in terror. There was no escape. Even if her crippled foot would allow it, there was nowhere to run. He had broken an ancient and powerful taboo by coming there. The high mesa was forbidden to all men. His motive was clear.

"You dare to come to this place?" Her voice shattered the silence. He stared at her for a long moment. Although his face remained expressionless, she saw the grief in his eyes. He clapped his hands together. Once. The sound ripped through her heart like an obsidian blade.

With a savage screech, the bird flew at her face. She stumbled backward, trying to shield her eyes. For a moment, strong arms protected her as the man rushed forward and seized her, crushing her to his chest. She felt his lips graze her forehead. Then with an abrupt, brutal motion, he shoved her away.

The ground disappeared beneath her feet. She flung her arms forward clawing empty air as she reached for him. The night sky tilted. She screamed his name, the sound drowning out the croaking of the raven as great jagged rocks rushed up to meet her.

"Lee, wake up!" Nick turned on the bedside lamp. "Honey! You're having a nightmare."

She sat up in bed, staring at her husband. "What?" She removed her foam earplugs. "Oh, God, it was so real."

"It must have been. You were moaning and thrashing around."

"It was one of those terrible dreams I've had for years. I was falling, I think from a cliff. But this time, there was more to it. Someone pushed me. A wild-looking man with long black hair. He had a bird, a huge black bird that attacked me. Slashed my face." Her hand went to her cheek, half expecting to find a bloody wound.

"Good lord," Nick stifled a yawn. "Vivid dreams can be triggered by spicy food. I read that in *Science Today*. Those *chile rellenos* you had for dinner made my eyes water from clear across the table."

"The bizarre thing about this dream was that the man was so familiar. He had a strange name. In fact, I was screaming his name as I fell. I can almost remember it…but then it slips away." She shuddered and pulled the covers up over her shoulders. "I know it must sound silly to you, but it was terrifying."

"Well, it was just a dream. Try to forget it, and go back to sleep."

"I don't think I can." *It was so realistic. The man was wearing some kind of leather outfit. I felt it against my cheek when he grabbed me. And necklaces. He was wearing weird necklaces. They were sharp—like pieces of bone. And the bird, it must have been a raven...*

"Babe." Nick interrupted her thoughts. "Fascinating though your nocturnal adventures might be, I need some sleep. I have an important meeting first thing in the morning." He turned off the light and rolled over.

"Well, excuse me for disturbing you, Dr. Lindsay. I'll try to keep my 'nocturnal adventures' to myself." She moved as far away from him as possible. *Is it too much to expect a little comfort?*

"Oh, come on. Don't be mad. I didn't mean to hurt your feelings. But it's the middle of the night."

Much to her surprise Lee started to cry.

"I don't believe this," Nick said in exasperation as he snapped the light back on.

"Honey, what's the matter with you? You had a bad dream. That's no reason to carry on about it."

"I don't know what's the matter with me! I was just so frightened. I was certain I was going to die in that dream. And then I felt myself falling. It just left me feeling so...sad." She reached for a tissue and blew her nose. "Go back to sleep. I'm okay."

"You sure?"

Lee nodded and Nick quickly turned off the lamp again. Within moments, he was snoring.

She replaced her earplugs, but her sleep was shattered. She lay awake for much of the night, staring into the darkness, replaying the dream in her mind, and wondering why it had shaken her so deeply.

When the alarm went off at six-thirty the next morning, Lee felt as though she had just gotten back to sleep. She forced herself up and into the shower. Half an hour later, still feeling groggy and out of sorts, she was dressed for work and in the kitchen.

Nick soon joined her, briefcase in hand. Tall and trim, he still resembled the handsome graduate student he'd been when she met him twenty years ago. Only the deep lines between his eyes and strands of silver in his blond hair hinted at middle age. At forty-four, Nick was an attractive and vigorous man. He gave Lee a quick kiss on the cheek before pouring himself a cup of coffee.

"Morning, gorgeous."

"Good morning," she said, setting out skim milk, three bowls and several varieties of sugar-free, cold cereal.

"How're you feeling?" he asked. "You had a pretty rough night."

Lee thought about her nightmare—vague memories of sharp talons and dark wings flying into her face. With an effort, she pulled herself back to the present.

"I'm okay. Sorry I disturbed your rest."

"I wasn't sleeping all that well anyway. Kept waking up, worrying about next week's rocket shot." He fixed himself a bowl of cereal before sitting down at the snack bar with the morning paper.

Lee poured two glasses of orange juice.

"Is it an important experiment?"

"It's critical. We're ready to launch that electron accelerator. That is, if bad weather doesn't add more delays." He glanced at his watch, then hurriedly ate his cereal while reading the sports page. His attention was still focused on the box scores when he added, "I have to leave for Fairbanks Friday morning."

"What? You're leaving for Alaska this Friday?"

He nodded, continuing to read while he drank his juice. "Afraid so. I'll need the weekend to get the station set up."

"So you'll miss the Buchanans' housewarming extravaganza Saturday night. I explained to you that it's important to the magazine. They're thinking of opening a second art gallery and they're one of our biggest advertisers."

He looked up at her with a puzzled frown that quickly dissolved into chagrin. "Uh-oh. That completely slipped my mind."

"Oh, hell, Nick," Lee said. "You promised you'd be home, when I accepted their invitation. Bob Buchanan's hobby is astronomy and he's fascinated by your work. He has a new telescope and said he wanted to talk to you about building an observatory. I was counting on you to schmooze him."

He stood up and walked around the snack bar. "I'm sorry, babe," he said, putting his arms around her. "Ray was scheduled to get the equipment set up, but he begged off. Out-of-town company or something. So I volunteered…"

"Of course, you volunteered. As usual."

"I agreed to leave a few days early," he continued, "in order to get things ready. Someone has to do it, and it has to be done right. You understand, don't you?"

"Would it make any difference if I didn't?" She knew she was sounding pouty, but it was just one more thing in a long list of work taking precedence over her.

"Come on, babe, don't make a big deal out of this. I said I was sorry. I'll make it up to you when I get back. Take you to The

Compound for an expensive dinner." He gave her a quick hug and released her.

"When will that be?"

"Oh, a couple of weeks."

"That long?"

"Like I said, this is a big experiment. Our funding for next year may depend on it."

"I see. "

What about the funding for my magazine, she thought, but didn't bother speaking the words. *Of course, that can hardly compete with national security.* She turned her back to him and poured a cup of coffee.

"What's on your agenda for today?" he asked, obviously wanting to change the subject.

"I'm going in to the office for about an hour, get some editing out of the way before my interview."

"Who are you interviewing?"

"Someone in a little village in the mountains."

"Really? How come?"

"I need some local history for an article I'm writing for the January issue. You remember that I'm working with a smaller staff right now—I had two good writers quit on me last month, and haven't found replacements for them yet."

Nick put down the paper and glanced at his watch. "That's not good."

"Are you even listening to me?"

"Of course I am. You're going out to a village for an interview."

"I talked to a man yesterday who gave me a lead…" Her voice trailed off as she saw Nick reach for his briefcase. "Never mind. Go on, I'll tell you about it tonight."

"Okay. Hey, where's Sara? Haven't heard a sound from her this morning."

"She's still asleep. There's a teacher's conference at the high school today, so classes are cancelled. I'm going to meet her downtown for lunch, after my interview."

With a quick wave, Nick was out the door. After clearing the snack bar, Lee hurried up the stairs to finish dressing. Running a brush through her short, naturally curly, blond hair, she peered critically at her reflection. *I look tired.* Her mind immediately returned to her nightmare. She shook her head, attempting to dislodge the disturbing memory. She dabbed a little concealer under her slightly puffy eyes, applied a smear of lipstick and quick coat of mascara. *That'll have to do. I'm running late.*

Grabbing her purse, she crossed the hall to Sara's bedroom.

"Sweetie?" Lee gently shook her sleeping fifteen year old daughter's shoulder. "I'm leaving now. Wendy's mom is dropping you girls off downtown later this morning, right?"

"Uh huh." Sara's voice was muffled with sleep.

"Okay. I'll meet you on the Plaza about one-thirty. Then we'll go somewhere special for lunch. Don't forget to lock the front door when you leave. Oh, and please feed Mister. He's outside stalking lizards. There's an open can of cat food in the fridge."

"Okay. Bye." Sara rolled over, her long brown hair fanning across the pillow.

Lee pulled out of the driveway and headed down the dirt road toward her office, two blocks west of the Plaza. As she drove, her thoughts returned to the Buchanans' party. She wasn't surprised that it had conveniently slipped Nick's mind. He hadn't really wanted to go. It would be the kind of thing he just suffered through when absolutely necessary, a collection of artists, writers, and colorful Santa Fe personalities. The "artsy-fartsy crowd," as he referred to her circle of friends and business acquaintances.

Oh, well, I'm certainly practiced at attending parties alone.

I'll just have to be extra charming to make up for his absence. Whether he understands it or not, socializing with advertisers is a vital part of the magazine business.

And the Buchanans' downtown gallery was one of the most successful in town. If they opened another one, this time on Canyon Road—"The Art and Soul of Santa Fe"—they'd no doubt increase their advertising. *Good news for the magazine.*

Lee pulled in the *Santa Fe Today* parking lot at eight o'clock sharp, noting that Annabel's car was already there. Annabel Garrett, her partner of almost ten years, was a hard worker and excellent editor. The only problem was Annabel's nosiness. She was a busybody, there was no getting around it, but she had a good heart. And, all things considered, they made a darned good team. They had succeeded in building the once floundering magazine into a thriving business with a full time staff of five and a sizeable pool of freelance writers. Lee was proud of what they had accomplished. It hadn't been easy.

Carrying her purse and bulging briefcase, she walked into the remodeled adobe building. Annabel, her stocky figure stuffed into a rhinestone studded denim jumpsuit, was bent over the front desk, shuffling through a pile of papers.

"Hi," Lee said,

Annabel jumped. "I didn't expect you in this morning," she said. "Aren't you interviewing some guy out in the boonies?"

"Not until eleven. I thought I'd edit a few articles first. Is Julie coming in?"

"As far as I know. I was just checking her 'in' box. I see there's a letter from her lawyer." She held it up to the light. "I can't believe that girl's going through another divorce. How many does this make so far?"

"I haven't been counting."

"I think it's at least five. Let's see, there was that flamenco guitar player—he didn't last long, did he? Then there was the bald guy who turned out to be gay. I heard that he..."

"Annabel," Lee interrupted, short on patience. "Julie is the best receptionist we've ever had. She practically runs this office. As long as it doesn't interfere with her work, I really don't think her love life is any of our business."

"My, my. You're a bit testy this morning."

Lee sighed. "I guess I am. Sorry."

"What happened? A fight with Nick?"

"No. I'm just tired. I woke up in the middle of the night and couldn't get back to sleep. Listen, I want to get these articles ready for the typesetter. I'll talk to you later." She hurried into her office.

Two hours later, Lee was driving north. The day was brisk and clear, perfect weather to take a break from the busy office. She'd long been intrigued by the history of the area, and was glad she'd made the decision to handle that story herself, rather than assigning it to one of her reporters.

She passed the sweeping roof of the world-class Santa Fe Opera and began the descent into the wide piñon-dotted Española valley. As always, she was struck by the grandeur of the landscape—a timeless, mystical quality that never failed to move her. Distant mesas loomed in the background like huge sacrificial altars. And beyond, thirty miles to the west, rose the magnificent Jémez Mountains, the forested remnants of an enormous ancient volcano. At their base, perched on a seven-thousand-foot-high plateau, sat Los Alamos, home of the world's first atomic weapons and the famed Los Alamos National Laboratories—Nick's employer since he'd earned his Ph.D. seventeen years ago.

She thought about that isolated scientific community as she drove. They had lived there years ago, when they were first married, in a government built apartment. Soon after Sara was born, Lee had persuaded Nick to move to nearby Santa Fe. The move had been a good one, as far as Lee was concerned. She loved the historic city's sophisticated, artistic ambiance and colorful mix of cultures. After working for several years as a freelance writer, she had bought a half interest in the almost defunct *Santa Fe Today* magazine.

Nick never seemed to mind the commute to Los Alamos. He said the drive gave him time to focus his thoughts. *And he's certainly focused. On his work, that is.*

She turned off the main highway and continued along a twisting, narrow road. In an effort to shake off her depressed mood, Lee popped a cassette into the tape player. Soon she was feeling better and singing along with Kenny Rogers:

Why don't we go somewhere and love
It's been a long, long time.
Why don't we just go somewhere and love
And leave the whole world behind.

Lee was becoming anxious, looking for some sign of civilization. Unless she'd taken a wrong turn somewhere, Cavado shouldn't be much farther. She'd been driving along isolated roads for half an hour and, except for a dilapidated pickup truck carrying a load of firewood, she hadn't seen another vehicle for miles.

The high desert landscape changed dramatically as the narrow road wound steadily higher, climbing past towering sandstone bluffs and rocky ravines into the forested foothills of the Sangre de Cristo Mountains. Rounding a curve, she was relieved to see a service station ahead on the left. She glanced at her gas gauge—almost half a tank, more than enough to get home. Still, she decided, better to play it safe. *It wouldn't do to be stranded in this remote area.* She pulled up beside the self service pump and got out of the car.

Two attendants were leaning against the building, watching her operate the gas pump. One of them, a tall, stoop shouldered Anglo, said something out of the corner of his mouth that caused his Hispanic companion to laugh.

Lee knew that she looked younger than her forty years. She took pride in her trim figure and good looks and usually appreciated the attention that they drew. But this was one of those times when she could have done without it.

The taller of the two men pushed his lanky frame away from the wall and sauntered toward her.

"Mornin'," he said, running his fingers through his disheveled hair in an unsuccessful attempt to tame it. "Need some help with that?"

"No thanks. I can manage."

"Good lookin' car," he said, patting the hood of her silver Subaru and moving closer. "Get good mileage?"

"Not bad." Lee stared at the flashing numbers on the gas pump gauge.

"Four wheel drive?"

"Uh huh."

"That comes in handy in this neck of the woods." Crossing his arms across his chest, he leaned against the car. "You from around here?"

"Santa Fe." Lee shifted her weight, moving away from him.

"Great town. Or used to be, before all them rich folks and movie stars moved in." He shot her a look and grinned, revealing a badly chipped front tooth. "Say, now, you look a little familiar, come to think of it. You some kinda celebrity?"

"I'm afraid not."

"Well, you look like you could be." He took a toothpick out of his shirt pocket and stuck it in the corner of his mouth. "Where you headed?"

Lee tried to ignore the odor of gasoline and stale sweat drifting toward her. With relief, she heard the click of the pump turning off.

"I have an appointment," she said, hanging up the nozzle and securing the cap on the tank. "In Cavado." She got back inside her car and handed him her credit card through the open window.

The attendant took the card and studied her.

"Cavado? That ain't much of a town to be having an appointment in." He chewed thoughtfully on the end of the toothpick. "Just a falling down church, few old houses, and a grocery store. And, of course, El Gallo. That's the name of the bar. Means 'the rooster'." He chuckled. "But you don't want to go in there. Rough spot. No place for a lady like yourself." He narrowed his eyes. "It ain't none of my business, of course, but who'er you seeing in Cavado?"

She hesitated. As a writer, she had learned to gather all the information she could, even from unlikely sources. "Juan Mascareñas," she replied. "Do you know him?"

"Sure, I know Juan. Everybody around here knows everybody else. But I have to say, you don't look like the sort that would be visiting him."

"What do you mean?"

"Just that you don't look like someone who would be seeing a *curandero*."

"A what?"

"A *curandero*. You know, a healer." He bent his head near the open window. "Well, at least they claim to be healers. They chant some kind of mumbo jumbo, and make medicines out of weeds. Most of the villagers swear by them. But me, I steer clear of that sort of thing. I ain't about to be treated by some witch doctor!" He laughed, blasting her with stale cigarette breath.

"Yes, I've read a bit about *curanderismo*. But I'm not going for any treatment. I'm interviewing him for an article I'm writing."

"A writer, huh? What kind of books do you write?"

"I write magazine articles. And I was told that Mr. Mascareñas would be able to fill me in on the history of this area."

"I guess so. After all, his people was here before God.

Descended from the *conquistadors*, they say. They grabbed up most of the land around here long ago and held onto it. Fact is, old Juan owns damn near all of Cavado. Got more money than he knows what to do with. Guess that's why he acts so high and mighty."

"He sounded nice enough on the phone."

"Yeah, he has fancy manners. But don't be fooled. He's way on the strange side. Be right back."

Lee watched him walk inside the station to write up the transaction. She reached for her note pad and wrote *Mascareñas —curandero?*

"Here you go," the attendant said, returning to the car. "Sign right here."

"How much farther is Cavado?"

"Couple miles. Just take that dirt road up ahead that cuts off to the right. You'll see a sign."

"Thanks." Lee started the engine and waited for him to move away from her car. Then she rolled up the window and drove away, following the winding track that passed for a road.

2

The road snaked up a hill and crested to reveal a village nestled in the valley below. The entire community consisted of no more than a dozen adobe buildings, their corrugated tin roofs shaded by ancient cottonwood trees. In the center stood the small adobe church. The weathered wooden cross on its bell tower leaned precariously to one side, giving the building a forlorn, forgotten look.

I'll run a photo of that church with the article, Lee decided. *It doesn't look like a thing has changed here for centuries. Not much action in Cavado.*

A raven circling above the silent village caught Lee's eye. It flew toward her, then swooped down, landing on a dead piñon branch about fifteen yards ahead. She slowed to look at it, feeling a chill. The bird evoked memories of her dream. *That's a huge raven. I've never seen one anywhere near that size.*

She pulled over to the side of the road and reached into the back seat for her camera case. A photographer had been assigned to the story, but she might as well take a few shots of her own. *A village untouched by time. That'll be my angle.*

Camera in hand, she walked down the road toward the raven. It watched her approach with unblinking eyes. *That's odd, that bird doesn't seem the least bit afraid of me. I wonder if it's tame?* She removed the lens cover and focused her camera. An instant after she took its picture, the raven flapped powerful wings and took flight. Soaring in a wide circle above her, it dropped toward the village and disappeared into the trees.

Lee continued walking. *This is a beautiful spot. Maybe I can drag Nick up here some Sunday for a picnic. Just the two of us. It's been I-don't-know-how-many years since we've done anything romantic like that.*

As she snapped shots of the village, Lee was struck by how quiet it was. *Too quiet. Where is everyone? Isn't anybody home in Cavado?* She detected no sound, no movement at all, not even a barking dog. Her uneasy feeling returned. I'd better locate Mascareñas, she thought, glancing at her watch. *Almost eleven o'clock.*

She hurried back to the car and drove down the hill. On the outskirts of the village, she saw an orchard of gnarled apple trees. Across the road stood a lifeless cottonwood tree, one side charred as though struck by lightning. Behind the tree was a small, ancient-looking adobe house.

Lee stopped to consult her directions: Five miles on dirt road—just before entering the village, first house on left. *This must be the place.* She parked beside a late model black pickup truck. *Boy, talk about the middle of nowhere.... That tree should be cut down before it falls over.*

She swung out of the car and took several more pictures, almost finishing the roll of film. Then she gathered her purse and what she would need—notebook, her favorite pen, tape recorder, a copy of the magazine—and walked up the dirt path to the house.

The front door was decorated with a string of garlic. *To keep away werewolves? Or is it vampires?* Lee tried to joke with herself, as she knocked on the wooden door, its weathered surface barely able to remember it had once been painted black. She glanced at the bleached canine skull grinning up at her from the top of a large dirt-filled clay pot beside the door. *That was one big dog. Or perhaps a wolf?* She took a deep breath and knocked again.

The door was opened by a tall, well built man wearing tight black jeans, snakeskin boots and a white Western shirt. His straight black hair was longish, covering his ears and shirt collar in the back, and showing a few white hairs near his temples.

"Señora Lindsay," he said in the deep voice that Lee remembered from their telephone conversation the day before. "I'm Juan Mascareñas. Please, come in."

Lee stepped across the worn wooden threshold into a dimly lit room. She blinked, waiting for her eyes to adjust.

"I appreciate your taking the time to see me, Mr. Mascareñas."

She extended her right hand and he grasped it firmly in both of his. As her vision sharpened, she noticed a half-inch long, reddish birthmark just under his left cheekbone. Shaped like a spider, it appeared to be crawling toward his neck. She suppressed a shudder.

Then she realized that he was older than his athletic appearance had first led her to assume. A deep network of lines creased his forehead and radiated from the outer corners of his eyes. *He must be in his early to mid-fifties. Obviously in good shape. Interesting face—handsome, actually, with those high cheekbones, aristocratic nose, and eyes so dark they appear to be black.*

Lee's smile wavered. Feeling ill at ease, she withdrew her hand.

"As I explained on the phone, *Santa Fe Today* is featuring articles on several villages in the area," she said. "Mr. Archuleta at the Española Chamber of Commerce suggested that I talk to you. He said that you're an authority on local history."

"Ah, yes. It is a small passion of mine. I will try to be of assistance. Please, come in."

Lee followed him into an even dimmer second room, noticing that the window shades were tightly closed. The only light emanated from several flickering candles. She looked around with growing interest. The room was filled with what appeared to be antique Spanish Colonial furniture. It was also cluttered with a startling collection of animal skulls, bones and various kinds of hides. A pair of black wings at least four feet wide were nailed to a wooden frame above a darkened window. *They grow ravens big out here!*

He helped her out of her jacket and hung it from a wooden peg on the wall. "Sit there," he said, indicating a sofa covered with a beautiful, but worn blanket. *Navajo, I would guess. An old Two Grey Hills pattern.*

Lee sat down, arranged her notebook and tape recorder beside her, then looked up. Resting on a table, just inches from her arm, was a diamondback rattlesnake, curled around two large, jagged, turquoise rocks. She let out a squeal, instinctively sliding away.

Juan chuckled. *"Descansa, Señora,* have no fear. *El serpiente* can not harm you. He is no longer in his body."

Lee hesitated, still squinting in the candlelight, before moving cautiously forward for a closer look. It was, indeed, just a carefully positioned mummified rattlesnake, its dried head and long string of rattles still attached.

Her voice trembled when she spoke. "You know, that's really not funny, Mr. Mascareñas. Someone could have a heart attack."

"If so, it would be no problem. I could cure them."

Oh, yikes, that gas station guy was right. This character is beyond weird. I'm going to make this as short as possible and get the hell out of here. Heart still pounding, she moved herself and her things to the opposite end of the couch, as far from the snake as possible.

"Former pet of yours?"

Juan smiled. "A pet? No, I wouldn't say that. Like all creatures, he was my brother." He seated himself across from her in a straight chair, stretching his long legs out in front of him.

"I see." Lee took a deep breath, fighting to control a rapidly escalating apprehension. Weird or not, she needed his input for her story if she was going to meet her own deadline. And she had never missed a deadline.

He sat quietly, studying her. The expression on his face was intense but unreadable.

No one knows where I am, she suddenly realized, not even Annabel. *I just referred to a small village outside of town—not even specifying which direction.*

She clenched her right hand, which had been tingling since Mascareñas released it. *Of course, Mr. Archuleta knows I was coming here. He just didn't know when. Surely he wouldn't have recommended this guy if he wasn't on the level. As an historian, anyway. So, get a grip, Lindsay. And do your job.*

"Are you familiar with *Santa Fe Today?*" She handed him a copy of the latest issue. "It has a circulation of fifteen thousand and is distributed throughout New Mexico, parts of Arizona and…"

"I have read the magazine," he interrupted, dropping it without so much as a glance onto the floor beside his chair. His eyes narrowed slightly as he studied her face.

"Oh. Well, that's good. Mr. Mascareñas…"

"Call me Juan. Please. And your first name is Lee. I remember from our telephone conversation.

"That's right." She tried not to squirm under his steady gaze. "First, I'd like a little background information on you, Juan, if you don't mind," she said, trying to ease into the interview. "I understand you're a *curandero?*"

He stiffened and his voice turned to ice. "Understand this, Señora. There is to be no publicity about me or my work. I agreed only to discuss the history of my village." He rose to his feet.

"Of course," she said quickly. "That's what I'm here for—

to talk about Cavado. Excuse me. I didn't mean to pry. I was only making conversation."

Juan moved across the room to a small hot plate where a teapot simmered. "*Bueno*, Lee," he said smoothly. "No need to apologize. May I offer you some tea?"

Relieved that the interview wasn't going to be terminated, Lee nodded. "Yes, thank you. My throat is a bit dry." She swallowed hard. *That was close. What a strange, touchy man! And this place is straight out of a horror movie.*

Juan handed her a steaming stoneware cup. As he leaned toward her, candlelight reflected off a heavy chain hanging around his neck. Lee got a glimpse of something silver hanging from it, hidden beneath his shirt. Then her gaze moved up to the spider-shaped birthmark on Juan's cheek. Something uncomfortable stirred in the back of her mind.

"Drink this," Juan said. "It will be good for you." He sat down again, facing her, watching as she took her first sip of the tea.

She tried not to make a face at the unexpectedly bitter taste. Instantly, her mouth and tongue began to tingle.

"I don't think I've had this particular tea before," she said. "What is it?"

"A special blend promoting strength and good health. It's from an old family recipe and tastes better after a few swallows."

Not wanting to appear rude, she forced another sip. The tea did, indeed, taste a little less bitter. In fact, it warmed her throat pleasantly. Reluctant to set the cup on the wooden arm of the antique sofa, she held it in her lap.

"Do you mind if I tape our interview?" she asked. Seeing him stiffen again, Lee began to talk faster. "I find that it helps me to keep my facts straight. Also, it's a little dark in here, and it would be easier than taking notes."

He leaned back in his chair. "*Bueno*. Use the recorder. Now, how may I help you?"

Lee punched the record button. "Well, for starters, how did the village get its name? What does Cavado mean?"

"It is both a Spanish and a Portuguese word," he said with a slight shrug of his shoulders. "It means sunken, hollow, concave. I suppose they named it for this spot where the village sits. But it may have had another name, long ago. There is a legend that this area was sacred to the Ancient Ones, the Anasazi, but for what reason, we do not know."

"That's interesting."

He nodded. "There are many secrets that are best left undisturbed." A small smile played at the corners of his mouth. Then it was gone.

Lee was dismayed to find that her hand was shaking slightly as she again brought the tea to her lips. She took another quick drink, hoping he hadn't noticed the disconcerting effect he was having on her.

"Could you tell me a little about the village?" she asked. "What's the population? I didn't see anyone on the streets down there when I drove in."

"At last count, it was sixty-three."

"You know the exact number?"

He nodded. "Cavado has always been a tightly knit community. Sadly, times have changed here. Like most of these small mountain villages, it is slowly dying as it loses its population. A man can no longer make a living by working a small plot of land. So while some commute to jobs in Taos or Española, many have moved away."

He shook his head sadly. "This was a lively place when I was a boy. But most of the houses around the plaza are now deserted, crumbling with neglect. And the plaza itself is overgrown with weeds. Only ghosts meet there now, after sunset, to talk of the old days."

"Are you saying that Cavado is haunted?"

"All places are haunted by the events and personalities of the past," he assured her.

She stared at him, puzzled. There was something about him, something vaguely familiar. In brief flashes she thought he reminded her of someone. But she couldn't quite place who that might be. She was both uncomfortable with him and at the same time, drawn to him.

"Of course our concept of time is just an illusion," he was saying. "Actually, the past, the present and the future all coexist in the Spirit World."

She frowned. "What? I'm sorry, I'm afraid you lost me there."

"I was just saying that there are many simultaneous realities."

"That's an interesting theory." She drank more tea to give herself time to think. Her mind felt strangely muddled. She cleared her throat, determined to get the interview back on track. "When did your family arrive here?"

"My forefathers came to this area from Spain in the mid-1600s, before the great Pueblo Revolt in 1680." He settled back in his chair, his eyes never leaving her face. "The local Natives were traditionally peaceful, but they tired of Spanish rule and of the forced conversion to Christianity. When they finally rebelled, they killed about four hundred Spaniards. Most of the Mascareñases managed to escape the massacre by fleeing south, to what is now El Paso. They returned after the reconquest by Don Diego de Vargas some twelve years later. We have been here, farming and ranching, since that time.

"So your family played an important role in the colonization of New Mexico."

He nodded. "The Mascareñas family roots are firmly attached to this rocky soil."

Lee leaned back against the sofa, feeling less tense. Although the setting was unnerving, the meeting was finally beginning to feel more like an interview. And Juan certainly knew his history.

"It's difficult to imagine the hardship and isolation the early settlers had to endure in order to settle this land," she said.

He shook his head. "You speak as though they succeeded in their efforts. That is an illusion, Señora. This land will never be settled, and it will never be conquered. These hills will tolerate and sustain us only as long as we respect them. We are guests here, not conquerors."

Lee stared at him, intrigued by the passion in his voice. She glanced down to make certain that her tape recorder was running. *That would be a great quote.*

"But you are right," he continued. "There was much hardship to be endured in those days. Drought and disease were frequent visitors. The Spanish learned many survival skills from the Natives of nearby pueblos, who brought gifts of food and medicinal herbs. And, because of the isolation, many old Spanish traditions and Native American beliefs have melded and endured here in Cavado."

Lee felt herself continue to relax as Juan talked, elaborating on the history of the area and telling anecdotes about his ancestors' lives. A feeling of peace and well being settled over her and she listened enthralled, as he went on to describe his strong attachment to the land.

"You must understand that Cavado is a very special place," he said at one point. "You can trust me when I tell you it is a highly spiritual place, a source of great power. It has been so since prehistoric times..."

He was interrupted by a knock at the door and politely excused himself to go into the front room. Lee turned off her tape recorder. She could hear a woman's voice and although her Spanish was minimal, she understood that the woman was ill. Lee strained to hear Juan's answer, but much of his rapid Spanish was incomprehensible to her.

He reappeared and filled a small plastic bag with a brown powdered substance that was stored in a jar on a shelf near the door. Then he returned to the front room. Lee heard him tell the woman to go home and rest. He would see her again tomorrow morning. The woman thanked him, and their voices grew muffled as Juan escorted her out of the front door and away from the house.

I guess he *is* some sort of healer, Lee thought, looking up at the bunches of herbs and plants hanging from the *vigas* above her. *I wonder how many people he treats? And for what ailments?* She looked at her watch. *Eleven-thirty! How can it be that late?* She'd been talking to Juan for thirty minutes. Strange, it didn't seem like that much time could have passed.

She frowned, trying to remember if she'd gotten the information she needed. She glanced through the carefully prepared questions in her notebook. *We covered the early history...relationship with Native Americans...drought and other hardships...the present day population...*

Heat radiated from a small wood-burning stove under the window. The dark room seemed to envelop Lee, making her feel drowsy. She yawned and leaned back against the sofa, closing her eyes.

She sat up with a start when Juan returned, shocked to realize that she had dozed off.

"I...I was just...resting my eyes," she said, feeling heat spread to her cheeks. She hoped the dim light in the room would keep him from noticing.

He paused by the sofa, looking down at her. Then, without a word, he retrieved her empty cup from the floor where she had put it and placed it on the table. He opened the drawer of an antique carved desk and withdrew a sheet of paper before returning to his chair. She turned her tape recorder back on, preparing to continue the interview.

"Turn the recorder off now," he said in a quiet voice. "And put away your notes." His dark eyes fastened on hers, willing her to obey.

"I..." Her voice died in her throat and she found herself doing as he instructed.

"I want to read something to you," he said. "Something I have written. I hope it will help you to understand who I am."

Juan's voice was low and intimate, caressing the words as he read:

I am night in the sleeping desert
I am morning on the windswept bluff

I beat my wings and fly through the ages
I am yesterday and all tomorrows to come
Look beyond what you see and you will know me
You will hear the song of my heart
And answer my voice as it awakens
Sleeping memories in your soul.

He finished reading and looked up at her. His eyes seemed to burn into hers.

"Do you understand what I'm saying?"

"That's beautiful."

"But do you *understand?*" His voice held a note of urgency.

"I…I guess I do." She felt confused, unable to think. *What exactly am I supposed to understand?*

"I knew you would." He moved his chair closer to her and leaned forward. "Look at me closely, Lee. Let me explain. I know many things about you. You are not simply who you appear to be. Trust me. There is a part of you that is yearning to be set free, to soar through the air and reconnect with the energies of the earth."

Lee tried to think of an appropriate response. Her head felt weightless, as though it might detach from her body and float away. She watched the candlelight play across Juan's face—his prominent cheekbones, his finely molded nose, and his full sensuous lips.

He smiled and scooted his chair even closer, until their knees were almost touching, taking one of her hands in both of his.

"I feel many things stirring in you," he said. "I feel your spirit struggling to be complete."

She experienced only a mild shock that he was holding her hand. Managing to unlock her eyes from his, she glanced toward the tightly closed window, wanting to open it. The air in the room felt oppressively warm and heavy.

"Look at me," he commanded sharply. "Don't look away. You are a special person, one who was given great gifts. When you free yourself of the burdens that hold you back, those gifts will blossom again. It is time now. It is time for you to get in touch with who you really are and to experience the powers that exist within you. You've been feeling the need to explore your spirituality, haven't you?"

Lee felt only a muted surprise at the strange turn the interview had taken.

"Yes...I..." she admitted. "How do you know that?"

"As I said, I know many things about you. But please, elaborate for me. In what way does the metaphysical interest you?"

"Well..." She struggled to gather her thoughts into some sort of coherent form. It was proving difficult. "I've always believed that ...that there is more to life than just the day-to-day world...the world we get caught up in." She knew she was speaking slowly, searching for words, but was unable to do anything else. "But for years I've been so...busy...publishing the magazine, raising my daughter and running a home. Lately, I've been thinking about...about setting aside some time to develop neglected...aspects of myself."

Her mind felt like it was operating on two levels, thoughts speeding by on one track encompassing all her deepest feelings about spirituality, and on the plane where she was trying to answer Juan's questions, things moved as slow as molasses.

"I guess...you'd say the spiritual aspects," she finally managed.

"Yes," he said firmly. "Yes, it is time. You have wisdom and powers that you are not yet aware of. Trust me. I can help you discover them." He leaned forward and took her other hand, holding both of them tightly. "I have a feeling that you have experienced other planes of reality," he continued. "Am I correct?"

Lee hesitated, flustered by the sudden intimacy that had developed between them and at the same time aware of a deep longing for that connection. She started to remove her hands, but Juan squeezed them encouragingly—all the while staring into her eyes. She swallowed hard.

"I...I'm sorry. What did you ask me?"

He smiled. "If you have experienced other planes of reality."

"Oh ..." she began, vaguely surprised by her willingness to confide in him, "I haven't...I haven't talked to many people about this...." *It would be such a relief if I could.*

"When I was a child I had some strange experiences." She hesitated, then forced herself to forge ahead. "Sometimes I felt I could leave my body. I'd float away from it, especially when things were upsetting at home." She shook her head, remembering. "It scared me...really scared me. I thought I was going crazy. I was only nine or ten years old." In her mind she could clearly picture the child she'd been. "I finally talked to a school counselor. She said that I had an over-active imagination and should just stop if it frightened me. So I did. I stopped, except...every now and then... As I grew older, I lost the ability." She was having real trouble getting words from her brain to her mouth. "I remember that feeling of detached freedom..." Her voice trailed off. "I sometimes wonder if I could learn to do it again."

She laughed, a soft, nervous laugh. "I don't know why I'm telling you this. I know it must sound bizarre...." She looked down at his large brown hands holding her smaller pale ones. She realized she had no desire to pull away.

"Lee, look at me. It doesn't sound bizarre. I am familiar with what you describe. I've heard so-called Anglo psychics call it astral projection, Natives call it soul travel. As children, we all remember much that we later forget. We lose important knowledge as we grow older and more attached to our current lives."

"Current lives?" *Is he talking about reincarnation?*

"We have all lived many lives," he said, "lives that influence who we are today. I think that your Deep Self knows this to be true."

She stared at him, fascinated. She couldn't take her eyes from his lips as they formed his words.

"I sense that you've had other spiritual experiences," he continued. "Tell me about them. Trust me. Share them."

Lee watched, fascinated, as he placed one of her hands on his knee and began caressing her forearm.

"You can trust me," he repeated.

It seemed as though time had shifted into slow motion. But she hardly knew this man. *Why am I letting him touch me like this?* And yet she felt no inclination to pull away. She wanted to hear more.

His eyes again captured hers, stilling the warning bell that was sounding faintly in her head.

"I…I don't know what's the matter with me," she stammered, "I keep losing my train of thought."

"You were describing your spiritual experiences."

"Oh… Yes…." She tried to recapture those thoughts and, with a sense of forced concentration, continued. "Something strange happened about twelve years ago. It was…something I've never been able to forget." She found herself eager to share what she'd always considered to be a very private experience. "You see…well, you need to understand…it was a rather rocky period in my life…before I bought the magazine."

It almost felt as though she was back there, back when her daughter was small, and her husband was gone most of the time.

"Nick's a scientist…." Suddenly, she found herself feeling she needed to defend him. "And his work…it's important and requires a lot of travel. I'm used to it now, but it was hard in those days." She shook her head, trying to focus. "Nick was out of the country… an experiment somewhere—New Zealand, I think—when I got word that my parents had been killed in a car accident." She felt emotions bubbling to the surface that she couldn't seem to control. "I took it very hard."

"You were close to your parents?"

She sighed and blinked back tears. "Very close to my mother. Dad had a lot of problems." She hesitated. "…an alcoholic… That's what caused the accident…too much to drink at a party. It was a head-on collision. Five people died…instantly…including my mother."

There was a long pause as she recalled the terrible days following the accident. "Dad died two days later."

Juan's expression was sympathetic. "You suffered much from that. Trust me, I understand loss."

"It was…" How could she tell him how deeply it had affected her? "It was a really difficult time. I started taking tranquilizers and sleeping pills…" Lee's arm tingled where Juan was stroking it. She forced herself to concentrate on what she was saying. "The pills left me feeling groggy…even more depressed. I realized I was on a dangerous downward spiral…."

He nodded. "You listened to your inner wisdom. Tell me how you changed your path."

She looked up at him but she was hearing her own voice, as if from a distance.

"I enrolled in a yoga class…then a meditation class." She stopped, feeling a little embarrassed. *What is making me say this to a stranger?* "Do you really want to hear this?" Her eyes searched his, longing for confirmation.

"Yes, very much," Juan assured her as he again took her free hand in his. "We all need someone to confide in, Lee. You can trust me."

She licked her bottom lip. Her mouth felt dry and her throat was tight.

"The classes…they really did help. I learned to relax myself to sleep at night and stopped all the pills." She suddenly felt a need to convince him that she had been serious about her metaphysical practice. That she'd been good at it. *He has to understand.*

"I was very good at meditation. I practiced with a candle… staring at the flame and trying to block out all thoughts. Then I would close my eyes and hold the image of the flame in my mind." She stopped and closed her eyes, remembering. She felt as if she were falling back into the experience itself. She groped for control but it was like swimming up from a murky depth, trying to reach the surface and the light, which remained just above her head, no matter how she struggled.

"I'm so thirsty," she managed to say. "Can I have some water?"

"You need more tea." He refilled her cup with the steaming liquid and returned. Again, he took her free hand and looked deep into her eyes.

"Now, please, continue," he said.

Lee sipped the tea. It soothed her throat and warmed her chest as it went down. She closed her eyes, absorbed by the sensation. When she opened them, he offered his other hand. She set her cup on the arm of the sofa and, without hesitation, took it. There was something very validating in the way he listened so intently.

"I get emotional just thinking about this."

"There is nothing wrong with feeling emotions," Juan said, taking her other hand and giving them both a gentle squeeze. "Trust me when I tell you that when we cut off our emotions, we cut off our Power."

His words touched something deep inside Lee, something that had been neglected for a very long time. Shaken by what she was feeling, she tried to look away, but Juan squeezed her hands more firmly, bringing her eyes back to his.

After a moment, she took a deep breath, torn by conflicting emotions. She couldn't understand what made her want to share these things, but she felt compelled by an unfamiliar sense of something close to desperation.

"One night while I was meditating…" she began, tentatively. "I've tried to tell myself that it was just a dream…but it was so vivid. It felt more like a memory than a dream."

She pulled one of her hands from his and took another fortifying drink of tea before continuing. She quickly took his hand again. She could feel his touch steadying her.

"I was small, just a child. I was sitting on the bank of a shallow stream with a group of other children and several women." The scene formed in her mind with startling clarity. She could feel the warmth of the sun on her face as she kicked her feet in the water, laughing.

"There was a woman with long black braids and a kind face kneeling beside me, filling a large clay pot with water. I remember that the pot was decorated with black rectangular designs," she told him. "The woman turned to smile at me, and I knew she was my mother. I felt very happy…" Lee's voice broke.

As she fought back tears, Juan gently squeezed both her hands in encouragement.

"A moment later," Lee continued, "I heard a scream. My mother pushed me down in the tall grass and crouched there beside me, looking toward the opposite stream bank. She motioned for me to stay where I was hidden. Then she crawled a few feet away. I lifted my head and saw men splashing through the water, coming toward us.

"From my hiding place in the deep grass, I saw my mother get to her feet and start to run. I saw a man—he was almost naked and had long, filthy-looking hair—running after her. He tackled her and threw her to the ground. A moment later he made an angry, snarling sound and moved on.

"My mother didn't get up."

As she spoke, the scene became even more intense and a wave of strong emotions engulfed her. She felt as though she were reliving it.

"I scrambled over to her. Her eyes were open and staring up at the sky. I shook her shoulder and her head rolled to one side and I saw the blood. It was all over the back of her head and on a sharp rock beneath it. I was old enough to know that she was dead." Lee could feel herself throw her little body across her mother's, crying.

"The grief I felt was unbearable, so intense that I jerked myself awake. Only I didn't think I'd been asleep."

For a long moment, she didn't say anything. Juan again squeezed her hands. She was slowly lifted from the flow of her emotions and able to continue.

"The scene was so painful and real that it made me wonder if I'd been reliving some past life. It really scared me. I stopped meditating after that, but the memory still haunts me. Lately, I've been thinking of trying it again...to see if I could remember anything else."

There was a pause and she slipped her hands from his. All the while, Juan's eyes never faltered, studying her. When he spoke, he seemed to be choosing his words with care.

"The veil between lifetimes is thin, Lee, and certain events can cause it to lift. The loss of your mother in this lifetime triggered the memory of a much older loss." He paused. "Some people have the ability to summon deep memories at will. I knew at once that you were one of those people."

"Really?" She found this intensely pleasing. "How?"

"I could feel it. I have an ability to know things. In fact, you'd be surprised at how much I know about you."

"Like...?" Lee reached for the tea and swallowed the last of it.

"Well, for example, I know that you have been through some health crisis recently. Am I correct?"

Lee blinked in surprise. She thought about the frightening appointment with her gynecologist several months ago. A lump in her breast had turned out to be a harmless cyst.

"I...I did have a recent scare," she said. "How could you know that?"

Juan smiled and reached once more for her hand. Without hesitation she took his, and immediately felt herself relax.

"I also know that you have a great connection to this land and a special communication with our animal brothers. Is that not true?"

His eyes were so dark in the dim room that they seemed to draw her soul in to their very depths. She tried to focus and answer.

"Yes. I do love this part of the country...and I've always been an animal lover. As a teenager, I spent weekends and summers working for a veterinarian." She paused a moment as images of the clinic flowed through her consciousness. "He used to say that I had a real gift for comforting sick animals."

"Ah, yes," Juan said with a reassuring smile. "I would have expected that. You have always had many pets."

"Yes...I was continually bringing home stray cats and dogs. It drove my poor mother to distraction." The images in her mind shifted to her childhood on the farm in southern Colorado. To her horse. "I had a horse...Moonbeam...a beautiful little palomino...my best friend until I left for college."

"And now? What lucky animals share your life these days, Lee Lindsay?"

She returned his smile. "Just one cat. He's unique...we're extremely close. My husband says...he says Mister and I read each other's minds."

"I wouldn't be surprised." His expression changed, becoming thoughtful. "There is no doubt. Trust me, you are ready, ready to awaken the powers within you. Listen to your Deep Self. It is telling you that the time has come."

"Hmmm..." She found herself unable to look away. "How would I do that...awaken my powers, I mean?"

"I will help you. I will guide you." He fixed her with a long, searching look. "But you must trust me, or you might lose your way. Do you trust me?"

Lee nodded. Without understanding why, she felt complete confidence in this compelling man whom she had met less than an hour before. On another level, she wondered why she felt no fear, no resistance.

"What will you do? I mean...guide me through what?"

"Through an ancient ritual. A ritual almost as old as these mountains. Its true name cannot be spoken, but loosely translated it means 'the Ceremony of Awakening'." He paused, watching her closely. "It requires great trust. The ritual consists of three parts, beginning with a sweating ceremony."

Something she had seen in *National Geographic* briefly slipped through Lee's consciousness and was gone.

"This ceremony is very different from those you have read about. It is far older. And far more powerful."

Is he reading my mind? I didn't mention that article....

"It involves anointing the body with a special oil and lying under a ceremonial sweat blanket," Juan continued. "The blanket is then tightly rolled, preserving the sweat and evil spirits that have been cast off." He shrugged. "Perhaps I should use a more modern expression, like 'self-doubt' or 'negative mindset'. The meanings are the same."

Lee stared at him. What a fascinating contradiction he was. One moment he seemed an archaic medicine man, the next he sounded quite contemporary.

"You look surprised," he said with a slight smile. "Perhaps I should explain that I became familiar with such terms when I studied psychology at the University of New Mexico."

"Psychology?" *Does that explain how he has drawn me into opening up like this?*

"For two years...until I realized that there is more wisdom in the old ways."

He released her hand and Lee again leaned back against the sofa. She wished she could kick off her shoes and make herself more comfortable. Her eyelids felt heavy.

"Tell me more about the Awakening Ceremony. What happens after the sweating part?" she asked.

"After the first ritual, on the night of the next full moon, I will shake the blanket to the four directions, freeing you of all you have cast off and preparing you for the spiritual awakening to come. That part of the ceremony will not require your attendance. In fact, I must conduct it alone." He hesitated. "This is a very important step, Lee, and should not be undertaken lightly. Trust me when I say that opening your awareness will change your life. But you must want it. You must desire the knowledge that comes with the awakening."

Lee was intrigued, and found herself eager to take this spiritual step forward. In that moment, there was nothing she wanted more.

He paused, watching her. "Then there is a final ritual, a most powerful ceremony. But we will speak of that later. If you trust me, tell me this is what you desire."

"Yes," Lee said. "Please...."

"Very well. First, you must be made ready. You must be cleansed of the limitations you've imposed on yourself. Perhaps then you will be strong enough to commune with the spirits who await you on the other side."

Lee felt relieved. He would help her. She relaxed and raised her hand to her mouth, covering a yawn.

"Trust me. I will lead you through the ceremonies and bring you to a place that will allow you to be in touch with your true identity," Juan continued. "You will gain new strength and wisdom." He leaned forward in his chair, his eyes fastened on Lee's. "This is a strong time for the ceremony," he said. "The moon will soon be full. We should do it now."

Her head nodded and Lee forced herself into a more upright position, fighting the languor that had completely enveloped her.

"Now?" She shook her head in an effort to find some clarity. "Oh, I...I can't...I mean...I don't have time. I have to..." *What was it I have to do? Sara! I have to meet Sara. How could I have forgotten?* She squinted, trying to read the dial on her watch. What time was it? The hands blurred and swam before her eyes. "I could make an appointment...come back later..."

"It's just twelve o'clock. The ceremony should only take half an hour. Trust me, Lee. This is important. We have time to do it now."

Although his voice was gentle and coaxing, Lee detected determination in his eyes.

"Your Deep Self knows that this is something you need, Lee. Listen to it. You want this. You need this. Trust me."

"I…I suppose I could…" she heard herself saying. Her voice sounded very far away.

Juan rose to his feet. "You must change into a ceremonial garment," he said, as he removed a rolled packet from under the table and unwrapped a folded length of buckskin.

She looked from the leather back to him in confusion.

"Can't I…just wear my own clothes?"

"I'm afraid not. The ritual must be conducted in the ancient, sacred way."

Lee hesitated, feeling a faint flutter of fear. *Do I really trust this man? Why should I trust him?* Their eyes met again and Lee felt her doubts dissolving and drifting away. Her mind seemed to be working on two levels, one logical, the other caught up in the charismatic power of this strange man before her. *If it's the "sacred way," it must be all right. And I want this. I need this. What harm can it do?*

"Where can I change?" she asked, rising unsteadily to her feet. "Do you have a bathroom?"

"I have only a portable toilet. You are welcome to use it."

Lee followed him into a small room. He gestured toward a toilet in the corner. "It doesn't flush, but there is no need for embarrassment between us." He handed her the folded deerskin.

"Remove all of your clothing," he instructed. "Everything."

"Even my underwear?"

"This is a ceremonial garment. To wear it with ordinary clothing would weaken its medicine." He turned and left her alone.

Alarmingly off balance and lightheaded, Lee leaned against the wall for a moment. She looked around the makeshift bathroom. Stacks of old books filled one corner. On a shelf above it were a few folded blankets and a basket filled with dried weeds and flowers.

As she undressed, part of her mind marveled at what she was doing. The other part was following Juan's instructions without question. She felt drawn to this unexpected experience, no matter how weird it might seem to be.

Lee discovered the soft "ceremonial garment" consisted of two parts: a small leather halter top and a primitive sort of wrap around skirt with a jagged hemline. She put them on and looked down at herself, momentarily dismayed. The halter, which tied at the neck and waist, barely covered her breasts and left her back bare. The skirt ended midway up her thighs. But then she heard Juan's voice in her head. *Trust me. You must trust me.* Lee opened the door.

Juan stood waiting. He wore nothing but a rectangular piece of leather, suspended from a thong around his waist and barely covering his genitals. Around his neck hung a silver pendant with three-inch wide outspread wings, separated by an intricate spiral design. On either side of the design, eye-shaped stones glowed blood red.

3

Lee stood frozen, feeling as though she had stepped into an unknown world—on one hand wary, on the other excited by the possibilities of awakening spiritually. Juan ignored her. Shifting his weight from foot to foot in a slow shuffling dance, he began to chant *"Na Yah He, Na Yah He, Na Yah He"* and shake the rattle. She was mesmerized.

After several minutes, he stopped and stood facing her. Candlelight played across his broad chest, highlighted his strange pendant and cast shadows on his solemn face.

"You must remove your jewelry," he said.

It felt like a dream. She slowly raised her hands to remove her silver and turquoise hoop earrings, her favorites, an anniversary present from Nick. Then she unfastened the clasp on her watch. She held them in the palm of her hand and looked up at Juan.

He glanced at her left hand, "All of it."

Slowly, reluctantly, she removed her diamond and platinum wedding band.

He took them from her and dropped the jewelry on a nearby table. Lee's eyes fell on a sharp-fanged skull—*a bobcat?*—that also rested there. The jaws of the skull were open in a rictus of perpetual laughter.

She glanced at Juan's exposed, firm buttocks as he walked to the middle of the room and felt her cheeks flush. But her embarrassment quickly turned to fascination as he began the ceremony.

He circled the dark buffalo robe three times, moving counterclockwise and shaking the rattle close to the floor. Then he stood tall, arms stretched overhead.

"The sacred circle is cast," he announced. "The space between the worlds has been created."

The space between the worlds…between the worlds…between the worlds… The words seemed to echo in Lee's head, distantly familiar. She felt momentarily displaced in time and encompassed by the emotions those words evoked.

Juan struck a match and lit a pipe, the long stem of which was decorated with feathers and beads. The ruddy bowl of the pipe was carved in the shape of a flying bird. He inhaled deeply and blew a cloud of acrid smoke into Lee's face.

She drew back, closing her eyes and struggling to suppress a cough. *What is it? It sure doesn't smell like tobacco.*

He leaned over and blew a second mouthful of smoke across her suede-covered breasts. Then he knelt and blew smoke across her stomach, legs and feet. He did the same for the back side of her body.

"I purified myself while you were dressing," he explained as he stood and took her hand. "Now you have been purified, as well. You may enter the sacred space." He guided her to the center of the invisible circle. "Kneel on *Cibola*, the sacred buffalo," he said. "Face toward the East, toward the window, while I invoke the guardian spirits of the four cardinal directions."

Eyes still burning from the evil-smelling smoke, Lee did as he instructed. *Invoke the spirits...* She closed her eyes, concentrating on the sound of his voice, although she understood none of his words.

Juan faced north and began speaking—harsh, unfamiliar words, punctuated by several grunts. Then he moved to face the west. More incomprehensible sounds. The performance was repeated facing south. Finally he stood behind her, facing east.

Lee fought to clear her head, wanting to take mental notes of the experience. The words and grunts continued, growing softer, until they were just a whisper.

For a moment there was silence. Lee resisted an impulse to look over her shoulder. *What's next?* She was eager to move on, to take the steps toward the promised awakening.

"Turn and face me," he said.

She started to get to her feet, but was hit by a wave of dizziness. Then she felt his restraining hand on her shoulder.

"No, remain kneeling, just turn toward me."

Lee pressed her hands into the dense fur of the buffalo robe and repositioned herself.

Juan knelt in front of her. He dipped his finger in a bowl of oil and applied it to her face—three slashes across her forehead, three on each cheek.

"This is to make you a strong warrior," he said.

Unguided, Lee's thoughts created a picture of Nick and his shock as she confronted him dressed in skins and war paint.

Juan rose, rattling the gourd above her head. Her eyes were level with his leather apron, which flapped up and down as he resumed his dance. He began to chant again, his deep voice resonating in the small dark room.

Lee stared at the huge black wings hanging above the window. They blurred as she tried to focus on them, then they appeared to flap slightly, keeping time with the chanting. She closed her eyes. Soon she was rocked by warm waves of relaxation and felt herself swaying on her knees. She could hear Juan chanting and feel vibrations through the wooden floor as he danced, vibrations that echoed in her body. The scene had acquired a distant, unreal quality.

"Drink," Juan said. His voice startled her out of her dream-like state. "It is water from the sacred stream."

Once again, he was kneeling in front of her, their bare knees touching. She sensed the heat of his body radiating around her. He handed her a small pottery bowl containing water and several small twigs.

She did as instructed, and then watched him refill the bowl from a leather canteen and drink the contents.

"Now we eat of the powder of life. Open your mouth."

He placed a pinch of something gritty—like cornmeal but bitter tasting—on her tongue. Lee rolled it around the inside her mouth. Her throat was too dry to swallow.

"Lie down," he said. "On your stomach."

She hesitated only a moment, turned again, and lay flat on the dusty hide, her head toward the window.

"First, the cleansing oil," he whispered in her ear.

Starting at her shoulders, he rubbed oil down her body to her feet. She stiffened when his hand slid under her skirt and over the curves of her buttocks.

"Trust me," he said. "Release your fear."

Her muscles went limp under his strong hands, and she lay placidly, the buffalo fur against her face.

"Now turn over."

Lee rolled onto her back and closed her eyes. His hands kneaded the muscles in her neck, then gently caressed her shoulders. When they slid over her breasts, she tried to fight her way back to awareness, realizing the halter had been untied at the neck. She opened her eyes and looked down at her breasts, bare and glistening with oil.

This isn't right! "No!" she said groggily, trying to sit up. "Stop…"

"*Descansa*," he said softly. "Lie back and relax. This is a necessary part of the ceremony. There is no cause for alarm. Trust me."

Trust him…yes. I should…trust him.

Juan pulled back, holding her with his gaze. "Trust, you must trust me," he whispered, as he gently, but firmly, forced to her lie back down. "Trust."

Almost immediately, another wave of relaxation rolled over Lee, numbing her anxiety. She lay completely still as he worked the oil into her thighs, knees and calves. When he reached her feet, he gently rubbed oil between each toe.

Lee felt herself being covered with a heavy warm blanket. Juan's voice came from somewhere above her.

"You are relaxed now," he said, "and feeling very safe. You have no cares or concerns. Your body feels heavy and is sinking deeper and deeper into the embrace of *Cibola*."

Lee floated in and out of a timeless state while soft chanting and the sound of the rattle resumed above her. When Juan accidentally stepped on her hand during his rhythmic dance, she tried to rouse herself. *I should open my eyes. I should watch what he's doing.* But her eyes wouldn't stay open, and she surrendered once more to the darkness.

Lee was only vaguely aware of Juan removing the blanket. Again she was rubbed, neck to toes, this time with a strong smelling oil that reminded her of rotting fruit and some kind of flower she couldn't quite identify.

"This is the sweating oil," Juan said. His voice was a whisper in her ear. "Now roll over, so I can rub it on your back."

Lee obeyed, and soon felt the blanket cover her again. Suddenly, she became aware that Juan was lying under it, beside her. She opened her eyes, startled, and tried to sit up. The halter, tied only at the waist, hung down into her lap. She tried to pull it up to cover her breasts.

"Rub the oil on me now," he ordered. "Do it quickly."

She fumbled to retie the halter straps around her neck.

"Quickly," he repeated.

She hesitated, wobbling, then took the small clay pot containing the oil. Pouring some of the golden liquid into her palm, Lee was again aware of the pungent odor. She felt a dim flash of alarm. *What's happened to me? Why am I doing this? I need to...* Then, reality retreated again and she found herself sliding her oiled hands over his strong arms, his broad back, naked buttocks and legs, aware of the sensual feel of those hard muscles beneath her fingers.

"You have strong hands," Juan whispered, as he rolled over onto his back. "I knew that they would be strong. Now my front, quickly. The oil. Quickly."

Lee saw then that his little apron-like covering had twisted, exposing his flaccid, uncircumsized penis. She was embarrassed but the sensation evaporated as she found herself obeying, spreading oil across his chest and arms and down his flat, hard stomach. Her eyes lingered on his penis—which even in its present state struck her as quite large—until he urged her to continue. She oiled the front of his legs and his feet.

"Lie down here beside me." His voice was soft but commanding. When she joined him, he pulled the heavy blanket over both of their bodies.

"Put your arms around me and hold on tight," he instructed. "You must squeeze me hard." His arms went around her, pulling her against his chest. "Now release all your tension and fear," he coached as he massaged her rigid back. "Trust me. You can let it go now. Let all of it go."

Lee was aware of soft fur beneath one cheek and the hard bones of Juan's cheek against the other. The smell of the sweating oil grew stronger.

Juan continued to chant in harsh exhalations,"*Huh Ya! Huh Ya! Huh Ya!*" as he held her.

At some point, he coaxed her to "squeeze tighter, tighter. The tighter you hold onto me, the more doubt and fear you release into me," he whispered against her cheek. "I will take it from you. Trust me. You can release the tension. *Bueno*. That's good. That's very good."

Lee tried to shift her lower body away from his, but he pulled her closer. His right leg slid over hers, capturing her. Only a vague awareness of her vulnerable position passed through her mind before she abandoned herself to his embrace.

She felt the hard muscles in Juan's stomach contract and relax as he began to chant again. The center of his body seemed to pulse against hers in time with the strange words. The rhythmic sound seemed to fill her entire being, to become part of her. She soon lost all thought and concern, content to float on the buffalo robe, her body pressed tightly against his, in a slippery embrace.

"What are you feeling?" Juan's whisper in her ear brought Lee back from her reverie.

"Peaceful," she said. "So peaceful." Even as she said it, images of her husband and daughter flashed through her mind, disrupting her tranquility. Dimly, she imagined their disbelief and horror if they could see her lying half-naked under a blanket. The thoughts disappeared as Juan whispered her name.

"Tell me more about what you are feeling," he insisted gently.

"I feel like I must be dreaming," she whispered.

She heard Juan laugh softly. His hand ran up and down her oiled back.

"You're starting to sweat now," he said. "That's good. Squeeze harder, harder." His hand rubbed the back of her neck. "*Bueno*. The oil is working well."

Lee felt an uncomfortable numbness in her legs. The weight of Juan's leg was cutting off the circulation. *How long have I been here?* Then his low, hypnotic chanting filled her head and she began to drift away again. Time lost all meaning. She was unable to hold a thought for more than a few seconds.

The chanting stopped, pulling Lee back to semi-awareness.

Juan released her and helped her into a kneeling position. He was close behind her as he drew the sweat blanket around both of them.

Feeling dizzy and disoriented, she closed her eyes. Juan fanned the blanket open and closed like giant wings and he continued to pray and chant.

"Open your eyes and look toward the light," he whispered in her ear. His voice had a strange urgency about it.

"What light?"

"Look at the candle!"

Lee tried to think. *What's happening? Why does he sound so agitated?* She stared at the flickering candle under the window.

"It is through the light that you will see your door opening. The door that leads into the void that is the Spirit World. You must concentrate. Which direction is the door facing?"

"I...I don't know," Lee said fretfully. "I can't tell." *I don't see a door. I don't want to go into any void....*

"We must try again," Juan said, and resumed his chanting. After a moment he repeated the question. "Which direction is your door facing?"

The answer came to Lee suddenly. "The south," she whispered. "It's toward the south."

"*Bueno*," Juan said.

Lee heard the triumph in his voice.

"Your Deep Self is awakening. The sacred direction of the South corresponds to fire and strong emotions, as well as to innocence and trust. That's the door we will go through during the next ceremony."

He continued to chant, fanning the blanket open and closed over their bodies. Lee shut her eyes and leaned back against him. It felt like they were flying. His arms tightened around her, across her breasts, as his chanting was interspersed with what sounded like an invocation. She tried to pay attention, to remember some of the strange words, but Juan's voice seemed to fade in and out.

He shifted his weight and stood up, startling Lee out of a half-formed dream. She rolled off her knees onto her left hip, trying to think. *Have I been asleep? I don't understand....* She closed her eyes, fighting dizziness.

"Drink," Juan ordered, touching a cool bowl to her lips. Lee took a small swallow, noticing again the twigs in the bottom of the bowl. *Sacred stream water, was that what he'd called it?*

Juan dipped his fingers into the remaining water and sprinkled it across Lee's chest. Only then did she realize that her halter top still dangled around her waist. With dazed eyes, she watched the iridescent drops cling to her nipples, then roll onto her deerskin skirt. She made no effort to retie the straps.

"Now, kneel at the other end of the sweat blanket," he instructed. "And roll it tightly toward me."

Lee rolled up the blanket, moving toward him on her hands and knees. She looked up at him. Juan's face seemed to shimmer in the candlelight. The silver necklace gleamed against his chest.

Once again he began moving counterclockwise, addressing the four directions in the mysterious language. After what seemed like a long time, he took her arm and helped her to her feet.

"The circle is open," he said.

Taking a cloth from a nearby table, he began at her face and very slowly and gently wiped the oil from her body. She closed her eyes and let herself drift with what felt like caresses. She could feel her body beginning to respond and that jerked her back to the present. *What on earth am I doing?*

Before she could follow that thought, Juan helped her to her feet, and they stood facing each other. He placed his hands on both sides of her face and gazed deeply into her eyes with what looked to Lee like longing. She could barely breathe.

Finally, he spoke. "It is done. You may dress now."

He led her into the back room and left, closing the door behind him. Lee dressed in a daze. Then she returned to where Juan sat quietly, wearing only his Levi's. The oil on his chest emphasized his muscles in the candlelight.

"That was a powerful ceremony..." he said, breaking the silence as he came to take her hand. "...the strongest I have experienced in a very long time. Do you want me to tell you why?"

Lee nodded, not trusting herself to speak.

"We have performed that ceremony before," he said. "In a previous lifetime. I recognized you. I knew that we had been together before, as soon as you walked through the door. I realized that was the real reason you had come."

She just looked at him.

"I know you didn't know this," he said, placing his hands on her shoulders, "at least not on a conscious level. But that's of no concern now. Tell me, how are you feeling?"

"I don't know...." she answered truthfully. She strained for clarity and almost achieved it. "This has been such a confusing experience. I've never done anything like this before."

"You don't think you have," he said. "But you must trust me. Perhaps the ceremony will unlock memories and reveal the truth to you." He gave her shoulders a little squeeze and then released her. "Drink this before you go," he said, handing her a glass of what looked like milk. "It will clear your head from the effects of the ceremony."

"What is it? Another old family recipe?"

He smiled. "As a matter of fact, it is."

Lee took a swallow, realizing that it was, indeed, milk. It tasted unusually good, as though it had been sweetened with something. She drained the glass.

"Come back a week from today," Juan said. "There is much to be done, much you must understand, before we continue."

"For another part to this ceremony?"

"That's right, although I must conduct the next part alone, on the night of the next full moon. After that, you and I must prepare for the final part of the ritual."

"What happens then?" She was beginning to feel more like herself, more like a journalist with questions.

"We will go through your door together, the door into the Spirit World. There your eyes will be opened, and you will reclaim your Power." He walked to the desk picked up a wooden fetish--about four inches tall. "This is *Ye-na-lo-he,* an ancient Native spirit," he said, handing it to her. "She offers great protection. You will carry her on our spiritual journey."

Lee held the strange carved figure. Dressed in red fabric, it had the body of a woman and the face of a sharp-billed bird. Tiny black feathers covered the arms and head.

"I will take this, my totem," Juan said, unwrapping a small black stone figure of a bird. "There are those who believe the raven is evil, but they are mistaken. Raven is beyond limited concepts of good and evil. He is a messenger between the earth plane and the Spirit World, a bringer of magic and healing energy." He pointed to the dark wings above the window. "His wings protect those who acknowledge him."

She handed the little fetish back to him, not liking the feel of it.

"Your necklace," Lee said, her eyes drawn once more to the red stones set between silver wings. "It's very...unusual."

"My amulet is certainly that. It is very strong medicine. It shields the wearer from danger. This one is very old. It belonged to my mother."

"The stones seem to glow. I've never seen anything like them."

"It's a rare crystal, found only in the mountains of northern Mexico. It carries great Power."

Lee looked away, feeling at a loss for words. "I don't know what to say...or think...about any of this," she said.

Juan gently touched her cheek. "It will all become clear to you in time. You are feeling well enough to drive?"

"I'm okay, I think."

"Come next week," he said, helping her into her jacket. "Next Tuesday." He collected her purse, tape recorder, pen and notebook, and handed them to her. They walked into the next room and Juan opened the front door.

Lee turned to go, feeling like someone awakening from a dream. The outside world looked a little unfamiliar. Dazzled by the bright sunlight, she shaded her eyes.

"Wait. You're forgetting something." Juan left and quickly returned with her jewelry. He pulled her against him in a quick embrace. "*Hasta luego*," he said in a husky voice. "Until we meet again."

Lee felt as though she were floating down the pathway to her car. She slid inside and relaxed against the headrest. After a moment, she remembered the jewelry in her hand and slowly put it on. It seemed to take a long time to locate the car keys in her purse and start the engine. She stared at the clock on the dashboard in amazement as the concept of time snapped back into her mind. *Sara and Wendy!* She would be at least twenty minutes late meeting the girls in Santa Fe.

She put the car in reverse and backed past the dead tree with its bare, ravaged branches. The sound of Juan's chants were echoing in her head as she shifted and drove away, over the wooden bridge and up the hill.

4

Lee sat in her parked car near the Santa Fe Plaza, startled as she realized that she had almost no memory of her drive back from Cavado. Unbelievable—the entire morning had been beyond bizarre. *That interview was the strangest thing that's ever happened to me. A 'sweating ceremony?' I've always done my best NOT to sweat, except in an exercise class. Still can't wrap my mind around it.*

She jerked herself back to the here and now, locked the car and hurried down San Francisco Street, waving to Sara and Wendy when she spotted them at their designated meeting place on the Plaza. The girls, dressed in their usual skin-tight jeans and denim jackets, were sitting on a white wrought iron bench, feeding popcorn to a flock of pigeons.

"Oh, Mom, there you are. Finally!" Sara tossed out the last of her popcorn and sprang to her feet. "Quick, before we go to lunch, I want to show you something."

Lee followed the girls across the brick paving of Palace Avenue to the Palace of the Governors. As usual, the full-length portal of the historic adobe building was crowded with tourists buying souvenirs from Native Americans.

Sara squatted in front of a jewelry display tended by a man wearing long braids, a black Stetson, and an expression of serene indifference.

"Aren't these great?' she asked, pushing her hair back and holding long, dangling beaded earrings to her ears. "Can I get them, please? Please? I'll save my allowance for two weeks to pay you back. Wendy thinks they make me look at least eighteen."

Lee shook her head. "Sorry. I want you to continue to look fifteen for a while longer. A lot longer. Now, come on. Let's go have lunch at The Shed. Where's Wendy?"

Sara sighed, returned the earrings reluctantly, and motioned to Wendy who was several displays away examining a turquoise bracelet.

"So," Sara said as the three of them continued up the street. "How was your morning?"

The lunch crowd had thinned, leaving the restaurant almost empty. Lee felt relaxed and oddly detached as she sat across the table from the girls.

Sara and Wendy chatted and giggled, ogling the busboy who filled their water glasses. Lee swallowed the last of her water and reached for her iced tea.

"I couldn't believe it when Lisa shaved the sides of her head," Sara said. "It looks totally gross. My parents would kill me if I did that. Right, Mom?"

Lee stared off into space, holding her now half-empty glass.

"Wouldn't you? Mom?"

She blinked and focused on her daughter. "What?"

"Wouldn't you kill me?"

"Kill you?"

"If I shaved the sides of my head. Like Lisa."

"I certainly wouldn't kill you, sweetheart. I'd just lock you in your room until it grew back. Oh good, here comes our lunch."

The waiter presented the two girls with cheeseburgers and Lee with her usual green chile chicken enchilada. She realized that the smell of it made her feel slightly nauseated. *I just had a small bowl of cereal for breakfast. I should be hungry…*

"Lisa's planning to get a tattoo next," Sara continued. "When she visits her father in Los Angeles. What about that, Mom?"

"Hmmm?" Lee put her napkin in her lap, wishing she had asked for more iced tea. *Don't know when I've been this thirsty.*

"What if I get a tattoo? Maybe a rose. Or a snake winding around my ankle."

"A snake winding…? What on earth are you talking about, Sara?"

"Earth to Mom," Sara said, frowning at her. "I was just teasing. Are you okay? You aren't eating anything and seem kinda out of it."

"I'm fine, honey. Just thinking about my interview." She took a small bite of her enchilada, trying to bring herself back to the present. After forcing a couple more bites, she put her fork down. "Well, are you girls all shopped out?"

"No way," said Sara, carefully removing the onions from her burger. "Do you think you could drop us off at De Vargas Mall after we eat? I need to find something totally devastating to wear to the Halloween dance."

"Totally devastating?" Lee felt a rush of affection for her daughter. "Well, I had planned to go back to the office this afternoon. But, what the heck, I haven't had an afternoon off in a long time. I think I'll play hooky and go with you."

"No kidding? Great!" Sara studied her mother approvingly. "You're sure in a mellow mood."

"I wonder if he's got a girlfriend," Wendy whispered, watching the busboy as he cleared the next table. "Maybe I should call him over and ask him."

"You wouldn't," Sara said. "I dare you."

Wendy motioned to the busboy. When he returned to their table, she turned crimson. "Could, uh, I have more water, please?"

Sara hid her face in her napkin. "Wendy," she said, giggling, "You are just too much. Isn't she, Mom?"

Lee smiled vaguely and smoothed the slightly oily curls at the nape of her neck.

Lee's mood of calm detachment lasted throughout the afternoon. She accompanied the girls to several stores in the mall, until she finally announced that she'd had enough and herded them, loaded with shopping bags, out to the car. When she passed The Camera Shop on her way back through town she remembered the pictures she'd taken in Cavado and pulled over to the curb.

"Do me a favor," she said to Sara. "Run this roll of film in and tell them I need to have the prints as soon as possible."

It was close to six o'clock by the time Lee and Sara had taken Wendy home and pulled into the driveway of their own two-story tan-stuccoed home. Lee hit the controls of the automatic garage door opener and the door rolled upward, revealing Nick's late model Volvo.

"Dad's home early," Lee said, suddenly feeling tired and more than a little edgy. She needed some time alone to think about what had happened in Cavado that morning and to decide how much she should tell Nick about it. One thing was clear: her husband would not approve of her encounter with Juan. She still wasn't sure how she felt about it herself. Her knees felt a little weak as she walked into the house.

Nick was standing behind the bar, opening a bottle of Wild Turkey, when Lee and Sara entered the large family room. He greeted them over his shoulder.

"Well, I don't have to ask what you two have been up to. Did you buy out the stores?"

"Hi, Dad. Wait till you see the really killer outfits I got!" Sara hurried up the stairs with her packages.

"Killer outfits?" Nick shook his head. "Whatever happened to nice little school dresses?"

"You're hopelessly out of date, dear," Lee said. "Why don't you fix me one of those?"

He raised an eyebrow. "I haven't seen you drink anything but an occasional glass of wine for ages. Rough day?"

"It certainly was an unusual one." She slipped off her shoes and sat on the sofa, staring out of the window at the nearby Sangre de Cristo Mountains. The aspens had begun to change color several weeks before, and now decorated the high green slopes with brilliant splashes of gold. It was an incredibly beautiful view, especially in the early evenings when the setting sun turned the mountains the deep salmon color that had given them their name, "Blood of Christ." But this particular evening the spectacular light did little to calm Lee's growing anxiety.

A gray cat with white markings came running down the hall, his feet making soft thumping sounds on the polished bricks. He jumped into Lee's lap, purring loudly.

"Hello, Mister," she whispered, stroking his silky fur. "How's my sweet furry purry?" Mister closed his eyes and pressed his head against her stomach, his front paws busily kneading her thigh.

Lee sipped the bourbon and water that Nick handed her, taking care not to disturb the blissful cat. She made a slight face as the liquid burned its way down her throat.

"This is going to knock me on my ear," she said.

Nick joined her on the sofa. "Well, now, tell me about your day. You said you had an out-of-town interview." He took a healthy swallow of his drink. "Where was it?"

"Cavado. It's in the mountains north of Chimayo."

"Hmm. How did it go?"

Lee felt a strong urge to talk about it—at least some of it.

"The strangest thing happened."

As she described her interview in Cavado, Lee knew she would have to do some serious editing where Juan was concerned.

"It was such a peculiar spooky little place. All the windows were closed and shaded. There was no light, except for candles. And there was the most lifelike snake on the table. At first I didn't realize it was dead."

Nick shook his head and took another drink, his eyes not leaving her face.

"Go on," he said.

I certainly have his full attention, she thought. *That's a rarity.*

"This is where it gets really interesting. After our interview, Mr. Mascareñas conducted an ancient 'Awakening Ceremony' for me..."

"What? How did he do that?"

"Well, he had me lie down on a buffalo rug and danced around me, shaking a gourd rattle and chanting."

Nick's expression changed from polite interest to one of shocked disbelief.

"Excuse me? You stretched out on the floor and let some weirdo dance around you?"

"He covered me with a heavy blanket to make me sweat. He needed my sweat."

Nick shook his head. "This is a joke, right?"

She wished it were. *Why did I say anything at all to Nick about the ceremony?*

"I know it sounds really strange. It wasn't that big a deal." She took another sip of her drink. And then another.

"Did you say he needed your *sweat*?"

"Well, yes. Juan said he would shake the blanket to the four directions when the moon is full. That's supposed to dispel all of my fears and self-doubt."

"So now it's 'Juan,' huh? It sounds like you two got fairly close. And I've never noticed you having much 'fear and self-doubt'."

"Well, maybe you don't pay that much attention these days."

"I'm going to pretend you didn't say that," he said with irritation. "Of course, I pay attention, and I know you pretty damned well. We've been together almost twenty years!"

"Eighteen. I'm sorry. Let's just forget this."

"*Forget* it? This is the craziest damn thing I've ever heard! Jesus Christ, Lee. How could you have put yourself in such a dangerous position? What the hell were you thinking?"

"It just happened. It was interesting...." It was obvious she needed to end the conversation as soon as she could.

"What do you mean, 'It just happened'?" Nick rose and stalked to the bar. He splashed more bourbon into his drink and stood staring at her. "I'm absolutely dumbfounded. You could have been raped! Murdered!"

"If I'd known you'd be this upset, I wouldn't have mentioned it. But you did ask."

"You didn't expect me to be *upset?* You sit here calmly telling me that you interviewed some freak in the middle of nowhere and ended up under a blanket on a buffalo rug. Of course I'm upset!"

"I told you, it was an ancient Native American ceremony...."

"Isn't that taking your writer's curiosity a bit far?"

Lee drained her glass. She could feel a headache coming on.

"Okay, okay," she said, rubbing her forehead. "It was a crazy thing to do. It just didn't seem dangerous at the time. Can we just forget it?"

"This is just so unlike you! I mean, you're usually so level-headed. Why were you even talking to this creep? I thought you were working on an article about the history of…what is it? Cavado?"

"I am. A man at the Española Chamber of Commerce suggested that I talk to Juan….Mr. Mascareñas. He's considered to be something of a local historian. I had no idea that he's also a *curandero*."

"A what?"

"*Curandero*. A folk healer. I guess they're fairly common fixtures in those little villages.

Nick walked back to the sofa and stood looking down at her. His face was flushed, the space between his eyebrows creased into deep frown lines. Then his expression softened, and he sat down beside her.

"I'm just glad you didn't get hurt, honey," he said putting his arm around her. "You certainly could have been."

Lee leaned against his shoulder and closed her eyes. Her head was really throbbing.

Nick sniffed her hair. "What's that smell?"

Lee pushed away and looked at him. "Probably some of the incense he burned," she said. *It must be the oil, or the smoke from Juan's pipe in my hair.*

"By the way, in spite of his ceremony, Juan isn't Native American." she said, hoping to put an end to the topic. "He's from an old Spanish family."

"I don't give a rat's ass about his family!" Nick said, his voice rising again. "Sane, civilized people don't dance around, trying to collect someone's sweat! I don't understand why you didn't run screaming out of there when he first suggested his little—what was it? —'awakening ceremony'?"

"I told you, I was interested." Lee pulled away and brought her fingertips to her temples, rubbing in small circles.

"How old is this character anyway?"

"I don't know. Somewhere in his fifties, I guess. Why?"

"What does he look like?"

"Well, as I said, he's Hispanic—dark hair and eyes. Could use a haircut. And he's about your height."

"Good looking?"

"I guess so, in a brooding sort of way."

Nick shook his head. "The world is full of nuts. You know that! And, my God, you're a beautiful woman. You shouldn't even be driving around those isolated little villages by yourself. Some of those folks up there don't take too well to *gringos*." He studied her face, frowning. "Your eyes look a little glassy to me," he said, feeling her forehead. "And you feel very warm. Are you getting sick?"

"I just have a headache." She scooted Mister off her lap and stood up. "I'm just going to stick some frozen lasagna in the oven and get some aspirin."

As she walked into the kitchen, Lee grabbed for the countertop, feeling faint. She held on, waiting to regain her balance.

Nick was right behind her. "What's wrong?"

"I don't know. All of a sudden I feel really sick." The dizziness passed, only to be followed by a wave of nausea.

"Forget dinner. Let's get you to bed," Nick said, putting his arm around her and leading her up the stairs.

Lee insisted on a shower in spite of Nick's objections. She washed her hair twice and soaped herself several times, leaning against the tile while hot water cascaded over her body. Then she dried off, toweled her hair, and pulled a flannel nightgown over her head. Shivering, she fell into bed.

Lee found herself in a long dark tunnel. She saw a dim light far ahead and struggled toward it. The air was dense, making it hard to move. Someone called her name, and the sound echoed around her.

She stopped, confused. That wasn't her name. And yet, somehow, she knew that it was. She turned in a slow, dream-like motion.

Juan materialized out of the darkness, his powerful body illuminated by an eerie light. As he drew closer, she saw that he was naked, except for the mysterious silver amulet shining around his neck.

"Trust me," he said. "Don't be afraid. It's time for you to awaken to who you really are. It's time for you to regain your Power." Then his arms were around her. His hands began to move on her body, and she pressed herself closer, aroused by his touch.

But something was wrong. With a shock she realized that his arms and shoulders were covered with feathers.

"Remember," he whispered. "Let yourself remember."

Suddenly there was a strong wind in her face, pushing her back several steps. Juan's face blurred. Round, blood-red eyes shone in the darkness. A long sharp beak opened and closed. Horrified, she watched Juan transform into a huge black bird. The sound of beating wings filled the tunnel.

"No! Get away!" She tried to run through the suffocating darkness, but her movements were slow and uncoordinated. He caught her, wrapping her in his wings.

"Lee?" Nick was shaking her shoulder. "It's all right, honey— just another bad dream." He felt her forehead. "You're definitely feverish. I'm going to get you some more aspirin. If you're not a lot better in the morning, I want you to call Dr. Zimmerman."

By morning, her temperature was almost back to normal.

"I'm feeling better," she told him. "But I think I'll stay in bed for awhile. I'll probably go into work this afternoon. Would you get my appointment book? It's in my office, on the desk."

"You look really pale to me," Nick said, as he handed her the thick book. "Why don't you spend the whole day in bed?"

"Too much to do. I took yesterday afternoon off."

"Annabel can cover for you. You've got to learn to take care of yourself, honey."

"You're a fine one to talk. Did Sara get off to school?"

"Mr. Wonderful just picked her up in his vintage hot rod," Nick said, arranging papers in his briefcase. "What's his name? The pretty one with the long, blond hair."

"Kevin," murmured Lee. "He's a nice boy."

"Well, I think he removed most of the gravel from the driveway when he took off. I'm going to talk to that kid about his driving." He bent to kiss her cheek. "Take care of yourself. Want me to put Mister out?"

"No, leave him in here with me." She stroked the sleeping cat. "He's a great bed partner."

"Well, each to his own. See you tonight."

Lee picked up the phone on her nightstand and dialed Annabel's home number.

"Hi, Annie. Listen, I'm afraid I've caught a bug. It seems to be going away, but I still feel pretty weak. Do you think you could cover for me this morning?"

She opened her appointment book. "Let's see. I'm scheduled to interview a freelance writer at nine-thirty. Richard Perry. He just moved here from Denver. Also, we need to follow up on that article about the Fine Arts Museum. Kirk Conners has that assignment, and it was due two days ago. We can't put up with that. Also, there are several stories on my desk to be edited, if you can get to them."

"Got it," Annie responded.

"Okay, thanks. I may be in this afternoon. Call if you need me."

She pulled the thick down comforter over her shoulders and

closed her eyes. Seconds later, she was sound asleep with Mister nestled against her stomach.

Lee swam slowly up out of a deep, dream-filled sleep. She moved her leg, waking Mister. He stood and arched into a graceful, feline stretch. Lee peered at the clock on her nightstand. Twelve-thirty. She groaned and rolled onto her back. Mister responded with a soft purr and walked across her chest. He put his nose down to hers, his whiskers tickling her cheek.

"We've been asleep all morning, Mister. Poor kitty. You must be starving." Lee sat up, which caused a soft throbbing in her temples. Mister jumped off the bed and walked to the bedroom door. Then he stopped and turned, waiting for her to follow.

"Okay, okay, I'm coming." She stood up and walked into the bathroom on rubbery legs.

Mister went into the laundry room to use his cat box. When he came out, Lee served him cat food and changed his water. She then fixed herself a cup of decaffeinated tea.

On her way back to the bedroom, she had another dizzy spell and gripped the banister. *There's no way I can go into work. I'm completely wiped out.* She put the tea on her nightstand and climbed back into bed.

A short time later, something pulled her out of another half-formed dream. A strong, familiar odor drifted through the room. Almost sickeningly sweet, like rotten apples. Mixed with…something else. Her eyes flew open, and she bolted upright in bed.

What's that smell? Then the realization hit her. *The oil. Oh, my God, I smell Juan's sweating oil! But that's not possible. I took a shower last night. I washed it all off. It's my imagination.* She lay back down, sliding under the covers. *I'm just sick, that's all.* She convinced herself that the bug had distorted her sense of smell, and took several deep breaths, trying to relax.

Moments later, Lee heard soft, padding, cat footsteps enter the darkened bedroom. She opened her eyes. Mister had stopped several feet inside the doorway, his body rigid. The fur stood up along his back and fanned his tail. He took a step toward the bed, and then turned his head sharply toward the sliding patio door. His ears flattened against his head as he hissed at the closed draperies.

"Mister? What…?"

Lee watched as the cat hissed again. Then, with eyes fixed on the door, he backed out of the room. She slid from the bed and opened the draperies to stare at the empty balcony beyond the glass.

"There's nothing here," she said out loud. "What scared you, Mister?" As she checked the double lock on the door, she was hit once more by the odor of sweating oil. A wave of dizziness washed over her, and she stumbled back to bed.

There must be a dog outside. One of the neighbor's Afghan hounds probably got loose again. Moments later, just as she was dropping off to sleep, Lee heard another hiss followed by Mister's low, threatening growl.

5

"Mom?" Sara peeked around the bedroom door. "Uh-oh, did I wake you?"

Lee opened her eyes. Her head was throbbing and her throat felt dry and scratchy. "That's okay. I've been sleeping most of the day."

"Gosh, you're really sick, aren't you? I'll bet it's the flu. Everyone at school has it." She sat down on the edge of the bed and tossed her hair over one shoulder.

Lee frowned at her daughter. Sara was dressed in tight Levi's and a faded T-shirt with *SUPERBITCH* stretched across her small breasts.

"Please tell me you didn't wear that shirt to school today," she groaned.

"Oh, Mom, don't get uptight. I wore my Levi jacket over it so only 'SUPERB' showed." She giggled.

"You're a real character," Lee said, managing a small smile.

"Thanks. I try." Sara stood up. "I'm gonna fix a snack. Can I get you anything?"

"Some ice water. Thanks, baby."

Sara started out the door. "What's wrong with Mister?"

"What do you mean?"

"He's hiding under the dining room table and won't come out. Acting really weird. I'll be right back."

Lee rolled onto her side and closed her eyes. The next thing she knew, the room was dark, and Nick was shaking her shoulder.

"Babe? I hated to wake you, but I was getting worried. How do you feel?" He placed a cool hand on her forehead.

"Oh, Nick. You're home already? What time is it?"

"Almost eight o'clock. You're still running a slight fever. Here, take these," he said, shaking three aspirins out of the bottle. "I meant to call to check on you today, but I got tied up in meetings."

"That's okay." She sat up and swallowed the tablets. "I've been zonked most of the day. Must be the flu."

"Well, if you aren't a helluva lot better in the morning, I insist that you call the doctor. We have to get you well." He hesitated. "Remember, I'm flying to Fairbanks day after tomorrow. I would hate to go if you were still sick."

"I'll be fine. I'm sure the worst is over now." She got out of bed and walked into the bathroom, surprised at how weak she felt. She splashed cold water on her face and peered into the mirror. Her face looked puffy and pale. She ran a comb through her tangled hair and brushed her teeth.

When she returned to the bedroom, Nick was sitting at his desk, sorting through papers.

"Can I get you something to eat?" he asked without looking up. "Some soup? Sara and I finished off the lasagna."

"No thanks. I'm just thirsty." She got back into bed and drained her water glass. "I feel achy all over, like something clobbered me."

"Well, you certainly had a rough night—all those nightmares."

"Nightmares?"

Nick glanced up from his paperwork. "You woke me several times, whimpering and thrashing around."

Lee stared at the ceiling as fragments of the dream came back to her. Juan was in it, wearing just his silver necklace. And there was something about a huge black bird. She shivered and snuggled under the covers. Then she remembered the sweating oil smell she had noticed in the early afternoon.

"Nick?"

"Hmm?" He was adding figures on his pocket calculator.

"Did you notice a strange odor in the house when you came home today?"

"Odor?" He glanced up at her. "What kind of odor?"

"I don't know, kind of sweet. And really strong. It's difficult to describe."

"I didn't smell anything." He went back to his columns of numbers.

"Just my imagination, I guess." Lee closed her eyes, determined to put it out of her mind.

Sometime later she felt Nick getting into his side of the bed. The lights were out, and the house was quiet.

She slept soundly through the night, not waking until the alarm went off at six-thirty the next morning. Her fever and headache were gone, but she stayed in bed, not wanting to get up. She dozed with Mister until Nick and Sara peeked in.

"We're both ready to leave," Nick said, "but I want a health update first."

"Yeah, Mom. How are you?"

"I'm on the mend, my darlings. Don't worry about me. You both have a good day. Love you."

"Love you more!" They shouted, the traditional family response.

After she heard the front door close, twice, Lee got up, lifted her arms over her head and bent from side to side. *Still achy, but not so bad. I'll go in to work a little later this morning.* She put on a warm robe and went downstairs, followed closely by Mister.

A short time later, she carried a steaming cup of herbal tea back upstairs and into her study. She stared at her notebook and tape recorder lying on the desk. *Nick is right. It was crazy to take part in that ceremony. Anything could have happened.* She rewound the tape and sat back in her chair to listen to the interview with Juan Mascareñas.

His deep voice hit her with a shock. Lee's hand jerked, spilling tea in her lap. She brushed at it, barely feeling the hot sting, and sat for thirty minutes as the tape played through. Her tea cooled, forgotten, on the desk.

I sound absolutely out of it! Stunned, Lee turned the recorder off and stared out her study window. Piñon-covered hills gently rolled beyond the house to the west. Across a sandy arroyo, several hundred yards away, she could see the light brown adobe home of her nearest neighbor. Santa Fe sprawled to the south, one of the oldest continually inhabited cities in the United States, now a center for art and culture. In spite of its international popularity, the city managed to preserve an intimate southwestern charm. Lee loved living on its outskirts and had always relished the location of her home. It offered privacy, views of the mountains and city, and yet was only minutes from the downtown Plaza. Now, for the first time, Lee felt uncomfortably isolated.

She picked up her notes on Cavado and studied them, trying to put the sound of her own voice on the tape out of her mind. *Better get going. Things are undoubtedly piling up at the office.* She walked wearily into her bedroom to dress.

"Hey! You doing okay?" Annabel's voice in the doorway jolted Lee out of her reverie.

"What? Oh, I'm all right. Just a little spacey, I guess."

"I'll say. Each time I've gone by this office today you've been staring at the wall, like you were lost in a dream. If I didn't know you so well, I'd say you were in love."

"Of course I am. With my husband."

"Right. But that's not the kind of love I mean." She peered at Lee over the top of purple-rimmed half-glasses perched on the end of her nose. "Seriously, Lee. If you aren't feeling well, go on home. Things are pretty much under control here."

"No, I'm okay. Just running in low gear today." She picked up her pen and glanced down at the papers in front of her, hoping Annabel would get the hint and be on her way.

"Well, if you're sure. How do those color separations for the museum story look?"

"Oh, God. I forgot to pick them up. Damn. They're due at the printer's in the morning."

"Relax. I'll send Julie out to get them. Take it easy, kiddo. I'm worried about you. You're obviously not over that bug."

"I'm fine, Annie. Don't fuss over me. Just let me get back to work."

Annabel was right. Lee's mind hadn't been on her work. Her thoughts kept returning to Cavado and Juan Mascareñas. She felt increasingly agitated as the afternoon wore on. *What on earth possessed me, to agree to that strange ceremony, to wear that revealing little outfit? It still makes absolutely no sense.* When she left the magazine office a little after five o'clock, Lee couldn't remember when she'd had a less productive day.

"For God's sake, Lee, let it go," Nick said, after Sara had left the dinner table. "It was a foolish thing to do, but you were lucky. Nothing terrible happened. Just let it be a lesson. Never rush into an interview without knowing what kind of situation you're getting into."

"That's a little easier said than done," she retorted. "People aren't that easy to predict. Their behavior doesn't fall into neat mathematical formulas. The point is that I've always shown good judgment in the past. I just don't understand how I let that happen."

"Well, I'd stop dwelling on it if I were you." Nick pushed back from the table. "What's done is done. Now, if you'll excuse me, I have to get ready for tomorrow's trip. I'll need to pack my woolies. Wouldn't want to freeze my buns off," he said with a wink. Then he patted Lee on the cheek and left her sitting alone at the dining room table.

The next morning was bright and cloudless, a preview of the perfect Indian Summer weather predicted for the weekend. Nick put his suitcase down in the sunny foyer and kissed Lee goodbye.

"I'll be home before you know it. You know how fast two weeks go by. I'll call you in a day or two."

She followed him outside to his car.

"Take care of yourself, babe. No more witch doctors!" he shouted and drove away, gravel crunching beneath his tires.

Lee got into her car and headed for work. It would be a lonely weekend. Sara was spending the night with a girlfriend and would be gone most of tomorrow. Even when she was at home these days, her daughter was too caught up in her teenage world to be much of a companion. Then Lee remembered the Buchanans' party. She sighed. *Oh, well. It'll give me something to do tonight. I can use a diversion.*

Lee stared at the blank screen of her computer. *I have to get this damned story written.* She flipped through her notes, then typed "Cavado: A Glimpse of the Past." She stopped and stared out of the window, remembering Juan's ramshackle, two-room adobe house. *He doesn't live there, I'd bet money on that. He must have a more comfortable house somewhere else in Cavado.* She closed her eyes, remembering the service station attendant's words: "Mascareñases was here before God…old Juan damn near owns Cavado…he's one of them *curanderos.*"

She stood up and crossed the room to the bookshelf. Finding her Spanish-English dictionary, she looked under "C" until she found:

Curandero*: Spanish. 1. a folk healer or medicine man who uses herbs or hallucinogenic plants, magic, and spiritualism to treat illness, induce visions, impart traditional wisdom, etc.*

So she'd been treated by a "quack" who wore a strange necklace, referred to it as an "amulet," and said it had belonged to his mother. She looked up that word in her Webster's New World Dictionary and spent a moment considering the definition. "Amulet: something worn on the body because of its supposed magic power to protect against injury or evil: a charm."

Magic power? Does Juan actually believe that his "amulet" has some sort of magic power? Come to think of it, he did say something about it protecting him from harm. But that's just superstitious nonsense. Surely he wasn't serious. After all, he's an educated man. He's been to college. But then, on the other hand, that ceremony of his was pure pagan—all that business about the sacred circle and invoking the spirits of different directions.

She sat back down and tried to concentrate on outlining the

story, but scenes of the Awakening Ceremony kept flashing through her mind. She remembered the feeling of his hands sliding down her back and over her buttocks, spreading the pungent sweating oil. The strength of his arms as she lay in his warm embrace on the buffalo hide rug. His command, "Hold me tighter, tighter," as he clasped her sweaty body against his.

Lee felt flushed and uncomfortably warm. Taking a deep breath, she closed her eyes and leaned back in her chair. Then her eyes flew open. What…?

She rose to her feet. Oh, my God, she thought as a sickeningly sweet odor filled the room. *No, it can't be! This is impossible. What's happening to me?*

Her heart was pounding as she fumbled through the phone book, then dialed a number.

"Is Dr. Mallory in?" Her voice shook. "This is Lee Lindsay. Please, it's urgent. I have to see him as soon as possible."

6

The carved wooden sign above the door read *James E. Mallory, M.D.* Lee stepped into an empty waiting room that was decorated in soothing tones of beige and brown. She sat in a chair near the door and nervously checked her watch. *Five-thirty.* The secretary had gone home, leaving her desk neat and cleared for the next day's work.

A side door opened and Jim Mallory stuck his head into the waiting room. His nearly bald crown shone in the overhead light. A few long strands of brown hair were carefully combed up from the sides and over the top.

"Hi, stranger," he said. "Come in."

Lee clasped the psychiatrist's extended hand and smiled down at him. She had forgotten again how short he actually was. His aura of quiet confidence distracted from his diminutive size.

"I appreciate you seeing me on such short notice," she said. "Especially after hours."

"Well, it's good to reconnect with you. It's been awhile. Almost two years, as a matter of fact. My secretary said that you sounded upset on the phone." He gestured toward the sofa. "Have a seat."

Lee sat down with a feeling of *déjà vu*. She had once spent many hours in that room, talking to this soft-spoken man with warm brown eyes. She had first come to see him seven years ago, after the death of her parents. In addition to the grief and rage she'd felt about the accident, she was disillusioned with her marriage. Mallory had gently guided her through that bleak period in her life, encouraging her to develop more emotional independence.

He had been a lifesaver. Without his support, she probably wouldn't have dared invest her small inheritance in the magazine. She had seen him occasionally since then for what she thought of as emotional tune-ups. He had always given her sound advice and a fresh perspective. She found herself hoping he hadn't lost his touch.

Mallory picked up a yellow legal pad and pencil from his desk before settling himself in the chair facing her.

"Catch me up," he said. "How's Nick? And Sara?"

"They're both fine. Sara's growing up much too fast. She's in high school and almost as tall as I am." She paused. "Nick's still on the go a lot. As a matter of fact, he left this morning for Alaska. To accelerate electrons into the aurora borealis, no less."

"I'm impressed. How are you handling his traveling?"

She shrugged. "Okay. I'm too busy to let it get me down."

"How's the magazine business?"

"It's hard work, and I love it. We made a nice profit last year."

"Great, keep up the good work. It's a snazzy magazine; I never miss an issue." He reached into a large glass bowl filled with hard candy. "Want a mint?"

"No, thanks."

"I've become addicted to them since I gave up the evil weed last year. Just substituted one addiction for another, I'm afraid. But

I decided I'd better stop smoking—before it stunts my growth."
He grinned and unwrapped a piece of the candy. Popping it into
his mouth, he leaned back in his chair, studying her. "It sounds
like things are going pretty well for you, Lee. Why are you here?"

She took a deep breath. "I need to talk about something
that happened during an interview three days ago. Something
very strange."

For the next thirty minutes, Lee presented an uncensored
version of her experience in Cavado. Mallory listened, occasionally
interrupting with a question and taking notes. By the time she
had finished describing the mysterious recurring odor, her hands
were tingling. She nervously rubbed them together while Mallory sat
quietly, watching her.

"That's quite a story," he said, after a long moment. He
uncrossed his legs and leaned forward in his chair. "Okay. A few
things seem obvious to me. For starters, I'm almost certain that
you were drugged during the interview. In addition, I suspect that you
were hypnotized."

Lee stared at him, surprised that hadn't occurred to her—or to
Nick. Of course, she didn't mention the tea to him.

"Let's talk about the drug first. There are some locally grown
drugs, including strains of marijuana that are incredibly smooth,
potent and long lasting. I think Mascareñas slipped that, or something
else, in your tea."

"My God, I never even suspected that. I smoked marijuana a
few times—years ago, in college—but I always hated the feeling and
couldn't wait for it to wear off. It frightened me to feel that I wasn't in
complete control of myself. I certainly didn't feel any of that panic in
Cavado. In fact, I felt relaxed and very peaceful."

"Of course. You had no reason to suspect that you were
drugged, so you didn't worry about it. You didn't spend time
analyzing your actions and reactions, like you did when you knew
that you were stoned. Besides, when marijuana is ingested, the

effect is far more subtle and gradual than when it's smoked. And as I said, I think your 'medicine man' gave you a dose of some very smooth, first-class 'medicine'."

"But why? What did he hope to gain by drugging me?"

"He got you under the blanket." Mallory grinned. "That was undoubtedly the highlight of his day. I'm sorry, Lee. I didn't mean to sound flip. But you are a very attractive woman. He probably just saw an opportunity and decided to take advantage of it."

"You obviously don't believe that Juan was on the level with his 'Awakening Ceremony' and story about our past life connection."

"No, I don't," he said. "Let me backtrack a bit, and I'll explain why. I've done considerable research on *curanderismo,* or Hispanic folk healing. The words '*curanderismo*' and '*curandero*' come from the Spanish verb '*curar,*' which means 'to heal.' *Curanderos* are generally very religious, and they believe that their healing powers come directly from God. They've played an important role, both medically and socially, for centuries in both Mexico and the American Southwest. After all, folk medicine is the source of much of our pharmacological knowledge. We didn't exactly invent medicine in the twentieth century, much as we'd like to take the credit.

"My personal experience with local *curanderos* has convinced me that there's still a lot they can teach us," he continued. "In fact, on occasion, I've referred Hispanic patients who don't trust modern Anglo psychology to a *curandero* who lives in Pojoaque. With excellent results, I might add."

He smiled at her surprise. "Old Manuel comes from a long line of healers. People used to travel up from Albuquerque to be treated by his father when he was alive. Anyway, Manuel's an ethical man, and he knows his herbs. From what I can tell, he uses standard *curanderismo* methods, which, by the way, assume supernatural causes of illness."

"Supernatural causes?"

"That's right. *Curanderos* attribute many illnesses to magic and witchcraft, which they have traditional methods of combating. Let me give you an example. A *curandero* might pass an egg, which is believed to have cleansing qualities, back and forth over a patient's body three times to remove the curse of the '*mal de ojo*' or 'evil eye' that he believes is causing depression or illness. Then he would break the egg into a bowl of water and place it behind the patient's head, instructing him to rest until the spell is removed.

"After a refreshing snooze, the patient would be served some soothing chamomile tea and—more often than not—they would experience a remarkable recovery." He shrugged. "It works because they believe in it. And if it works, who can knock it?"

"Do you know of any *curanderos* here in Santa Fe?"

"As a matter of fact, a *curandera* called Tia Delfina lives on Salazar Street, just off Agua Fria. I haven't met her. But I understand she's a delightful old lady, who cheerfully dispenses herbs, massage, and a little benevolent magic." He paused, his smile fading. "But I've also encountered a few unethical and even dangerous self-proclaimed *curanderos*. In fact, I did a psychological evaluation on one years ago that made my hair stand on end."

"Really?" Lee tried not to smile at the mental image of Mallory's few long strands of hair spiking out from his temples.

"It was during the trial of Leroy Martinez, who was convicted of poisoning his uncle in Pecos. Does that ring a bell?"

"No, I don't think so."

"It might have been while you were still living in Los Alamos. But it got a lot of local publicity at the time. Leroy admitted to poisoning his uncle. Used rat poison, in fact. But he maintained that he did it against his will. He claimed he was bewitched into doing it by a local *brujo* who hated his uncle."

"*Brujo*?"

"A *brujo*—a sorcerer, a practitioner of the so-called black arts. I'll let you in on a well-kept secret. Witchcraft is alive and well here in the Southwest."

Lee stared at him in amazement. "Of course, I've heard folk tales. But I assumed that's all they were."

"Most Anglos are unaware of the old Spanish and Indian traditions that still flourish around here, especially in the rural villages and pueblos. Those people are understandably reluctant to discuss their supernatural beliefs and experiences with outsiders." He leaned back in his chair. "Examples of the belief in witchcraft are all around us in New Mexico, although most people these days don't take them seriously. For instance, there's the ancient tradition of painting doors and window frames blue. Do you know how that originated?"

"I've read that it's supposed to ward off evil influences. But isn't that just colorful Santa Fe lore?"

"There's more to it than that. For centuries the Spanish have used blue, the color traditionally associated with the Virgin Mary, to protect their homes from witches. Many still do. And Native Americans have long believed that turquoise, the stone and the color, offered protection from evil." He stood up and walked to a coffee pot sitting on a table by the door. "How about some coffee? It's strong enough to melt bullets by now."

"No, thanks," Lee said. "I'm trying to cut down on caffeine."

He chuckled as he poured himself a cup. "Oh, that's right. You prefer the local tea."

Lee smiled. "I have to say, it feels good to be able to joke about it."

Mallory returned to his chair and took a cautious sip of the steaming coffee.

"Now, let's see, where was I? Oh yes, I started to tell you about Leroy Martinez and the *brujo*. Well, Leroy swore that this *brujo*—Pedro Armijo was his name—had put a spell on him, causing him to murder his uncle. He maintained that Armijo had caused the deaths, in one way or another, of five or six Pecos residents throughout past decades. Most of the villagers came forward to support Leroy's story and to insist that Armijo, rather than Leroy, be brought to justice."

"Are you serious?"

"I'm afraid so. There was such an uproar that the court ordered a psychological evaluation of Armijo." Mallory shook his head, remembering. "I have never encountered a more cold-blooded bastard in all my years of practice. He tested out as a textbook sociopath. Absolutely no conscience. Naturally, he denied having had anything to do with the murder. He admitted to being a *curandero*, but denied any connection with black magic. However, he expressed absolute glee over the uncle's death. Said the entire Lopez family deserved to die. It was obvious during the trial that Leroy and his family were terrified of Armijo. They wouldn't even look at him."

"What happened?"

"Leroy was convicted of first degree murder. Nothing could be proven against Armijo. He left the courtroom smiling ear to ear." Mallory grimaced. "As far as I know, he's still living in Pecos, terrorizing the community."

"You don't really believe that he was or is a...*brujo*?"

"I believe that he thought he was. And he'd certainly managed to convince the Pecos community of his supernatural powers."

"Just a minute. You aren't saying that you think Juan Mascareñas could be some kind of sorcerer?"

"I don't believe in the supernatural," Mallory said, "but from what you've told me, I don't believe Mascareñas is a simple, well-meaning *curandero*, either. In the first place, reputable *curanderos* don't drug journalists and talk them into taking off their clothes. They don't need to drum or rattle up business, if you will forgive the pun. You would have to request treatment. And since you are a '*gringa*'— an Anglo—a typical *curandero* would probably refuse."

Mallory reached into the candy bowl. "Also, most *curanderos* carefully avoid anything that smacks of the occult, in order to protect their reputations." He put another mint into his mouth. "You mentioned that he referred to the raven as having some special significance to him?"

"That's right. He said it was a 'powerful spirit,' or something like that."

"Well, a raven is almost universally associated with magic. Legends about them certainly abound in this part of the country. A prevalent belief is that witches can assume the form of an animal. When they're up to mischief, they often turn themselves into an owl, a crow or a raven."

"People in this day and age actually believe that sort of thing?"

"You'd be surprised. A friend of mine, who happens to be a brilliant and successful lawyer, grew up in one of those isolated little villages. He once told me that, as a child, he had trapped a *bruja*."

"Trapped her? How?"

"By placing a pair of scissors, opened to form the shape of a cross, under her chair. He swears that the woman was unable to stand up until someone removed the scissors."

Lee shook her head, smiling.

"He was very serious. Apparently lived for years in terror of her retaliation. To this day, he suffers from a phobic fear of birds."

Lee couldn't hold back a giggle.

"I know, it's hard to believe. But my point is that a deep-seated, cultural belief in witchcraft still exists, even among many educated, professional people. Now, let's get back to your experience in Cavado. Based on all that you've said, especially Juan's reference to the raven, my guess is that he aspires to be more *brujo* than *curandero*."

"There was something else. He was wearing a very unusual necklace. He referred to it as an 'amulet'."

"What did it look like?"

"Well, it was silver in the form of two outstretched wings and in the center were reddish stones that looked like eyes. There was a spiral design running between the two stones. The tips of the wings were attached to a heavy silver chain."

"Interesting."

"There were also black wings nailed to the wall in his little house. And he talked about each of us taking a raven fetish with us when we do the second ceremony."

"I certainly don't like the sound of that," Mallory said. "I assume you don't plan to see him again. I think you would be asking for serious trouble if you participated in his next ceremony."

"What do you mean?"

"I expect it would involve a hallucinatory drug, probably peyote or datura. And I'd be willing to bet that this time the ceremony would include having sex with the medicine man."

Lee felt her face flush. Anxious to change the subject, she asked, "How do you explain the odor of that sweating oil? I smelled it twice, the day after the ceremony and this afternoon when I was in my office."

"I said I also suspected that you were hypnotized. I think the smell is an after-effect of the hypnotic experience. It's surprisingly easy to hypnotize most people and it doesn't require swinging a watch back and forth in front of their eyes. A soothing tone of voice in a darkened room will usually do the trick. A low, repetitive chant or the repeating of a word or phrase is also very effective."

"But would I be able to remember the experience if I'd been hypnotized?"

"Sure you would, if you weren't under that far. Hypnosis is simply an altered state of consciousness, similar to a meditational trance. It's a slowing of brain waves. And there are many different levels. It's only deep hypnotic trances that produce amnesia or hallucination. A mild hypnotic state would just make you feel very relaxed and would slowly wear off. But combined with your mysterious toddy, it might well leave you open to suggestion, to say the least. And you could certainly experience after-effects for several days. Like smelling the sweating oil."

"The first time I noticed the smell, I thought it was just because I was sick."

"You were sick? When?"

"It hit me that night after the interview." She frowned, remembering. "I felt fine before I went to Cavado. And I was okay all afternoon after the ceremony, except for feeling a little spacey and having no appetite when I took Sara and her girlfriend to lunch. Then I took the afternoon off, and we went shopping. I remember thinking that I felt unusually relaxed." She paused. "Come to think of it, I bought Sara several outfits that I normally would have vetoed. I must have been drugged!" She gave a small laugh.

"When did you start feeling sick?"

"Early that evening, when I was describing the experience to Nick. I gave him a rather edited version, omitting a detailed description of the brevity of the 'garment' and that Juan joined me under the blanket. It's a good thing I did, too. Nick went ballistic, ranting about what a stupid and dangerous thing I had done. That was before dinner. As a matter of fact, I skipped dinner, too. My head started pounding and I felt dizzy. I just showered and went right to bed."

"How long did the symptoms last?"

"I slept most of the next day. I had a headache and felt very weak. I assumed it was the flu."

"Did you feel dehydrated? Thirsty?"

"Why…yes, I did. Almost right away, and for a couple of days afterward. But I attributed that to the fever I was running."

"And then your fever was gone and you were better? Let's see, that was yesterday, right?"

"That's right. I still felt a little weak and very nervous. I couldn't stop thinking about what had happened. I felt like a gullible fool. Then when the smell returned, I panicked."

"I don't think you had the flu. I think you just reacted to whatever was in the tea and possibly the water you drank during the ceremony. And didn't you say you ate some kind of powder?"

"I thought it was cornmeal."

"Maybe. But maybe not. Mind-altering drugs, even in mild

doses, can have a dehydrating after-effect. Sometimes severe enough to cause serious illness. And we don't know what he gave you."

"I almost forgot—I also drank some milk. Very sweet tasting milk. Juan said it would clear my head from the effects of the ceremony."

"One for the road, huh?" Mallory shook his head. "Heaven only knows what combination of drugs you ingested. I think that explains all your symptoms since Tuesday night, including the sweating oil smell. Also, dramatic events sometimes leave a recurring reaction. For example, people who survive auto accidents sometimes report smelling gasoline or burning rubber weeks later. They're just re-experiencing vivid memories of the accident. It could be something like that. Anyway, it's nothing to worry about. It probably won't happen again."

He glanced at the clock on the wall behind her. "We're going to have to stop now, Lee. Keep far away from this Juan character in the future. He's undoubtedly bad news. And try not to feel bad about what happened." He smiled at her. "Look at it this way. You were given a peek into a world that is closed to most Anglos, a cultural phenomenon and a fascinating experience. It'll make a great magazine article."

Lee grimaced. "Someone else can write it. I feel like such a fool. Talk about losing control of an interview! My God. I go in there with my notepad and tape recorder, and half an hour later I'm on a moth-eaten buffalo rug—allowing an almost naked man to rub me down with snake oil! I'd be laughed out of town." She stood up. "Dr. Mallory, thank you. I feel sane again."

"I'm glad I could help. Call me again if you need to talk more about it." He hesitated. "You know, it might be interesting to talk to Socorro Tafoya-Hall about your experience. Do you know her?"

"Only professionally. Her gallery advertises in the magazine."

"Socorro and her husband, Howard, own Galería on Canyon Road. Howard's from Dallas and a real character, usually wears a big Stetson with a turquoise-studded hatband. Nice guy." He smiled.

"Socorro and my wife are close friends. As you may know, Socorro's Native American. She's a fascinating woman—very bright, with a master's degree in art history. She might be able to shed some light on Juan's so-called 'awakening ceremony.' At any rate, it would be interesting to get her reaction. She grew up with that sort of thing."

"You don't think she'd mind talking to me about it? I know that Native Americans are sometimes reluctant to discuss their ceremonies with outsiders."

"Tell her that I suggested it. You can usually reach her at the gallery. And just so you'll be prepared, Socorro also claims to be psychic."

"A Native American psychic with a master's in art history, "Lee laughed. "Sounds like a typical Santa Fean."

"She's anything but typical. Incidentally, 'Socorro' means 'help' in Spanish. See if she lives up to her name. And let me know what happens. Please call if you have any more problems with this experience."

"I will," Lee said, moving toward the door. "Thanks again."

The small side street where Lee had parked her car was deserted and gloomy in the early evening darkness. She hurried along, glancing over her shoulder and fumbling through her purse for her car keys. There's no reason to be so nervous, she chided herself, as she located the key and unlocked the car door. *As Mallory said, it was an interesting experience, but now it's behind me. No real harm done.*

She locked herself inside and took a deep breath before starting the engine. Then she drove carefully through the narrow winding streets of downtown Santa Fe, eager to get safely home.

7

The house was dark when Lee drove into the driveway, and she felt a stab of alarm before remembering that Sara was spending the night with Wendy. She waited until the garage door closed safely behind her before getting out of the car.

Mister came running down the hall to meet her in the kitchen.

"Hi, sweet kitty." She bent down to rub him under his chin. "Could I interest you in a little dinner?" He wound himself around her legs, purring happily as she filled his bowl. "It's just you and me tonight, little buddy. Good thing we enjoy each other's company."

Although Lee was cautious about alcohol because of her father's addiction and made it a rule not to drink alone, she felt compelled to pour herself a glass of white wine before going upstairs to undress. I certainly need something to calm my nerves, she rationalized. After slipping into her flannel robe, she carried her wine out onto the upstairs balcony of the master bedroom.

It was her favorite part of the house. She relished quiet moments spent there, unwinding and thinking private thoughts. Leaning against the balcony wall, she gazed out across peaceful moonlit hills at the lights of Santa Fe glittering below. The crisp air was perfumed by the aroma of piñon wood burning in some neighbor's fireplace. What a beautiful night, she thought, looking up at a black velvet sky crowded with stars. She took a deep breath and, ignoring a wave of loneliness, sank into a redwood deck chair, sipping her wine. Pulling her robe tighter around her, she began to review her session with Dr. Mallory. His words replayed in her mind. *"You were drugged...hypnotized. He sounds like a* brujo *to me...a* brujo. *"*

She took another sip of her wine, and then another. A furry body suddenly leaped out of the darkness and into Lee's lap.

"Mister!" she exclaimed. "You scared me! And you spilled my wine." She put her empty glass on the table beside her and stroked the cat. Suddenly, the quiet night seemed ominous and the lights of Santa Fe much too far away. "Let's go inside," she said, scooping him up. As she got to her feet, she heard the phone ring in the bedroom.

Hurrying inside, she dropped Mister onto the bed and lifted the receiver. "Hello?"

"Lee?" The deep, familiar voice hit her like a slap. "Is this Lee Lindsay?"

She stood frozen with the phone to her ear. When she finally found her voice, it was little more than a whisper.

"Juan?"

"You recognize my voice," he said approvingly. "I'm flattered."

"How did you find me? I mean, how did you get my home phone number? It's unlisted."

"I called your magazine office this afternoon. I explained to your receptionist that you had interviewed me. I told her that we had unfinished business." He paused. "She was most cooperative."

"She was?" Lee frowned. Julie usually showed better judgment. She was certainly going to hear about this!

"You are alone," Juan said. It was a statement not a question.

"How do you know that? How do you know I'm alone?"

"I told you. I know many things about you."

Lee sat on the edge of the bed, speechless and somehow powerless to hang up the phone.

"I had to speak with you," he continued. "You have been... how shall I say it? You have been strong in my mind the past few days. How are you feeling?"

"Better now. But I've been ill."

"Yes. That was from the ceremony. The body is sometimes shocked by an awakening process. The weakness will soon pass, and your strength will return. You will be stronger than ever." Another pause. "It was a very powerful ceremony."

"You should have warned me that it would make me sick." Her voice shook with emotional turmoil and it took an effort for her to say, "I haven't known what to think about our...ceremony. It left me confused and frightened."

"I must be honest with you. In some ways it frightened me, too."

"What?"

"The power of our ceremony—it moved me very much. More than anything has in a long, long time."

"What did you do to me? Did you drug me?"

"Drug you?" He laughed softly. "No, trust me, I didn't drug you. Why do you ask?"

"Because it's so unlike me to..."

"Listen to me," he broke in. His voice suddenly had a hard, impatient edge to it. "You must open to your real self, to your Power. As I told you, you are much more than the person you appear to be. The time has come to cast aside the illusions of this life and get in touch with who you *really* are." His voice softened. "But we must be patient. Trust me, the understanding will come."

"What understanding? What are you're talking about?" Lee

couldn't understand why she was having so much trouble expressing her anger. She had a vague realization that she also felt betrayed.

"You ask too many questions," he said with growing irritation. "It is a way of avoiding the truth. Just listen. Trust me. In two nights the moon will be full, and I will go into the hills to perform the second ceremony. I will shake your sweat blanket to the four directions and scatter your fears. You will feel your strength return soon after that. And you will return to Cavado on Tuesday morning."

"Oh, no! I…I can't." Lee felt a sense of rising trepidation.

"We must meet again," he said in a soothing voice. "You know that, don't you? You and I have much unfinished business. You aren't aware of it yet, but already my mind is connected to yours. This is not something to fight. Trust me, it is a very special blessing."

His voice, so intimate and coaxing, held her—somehow scattering her thoughts and dissolving her fear. It would be so easy to agree….

"No!" she said, struggling to maintain her resolve. "I can't do the next ceremony. I mean, I don't want to. I won't."

"I won't rush you. The final ritual can wait. It can be postponed until you are ready. But I must see you. Soon."

"I don't think…"

"Tuesday morning. I will be waiting. Trust me, Lee. *Trust me.* I can tell you are tired. Very tired. It is time for you to just relax, time for you to sleep. Go to bed, Lee, and sleep. Put all your fears to rest. Sleep. *Buenas noches.*"

The line went dead. Lee sat motionless, staring into space, then slowly replaced the receiver. She felt weak and disoriented. I need to sleep, she thought numbly. *And put my fears to rest.*

She untied her robe and let it fall to the floor before climbing naked into bed. Almost immediately, a black wave of sleep carried her away.

8

Lee sat up in bed the next morning, surprised to discover that she was nude. She always slept in a nightgown, even on the warmest summer nights. For a moment she felt utterly confused, as though she'd just returned from a long journey. The next thing she noticed was that the draperies, which she always closed before sleeping, were open.

What day of the week is it? She stared at the clock on the nightstand until she got her bearings. *Six-twenty. Saturday.* Her mind returned to the mystery of her missing nightgown. *There's some sort of big gap in my memory! I can't remember even going to bed last night. I was out on the patio....* Her breath caught in her throat as memories of Juan's phone call returned. She slid back under the protection of the warm covers, trying to reconstruct the strange conversation of the night before.

It was downright creepy. He seemed to know that I was alone. How could he know that, unless he's been spying on me? He insisted that I come to see him again next Tuesday morning. And he paid no attention to my refusal. He was so damned insistent.

"Oh, God," she groaned aloud. "Why couldn't I just tell him to get lost?"

At the sound of her voice, Mister raised his head from the comforter at the foot of the bed. He rolled onto his back, exposing a fat gray and white striped belly. After a long stretch, he rolled upright and walked to the head of the bed. His cool nose touched Lee's and he began a deep-throated rumbling purr.

"What do you remember about last night?" she asked, scratching his head. Mister's amber eyes just stared into hers.

Lee rose and went into the bathroom. Moments later, she picked her robe from the floor, put it on and walked to the sliding glass door. *Unlocked? And I didn't close the draperies? Something obviously wiped me out. Could it have been the wine? No, I just had a few sips. More after-effects from my Cavado visit? From the drugs and hypnosis? Maybe just hearing Juan's voice on the phone…*

She opened the door and walked out onto the balcony. The sky to the east was rosy gold, with shafts of sunlight lancing between the purple clouds that covered the tops of the Sangre de Cristo Mountains. Savoring the cool morning air, she took a deep breath and stretched her arms out wide.

I feel fine today, physically. Completely recovered. But I must have spent the whole night in one position. I'm as stiff as a board. Better do a little yoga.

Lee walked back into her bedroom and, as her robe slipped from her shoulders, her anxiety about the night's happenings somehow slipped away with it. It was as though a curtain had been drawn.

She stood naked in front of the tall mirror in her dressing room, studying her body. *Breasts beginning to sag a bit. But they don't look bad, for a middle-aged broad.* She ran her hand over a reasonably flat stomach that was laced with faint stretch marks from her pregnancy and a long, thin scar from the hysterectomy performed for endometriosis, ten years ago. She turned a little, frowning. Something was definitely happening to the back of her thighs. *Cellulite. That does it.* She sat down on the carpeted floor. *Time to get on a serious exercise program. Long walks, maybe an aerobics class. Daily yoga.*

She closed her eyes and did some deep breathing. For the next twenty minutes, she concentrated on a routine of slow stretching. Afterward, she dressed quickly in a sweatshirt and pants before following an impatient and loudly complaining Mister down the stairs and into the kitchen.

While Mister ate his breakfast, Lee fixed herself a pot of coffee. She ate half a grapefruit and a bowl of yogurt while she read the morning paper. Then she cleaned the Mexican tiles decorating the kitchen countertops and shook out the Navajo rugs that covered the hall and foyer floors. Finally, she climbed the stairs and went into her study. She'd put it off long enough. It was time to get started on the Cavado article.

Bracing herself, she sat down and listened again to the tape she'd made in Juan's strange little house. She sat quietly for a moment after it was over. Then she partially rewound the tape. She hit the play button again, feeling an odd thrill as Juan's deep voice filled the room.

"There was much hardship to be endured in those days. Drought and disease were frequent visitors. The Spanish..." Lee hit the fast-forward button. *"...many old Spanish traditions and Native American beliefs have melded and endured here in Cavado,"* Juan's voice concluded.

"Yes, yes, hmmm...I see." Lee frowned at the sound of her own voice, again struck by how strange she sounded. Rather detached. And sleepy. She replayed the last ten minutes of the tape, leaning forward in her chair.

"Cavado is a very special place," Juan's voice continued.

"...source of great Power. It has been so for..." There was a faint
knocking. *"Will you excuse me for a moment?"*

"Ummmm...yes...of course." A quick click as the recorder
was turned off. Another click. Then Juan's voice. *"Turn the recorder
off now. And put away your notes."* Click.

Lee sat staring at the recorder as the tape continued to run
soundlessly. "Well, I'll be damned," she said aloud. "I do sound
stoned. Mallory, you were right."

She glanced at the clock on the wall and made a quick
decision. It would be interesting to talk to someone else about this.
Who knows, it might even be helpful. She reached for the telephone
book and found the number.

"Galería on Canyon Road. May I help you?" The voice was
soft and slightly husky.

"Hello. May I speak to Socorro Tafoya-Hall, please?

"Speaking."

"Socorro, this is Lee Lindsay, from *Santa Fe Today* magazine.
Jim Mallory suggested that I call you. There's something I really need
to talk to you about. I know this is short notice, but would you have
any free time today?"

Socorro suggested that they meet for lunch at The Pink Adobe.
Lee hung up the phone and turned off her computer. The story would
have to wait. She hurried to shower and dress.

The historic restaurant. housed in a three hundred year old
adobe on the Old Santa Fe Trail, was filling with people. Some looked
familiar to Lee as she sat alone at a small table near a fireplace. She
recognized the handsome face of a former soap opera actor sitting
several tables away. And the woman at the next table also looked
familiar, an actress maybe? You never knew whom you might see in

Santa Fe these days. It had become a popular hideaway for the rich and famous.

Lee felt a vague uneasiness creeping into her mind. *Why am I suddenly nervous?* She glanced at her watch. Socorro was already fifteen minutes late. Sipping a glass of mineral water, she watched the door.

A dark complexioned, attractive woman dressed in red suede pants and matching tunic top paused in the doorway, her eyes searching the tables. She wore a massive turquoise and silver concho belt around her slender waist. Large silver hoops hung from her ears and silver bangle bracelets decorated both forearms. Her black hair cascaded from a middle part and flowed across her shoulders. Lee estimated the woman's age at somewhere around thirty-five, although she had the type of exotic good looks that made it hard to pinpoint.

"Socorro!" A man with his hair pulled back in a ponytail waved from a crowded table by the window.

The woman waved back. "Hello, David. Why aren't you in your studio working? Your clay baskets sell as fast as I get them in."

"I'll be back at it, right after lunch," the man retorted. "Even artists have to eat, occasionally." She joined in the laughter that arose from his table and blew him a kiss.

Their eyes met and Lee raised her hand in greeting as she watched Socorro glide through the tables toward her.

"Hi," Socorro said, pulling her chair out and sitting down. "Sorry I'm late. It's been a frantic morning at the gallery. But don't get me wrong, I'm not complaining. I hope the tourists keep flooding into town."

"So do I. They keep all of us in business." Lee hesitated. "I really appreciate your meeting me today," she continued. "As I told you on the phone, Jim Mallory said you might be able to help me with something."

"I'll try." Socorro smiled. "Jim and Edie are two of my favorite people. I met Edie about ten years ago, when we were both enrolled in a photography course at the College of Santa Fe. We've been good friends ever since."

"I've never met Edie. But I've known Dr. Mallory for quite a few years. I think he's terrific. He's helped me through some pretty rough spots."

"You're going through a rough time right now, aren't you?" Socorro's large, dark eyes studied Lee's face.

"Why, yes, I am. Does it show?"

"Your aura is cloudy. You're confused...maybe even frightened."

Lee stared at Socorro across the table. "Dr. Mallory did say that you're a psychic."

"Did he? I can't believe that's the reason he wanted you to see me." She smiled and leaned forward, her elbows on the table. "The good doctor has made it very clear that he doesn't believe in that sort of thing."

"Well, actually, it's more because of your Native American heritage. He thought you might be able to shed some light on something that happened to me in Cavado last week."

The smile froze on Socorro's face. "Cavado?"

"Yes. I was there to gather historical background for an article I'm writing. I interviewed a man named Juan Mascareñas. Do you know him?"

"No, I don't. But Mascareñas is an old and distinguished name around here. They were among the first Spanish settlers in northern New Mexico." Socorro hesitated. "I can tell you, however, that Cavado is a strong vortex of psychic energy, much of it evil. I've only been there twice, and both times I was very uncomfortable. The last time, I actually felt sick. It's a real power spot, psychically speaking." She picked up her menu. "Let's order lunch. Then I want to hear exactly what happened to you in Cavado."

Over a steaming bowl of *posole*, Lee gave a brief, edited description of her experience in the isolated village. Socorro picked at a spinach salad, listening intently.

When Lee was finished, Socorro sat quietly, chewing on her full lower lip. When she spoke, her voice sounded strained.

"I'll tell you right now, I really don't like the sound of this."

Lee's stomach clenched. For a moment, she thought she might throw up. *Deep breath. Deep breath.*

"Tell me more," Socorro urged.

"Well, I...I was feeling so strange, light-headed and confused. The truth is, my memory is hazy about some of it."

"Was Juan wearing any special jewelry?" Socorro's eyes narrowed at the description of Juan's amulet. "Okay, I'll want to get back to that. First, did he drum during this ceremony?"

"No. Just a rattle, some sort of a gourd rattle, while he was chanting."

"That could explain why you felt so out of it. A shaman, a good one that is, can easily induce an altered state by using a rattle, a drum, or just by chanting."

"That's what Dr. Mallory said. He feels certain I was hypnotized."

"I'm glad that Jim and I agree." She grinned. "It's encouraging to see medical science making such strides."

"He also thinks that I was drugged by Juan's tea."

"I wouldn't be surprised. How long did your illness last?"

"A couple of days. Let's see," Lee took a moment to put her thoughts in order. "I got sick Tuesday night, after the ceremony. And I still felt..."

"Tuesday?" Socorro interrupted. "You went to Cavado on Tuesday?"

"That's right."

"Tuesdays and Fridays are known by my people as 'witches days.' Any magic worked on those days is especially potent. How did you feel on Friday?"

"Yesterday...Friday...I didn't really feel sick by then, just a little weak. But I certainly felt off balance. In fact, something happened that sent me running to Dr. Mallory."

Lee told Socorro about the distinctive odor that had filled her office Friday morning.

"It smelled like the sweating oil Juan rubbed on me. A strong, rotting fruit smell, mixed with something else. Some kind of flower or weed. It happened twice, just coming out of nowhere. The first time was Wednesday afternoon, just before I fell asleep. I thought it was my fevered imagination. But then, when I smelled it again, it really scared me."

"It should have." Socorro studied Lee for a moment, then put her hands on the table toward Lee, palms up. "Give me your hands," she said.

Lee hesitated, then put her hands in Socorro's. Socorro's skin felt dry and cool. Lee looked at her expectantly.

"Now, I want you to close your eyes and think of Juan. Fix him in your mind. Visualize his face, recall his voice."

Lee resisted the temptation to glance around the room and did as Socorro instructed, hoping no one was watching. She had no trouble remembering Juan's face or his deep, intimate voice. A long moment passed before Lee hesitantly opened her eyes. She stared across the table, fascinated.

Socorro was sitting erect and motionless with her eyes tightly shut. Although the restaurant was cool, her forehead was shiny with perspiration. Lee watched her frown, shake her head slightly, then frown again. Beads of perspiration appeared on her upper lip. Lee was uncomfortably aware of her hands in Socorro's firm grip. They were feeling very warm, almost hot. She forced herself to sit still.

Finally, Socorro opened her eyes. She blinked several times and took a deep breath. Her hands tightened on Lee's.

"I felt a great psychic force," she said, her voice shaking slightly. "Something dark and fierce."

"What do you mean? What is it?"

Socorro released Lee's sweating hands and looked into her eyes.

"I fear for you, Lee," she said in a hushed voice. "You

encountered a *brujo*. A dangerously powerful one. I will do what I can to help you."

Lee found herself at a loss for words. Socorro certainly didn't look like she was joking. In fact, she looked genuinely shaken. And her assessment matched Dr. Mallory's. Before Lee could think how to respond, Socorro glanced at the check and reached for her purse, obviously eager to leave the restaurant.

"No, please," Lee said. "You're my guest."

"Thank you. Now I must go. I need time alone to meditate, to confer with my spirit guides, before I go back to the gallery."

"Spirit guides?" Lee asked in confusion.

"Yes. They help me to see beyond the distractions of the physical world," she explained matter-of-factly.

"Wait...are you saying you actually talk to spirits?"

"Yes, I do. My guides have been with me since I was a child."

"No kidding? Who do you think they are? And how do they...?" Lee stopped embarrassed. "I'm sorry. I don't mean to pry. I'm just curious."

"I understand. And I don't mind talking about them, not to people who are genuinely interested. Perhaps I'll tell you more about my guides someday when we have more time." With a quick graceful movement, Socorro was on her feet. "I'll do some checking around, find out what I can about Juan Mascareñas and get back to you."

"Great." Lee opened her purse and took out a business card. She wrote her home number on it and handed it to Socorro. "You can reach me at home or at the office."

Socorro took the card and gave Lee's hand a quick squeeze. "Try not to worry. But don't ever go back to Cavado. Don't even talk to Juan again. Hang up if he calls you." She started to go, then turned back to Lee. "I would advise you to light a candle or two in your bedroom at night, at least an hour before you go to sleep," she said. "In fact, light one during the day, too, at work. Candlelight has a purifying effect. It will weaken any negative influences that might still be affecting you." She brushed long black strands of hair away from her face. "I'll talk to you soon."

Lee sat alone at the table, staring into space. Dr. Mallory had been right. Socorro did add to her information about Cavado. But now the experience seemed more mysterious than ever. *Spirit guides. Brujos. This whole thing is incredible. Absolutely unbelievable.*

She paid the bill and left the restaurant. On the way home, she stopped at the grocery store.

Pushing her cart past the produce section, Lee froze. Several feet away, standing with his back to her, was a tall, well-built man with dark hair hanging past his collar. When the man turned and walked past her, Lee felt weak with relief. *Not Juan. He doesn't even look that much like Juan.*

She turned her cart around and hurried to the checkout counter forgetting the other items she'd planned to buy. Her hands were shaking so hard she had trouble writing the check. Grabbing her sack of groceries, she almost ran to her car.

I've got to get a grip on myself, she thought. *Somehow I have to put this craziness out of my mind.*

But something deep within her knew it wasn't going to be easy.

9

Rock music blared from the second floor as Lee walked into the kitchen. She put the groceries away, then climbed the stairs and knocked on Sara's door.

"Hello in there!" she shouted over the music.

Sara opened the door wearing a lavender bra and matching bikini panties. Her hair was pulled back with a rubber band, and her face was plastered in a partially dried oatmeal masque.

"Hi, Mom," she murmured, trying not to move her mouth. "I can't talk."

"Eeek!" Lee pulled back in mock horror "An alien! What have you done with my little girl?"

"Don't make me laugh!" said Sara, struggling to keep her face still.

"I wouldn't dream of it." She grabbed Sara around her slender waist, tickling her ribs.

Sara pressed her lips together, squealing. Lee was struck by how frail Sara felt in her arms. She was still so young, so vulnerable. *And trying to grow up too fast.* Lee hugged her daughter hard for a moment, blinking back tears.

"Did you have a good time at Wendy's last night?" She tried to keep her voice light.

Sara nodded, her hand over her mouth.

"Great. Tell me about it later. I'm going into my study to write for a while. And I have to go out for a couple hours tonight. One of my advertisers is having a housewarming party. Didn't you say you have a date with Kevin?"

Sara nodded again.

"Okay. And don't forget, it's your turn to vacuum and dust downstairs."

Lee walked down the hall into her bedroom and kicked off her shoes. She exchanged her silk blouse and slacks for comfortable jeans and a sweatshirt. Then she closed herself in her study, telling herself she'd feel better if she could get some work done. *Finishing the article about Cavado will make me feel more in control.*

The rest of the afternoon passed quickly as she wrote. She was only vaguely aware of the whir of the vacuum cleaner and Sara's phone ringing from time to time.

Finally, she leaned back in her chair and looked at the clock. *Five-thirty.* She reread what she had written with satisfaction. *That came together easily enough. Stoned or not, I managed to get enough information for a good article. Some final polishing and I'll get it to the typesetter on Monday, four days ahead of deadline!*

Lee was in her bathrobe, debating what to wear to the Buchanans' party, when Sara walked into her bedroom an hour later. She was wearing black stretch pants and an oversized hot pink sweater.

Iridescent pink eye shadow gleamed under her eyebrows and across her eyelids.

"Kevin will be here any minute," she said. "How do I look?"

"Beautiful. Except for the eye shadow."

"It's called *Raunchy Rose*. Wendy and I found it last week at the drug store. Isn't it wild?"

"Wild. Rub at least half of it off."

Lee had decided on a long-sleeved black jersey dress for herself, accented by her mother's pearls. Small silver hoop earrings. Nice but understated.

"Will you zip me up please, sweetie? Where are you and Kevin going?"

"For a pizza, then to a movie. Will you be out late?"

"No. I just have to put in an appearance, schmooze a little. Business politics." She slipped her feet in black suede boots and grabbed a red wool shawl to drape over her shoulders.

Lee went into the bathroom to her dressing table, moved Mister off the stool and sat down, staring at herself in the mirror.

Sara followed her. "Mom? Did you know right away that you were in love with Dad?"

"Hmmm? Well, let me think. I liked him right away. But it took quite a few months to get to the 'in love' stage. Why?"

"I was wondering. About being in love, I mean. How do you know for sure when you are?"

"Oh, honey," she said to Sara's reflection. "That's a tough question. People have been trying to figure that one out for a long time. There are so many different kinds of love. And at your age..."

The doorbell rang and Sara jumped to her feet. "He's here!"

"Sara, that eye shadow!"

"Mom, please. I'll fix it in the car." She gave Lee a quick kiss on the cheek. "Bye!"

"Have fun, be careful and home by eleven-thirty."

Sara ran down the stairs.

Lee walked to the window, watching the battered red Mustang spray gravel in the driveway and then turn right on the dirt road toward town. *Oh, Sara. Don't be in such a hurry to fall in love. It's rarely all that it's cracked up to be.* She quickly glanced in the mirror, added a little makeup, told Mister goodbye, and left the house.

Bill and Samantha Buchanan's new home was spectacular. Perched on a hill west of town, the sprawling hacienda-style structure commanded 360 degree views of the surrounding mountains and high-desert terrain. The inside was filled with expensive art and Southwestern antiques.

"This place looks more like a museum than a private home," Annabel said, joining Lee, who had grown weary of conversations with the Santa Fe elite and was catching her breath in a quiet corner of the massive living room. "The Cowboy Hall of Fame or something."

Lee grinned. "It's something all right. How many square feet do you suppose?"

"Yara Pitchford is their decorator. She told me there's close to six thousand, and that doesn't count the guest house. Apparently, Bill and Samantha need that much space in order to live under one roof. I've heard they fight like cats and dogs."

"You should be writing a gossip column, Annie. *The Santa Fe Scoop* or something."

Annabel snorted. "You'd better be glad I'm not. I'd have to write about George Jennings, your tireless admirer. Brace yourself, kiddo. Here he comes."

Lee groaned. "God, I'm not up to George tonight. Where are the Buchanans? If you'll stay longer and continue to schmooze, I'll make my excuses and turn into a pumpkin." As she turned to go, she felt an arm slide around her waist.

"Lee, you gorgeous creature. I was hoping you'd be here."

"Hello, George." She turned her head so that his kiss landed near her ear.

"Your glass is empty. Let me get you more champagne. Where's Nick? Out of town I hope."

Lee ignored his question. "Thanks anyway, but I was just leaving. Another engagement. See you Monday, Annie. Goodbye, George." She extracted herself gracefully from his embrace and moved off through the crowd.

Lee walked into the house and sighed. It had been a long day. Mister came running down the hall to greet her.

"Hi, old buddy," she said, bending to pick him up. "Did you miss me?" Mister purred loudly, pressing his nose to her cheek. "I can always count on you to be here for me, can't I?" She buried her face in his fur for a long moment, and then carried the cat up the stairs.

Lee put on the faded flannel nightgown she usually wore when Nick was out of town and climbed into bed with a book. Engrossed in the novel, she jumped when the phone beside her rang an hour later. Hesitantly, she picked up the receiver.

"Lee? How are things there?"

Nick's voice sounded very far away.

"Oh, hi. Everything's fine. I went to the Buchanan bash for a little while tonight."

"Oh, yeah. How was it?"

"Very posh. A mob of people. I escaped as soon as I could. I'm in bed now, with Mister and a book."

"Sara's out with Mr. Wonderful?" Nick said sarcastically.

"That's right. Pizza and a movie. How's Alaska?"

"Cold. I've been setting up the experiment all day. Just got back to my room."

"What did you have for dinner?"

"I feel guilty telling you," he said. "A mountain of king crab."

"Sounds like rough duty."

"Well, someone's got to do it."

Lee knew her laugh sounded strained. "Is everything going according to plan?"

"So far. The first rocket shot is scheduled for early Tuesday morning. Of course that could change if we get bad weather."

"Well, good luck. Don't freeze or overdose on crab."

"I'll be careful on both counts." There was a short pause. "Everything's okay there? You're feeling all right?"

"I'm fine."

"You haven't had more interactions with demented witch doctors, have you?" he asked in a teasing voice.

"None worth mentioning," she forced herself to joke back. She hesitated, she wasn't about to say anything about her visit to Dr. Mallory, or her lunch with Socorro. "Everything's under control here," she said, striving to keep her voice casual.

"That's my girl. Well, hold down the fort."

"Okay. Stay safe." She hesitated. "Nick?"

"Yes?"

"I miss you."

"Miss you, too, babe."

"And I love you."

"Back atcha. Talk to you soon."

Lee hung up the phone, feeling very alone and suddenly depressed. She bent down to the foot of the bed to pick up a sleeping Mister. Then she lay back, staring at the wall and cradling the purring cat against her chest.

At eleven thirty-five, Lee heard the front door open and close. Sara walked up the stairs into her mother's room, rubbing at her eye shadow.

"Hi, I'm home."

"Hi, yourself. Did you lock the front door?"

Sara nodded. "We saw the coolest movie...."

"Did you remember the dead-bolt?"

"Yeah." Sara shot her mother a concerned look. "You okay? You're acting a little uptight. Paranoid, in fact."

Lee closed her book, a romantic thriller that wasn't holding her interest despite its gratuitous sex, and put it on the nightstand. I'm fine, honey. Just tired. Guess I'm not completely over that bug I had last week. Tell me about the movie."

"It was really neat. Kinda violent though. You would've hated it."

"No doubt. I can't handle blood and gore. Your dad called."

"Yeah? Where is he this time? I can't keep track."

"Alaska. Studying the ionosphere and eating king crab."

"I could go for the crab part." She bent to kiss Lee's cheek. "Night, Mom."

"Sleep tight, honey."

Lee turned out her light. After forty-five minutes, she was still wide awake. Finally, she sat up, remembering Socorro's suggestion about lighting a candle. *What did she say? Candlelight chases away evil spirits, or something like that.* She shrugged and got out of bed. *Well, why not?*

She picked up one of the candles on the bathroom shelf. *It can't hurt.* She lit it, placed it on the nightstand and stood in the darkness, watching the flickering light. *I ought to try some meditation, too. See if I can still do it. It might help me relax.* She hiked up her nightgown and sat cross-legged on the carpet, staring at the candle and concentrating on relaxing every muscle in her body. The flame seemed to grow larger and brighter, slowly filling her mind as her eyes began to close.

Her legs felt stiff from sitting too long in a cross-legged position. The only light came from a small fire burning before her. The air was thick with the smell of smoke and sweat. Where was she? Some kind of cave? As her eyes grew accustomed to the darkness, she could make out the shapes of ten or twelve people, sitting with her in a circle around the fire. They were swaying to the throbbing sound of a drum. And someone was chanting. From behind her came a deep, rhythmic, "Hi-yuh-yuh-yuh! Hi-yuh-yuh-yuh!"

Adjusting her legs, she was aware of sitting on a pelt of thick dark fur. She looked down at the short skirt covering her stomach and upper thighs. Except for a necklace of multicolored beads, she was naked from the waist up. Her skin felt sticky, covered with a rancid-smelling oil that made her heavy bare breasts glisten in the firelight. She stared down at her large dark nipples. Long black hair tickled her shoulders and back when she moved her head. A drop of perspiration ran between her breasts and onto her skirt. She brushed it away, touching soft leather.

Smoothly, the drumbeat and the chanting built to an intense climax, then suddenly stopped. Her heart raced with excitement. The time had come. She stood, her feet bare in the fur, and slowly raised her arms above her head as a howling animalistic song burst from her lips. An answering chant rose from the shadowy group seated around her. She began to sway to the new chant, shifting her weight from foot to foot.

A tall figure stepped forward, wearing a shoulder-wide headdress of deer antlers. His only other garment was a length of leather, tied around his waist and reaching halfway down his muscular thighs. His broad forehead was painted with white zigzag lines, and his straight black hair hung down his bare chest almost to his waist. The strand of beads around his neck was identical to the one she was wearing. As she stared up at him, her eyes fastened on a ruddy, spider-shaped birthmark that spread across his lower left cheek.

His dark eyes relayed a silent message of encouragement. She allowed her fingers to linger on his as she took a small stone bowl from his hands. Then she poured some of the sand-like mixture from the bowl into her palm and threw it on the fire.

The flames flared. She tossed her hair out of her eyes and began to dance in a widening circle, as the drumbeat and chanting grew steadily louder.

Lee jerked backward, catching herself on one elbow. She looked wildly around the room. The candle had burned halfway down; wax was overflowing the candleholder and puddling on the nightstand. She scrambled to her feet and flipped on the light.

Mister stared at her from the bed. She ran her hand through her damp hair and looked down at her sweat-soaked nightgown.

"What on earth?" she mumbled to herself. "Did I fall asleep? I must have been dreaming." She shivered, suddenly chilled, then struggled out of her nightgown and stumbled into the bathroom.

Her face, flushed and damp, stared back at her in the mirror. Trembling with exhaustion, she stood for a moment staring at her small naked breasts. Then she slipped on a fresh nightgown and hurried to bed, leaning to blow out the candle before tumbling into a deep, dreamless sleep.

10

By seven-thirty the next morning, Lee was up, dressed in a warm-up suit and running shoes. She grabbed a lightweight ski jacket and left the house determined to begin her day with some exercise.

Swinging her arms, she walked down the driveway and cut across the arroyo toward Camino Encantado. She quickened her pace on the deserted road, listening to the cheerful chatter of sparrows in the piñon trees and taking deep breaths of the invigorating morning air. An elderly woman in a white bathrobe waved and bent to pick up her Sunday edition of *The Santa Fe New Mexican*. A tiny brown poodle ran to the edge of the driveway, yipping furiously.

"Macho, stop that!" the woman called. "Bad boy! You come back here!"

Lee smiled and waved. She was already feeling better. The disquieting dream of the night before seemed less threatening in the clear morning sunshine. Of course, it must have been a dream, she assured herself. *But I have to admit it didn't feel like one. At least, not like an ordinary dream. It was more like the other candle-meditation dream I described to Juan—complete with smells and physical sensations. Could they really be past life memories?*

Needless to say, Nick's reaction to her interest in reincarnation was amusement and absolute skepticism. Just far fetched nonsense. She knew he would laugh at her if he'd been there this morning and tell her she was letting her romantic imagination run away with her.

And he could be right. I've been a basket case ever since encountering Juan Mascareñas. No doubt about that. Well, it's time to put that experience behind me. She went on walking, trying but not succeeding in distracting herself. *On the other hand, I stumbled upon a fascinating story.* Witchcraft in New Mexico, Past & Present. *It would make a great magazine article—deserving some research, but not all this emotional turmoil.*

Lee's leg muscles were tingling with pleasant fatigue when she returned to the house an hour later. She found Sara sitting at the snack bar in a faded cotton nightshirt, eating English muffins and reading the Sunday comics.

"Wow, it's Mom, the superjock," she said sarcastically. "How many miles did you log?"

"Close to three."

"I'm impressed. What are you training for?"

"You never know, sweetie." Lee poured herself a glass of ice water. "You just never know."

Lee spent the afternoon in the public library, researching witchcraft. She was surprised to find several books dealing with the subject in the American Southwest. She sat at a table in the back of the room, reading and scribbling occasional notes. Although she found scattered references to various occult ceremonies, she was disappointed that none of them described the ceremony that Juan had performed with her. She opened another book and read:

> *Witchcraft in the American Southwest is a combination of European beliefs (brought to New Mexico by 16th century Spanish explorers) and ancient Native American practices, which date back to prehistoric times.*
>
> *Witchcraft* (brujería*) and sorcery* (hechicería) *remain integral parts of Mexican folk culture and continue to be practiced, especially in rural villages, in both Mexico and the Southwestern United States.*
>
> *Witches are called "brujas" or "brujos," depending on sex. They are believed to possess supernatural powers capable of causing illness, injury, even death. They are also believed capable of curing illness and injuries.*
>
> *Food or drink offered by a* brujo *may be contaminated and is often suspected to be the source of supernatural illness or affliction.*

Lee thought of the tea Juan had given her during the interview. The source of a supernatural affliction? She certainly preferred Mallory's theory that it had been laced with marijuana or something like it. Frowning, she continued to read.

> *According to ancient belief,* brujos *can transform themselves into birds and animals, as well as cast magical spells. Pueblo Indians in northern New Mexico still associate crows, ravens and owls with witchery.*
>
> Brujos *have been accused of preparing*

*love potions and seducing unsuspecting victims. An
ancient legend refers to a sacred plant that was boiled
into a tea for the purpose of seduction....*

At this mention of the tea, the hairs rose on the back of Lee's
neck. She glanced at her watch. *Almost five o'clock! How did it get to
be so late?*

She checked out one of the books and left the library, glancing
up at the darkening sky as she buttoned her jacket. A chilly breeze was
sweeping down from the mountains, pushing dead leaves along the
quiet street. She hurried to her car in the almost deserted parking lot.

The house was quiet as Lee opened the garage door and
walked into the kitchen.

"Sara? I'm home," she called.

No answer. She dropped her notebook and book on the snack
bar. There was a note from Sara stuck to the refrigerator door. *Mom—
Kevin invited me to his house for spaghetti. I couldn't wait for you to
get back. Home by 9:00. Hugs and kisses, S.*

Lee sighed and bent to stroke Mister, who wound around
her legs.

"Well, at least I have you for company, old buddy," she
said. Still wearing her jacket, she wandered out onto the patio.
Mister followed closely behind and jumped up on the four foot
wall to look out into the arroyo. A brilliant tangerine-and-gold
colored sunset lit up the sky as the sun dropped behind the hills. Lee
filled a large plastic watering can and began to water the dwarf
evergreens that grew in clay pots on the patio. The mild weather
couldn't last much longer. Last year it had snowed on Halloween.
She'd had a real battle convincing Sara to wear a ski parka over her
gypsy Halloween costume.

She refilled the watering can and started toward the potted shrubs at the east end of the patio. A full yellow moon was rising over the mountain peaks. Lee stopped, her breath caught in her throat. As she stared at the moon, she suddenly saw Juan in her mind's eye—*standing on the top of a lonely hill, holding her sweat blanket high above his head. The cool night breeze ruffled his dark hair and plastered his shirt against his muscular chest. Chanting mysterious words, he began shaking the blanket to the four directions.*

Lee shivered as the vivid image slowly faded from her mind. She put down the watering can and hurried into the house with Mister, locking the sliding door behind them. Feeling unnerved, she poured herself a glass of wine. I won't let this become a habit, she promised herself. *But desperate times call for desperate measures.* She carried her drink into the living room where she sat with Mister in her lap, staring out the window at the moon as it cleared the dark outline of the mountains and floated across a deep lavender sky.

Sometime later, Lee realized that her glass was empty. How long had she been sitting there? She lifted a sleeping Mister from her lap, closed the wooden shades and walked into the kitchen. Pausing in front of the refrigerator, she debated whether or not to have more wine. *Why not? Maybe it'll help me relax.*

The phone on the kitchen wall rang, causing her to jump. She quickly poured herself another glass of wine and picked up the receiver.

"Lee? It's Socorro. How are you doing?"

"Oh, hi. I'm okay, I guess. A little spooked."

"That's understandable. Listen, I called a few of my psychic friends here in town. None of them know Juan Mascareñas. But one of them—you may know her—Clarity Light?"

"No, I don't think so." *With a name like that, I'm pretty sure I'd remember.*

"Well, anyway, Clarity agreed that Cavado is a very negative place. She said that she stopped for a picnic there one day last month on her way to Taos, but got such a headache she had to leave. The psychic vibrations were just too strong."

"Really?" Lee tried to hide a slight impatience. She wanted facts, not psychic mumbo-jumbo.

"I'm going to visit my grandmother at Santa Clara Pueblo tomorrow. I'll ask around there and see what I can find out. If Juan's a *brujo*, Grandma will probably know about him. She's eighty-six and knows everything that has ever happened within a two-hundred-mile radius of the pueblo."

"Thanks. I'd appreciate any information you can uncover. I feel absolutely obsessed by this thing. I can't seem to think about anything else."

"I was afraid of that. Lee, did you leave anything in Cavado? Clothing or any personal object?"

"No. I almost left my jewelry, but Juan gave it back to me as I was leaving. Why?"

"He returned your jewelry? That surprises me. *Brujos* need something belonging to a person in order to cast a spell on them. Of course, he does have your perspiration on the sweat blanket. If he's as powerful as I think he is, that might be enough."

"How about urine?" Lee said, thinking of what she'd read.

"What?"

"I used Juan's portable toilet. It doesn't flush."

There was a long silence. "That explains it." Socorro's voice was strained. "He didn't need the jewelry. With your urine, he could cast one hell of a spell."

"You don't really believe that he put a spell on me, do you?"

"It's looking that way. I'm getting very disturbing readings. And you just admitted to feeling obsessed."

"Well, sure, I'm preoccupied with all this. Who wouldn't be?" Lee's voice was shaking. "I mean, I can accept being drugged and maybe even hypnotized, but a *spell*? That's just too damned freaky!"

"I'm sorry. I didn't mean to upset you. Try not to worry. I'll see what I can find out tomorrow."

Lee took a deep breath. "All right. Thanks, Socorro. I really do appreciate what you're doing. This whole thing has me very strung out."

"I don't blame you. Take care, and remember to keep candles burning in your house. It would also be a good idea to take frequent baths or showers. Water drains off negative psychic forces. I'll call you soon."

Lee hung up and finished her glass of wine. Although she wasn't really hungry, she forced herself to eat a bowl of soup. She hoped she hadn't been rude on the phone. Socorro had some pretty strange ideas, but she seemed sincere about trying to help.

Lee continued to be on edge. Two glasses of wine, which she would normally feel, had done nothing to calm her nerves. As she walked through the large house checking the locks on doors and windows, she found herself wishing for an alarm system. Nick had talked about having one installed, but they'd never gotten around to it. She made a mental note to call the alarm company. *Better safe than sorry. The crime rate is up everywhere, even in Santa Fe.*

She remembered the .32-caliber handgun that Nick kept loaded and hidden on the top shelf of the closet, behind his ski boots. She knew how to use it. Nick had insisted she accompany him to the target range for practice sessions several years ago. He'd maintained that the gun would give her a feeling of security when he was gone. But Lee tried not to think about it. Just knowing the weapon was there in the closet gave her the creeps. Heaven forbid she'd ever find herself in a situation where she had to use it.

Feeling a need to keep busy, she hurried up the stairs into her study. After doing some final editing on her Cavado story, she went back down. Dr. Mallory would call this compulsive behavior, she realized, as she rechecked all the locks. *I'm acting neurotic as hell.* Mister followed her from room to room, nervously twitching his tail.

Finally, Lee settled herself in bed with two pillows at her back, pulled up the covers and reached for the library book on her nightstand, *Native American Witchcraft: Sorcery and Spells.* She opened the book and began to read:

> *Sorcery is essentially an enchantment by spell. The sorcerer need not encounter his victim personally. All that is required is an item of the victim's clothing or, better still, something from the victim's body, such as hair, fingernail clippings, feces or urine...*

There it is again—"urine." Lee fought a rising wave of anxiety. *This author forgot to mention sweat.* She took a deep breath and continued reading:

> *...the sorcerer can enhance the power of spells by casting them in proximity to a lightning-struck tree...*

A lightning-struck tree! She felt goose bumps rise along her arms as she remembered the half-charred cottonwood in front of Juan's house. Okay, okay, calm down, she ordered herself. *That's just a coincidence. Lightning strikes trees all the time. It doesn't mean that Juan uses that tree to... Knock it off, Lindsay. You're letting your imagination run away with you again!* She slid farther under the covers before continuing:

A spell cast in this manner may cause the victim to be under his control and sometimes to sicken and/or die.

Lee skimmed the next page until her eyes fell on the words:

...Sorcerers are said to cast spells while stepping over the body of an unsuspecting victim.

An image of Juan stepping back and forth over her body as she lay under the sweat blanket flashed into Lee's mind. And he'd been murmuring, chanting to himself the whole time! She made herself continue:

Some chants may be used to bewitch. Chants are instruments of great power, which are usually intended for good. But an evil medicine man may use the power of chants for his own malevolent purposes.

Lee closed the book. *Okay, that's enough. This is not the best time for witchcraft research. Not at night. Not when I'm alone.* She returned the book to her nightstand and reached for the television remote control. *Murder She Wrote* was half over. For a moment, Lee watched Angela Lansbury follow a suspect through a dark, deserted building. Then she switched channels until she found a lighthearted sitcom.

An hour later, after Sara was safely home and in her room, Lee was still wide awake. She got out of bed and walked to the large bedroom window, parting the draperies to look outside. The full moon flooded the silent hills with a ghostly radiance. Lee felt a chill. Was Juan really out there somewhere chanting to his ancient gods? Hugging herself, she turned away from the window. She climbed into bed she curled close to Mister, grateful for his purring warmth and companionship.

Mondays were always busy at *Santa Fe Today*. When Lee arrived at eight-fifteen, all three telephone lines were ringing. She waited by Julie's desk until the receptionist had handled the calls.

"I need to talk to you about something," she said.

"Just a sec." Julie scribbled a short note to herself. Then she looked up, smiling.

"Julie, I'm going to tell you again—please do not give my home number to people who call here. Nick gets very annoyed when work-related calls start coming in at night. That's why I have an unlisted number. Just take a message, and tell them I'll get back to them."

Julie looked puzzled. "That's what I always do. I've never given your number out."

"You didn't give it to a man who called on Friday? A man who said that I'd interviewed him earlier?"

"I wouldn't do that."

"Could anyone else have talked to him?"

"I was the only one answering the phones. Bruce was on vacation. Pat was sick. Marcia and Al were out on assignment most of the day."

"But he said…"

"Who?"

"Never mind. Just forget it." Lee hurried into her office and closed the door.

She hardly looked up from her desk all day long. By throwing herself into her work, she was able to bury—at least for the time being—the disturbing thoughts that haunted her.

On her way home late that afternoon, Lee made a quick stop at *The Camera Shop*. Her Cavado prints had been ready for several days.

That's strange, she thought, shuffling through the pictures a second time. *I know I took a picture of that huge raven, just before it flew away. It was right before I took those shots of the church. I wonder why it didn't turn out?* She blocked a thought that tried to form by turning her attention to the shots looking down into the village. *Not bad. I should have used the telephoto lens, though.* She put the prints in her purse and drove home.

After Sara had gone to bed that night, Lee decided to do some yoga exercises. Slow stretches were relaxing. Maybe they would help her get to sleep. She stripped to her panties and sat on the carpet in front of the floor-to-ceiling mirror in her bedroom.

Raising both hands over her head, she pressed her palms together and turned slowly to the right and then to the left. Next, she bent toward the floor, her arms out straight behind her. Suddenly she stopped, staring down at her small breasts and pink nipples.

Her mind slipped to a mental image of dark brown nipples seen from the same angle. *Heavy, brown breasts, shining with oil and perspiration.* Her scalp began to tingle. She hadn't allowed herself to think about her candle meditation dream since her walk yesterday morning. *Was it just a dream?* Even though the body she'd seen had been unfamiliar, she had somehow felt it was hers. Vivid memories flooded her mind—smoke burning her eyes and nose, the rancid odor of her skin, the weight of her breasts as she swayed and danced.

Juan's voice echoed suddenly in her ears, "*It's time to get in touch with who you really are. The memory and the understanding will come. You and I have performed that ceremony before, in a different lifetime. Trust me.*"

In a different lifetime... She frowned, recalling long black hair sticking to her sweaty shoulders. She'd been topless in the "dream," wearing only a short leather skirt similar to the one that Juan had given her for the Awakening Ceremony.

She closed her eyes, trying to recall the face of the painted, antler-bedecked man who had handed her a small stone bowl. He'd looked Native American, his bronze-colored forehead decorated with white paint. She had a fleeting memory of straight black hair and piercing dark eyes. And on his cheek had been a strange red mark. Her eyes flew open. *He'd had a spider-shaped birthmark, exactly like Juan's!*

Lee stood up and put on her robe. She paced around the bedroom, her mind racing. *Were those memories from a past life? Or am I just going off the deep end?*

She thought of the dream—or flashback—she'd experienced ten years ago—the violent death of a woman with long black braids. She'd been practicing candle-meditation when that happened, too.

When she'd described that experience to Juan, he didn't seem at all skeptical. In fact, he'd said something about her having the ability to summon "deep memories." And he said several times that she'd be amazed at how much he knew about her. *What was he hinting at? Could he possibly have information about my past lifetimes?* Suddenly, that thought didn't seem quite so incredible.

A decision was already forming in Lee's mind, overriding her fear and good judgment. It was almost as though the decision was being made for her. *They'll have to get along without me at the office tomorrow. I'm going back to Cavado. I have to go back—despite Socorro's warnings. And Dr. Mallory's. There's something going on here, something that won't let me rest. And I have to get to the bottom of it. I won't have any peace until I do. It'll be all right. I'll be very careful this time. I won't eat or drink anything, I won't pee in his port-a-potty and I certainly won't participate in any more ceremonies.*

Lee saw Juan's face in her mind—his sensuous smile and dark compelling eyes—and felt an unwelcome thrill of excitement. It can't hurt to just talk to him again, she convinced herself. *I won't be in any danger. Surely. He's just a village* curandero. *This* brujo *business is nonsense. Superstitious nonsense. Besides, I don't really have any choice. I want answers and there's only one way to get them. I have to see Juan again. But I'll sure as hell keep my clothes on this time!*

11

Lee fought with herself as she drove toward Cavado the next morning. *I have to do this. I know it's nuts, but I want some answers and Juan's the only one who can give them to me. But what if he really is dangerous?* She remembered the alarm on Socorro's face after her trance—or whatever it was—at lunch. *"I fear for you, Lee,"* she'd said. *"You encountered a brujo."*

Socorro had also said something about Tuesdays and Fridays being "witches days," days when any magic being worked was especially potent. *It is Tuesday...but that's just a coincidence.*

For a moment, Lee reconsidered. There was still time to change her mind, to just turn the car around.

"I can't!" she said out loud. *Can't? Or won't?* the voice in her head asked. Whichever, the compulsion to see Juan again was too strong. *If I don't follow through with this, I'll never know the truth about our possible past life connection. And I would always wonder. Getting the truth out of that bastard is the only way I'll ever be completely free of him.*

Again, she saw Juan's face, his penetrating eyes, and the graceful movements of his muscular body as he danced around the buffalo hide. Something deep within her—something wild and dangerous—stirred in response to that memory. In spite of the cool day, Lee suddenly felt flushed. She cracked the car window to get some air.

The closer to Cavado she got, the more her mental turmoil grew. *What am I doing? Every instinct and rational thought I have is telling me to stay away from Cavado. An yet, I can't seem to do that. I'm almost there!* And then a thin thread of reason told her she needed to talk to someone who knows Juan. Someone who could shed a little light on who—or what—he really is. When she came to the gas station, she pulled in beside the full-service pump.

The tall, thin attendant she'd talked to before sauntered over.

"Thought it was you," he said with a grin. "Recognized the car soon as you came around the bend."

"I need to ask you a few questions. And I might as well get some gas, too."

"Sure thing. Fill 'er up?" She nodded.

He put the nozzle in the gas tank and walked around the car, wiping his hands on a dirty rag. He rested an elbow against the top of the door and bent down level with Lee's face.

"Now then. What can I tell a city gal like yourself that you don't already know?"

Lee pulled back slightly, but mustered a pleasant expression.

"As I told you last week, I'm writing about this area. I thought you might be able to provide some local background."

"I'd be happy to provide you with anything you might need, pretty lady. You can count on that."

She ignored both the comment and accompanying leer.

"Last week you said that Juan Mascareñas is a *curandero*. What else can you tell me about him?"

"Not a whole lot. He drops by to gas up that black pickup of his is all. Don't say much. Kinda keeps to hisself. Now, Pablo— he's from Cavado—bet he could tell you more about him. He's around back, working on that rattletrap low rider of his. Hold on. I'll get him."

Pablo was small and brown, with close-set, darting eyes. He reminded Lee of a fox. Obviously reluctant to talk to her, he approached cautiously and stopped several feet from her car, arms crossed defensively in front of his chest.

Lee opened the car door and got out.

"Hi. I won't take much of your time," she said. "I just wondered what you could tell me about Juan Mascareñas, the *curandero* in Cavado."

Pablo's eyes were suspicious slits. "Why do you want to know about him?"

"I'm writing a magazine story about Cavado. And he seems to be an important person there."

No response.

"Isn't Juan the village *curandero*?"

He nodded, mouth tight and grim.

"Do you know him well?"

"No, Señora."

"Has he ever treated you?"

"No."

Lee sighed. This was like pulling teeth. Pablo wasn't going to volunteer a thing.

"But he saved my little sister's life."

Lee blinked in surprise. "He did? How?"

"She fell from a tree. Hit her head, very bad. Blood came from her ears and nose. There was no time to drive to the hospital in Española. My mother took her to Juan, and he saved her."

"How? How did he save her?"

Pablo shrugged. "He has ways. Treated her for two days. On the third day she was climbing trees again." He smiled a tentative smile, showing discolored front teeth.

Lee smiled back, feeling reassured. "I'm glad to hear that. This information is very helpful. Thank you."

"*De nada.*" Pablo turned and walked away.

Lee paid for the gas and got back in the car. The Anglo attendant waved goodbye.

"You come back real soon now, doll," he hollered. "You hear?"

Don't hold your breath, buster, Lee thought. She pulled out of the station and turned down the dirt road that led to Cavado.

Juan's pickup was parked beside the tiny adobe house with its drawn window shades. Lee parked her car beside the dead tree and turned off the engine. As before, she was acutely aware of the silence. Except for a bony, black dog trotting down the dusty road, she could detect no signs of life in the village down the hill.

She sat in the car for a moment, trying to calm her racing heart. There's nothing to be afraid of, she told herself. *He's a healer. Pablo just confirmed that. I've come this far, I may as well go in and talk to him. Just talk. No more ceremonies.*

A memory of Juan blotting sweat from her naked breasts made her mouth go dry. A sudden wave of fear overcame her lust. *Dear God, how did I get into this? No one who knows me would believe it. I really don't believe it myself. I don't know what's happened to my judgment.*

At that instant, a self-protective part of Lee's mind kicked in, rebelling against her earlier rationalizations. *Get the hell out of here! Go! Go!*

She started the engine again, and began to back up. Then, looking over her shoulder, she saw Juan, stepping from behind the dead tree. In an instant, he had opened her car door and it was too late.

"I've been waiting for you." Juan grabbed her elbow and half-pulled her out of the car. His arm was firmly around her shoulders as he hurried her down the dirt path.

Lee managed to find her voice. "Wait! My purse!"

"You don't need your purse. Believe me, no one would dare bother it here."

An instant later, Lee found herself inside Juan's candle-lit front room.

She blinked, momentarily blinded. As her eyes began to adjust to the darkness, she raised them to Juan's face. Words stuck in her throat as she stared up at him. The corners of his mouth lifted in a smug smile.

"I knew you would come," he said, pulling her close. His dark eyes locked on hers as he ran one hand up the back of her neck, cradling her head.

She tried to pull away. "No! Don't. I…I need to talk to you."

"Later, *mi vida*," he whispered, holding her fast. "This is not a time for words." His warm, moist lips fastened on hers.

Lee felt something like an electric shock run through her body. Her knees felt weak. Frantically, she jerked her head to one side.

"Let me go! What do you think you're doing?"

"You know what I'm doing and you want it, as much as I do." He clasped her chin, forcing her to look at him. "Trust me. You must trust me." Juan's dark eyes held her, awakening feelings too deep and compelling for her to identify.

Once again, his lips met hers. Lee struggled for only an instant before all strength and reason deserted her. As if she had fallen into a dream, Lee closed her eyes and leaned against him. She was only dimly aware that her jacket had been removed and dropped to the wooden floor.

He kissed her gently, unhurriedly, his lips moving softly as his tongue explored her mouth. A tidal wave of desire surged through Lee, drowning all rational thoughts. The outside world slipped away, leaving only Juan's searching lips. All at once, she was aware of his hands unfastening the buttons on her blouse.

"No! Juan, no…" His lips stopped her words and her blouse fell open. He pulled back to slide it off her shoulders. She dropped her arms and let it go. Her eyes followed its fall, and she noticed that his feet were bare.

"Wait a minute! Don't…" she whispered as the last shred of her resistance unraveled.

Ignoring her words, he drew her to him once more, pressing warm kisses down her neck as he unbuttoned her trousers.

"Trust me, Lee. This is for you. It is for us."

The trousers followed her blouse and he took her hand to help her step out of them. She left her shoes behind as she did. When he pulled her back against him, she tried feebly to twist in his embrace.

"No! Stop! I can't…" It was almost a sob, but her will to resist faded with the sound of her voice.

Juan bent and slipped one arm under her knees, lifting her effortlessly.

"Don't fight it, *querida*," he said in a soft voice, as he carried her into the back room. "You don't want to fight it. Trust me."

He lowered her gently onto the buffalo hide rug and straddled her as he slowly unbuttoned his shirt and tossed it aside. He smiled down at her, his hands caressing her breasts before he deftly unfastened the front hook of her bra. His hair shone blue-black in the candlelight as he bent toward her. Slowly, his tongue teased each nipple before sucking it into his mouth. Lee shut her eyes as pleasure shuddered down the length of her body and she gave herself to the sensations.

"Lift your hips," he said. "Quickly." The next thing she knew, he had pulled her panties down past her hips and slid them off. She felt his lips brush back and forth across her quivering stomach. Then, in a swift movement, he rose to his feet and removed his Levi's, leaving him naked, standing above her like some dark angel on a mission from the gods.

Lee looked up, feeling the inevitability and no longer wishing to avoid it. She was entranced by the light and shadow that emphasized his well-muscled body and felt a thrill of desire as candlelight flickered across his impressively erect penis. *Is this really happening? My God, am I really doing this? Yes…*

Juan smiled. "Yes, Lee. This is real. You want this as much as I do. Trust me."

Before she could wonder if he'd read her mind, he was lying beside her. She made one last attempt to break away, to fight her way through the mindless passion that engulfed her. But he held her, pressing her back into the springy fur of the buffalo, his eyes locked on hers.

"Trust me, *querida*," he whispered. "Trust me."

Nothing made sense to Lee in that moment. She felt disconnected from the self she'd always known. And when he began to kiss her again, nothing mattered but surrendering to a fierce and altogether alien passion. She ran her hands across his smooth wide shoulders and up his neck, burying her fingers deep in his hair.

"At last, at last," he murmured, between passionate kisses. "You are mine again, at last." His words barely registered as she pressed against him, her mouth searching for his.

"I can wait no longer," he panted. "Open to me." She was vaguely aware of her own sobbing breath as she spread her legs and locked her feet across his back. She felt his hands slide under her hips and grasp her buttocks. She gasped as he thrust into her. The room beyond his shoulders became a shadowed blur as her body began to move to his rhythm.

Her eyes fastened on the dark wings nailed to the wall above the window. They seemed to move as the candlelight cast flickering shadows on the wall. Juan's body suddenly tensed and jerked convulsively. He buried his face in her hair and cried out something she couldn't understand. Then her own climax exploded, shattering all thought.

Afterward, they lay side by side. Lee felt stunned, totally unable to deal with what had happened. Juan propped himself up on one elbow, looking down at her. The amulet dangled, its red crystal eyes glowing.

She turned away from him. "Oh, dear God," she groaned. "I can't believe..." Tears rolled down her cheeks.

He gently turned her face back toward his and brushed her tears away with his finger.

"Yes, you can *mi vida*," he whispered. "You can believe what is true."

"Juan," she whispered, searching his dark eyes. "What have you done to me?"

He pulled her against his chest. "Some things are meant to happen," he said. "They cannot be controlled any more than the wind can be commanded not to blow."

She drew back, doing her best to focus on him. Her vision, as well as her mind, seemed blurred. "But...but I had no idea when I came here this morning that we would...that any of this would happen." She laid back, her head on his upper arm. "I'm so confused. I came here today...to ask you questions. To try...try to find answers."

"And did you not succeed?" His voice sounded faintly amused. "Doesn't the passion that we shared answer your questions about me? About us?"

"No," she said, shaking her head. "I feel more bewildered than ever. I'm mystified by what just happened—by how I could have let it happen."

His hand caressed her cheek, turning her head toward him.

"You must not feel regret, *querida*," he said. "We have no time for regret." He kissed her, gently at first, then with rising passion.

Lee felt her body respond. "You must be a *brujo*," she whispered, "to be able to do this again...so soon."

"I am a man who has waited for a long time," he said. "A very long time."

I can't believe this is happening...can't believe how much I want it to happen, she thought, as they began making love again.

They lay exhausted in each other's arms. After a few moments, Juan pulled away and rose to his hands and knees, reaching for a blanket that was rolled against the wall. He shook it open and laid back down, drawing it over their sweaty bodies.

Lee tried to pull out of her dream-like state of mind.

"Is...is this another part of the sweating ceremony?"

Getting no answer, she turned her head toward him. Juan's profile was sharply outlined in the light of the single candle still burning on the table by the sofa. His spider-shaped birthmark seemed to cling to the hollow of his cheek. An image of deer antlers above another shadowed face flashed in her mind, and she closed her eyes. When she opened them a few seconds later, he was studying her with an unreadable expression on his face.

She managed to push herself up to a sitting position, gathering the blanket to her chest. A wave of dizziness forced her to lie back down.

"Why do I feel like this?" she asked. "I didn't drink or eat anything, but you're still hypnotizing me...aren't you?

"You continue to believe that?"

She was surprised by the hurt and disappointment in his voice.

"I don't know what I think, Juan. Help me."

"Of course. How may I do that?"

"You can answer some questions," she said tentatively.

"All right. What questions?"

Lee frantically tried to organize her scattered thoughts. "Well...for starters...are you married?" Her irrational laugh surprised her. "This isn't funny. It's just so... unreal... so unbelievable. We've made love twice this morning, and I don't even know if you're married."

"I have no wife." He was silent for a moment and when he spoke again, his voice was husky. "This lifetime has been a solitary one for me." He turned toward her and brushed her hair back from her forehead. "Sometimes it is necessary to be lonely. There is an old Spanish saying, *'Lo que no sé puede remediar, hay que aguantar'*. It means 'What cannot be cured must be endured'."

Lee found herself getting lost again in his dark eyes. *Think! Think!*

"Where do you actually live? I'm guessing not in this little building."

"You are correct. This is just where I work. My home is not far from here, on the other side of the village." He paused. "You're shaking, *querid*a. Are you cold?"

When Lee shrugged, Juan pulled the blanket back up over her shoulders.

"That's just your body's reaction to deep feelings breaking through. It will soon pass."

"More...tell me more about your house," she said. She needed answers...even if she was having trouble forming the questions.

"I live in a *hacienda* built by my grandfather, Don Antonio Mascareñas. It has been added onto from time to time over the years. Now it is quite large."

"Do you live there... all alone?"

A shadow seemed to pass across his face. "My mother lived there, too, until she passed from the flesh many years ago."

Keep going, keep going, she urged herself. *Don't stop now. This is your chance...*

"You have no other family? Brothers or sisters?"

"I was an only child. My father died before I was born." He raised himself on one elbow, looking down at her. "Now, tell me about yourself. Do you come from a large family in this lifetime?"

In this lifetime... Lee shook her head, trying to clear it.

"I have an older sister. And a few relatives...in Arizona, that I've been out of touch with since my parents died."

"You will be reunited with your parents someday. In new relationships, a new lifetime.

"You keep talking about that. Do you really believe it?"

"I know it to be true," he assured her. "And soon you will, too." He abruptly changed the subject. "Your sister, are you close to her?"

"She moved to Boston when I was still in high school. We've never really had a chance to know each other as adults."

"So you have only your husband and a daughter." He smiled slowly, and then bent to kiss her neck, brushing his lips down and across her collarbone.

Through her fog, Lee was struck by the strangely ominous tone of his voice. She fought to turn the subject away from her family.

"Tell me...about your work. What exactly does a *curandero* do?"

"People come to me to be helped, to be healed. I do what must be done for them." He gently ran a finger up and down the side of her neck. "I accept no money for what I do. When money is exchanged, it weakens the medicine."

She realized that she hadn't noticed a telephone in either of the small dark rooms. "Do they call here for an appointment?"

"Not here. I allow no electronic interruptions while I am working. The number you have is for my telephone at home."

Feeling a little clearer, Lee pressed on. "What...sort of illnesses do you treat?"

"Injuries, aches and pains. Sometimes the *mal de ojo*."

"*Mal de ojo?* "

"The Evil eye."

"Are you talking about removing some kind of spell?"

"You might call it a spell. It is a sickness certain people can cause by their jealousy."

Juan's fingers and his lips continued to move over her skin, making it difficult for her to concentrate.

"How did you learn these things?" she asked.

"From my mother. She was an exceptional woman. Most exceptional." His expression turned to one of concern. "You're still shivering. I'm going to get you another blanket," he said, getting up. "You must not catch a cold." Then he smiled down at her. "Of course, if you do, I will be happy to treat you."

She responded with a slight smile, and watched Juan walk naked into the tiny back room where she had used the portable toilet during her previous visit. He came right back, carrying a soft woolen blanket that he draped carefully around her shoulders.

"Would you like some tea?" he asked.

"No! No tea." She looked away.

He laughed. "Oh, yes...you believe I put something in your tea. You think I drugged you. Lee," he said, kneeling beside her. "You must trust me." He caressed her cheek. "Trust me. I would never hurt you."

She stared at him. *Is that the truth? What kind of man are you, really?* His face revealed nothing.

"How about a beer instead? It would be good for you...to calm your nerves." Without waiting for an answer, Juan continued, "I have some cold."

Lee recalled seeing a small refrigerator in the back room. *So, medicine men drink beer?*

When he returned, he made a point of opening the bottles in front of her. "So you don't worry that I spiked them with something," he said, treating it as a joke. "To put your mind completely at ease, I insist that you choose your bottle."

Lee didn't find his teasing amusing. She accepted one of the bottles, took a deep drink and then another, realizing how thirsty she was. After a moment and another drink, she felt considerably better. The dizziness and disorientation seemed to be gone.

"This tastes good," she said. "I haven't had a beer in years."

"No?"

"I usually drink white wine. Beer's too fattening."

"You worry about that? That you will be fat?" He looked amused. "You are *muy flaca*, my love. Very skinny."

"I guess I can thank my metabolism for that," she said, taking another sip. "I've always been slender."

"No, not always," he said, watching her.

"What do you mean?"

"When we were together before, long ago, you were not skinny," he said in a soft, matter-of-fact voice. "Your body was much fuller then."

She lowered her beer, staring at him.

"You're remembering, aren't you? The memories are breaking through, I can see it in your eyes." He moved closer to her, putting his arm around her shoulders.

Lee's stomach twisted into a hard knot, threatening to bring up that last swallow of beer. She had a sudden bitter taste in her mouth, and set her half-empty bottle aside on the floor just beyond the rug.

"Juan," she said, "you scare the hell out of me."

She lay back in his arms and described what had happened late Saturday night as she meditated. When she finished, she turned to look at him.

"I tried to convince myself that it was just a dream, that I'd fallen asleep." She watched him shake his head. "You don't think so though, do you?"

Juan was silent for a moment. When he spoke, his voice trembled slightly.

"You were beautiful then, as you are now," he said. "But you had a different kind of beauty. Your name…it meant She Who Talks to Animals. You were very gifted, a most powerful medicine woman."

"I was Native American?"

"We both were, living on a mesa beneath what we now call the Jémez Mountains."

She sat up and turned to stare at him. "You mean Los Alamos?"

"Near there. Even the ruins are gone now. It was very long ago." He caressed her partially exposed shoulder. "But I have said enough. It is better that you remember for yourself."

"That's it? That's all you're going to tell me?"

"*Descansa*, Lee. Just relax. I have told you, it is necessary that you trust me."

"Relax? How can I relax?" She pulled away from him, her voice rising. "This is just too damned creepy. I mean, I can't even believe I came back here. Much less that I've been screwing my brains out with someone I hardly know."

"Is that what you think?" His expression changed in an instant, becoming threatening. "That I am someone you hardly know? You try my patience, woman! Stop hiding from yourself."

Lee suddenly felt fear. She yanked the blanket up, trying to cover her naked shoulders. *This is insanity! I've got to get out of here.* She tried to get to her feet, but her legs were tangled in the blanket, and her vision was blurred by sudden tears.

The weight of Juan's hand on her shoulder stopped her struggle.

"*Lo siento,*" he said. "I'm sorry. I spoke too harshly. Sit back down, please."

Engulfed by shame and confusion, Lee wept, hiding her face in the blanket even as she felt herself drawn once more into Juan's strong embrace.

"Trust me, *querida*," he whispered in her ear. "Let me take your unhappiness from you. This is not a time for tears. It's a time for rejoicing. We are together again. And you are growing stronger, more in touch with who you really are."

He placed a hand on each side of her face and looked into her eyes. "Your sweat blanket was heavy with the demons of self-doubt and fear. They clung to the blanket as I shook it. But when the ceremony was complete, I felt your strength began to grow." He paused. "It will soon be time for the final ceremony—time for me to take you through the door."

Alarm blossomed into panic. "No! I told you, I don't want to do that. I won't do it! I'm afraid...."

"Shhh. *Descansa, mi amor*. You will not be afraid when the time comes. But do not let that concern you now. There is no rush."

"I mean it, Juan. I'm not going through any so-called door with you."

He bent to kiss her shoulder. "Don't upset yourself. We have time. And I have much to teach you."

"No!"

"Yes. I'm going to teach you to get back in touch with the earth, to regain the secrets that you have forgotten. You will remember how the plants feel and how to communicate with animals." Juan's eyes glistened with a strange passion. "I will teach you to talk to the birds again. I will return your medicine power to you. Together, we will be as we were before."

"What are you talking about? I don't understand."

"I will take you to my mother's people in the mountains of northwestern Mexico. I lived with them for two years after I left the university. They have powers that will amaze you, powers they will impart to you."

Lee's stomach clenched. "Mexico? Your mother came from Mexico? I thought your family had lived in Cavado for generations."

"My mother was of the Yaqui people. My father met her on a trip to Chihuahua."

"That explains your connections to Native American traditions."

"My knowledge comes from all my people, both Hispanic and Native. But you will soon understand this. Trust me. This and much more. I will make special ceremonial skins for you before we leave."

"Leave?" The impact of what he was saying finally hit her. "Wait a minute. What are you talking about? I can't go to Mexico with you. That's impossible. I have a life! A family, a husband and a daughter. Not to mention the magazine..." Her voice trailed off as she stared at his frozen face.

"Listen to me," he said in a sharp voice. "Our souls were bound together long ago. We made a sacred pledge. It cannot be undone. You belong to me!" His tone softened. "Forgive me. It is just that I have waited so long for you. But never mind. You will come to understand that."

Lee felt as though she couldn't breathe. *I have to escape! Where are my clothes?*

"I have to go now," she said. "I...I have an appointment in Santa Fe. I can't be late."

Juan's face was expressionless. "If you must go, I will get your things," he said, helping her to her feet. "Most of them are in the front room."

Lee dressed quickly, managing to button only a few of the buttons on her blouse. "Goodbye," she murmured, moving past him to the door.

He caught her arm.

"You will return soon, *mi vida*," he said. "Trust me." He held her face in both his hands, forcing her to look at him. "And I will be waiting." Then pulling her against his naked body, he kissed her cold lips.

She broke away, grabbed her jacket, and opened the door, shading her eyes from the glare of bright noon as she ran to her car. In seconds she was safely inside, speeding down the dusty road, frantic to get away from Cavado—and from Juan.

12

Lee drove back to Santa Fe in what she recognized was a state of shock. The passion she had experienced in Juan's arms had been overpowering. She wouldn't have believed it possible to be swept away like that. It had almost felt as though her body belonged to someone else.

At last she was home. She parked the car in the garage and glanced at the clock on the dashboard. One-thirty. *Not counting driving time, I spent three hours with Juan. Three incredible hours.*

Lee gave Mister a quick scratch on the head and went up the stairs to her bedroom. She kicked off her shoes and collapsed, fully clothed, on the bed. Pulling the comforter up over her shoulders, she closed her eyes. Images of Juan's face and naked body circled through her mind as she sank gratefully into oblivion.

She was hurrying uphill, following a narrow path worn deeply into the pale sandstone face of the high mesa. It wasn't much farther. She was almost home. A thin trail of white smoke rose into the air from the cooking fire above.

She paused on the edge of a flat stone ledge and adjusted the shoulder strap on her back sling. It had been a successful day, yielding a good harvest of roots, herbs and berries. As she gazed across the rocky canyon far below, a gust of wind blew her long black hair across her face. She brushed it out of her eyes and inhaled the good rain smell. It was coming. The long dry season was ending. It would be a strong, cleansing storm.

The sky darkened as massive purple thunderheads obscured the sun. There was no time to waste. She felt the first drops of rain strike her bare arms as she scrambled up the path and turned to the sheer cliff face. Using familiar toe and finger holds worn into the rock, she carefully balanced her weight as she reached for the thick exposed root overhead, and wedged her yucca sandal into a small space between two tall boulders, pulling herself up.

With a loud snap, the root broke in her hand. She gasped, digging her fingernails into the hard sandstone surface, frantically searching for a hold. For a long moment she clung to smooth bare rock. Then, her fingers sliding and scratching, she began to fall backward. She screamed as she felt her right ankle twist and snap. Sharp pain flooded her senses, followed by a bright red flash as she smashed against the ground.

She lay still, unable to open her eyes, but aware of throbbing pain in both her ankle and her head. From far away came a ringing sound. She allowed herself to drift into a cloud of darkness. But gradually a cold, wet sensation nagged her to awareness. Rain. It was raining hard. Pain stabbed her scalp as she jerked her head to one side. Her hair was caught on something. Squinting through wet eyelashes, she stared at sharp branches close to her face. She was cold. Somehow she must get to her feet and continue the journey up the trail. Warmth and safety waited above.

A small grey owl swooped toward her and landed on the ground, within inches of her face, flapping its wings against the rain.

"Bright Eyes," she whispered, "help me." She focused through her pain and reached into the bird's mind. "Go at once," she ordered. "Fly to your master. Tell Kamulko that I am injured. Make haste, Bright Eyes, make haste."

The owl's yellow eyes locked on hers for just an instant, then flew upward, toward the village on the mesa above.

She lifted her arm to shield her eyes from the rain. The irritating ringing sound was growing louder. She frowned, trying to identify it. The high-pitched call came from no creature that she could identify. But it seemed to be coming from nearby, growing louder. She cried out as she tried to move her ankle. Thick blackness engulfed her, blotting out the rain and the wetness. She felt herself leaving her body, slowly floating upward.

Ring…ring…ring.

Lee sat up, gasping, her head pounding, and stared at the phone. She ran her hand through her short hair and frowned. *My hair. What happened to my long black hair?* She shook her head. It had seemed…

"Oh, sweet Jesus," she whispered to the empty room.

Another ring. She lifted the receiver.

"Lee? Is that you?" It was a woman's voice.

"What? I…Yes?"

"Hi, it's Socorro. Are you all right?"

"I…I don't know. I was asleep. Dreaming, I guess. I heard the phone, but I couldn't seem to wake up." Lee reached under the covers to rub a dull ache in her right ankle.

"Oh, I'm sorry. Shall I call back later?"

"No. It's okay." She glanced at the bedside clock and saw that it was almost three o'clock. Sara would be home from school soon. She threw the covers back and stared at her ankle as she rotated her foot in a slow circle.

"You sound strange," Socorro said. "And I'm getting some really bad vibrations. Are you sure you're okay?"

"I'm just a little groggy." She stretched her leg out straight and took a deep breath. *There, my ankle seems all right now. The throbbing is gone. It must have been some sort of cramp.*

"Well, if you're sure," Socorro said in a concerned voice. "Listen, I need to talk to you. As soon as possible. I have some information about Juan Mascareñas."

Lee swallowed hard. She wasn't sure she wanted to hear what Socorro had to report.

"It's important," Socorro said urgently.

The tone of Socorro's voice caused Lee's stomach to lurch. "I'm going to be home in the morning," she heard herself say. "Can you come by?"

"Is eight-thirty too early?"

"That'd be fine." By the time she'd given directions to her house, Lee was feeling queasy. There was a terrible pounding in her temples.

"I've got to go. See you tomorrow."

Lee hung up the phone and lay back on the pillow, her forearm over her eyes. She felt physically ill. Aching and bruised—as though her body had actually experienced that terrible fall.

She was still in bed with a cold washcloth across her forehead when Sara came through the front door.

"Mom? I'm home," she called as she came upstairs.

"In here, honey." Lee's head and body still ached, but her nausea was gone. She tried not to think about her morning with Juan or Socorro's phone call, but images from her dream continued to dance through her head. *Stark bluffs. The storm. And an owl with shining golden eyes.*

"Bright Eyes?" She whispered the word and shivered under the warm covers.

Sara burst into the room, carrying Mister. "This cat is definitely gaining weight," she said. "If he gets any fatter he won't be able to jump over the courtyard walls." She stopped, her smile fading, when she saw Lee. "You sick again, Mom?"

"Just a headache. How was school?"

"Okay. The usual grind. I lived through the algebra exam. Just barely." She dropped Mister onto the bed. "I think I passed it, though."

"Good for you." Lee dropped the damp washcloth to the floor beside the bed and sat up. She held out her arms to her daughter. "Come here, baby," she said. "I need a hug."

Lee awoke the next morning feeling groggy and depressed. But her aches and pains had disappeared. It was almost eight o'clock. Sara had left for school without waking her. She rolled over on her back, staring up at the ceiling. Oh dear God, she thought as memories of the previous day returned. *It really happened. Juan and I made love. No, not 'made love.' We had sex. Incredible, almost savage sex. Twice.* She pulled the covers up under her chin.

The thought of Nick entered her mind for the first time in almost twenty-four hours. She caught her breath. I've cheated on my husband, she thought in amazement. *After all these years of being a faithful wife. And with someone who may be a witch, for all I know.* She buried her face in the pillow. *I have to get a firm hold on myself, deal in reality. I don't believe in witchcraft. Juan's a* curandero, *a healer. It's crazy to believe that he's anything else. After all, he healed that station guy's little sister. And that woman came to him with a stomach ache during the interview.*

She rolled over and stared at the ceiling. It was time to get out of bed and pull herself together. Socorro would be arriving soon—Socorro, with her spirit guides and vortices of evil. I know she means well, Lee thought, and I can't help but like her. *But, let's face it, the woman is a little nutty. "Meta-fizzled," as Nick would say.* Lee frowned, wondering what urgent news Socorro was bringing. *Why did I tell her she could come? I don't want to talk about Juan, right now. To anyone. I need to get him out of my mind.*

But Lee's mind, seemingly against her will, returned to Juan's lovemaking. *It was incredible, unlike anything I've ever imagined, much less experienced. Sex with Nick, when it happens—not so often these days—is something I usually enjoy. But the raw passion I felt with Juan is something else, a completely new emotion. And I'm not sure I even like the man. I certainly don't trust him. But when he touched me—God, help me, the way he made me feel! It was as though my body came alive, for the first time.*

She closed her eyes, remembering. *He was strong and demanding, yet gentle when I needed him to be. It was as though he read my mind and knew my sexual fantasies.* Her hand slipped under her nightgown, and she began to caress herself. The memory of those secret hours with Juan left her aching with desire. She clenched her hand into a fist as guilt washed over her. *Nick would never believe this. His wife fucking some backwoods* brujo *simply would not compute. It doesn't even compute with me!*

She sat up and noticed Mister watching her thoughtfully from the foot of the bed.

"Oh, sweetie," she said to the cat. "I can see that you're worried about me. Well, that makes two of us. Poor kitty, I'll bet Sara didn't feed you before she left. Come on," she said, swinging her legs out of bed. "Let's go rustle up some tea and cat food."

The doorbell rang promptly at eight-thirty. Socorro stood there, wearing a fringed leather shirt and masses of silver Indian jewelry. She was a knockout, Lee had to admit, even at that early hour. Her black jeans were tucked into tall snakeskin cowboy boots, and her hair hung in a thick dark braid over one shoulder. She was carrying a small drum and large canvas tote bag.

"Hi. Come in," Lee tried to sound more cheerful that she felt. She looked at the drum and bag. "What's all this?"

"I'll explain in a few minutes," Socorro said, stepping into the foyer. "First things first."

"Let's sit in the kitchen," Lee suggested. "Can I get you something to drink? Coffee? Orange juice?"

"Juice would be great."

Socorro sat at the kitchen table, watching Lee fill two glasses.

"You're not doing well this morning, are you?" she asked.

Lee grimaced. "So much for my acting abilities. Is it that obvious?"

"It is to me. Your aura—or Spirit Body, as I prefer to call it—is muddy, almost grey."

"I'm just tired," Lee said, feeling uncomfortable under Socorro's searching gaze. "I had a hard time getting to sleep last night." She carried the glasses to the kitchen table and sat down.

Socorro raised an eyebrow. "Are you burning a candle in your bedroom, as I suggested?"

"No. Actually, I did try it...one night. But I'm afraid I'll fall asleep and burn the house down."

"Well, I think I have a remedy for that." Socorro reached into her bag and pulled out a small, gaily wrapped box."

"What's this?"

"Open it."

"A present? What's the occasion?"

"I don't need an occasion to give someone I like a gift. It's just something I picked up for you at the Wicked Wick."

Lee unwrapped the box and looked inside. "A vase? It's beautiful."

"No, it's not a vase. It's a pottery candle."

Lee took the candle out of the box and put it on the table between them. It was dark blue, with a small white lizard painted on one side.

"Animals—all creature beings—are our teachers," Socorro explained, her fingernail tracing the reptilian tail that curved up the bowl of the candle. "We need only pay attention and be willing to learn. My people honor the spirit of the lizard because she's a survivor. If she loses her tail escaping a foe, she wastes no time regretting it. She simply grows another one. We could all learn a lesson from the lizard."

She smiled at the thoughtful expression on Lee's face.

"The candle's easy to use. Just fill the base with lamp oil and pull the wick partway up through the hole in that little ball so that you can light it. It'll burn for several days, until you need to replace the wick or refill it with oil. There are extra wicks in the box." She patted Lee's hand. "Now you don't need to worry about candle wax dripping while you sleep. And perhaps the spirit of the lizard will give you courage."

Lee's eyes filled with tears. "Oh, Socorro," she said in a choked voice, "thank you. I know you're really concerned, and I appreciate it."

"You're very welcome. I had it blessed by Dream Singer, a

Cheyenne-Arapahoe medicine man. It should provide you with some protection."

"Protection?"

"Let's just say that you shouldn't sleep in total darkness for awhile." She paused. "I drove to the pueblo Monday morning and talked to my grandmother about Juan Mascareñas."

Lee felt her body tense.

"I'm afraid I was right about him being more than a *curandero*," Socorro continued. "He's the son of Sinopa Mascareñas, known in these parts as a notorious Mexican *bruja*. She's dead now, but the elders at the pueblo still cross themselves when they speak of her. They remember the old rumors."

"What rumors?"

"Well, there are those who believe that she killed her husband, Juan's father, when he discovered she was practicing black magic and tried to put a stop to it. And there was another story about a Cavado woman who died mysteriously, in terrible pain, after accusing Sinopa of putting a 'sex spell' on her husband."

Her words sent a chill through Lee. *Sex spell?* "What…what happened to the husband?"

"No one knows. The story is that he disappeared and was never heard from again."

Lee sat frozen in her chair. *Did he go through a spiritual door?*

"Anyway, apparently there were no formal charges in either case. The Mascareñas name and wealth protected Sinopa."

Socorro laid her hand on Lee's arm. "Now listen, my friend. *Brujeria*, or sorcery, is usually passed from one generation to another. It's almost certain that Sinopa passed her powers on to Juan before she died. I have to tell you that I'm worried. My spirit guides agree that you are in grave danger. You must never," she paused for emphasis, "*never* go back Cavado."

Lee managed a deep breath. "This is all so hard to believe," she whispered.

Socorro's eyes filled with compassion. "I know it is," she said. "You've entered a world you don't understand. But please believe that Juan is not a man to be taken lightly. In my view, he's as dangerous as a rattlesnake."

Lee shuddered as her mind flashed back to the mummified snake on Juan's sofa table. Did your spirit guides have any more info on Juan and his motives?"

"No. And I'm getting conflicting readings. At first I thought he might be a spirit-sucker. But now I'm not so sure."

"A what?" Lee almost laughed.

"I know," Socorro said with a slight smile. "It does sound obscene." Her eyes narrowed. "And believe me, it is. A spirit-sucker is a sorcerer—of either sex—with the ability to steal another person's spirit. The spirit-sucker then has control over that person."

"Are you serious?"

"Very serious. Victims have no choice but to do whatever the spirit-sucker wishes. They are *embrujáda*, bewitched. Only the death of a spirit-sucker can free them. And those who have encountered one will tell you that a spirit-sucker doesn't die easily."

"That sounds like something out of a horror movie."

"Let me explain about magic," Socorro said, "and about the different kinds of so-called 'witches.' Magic most certainly exists. Simply put, it's the ability to influence events through extraordinary means such as ceremony and focused will. It's been around for a long time. In fact, methods of moving into and utilizing a hidden reality are probably more than thirty thousand years old. But the concept is terribly misunderstood in the present-day Anglo culture.

"You see, the power of magic is in itself neither good nor evil. It's a neutral force, like electricity. We use electricity to enhance our lives. But it can be a deadly force if proper precautions aren't taken. You wouldn't condemn lightning as evil for striking someone standing under a tree in a rainstorm, would you? And it's the individual operating the electric chair that makes it an instrument for destruction, not the current itself.

"Like electricity, magic can be used for good or for evil, depending upon the intent of the person using it. And any form of magic which manipulates or harms another person is black magic—a misuse of the Power."

"You're talking about 'white' versus 'black' witchcraft? Seriously?"

"You'd better believe, seriously. Unfortunately, we've been conditioned, in these modern times, to think of all 'witchcraft' as evil. In truth, the Power can be—and most often is—used to promote good. To bring about healing or good fortune. Ethical as well as unethical 'witches' have been part of all societies since prehistoric times. The ethical 'white witches' have been the healers, the midwives and the psychics."

"Psychics?"

"Sure. Psychics are just people who are born with an unusual sensitivity to what goes on in other people's minds, plus a talent for tapping into the Universal Intelligence. There are many people who would consider me a witch because of my psychic abilities. The point is that those practicing white magic are careful not to cause harm. In fact, most witches believe that whatever kind of magic they work will come back to them three-fold, if not in this lifetime, then in another. That belief prevents a lot of black magic."

Lee tried to assimilate what she was hearing. She knew what Nick's rational mind would do with the information, and imagined his reaction. "Give me a break," he'd say. "What century does that woman live in? She's obviously as nutty as the medicine man! What's going on with you, babe? Why are you opening yourself up to fruitcakes? What's happened to my level-headed, I-can-handle-it-all wife?"

Lee felt a sudden, intense longing for Nick and gratitude for the life they had built together. And Sara! *Sara is the center of everything.*

Socorro's voice broke through her thoughts.

"But there's a completely different magical tradition, an ancient Native American tradition of the evil sorcerer—or spirit-sucker—that far predates the European 'witch' traditions brought to New Mexico by the Spaniards—no doubt under the influence of the Catholic Inqusition. I'm afraid a spirit-sucker isn't inhibited by fear of karmic reprisal. He doesn't hesitate to work magic for his own selfish ends."

Lee was suddenly feeling almost desperate for Socorro to leave. *I just want to block it all from my mind!* But, after a couple deep breaths, the moment passed, and her curiosity returned.

"Okay," she said, "assuming, for the moment, that such a thing is possible, that Juan is some sort of spirit-sucking *brujo*, how would he go about it?"

"That's one thing that's confusing me as far as Juan is concerned. *Brujos* usually use sex magic to steal a woman's spirit. But you said that Juan didn't try to have sex with you after your interview."

Lee shifted in her chair, unable to meet Socorro's eyes.

"So, I just don't know," Socorro continued, lost in her own thoughts. "And there are other inconsistencies. I can't seem to get a clear reading on Juan. My intuition tells me that his motives are complicated." She glanced at her watch. "Okay, it's time to get down to business. We have serious work to do. But first, drink that juice. You need to keep up your strength."

Lee drained her glass. "I'm afraid my strength is already about gone, Socorro. All of a sudden, I feel so tired. Can't we put this off?"

"Your physical weakness is all the more reason to do this now. Frankly, I don't dare delay. Please, just bear with me."

Without waiting for a reply, Socorro began unloading the contents of her bag onto the kitchen table: an old beaded eagle feather, a decorated leather pouch, a cigar-shaped bundle of what looked like dried weeds, held together with a red string and resting in a large abalone shell, and finally, four grapefruit-sized rocks painted with strange symbols.

Then she grabbed Lee's hand and gave it a hard squeeze before releasing it.

"I'm not trying to scare you—or maybe I am. You must take this seriously, my friend. You are, as the saying goes, in deep shit. I think I can help. Anyway, I'm going to give it my best shot. First, I'll draw a protective circle around this house. Enclose it, actually, within a medicine wheel. That will create a sacred space and provide some psychic protection."

"How? What exactly is a 'medicine wheel'?"

"As a circle, it's probably the most ancient and universal religious symbol on earth. Because it has neither beginning nor end, the circle has represented life and the Creative Force in many cultures for thousands of years. To Native Americans it is still a powerful protective and healing symbol. I'll place these rocks at proper points on the circle."

"What's painted on them?"

"Ancient symbols, representing the four cardinal directions. Briefly, the East is represented by this yellow morning star symbol, the South by the red sun, and the West by the black half moon. The North is depicted by a white spiral, which symbolizes the continuing cycles of life and death."

...cycles of life and death..."Socorro," she interrupted. "Do you believe in reincarnation?"

"Absolutely. It's the only thing that makes any sense to me. You can't graduate from college by taking just one class. Besides, my spirit guides warn me that I'm doomed to keep on doing it until I finally get it right." She smiled, and then stood up. "Now, let's get started. While I'm doing my thing outside, I want you to take a long shower."

"But I just took a shower. Look, my hair's still wet."

"Well, I'm asking you to take another one. And this time close your eyes and visualize the water as a healing spray of golden light. See it cleansing you, inside and out, from head to toe. Ask the light to go to all of those places within you that need healing—releasing emotional pain, anxiety and fear. Picture your entire body filling with that warm golden light. Hold that image, and stay in the shower until I come and get you out. Where's your bathroom?"

"Upstairs. But I don't know about this. Is it really necessary?"

"Humor me, dear. I won't be long."

Lee watched from the living room window as Socorro began walking around the outside of the house, drawing a circle with a sharp stick as she went. Her lips were moving as though in prayer.

Lee slowly climbed the stairs, wondering what had happened to her nice, sane life. *Now I'm living in a medicine wheel and showering in golden light. I really don't know Socorro that well. Why am I letting her take charge?*

On the other hand, she argued with herself, I did ask for her help—on Dr. Mallory's recommendation. *She's gone to a lot of trouble for me, and she seems so sincere. I certainly need all the help I can get. I may as well go along with her, see where this leads. If nothing else, I'm getting a crash course in ancient beliefs and practices.*

Lee stripped off her clothes and turned on the shower. As she stood under the cascading water, she tried to visualize, with minimal success, golden light coursing through her body—washing away her obsession with Juan and putting a stop to her disturbing dreams. *Or "nocturnal adventures," as Nick so dismissively described them.* The thought of Nick and the guilt it evoked depressed her even more, and she tried to block it. *I'll have to deal with that later. Thank God my husband is out of town.*

Just as Lee had decided she'd had enough of the golden light, which had faded to just a glimmer, anyway, she heard a loud knocking on the bathroom door.

"You can come out now," Socorro shouted over the noise of the water.

Lee turned off the water and stepped from the shower stall, reaching for a towel.

Socorro came on in. "Wait, let me look at you," she said, squinting her eyes and staring intently at Lee's naked body.

Flustered, Lee froze. She'd always been rather modest. *But now I'm taking my clothes off for another person I hardly know?*

Socorro nodded. "That helped. Your Spirit Body looks a little brighter."

Lee quickly wrapped the towel around her. "What exactly do you mean by my 'spirit body'?"

"It's really very simple. The Spirit Body is an energy field surrounding the physical body. It responds to thoughts and feelings, our own and those of others. And its color reflects the energy that's collected and stored there."

"You can actually see it?" Lee asked skeptically.

"Yes, I can. When I arrived this morning I could tell by the darkness and density of your Spirit Body that your energy was blocked. You were obviously exhausted and depressed. You're a little stronger now, but we still have work to do. We must restore your Power by building your inner strength and stamina. Dry off, put on some clothes and come downstairs for a healing ritual."

Lee sighed. "Oh, geez, Socorro. I'm not up for another magical ceremony."

"It won't take long. And I promise it won't resemble anything that Juan put you through. His ceremony depleted your Power. I'm trying to restore it."

"I know you are. And I appreciate your efforts. I really do. It's just that this is all so strange to me." She sighed. "Okay. I'm at my wits' end. Obviously, I'll try just about anything to regain control of my life."

"This is called a smudge stick." Socorro lit the bundle of dried sage and cedar, tied with a red string. "Bathing in smoke is a time-honored means of purification."

Lee tensed as she remembered Juan blowing evil-smelling smoke in her face and on her body, to prepare her for the sweating ceremony. Whatever his intent, she doubted it had anything to do with purification.

Socorro removed a quartz crystal from the leather pouch and passed it through the smoke several times. Then she moved slowly around Lee, fanning the smoke from her feet to the top of her head. Socorro asked Lee to do the same for her, before extinguishing the smoldering bundle in the abalone shell.

After requesting a blanket, Socorro instructed Lee to lie on her back on one of the Navajo rugs.

"Get comfortable," she said, covering Lee with the blanket. "Are you warm enough?"

Lee flashed back to Juan and his blankets. Although she wanted to trust Socorro, her thoughts about magic—white or black—were still so conflicted. She couldn't help feeling apprehensive.

"The crystal will open your third eye and increase your visionary powers," Socorro said, placing the cool stone on Lee's forehead. "While all natural objects are manifestations of divine energy, crystals have the ability to generate that energy and pass it on to us."

"Juan's amulet had red crystal stones," Lee said. "He told me it was found only in the mountains of northern Mexico."

"Did he say what it was?"

"No, just that it was rare. Why?"

"My grandmother has spoken about a powerful red-colored crystal, found near a sacred mountain to the south, in Mexico. According to legend, it has miraculous healing powers. It was said to have been used by Aztec priests to heal injured warriors after battle." She shrugged. "Who knows if the crystals ever existed? It may just be a legend. Still, I'd like to get a look at Juan's amulet. Tell me more about it. You said it was shaped like wings. Do you remember anything else?"

"Well, the stones were shaped like eyes. They seemed to glow, to deepen in color, especially when the candlelight hit them a certain way. Between the stones was a spiral design."

"The symbol of the North!" Socorro exclaimed. "Remember I said that the spiral is an ancient symbol representing the cycles of life and death. Did Juan happen to say where he got this amulet?"

"From his mother."

"Sinopa's amulet." Socorro's voice was grim. "It all fits. We have our work cut out for us, girlfriend. Roll over on your stomach, and we'll get started."

Feeling too confused and exhausted to do otherwise, Lee followed Socorro's directions.

Socorro was silent for the next few minutes, as she brushed the eagle feather back and forth across Lee's head and body. "Now turn over on your back. The feather brushing continued.

Then Socorro took off her boots and sat cross-legged on the floor, close to Lee.

"Close your eyes," she instructed as she placed the crystal on Lee's forehead, "and try to relax."

She began beating a soft one-two-three rhythm on her drum. After several moments, she began to speak, her voice calm and soothing over the hypnotic beat of the drum.

"Lee, I want you to envision a ball of golden light above your head.

Lee groaned inwardly. *More light?*

"Now," Socorro continued, "pull that light through the top of your head in a straight line down to your feet. See the light filling each toe, moving through your feet and into your ankles. That's good. Now bring the light up both legs. Feel it warm your calves, your knees, and your thighs. Bring it on up, into your buttocks and your belly.

Take your time. See the light filling your chest. Feel its warmth. Now the light is moving into both arms, into your hands and each finger. It's traveling up your neck and filling your head, warming and healing you."

Lee was beginning to feel a little more relaxed. She tried hard to focus on Socorro's words.

"That's it. Get a clear image of the light filling you—warming, healing and strengthening every cell of your body. Concentrate on this image for awhile."

The drumming continued—ONE-two-three, ONE-two-three, ONE-two-three.

"Now, expand the light, extending it in all directions, about twenty inches beyond your physical body. Recognize this light as a field of energy, as your Spirit Body. Notice its brilliance. Feel its power. It is filling and surrounding you, healing and protecting you.

"Be with your Spirit Body for a few moments. Extend it out a few more inches. Good. Pull it back to where it was. Make your Spirit Body expand and contract for awhile, until you have a clear sense of it."

The drumming continued for some time, as Lee did her best to follow Socorro's instructions.

"Your Spirit Body also acts as a psychic shield, my friend," Socorro continued. "Keep it brilliant. Keep it strong. Allow no negativity or evil to penetrate or weaken it." The drumming stopped.

Lee felt the crystal being removed from her forehead. She opened her eyes and turned her head to meet Socorro's warm and steady gaze.

"How do you feel?"

"Pretty wiped out. But better than I did before you came. Thank you."

Socorro rose to her feet in a swift, graceful movement and put on her boots.

"I'm happy to do whatever I can to help you," she said,

returning the crystal, feather, smudge stick and abalone shell to her tote bag. "I will work with you again in the days to come, until you learn to cleanse and guard your Spirit Body by yourself."

She helped Lee to her feet and gave her a hard hug.

"I must run," she said. "I'm meeting Dream Singer for lunch."

"Why do I know that name? You said that he's a medicine man?"

"He's also a well-known potter. We carry his work in the gallery. Dream Singer is an incredible man, a great teacher. Not to mention that he's the youngest eighty-six-year-old I've ever known. If I wasn't happily married, I'd run away with him in a minute."

Lee walked her to the front door.

"Socorro, before you go, what can you tell me about ravens? Dr. Mallory said that they're associated with black magic."

Socorro shook her head. "That's only part of the story. Ravens have, indeed, always been associated with magic, both black and white. Apollo had his raven messenger, as did Merlin and many of the early Celtic wizards. As I said earlier, animals—all animals—are our teachers. They are neither good nor evil. They are just who they are.

"Raven medicine is magical and very powerful. Properly used, it is a healing medicine. Certainly, it can be used for evil ends. Those who are called by Raven must use great caution to utilize the magic only for the greatest good. I don't think that is the case with Señor Mascareñas. Take care, Lee."

"I will. Thanks again, Socorro. I do feel a little stronger."

Socorro smiled. "I'll talk to you soon. Guard your light, my friend. And stay clear of the spirit-sucker." She walked through the courtyard and climbed into her Jeep. "Don't forget to burn your candle," she called through the open window before driving away.

Lee stood in the doorway, Socorro's warning echoing in her ears. "Spirit-sucker...stay clear of the spirit-sucker." Too late, Socorro, she thought. *I'm afraid I'm already screwed—twice. And none of your rituals can undo that.* Fighting back tears, she closed and locked the door.

"May I interrupt for a minute?" Julie stuck her head into Lee's office, late that afternoon. "I need your signature on a few things."

Lee looked up from a stack of correspondence. She shoved it off to one side of her cluttered desk.

"Sure. Come on in."

"I know you usually pay these bills," Julie said, handing her a stack of checks. "But it's getting late in the month, and I noticed that they were still sitting in your 'in' box. So, I went ahead..."

"Oh, God," Lee groaned, glancing up at the calendar. "You're right. Thanks. The last week has really gotten away from me."

"Anything else I can help you with?" Julie asked, eyeing the disorganized state of Lee's desk. "I know you haven't been feeling well."

Lee suddenly found herself near tears.

"As a matter of fact, you can help with all of this. Most of this mess is just correspondence. A few queries from writers. Would you go through it, take care of what you can, and organize the rest into separate piles for me? I...I can't seem to get anything accomplished this afternoon."

"Are you okay? You seem so upset."

"I guess I'm not completely recovered from that bug I caught last week." She grabbed her purse and headed for the door. "When Annabel comes in, tell her that I went home."

"Have you seen a doctor?"

"There's nothing much they can do for this sort of thing. For a virus, I mean."

"Well, it might not hurt..."

"Thanks, Julie. I'll see you in the morning." She hurried out to her car.

Lee undressed and put on a warm-up suit and running shoes. She had at least an hour before Sara got home from school, time for a long walk. Maybe that would help to dispel the confusion and restlessness she was feeling.

She walked around her house, following the faint circle drawn in the sand and locating the four rocks marking the directions of the medicine wheel. She stood for a moment, wondering if Socorro's efforts really could affect Juan in any way. Shaking her head in confusion, she took off down the road.

By the time she got home, almost an hour later, Lee felt somewhat calmer. Socorro's description of spirit-suckers had unnerved her more than she wanted to admit, even to herself. Somehow, she had to put it all out of her mind. She was determined never to see Juan again. And she would certainly never tell anyone about yesterday. There was no need to. It all seemed unreal now, anyway. Like a dream. She would try to think of it that way—as just a weird romantic fantasy. *Nick can never know. Never! He'll be home before long, and things will return to normal.*

As she walked into her brightly decorated living room, Lee was assailed by thoughts of Juan's dark, cluttered rooms. Vivid images flashed through her mind: antique tables covered with an assortment of skulls, feathers, bones. Ceremonial paraphernalia. The worn buffalo hide rug. The mummified snake. Black wings moving on the wall as she rocked in Juan's embrace.

She leaned against the wall as the images of Juan grew stronger—almost as though he were there in the room with her. She closed her eyes, feeling his arms around her and the smooth muscles of his naked back. Smelling the warm musky odor of his skin. Her eyes flew open and a nameless emotion, part fear, part sexual excitement, pricked her scalp. She felt her upper body flush and a warmth spread down her thighs.

"No!" she said aloud in a choked voice. "I can't let myself think about Juan. I have to get him out of my head and keep him out!"

Lee made a spur-of-the-moment decision to take Sara out for dinner and almost ran up the stairs. What the hell? I'll visualize the golden light again, she thought, preparing to take her third shower of the day. *If this keeps up, Nick will be complaining about the water bill.*

13

"I just love it here," Sara said, looking around the cozy, candlelit room. "La Casa Sena is my favorite restaurant in the world."

"I like it, too," Lee said. She was determined to overcome her anxiety and spend some quality time with Sara. "And I'm glad we could get our usual table by the fireplace."

"That's right! We sat here, you and Dad and me, at my birthday dinner. I can't believe that's already been—let's see—almost three months ago! Wow, I've been fifteen for three months. Time really flies when you get older, doesn't it?"

Lee smiled. Sara looked so beautiful. And so grown up, Lee realized with a start. *She really does look like a young woman tonight. There's just a trace of the child she was only yesterday. Soon she will be gone, leading a life of her own.* Oh God, Lee thought, what would life be like without Sara? *How will I bear the lonely evenings when Nick is away on one of his trips?*

Sara frowned at her across the table. "What is it? You look like you're about to cry."

"It's nothing baby," Lee said in an unsteady voice. "I was just realizing how much I'll miss you when you go away to college."

"Oh, Mom, that won't be for eons. I'm just a sophomore." She opened the menu. "Now, let's see. What looks the yummiest? Maybe the trout baked in clay? Or…hey! How about shrimp Creole?"

They returned from dinner at seven-thirty. Lee felt better, considerably more relaxed. She was acutely aware of what a comfort and anchor Sara was in her life.

"Thanks, Mom, that was great," Sara said, hanging her coat and scarf in the hall closet. "I'm stuffed. I probably gained five pounds."

"Me, too. I'd better walk an extra mile in the morning to undo the damage. Speaking of food, Mister hasn't had his dinner." Lee opened the front door and called, "Kitty, kitty," into the darkness.

When the cat didn't come running, she went to the back of the house and opened the sliding glass door that led to the redwood deck. "Mister? Kitty, kitty, kitty?"

She came back into the family room, frowning. "Sara, have you seen Mister? I can't find him."

"He's probably terrorizing mice in the arroyo." Sara kept her eyes on the television set. "Don't worry. He'll be crying at the door any minute. Old Mister never misses his dinner."

But Mister didn't respond to repeated calls as the hours passed. By bedtime, Lee felt heavy with apprehension. Sara joined her on the bedroom balcony.

"This just isn't like him," Lee said. "He always comes home before bedtime."

"He'll be here in the morning," Sara said. "He's just out cattin' around somewhere."

"I hope you're right. But I worry about coyotes coming down from the hills after dark. They were really howling out there a few nights ago. And Mister's too fat to run very fast. I had just about decided he would have to adjust to being an indoor cat."

"I'm sure he's okay," Sara said, suddenly not sounding so sure. "Get some sleep, Mom."

Lee locked the sliding doors and reluctantly went to bed. She knew she had to get some rest. The emotional exhaustion she felt was taking its toll. After a few minutes of deep breathing exercises, she fell into a restless sleep.

The next thing she knew, Sara was shaking her shoulder. "Mom! Mom, wake up! You're having a nightmare. Geez, you scared me to death."

"What?" Lee looked around the dark room, trying to get her bearings. Her nightgown and hair were damp with perspiration.

"You were screaming. Are you okay? Are you awake now?"

"What time is it?" Lee fumbled for the bedside lamp.

"Twelve-fifteen," Sara said, looking at the numbers on the digital clock radio. "That must have been some nightmare. I almost had a heart attack. I thought you were being murdered."

"Oh, honey, I'm sorry I woke you." Lee held her head with both hands. "My head is killing me. Would you get me a couple of aspirin?"

"I've never even heard you talk in your sleep before, much less scream. What were you dreaming about?" Sara asked, returning with the pills and a glass of water.

"Mister. Would you see if he's at the front door or the deck?"

Sara ran down the stairs. Lee could hear her calling, "Mister? Here, kitty, kitty."

Lee lay back and closed her eyes. Then she smelled it. The sweating oil! She jumped out of bed, her heart pounding.

"Mister's not there," Sara said. "But I'm sure he'll be back in the morning. What's the matter, Mom? Why are you looking like that?"

"Do you smell it?"

"What?"

"That strange odor. Can't you smell it?"

"I don't smell anything." Sara sniffed and stared at her mother, a worried expression on her face.

Lee sat on the edge of the bed. "I don't smell it now, either. It must have been my imagination …probably triggered by the dream."

"Boy, that must have been some freaky dream."

"It was terrible. A huge raven was attacking Mister. Then I became Mister. It caught him—or me—down in the arroyo." She shuddered. "It sounds crazy, I know. But it was so real." She managed a small apologetic smile. "It was a dream, that's all. Go back to sleep. I'm okay now."

"Well, if you're sure." Sara stood beside the bed, looking down at her mother, a slight frown on her face. "I think you've been working too hard, Mom. You've been really stressed lately."

"I'm fine, honey, really," Lee said, reaching to squeeze Sara's hand. "Go back to bed."

Lee lay awake in the darkness. There wasn't any odor, she told herself. *Sara didn't smell it. It was just my imagination working overtime.* She closed her eyes, trying to shut off her thoughts. But the nightmare remained with her. *The pain of talons ripping into her back and neck—and the terrible sound of Mister's screams.*

Mister didn't come home for breakfast. Lee walked around the outside of the house several times, calling his name. She reluctantly left for work at eight-fifteen, realizing she was already late for the weekly staff meeting.

At noon, she broke a lunch date to go home. *Surely Mister*

JANN ARRINGTON - WOLCOTT

will be there by now. He's probably sitting on the wall, waiting to be let into the house.

"Here, kitty, kitty," she called around the front of the house. She sat on a bench in the courtyard, blinded by a rush of tears.

"Oh, Mister," she whispered, "please come home." After a few moments she stood up. *I've got to pull myself together. Stop overreacting. Mister will come back. He probably just wandered too far and got lost. He was wearing his collar with our phone number on it. Surely someone will find him and give me a call.* She went back into the house to grab a banana for lunch, before returning to the office.

There was still no sign of the cat when she got home late that afternoon. Heartsick, Lee climbed the stairs to her bedroom. She unlocked the sliding glass door and walked onto the balcony.

"Mister? Mister?" she called, her eyes searching the peaceful landscape. Santa Fe sparkled in the distance, bathed in warm October sunshine "Oh, sweet buddy," she whispered. "Where are you?" She grabbed her jacket and left the house, walking through the neighborhood and pausing frequently to call Mister's name.

Lee was in bed trying to concentrate on a book when the phone rang at nine-thirty that night.

After a few minutes, Sara called down the hall, "Mom, it's Dad."

She braced herself and picked up the phone. "Hi," she said in what she hoped was a normal tone of voice.

"Hi, babe. How are you?"

"I'm okay. In bed, reading. How's the experiment going?"

"So far, so good." His voice sounded tired. "Everything went off on schedule early Tuesday morning. I think we got some good data. We have another rocket launch scheduled for Monday."

"I'll keep my fingers crossed for you." She felt a pang of guilt as she realized how seldom Nick had entered into her thoughts during the week he had been gone.

"I meant to call last night, but I was going over the data and lost track of time. Then, with the time difference, it was too late."

"It's okay, I knew you were busy."

"You sound depressed." He paused. "Sara told me about Mister."

"I've looked everywhere for him. I'm afraid he's gone. I guess a coyote got him."

"That's too bad. I know how crazy you've always been about that cat."

"Yeah," Lee sighed into the receiver.

"Well, it was bound to happen one of these days. After all, Mister was getting old."

Lee felt a flash of annoyance. "That doesn't make it any easier," she snapped.

"No, I guess not." Another pause. "How are things at work?"

"Fine, everything is fine," she said, eager to hang up.

"Well, have a good weekend. I'll call the first part of next week."

"Okay." She took a deep breath and tried to soften the edge in her voice. "Take care of yourself."

She hung up and lay back on the pillows, fighting tears. *God, what will I do when Nick comes back? I don't know how I'm going to face him.*

Her feelings about Juan and what had happened between them were a mystery to her, a jumbled mass of contradictions. One minute she felt almost normal, determined to put it all behind her. The next, she was overwhelmed with feelings of desire, followed by shame and a deep, pervasive fear.

She sat up, rubbing her temples. *I don't know how I feel about anything. I can't seem to think straight anymore. I'm afraid Socorro's healing ceremony didn't take.* She pressed her fingertips against the tight muscles along the back of her neck. *I'm just wiped out. And Mister...Oh God, I can't bear to think about Mister.* She buried her face in her pillow and cried.

Lee woke up before the alarm went off. She slipped on her robe and slippers and hurried out to the front courtyard. No sign of Mister. She called his name repeatedly, over the courtyard wall. After a few minutes, she was joined by Sara. "Still no sign of him?"

"No."

Tears filled Sara's eyes and ran down her cheeks.

"I'm afraid something's happened to him. He's never not come home at night. It's just so sad. He's been with us all my life. I know he was mostly close to you, but I loved him, too."

"I know you did." Lee put her arms around Sara and tried to turn her attention back to her teenaged life. "How did you sleep?"

"Fine. I got up early to do my hair a new way. I saw it in a magazine. You braid the back into three braids, then wind them around in a big loop."

Lee hugged her daughter close. "Sounds pretty exotic."

"I hope so. Maybe it'll make me look older. I'm so sick of looking like a child. Gotta hurry." She squirmed out of Lee's embrace. "I'll keep praying for Mister." She dashed back into the house.

Lee made a complete circle around the house, continuing to call Mister's name, before giving up and dressing for work.

"Look, kiddo," Annabel said, settling her plump frame into the chair in front of Lee's desk. "We have to talk. I'm worried about you and so is Julie. She said you were weepy when you left here yesterday. What's going on?"

Lee sighed. "My energy level is still low from that bug I caught last week. I'll be fine."

"Come on, partner. Don't pull that 'fine' crap with me. I know you pretty well, having worked with you five days a week for the past ten years. There's more going on with you than a virus." She studied Lee for a minute. "Is it Nick?"

"No. Nick and I are fine." She grimaced. "There's that word again. Nick and I are okay, the same as always. I'm just going through a rough spot."

"Emotionally, you mean."

"Mister has disappeared."

"Oh, no." Annabel stood up to give her a hug. "I'm so sorry. How long has he been gone?"

"Two nights. This has never happened before."

Annabelle shook her head. "I know how much he's meant to you. How old was...I mean is he?"

"Fifteen. Just a few months older than Sara."

"Well, let's not give up hope," Annabel said before sitting back down. "Cats are so independent. Maybe he came across some flirty feline and followed her home. " She paused. "But, honey, you've been a nervous wreck for longer than three days. Look, it would be understandable if you were suffering from some sort of burn out. You've worked your ass off here for years. And you almost never take a vacation."

"I took one last spring."

"Tagging along with Nick to some physicists' convention in San Diego doesn't count. You said yourself you never had a minute alone with him. Why don't you take some real time off and just relax together? Not to hurt your feelings, but we could manage without you. Just barely, of course."

"To tell you the truth, I really don't want to spend time

alone with Nick right now. I'm in such a funk I wouldn't be good company."

"Do you remember what a mess I was two summers ago? Snarling at everyone, crying at the drop of a hat, even threatening to divorce poor Milt. It felt like I was on an emotional rollercoaster. And then there were the physical symptoms: hot flashes, night sweats, migraines. Also, I was absent-minded as hell. Couldn't seem to focus on anything."

Lee smiled. "Is this your subtle way of suggesting that I might be menopausal? I hate to remind you of this, but I'm nine years younger than you are."

"Some women go through the change at forty. Liz Eaton was just thirty-eight. I heard that she…"

"Annie, for heaven's sake! I had some kind of flu. It knocked me for a loop. And then Mister disappeared. Look, I do appreciate your concern. And if I don't feel better soon I will take a few days off."

"Are you sure everything is okay between you and Nick? You never complain about it, but with all his traveling, it must get lonely…."

"You would have made a great therapist, but I already have one. Stop worrying. My marriage is fine. My hormones are fine. Really. Now, get out of here. I have to interview that Arizona artist on the phone this morning, the one that shows at Wild West Gallery. The writer assigned to that story broke up with her boyfriend and left town. There's no time to reassign it, so I'll just write it myself."

"All right! Now you're sounding like your usual take-charge self." Annabel heaved herself out of the chair. "I'd better edit the two pieces that came in yesterday. Thank heavens this is Friday. I'm ready for the weekend. See you later." She left the office, closing the door behind her.

Lee shook her head. Annabel was a well-meaning person and a good friend. If only she didn't have such a big mouth. There was no way Lee could confide in her. It would be like putting an announcement in the newspaper.

She pulled out a notepad, intending to get the telephone interview over with. Reaching for the phone she changed her mind. The interview could wait. First, she'd call a few of her neighbors. Maybe one of them had seen Mister.

"I'd appreciate it if you'd keep an eye out for him. No, he's never done this before. I know. Yes, I called the Bloombergs a minute ago. Well, thank you. I hope so, too. Goodbye."

Lee hung up the phone, feeling more depressed than ever. Just because no one had seen Mister didn't mean that he wasn't nearby, injured or...worse. After all, the houses in her neighborhood were situated on lots of at least one-acre.

Fortifying herself with another cup of coffee, Lee called the artist in Tucson. Thirty minutes later she felt confident that she had enough information on the artist's background and work to write a respectable article. But the words wouldn't come.

Two hours later she was still struggling with the same paragraph. Rereading what she had written, she groaned.

"To hell with it!" she said, switching off the computer. Then she surprised herself by bursting into tears.

When the phone rang a little before noon on Saturday, Lee was still moping around the house in her bathrobe. She'd been awake since early morning, unable to shake the depression that gripped her. Sara was spending the weekend with a girlfriend, and the house seemed unbearably empty. She sighed and picked up the receiver.

"Lee? Hi, it's me. Socorro."

"Oh, hi."

"I hoped to hear you sounding better. What's going on?"

"I'm just down. Things haven't been going so well."

"Has Juan been harassing you?"

"I haven't heard from him."

"Then what's wrong?"

"My cat is missing. He's been gone since Wednesday night. Oh, Socorro, I'm just heartbroken. He was such a companion to me."

"Has he ever been gone this long before?"

"Never. Mister goes outside, but he always stays close to the house."

"Well, maybe he felt overdue for an adventure." Socorro's voice was thoughtful. "Cats sometimes need to just take off by themselves. Although they might live with us, animals have secret lives. They are a separate nation."

"I suppose so. But this is totally unlike Mister. I just know that something's happened to him."

"Are you sleeping?"

"Not well. I've been having really bad dreams. In fact, the same night Mister disappeared I had a terrible dream that he was killed by a giant raven. And when I awoke I smelled Juan's sweating oil. Or at least I thought I did. Sara didn't smell it, so it must have been my imagination."

"Lee, I don't like the sound of this. Your defenses are being beaten down. You must get some rest so you aren't so vulnerable."

"I took a sleeping pill last night."

"That's the worst thing you can do," Socorro said. "Drugs put a barrier between you and your Higher Self. They block your intuition, your inner knowing. Right now, you need all the spiritual and emotional support you can get."

"I sure need something. I'm in such a funk I can't even work. That's never happened to me before."

"On top of everything else, you're grieving for your cat. Give yourself permission to do that. But stay connected to your center. Meditate. Spend quiet time outdoors."

"Okay. Thanks, Socorro."

"Is your husband still gone?"

"Yes, for another week."

"Well, speaking of husbands, mine is waiting to take me to the Coyote Café. Howard and I always have a lunch date on Saturdays."

"That's nice," Lee said, feeling a twinge of envy. "Have a good time."

"We always do. I'll talk to you soon. Meanwhile, I'll send you energy—a big, golden wave of it. And I'll send good thoughts to your Mister."

Lee smiled. "Thanks. Goodbye."

She hung up the phone, feeling somewhat better. Socorro was beginning to have that effect on her.

Early the next morning, Lee took another walk. Socorro might be a bit off the wall about some things, but she was certainly right about spending time outdoors. She was right about sleeping pills, too. Although Lee had awakened several times last night, she didn't feel drugged this morning. Her tight leg muscles complained as she left the dirt road and began jogging up a slight hill that marked the end of her property line.

Sometime later, after climbing out of the deep arroyo that ran behind her house, Lee paused to get her bearings. Suddenly, a strip of red caught her eye—it was just ahead, dangling from a ground-level branch of a juniper. She rushed forward, knowing even before she picked it up that it was Mister's collar. The brass tag with his name and their phone number dangled from the strip of mangled red leather in her hand. The leather had been ripped through, with scratches in several places.

"Oh, no!" she cried aloud. "Mister, what happened to you?"

Images from her dream flooded her mind. Running. Gasping for breath. Heart pounding, a dull ache in her chest. Sharp, twisting pain as talons sunk into her neck and back…into Mister's back…her back.. *Stop it!* She clutched the collar. *Mister's collar got ripped off. Somehow. That doesn't prove…* Unable to finish the thought, she ran the rest of the way home.

The phone was ringing when she let herself in the front door. Lee hurried into the kitchen and picked up the receiver. "Hello?"

"I'm glad I caught you. I was about to hang up."

"Hi, Socorro. I was out walking."

"Did your cat come back?"

"No." She paused, swallowing back tears. "But I just found his collar."

"His collar? Where?"

"In the arroyo behind the house."

"Does it look like it was torn off?"

"It was sliced clear through, with deep scratches in three places, obviously made by something very sharp. Oh, Socorro, I'm just sick. I keep remembering the dream I had about the raven catching him—it was as if I *was* Mister. I could feel his pain and terror…" Her voice broke.

"Listen to me, Lee. This is important!" Socorro's voice was firm. "You mustn't allow your psychic shield to be so weak. Especially now. If Mister can, if he's still on the earth plane, he will return to you. In the meantime, you must focus all your energies on strengthening yourself."

"I feel too depressed to focus on anything. And the thought of Mister lost or injured… or worse…"

"What have you eaten today?" Socorro interrupted.

"A piece of toast. Early this morning."

"Good. Don't eat anything else. But drink lots of fluids, water and juice. Herbal tea is fine. I'll pick you up about six o'clock tonight. Wear a warm jacket and hiking shoes."

"Why? What are you talking about?"

"Dream Singer is conducting an *inipi* in the mountains. I want you to come with me. It's a powerful cleansing ceremony, more healing than any I could conduct. I think it's just what you need."

"Oh, no. Absolutely not. Please, no more ceremonies."

"Your spirit is under attack, Lee. You have a real fight on your hands, and you need help. Will you allow me to help you?"

"Oh, God." Lee's voice was little more than a whimper.

"Good. Now, you will need to prepare yourself. Rest this afternoon. Visualize and strengthen your psychic shield. Take a long shower about five-thirty. Dress warmly. Oh, one more thing, you'll need to bring something for your Give-Away."

"My 'Give-Away'?"

"It's an integral part of Native American ceremony. Before asking for something from the Great Mystery, which is the unknowable aspect of the universe, we prepare by giving something to it. A Give-Away symbolizes the harmonious give and take in all of nature."

"But what should I give?"

"A packet of American Spirit tobacco would be fine. You can get it at the Market Place on Alameda. But it has to be all-natural American Spirit, the pow-wow blend."

"Did you say 'pow-wow' blend? That sounds like it should be illegal."

Socorro laughed. "Don't worry. It's just tobacco blended right here in Santa Fe with red willow, sage and spearmint. All perfectly legal. Okay, I've got to run now. I'll pick you up at six o'clock."

"Wait a minute. What am I letting myself in for? I've never heard of an ini—what did you call it?"

"*Inipi*. That's a Lakota word meaning sweat lodge ceremony."

"More sweating? Are you kidding?"

"See you tonight." Then the line went dead before Lee could respond.

Sara was sprawled across her bed, head hanging over the side and hair trailing down onto the floor, talking on the phone. Lee stuck her head around the door just before six o'clock.

"Bye, sweetie. My friend will be picking me up in a minute."

"Hold on, Wendy." Sara put her hand over the phone. "Where did you say you're going?"

Lee hesitated. She hated being dishonest with her daughter, but a sweat lodge ceremony would be difficult to explain. And it would probably get back to Nick. That would never do.

"Just over to a friend's house," she said, carefully choosing her words. "She's having a little get-together and insisted that I come along. I'll be out of touch, her phone line is down. Don't worry if I'm not home by your bedtime."

"Okay, see you later." Sara resumed her conversation, saying "I'm back."

"I've locked all the doors," Lee continued, "and turned on the outside lights. I know I've told you this before, but Sara—honey, are you listening? Don't ever open the door to anyone you don't know when you're here alone."

Sara giggled into the phone.

"Did you hear what I said? If anyone you don't know comes to the door…"

"Right. I heard you, Mom. I'll be fine. I've been babysitting little kids for over a year now, remember? I can certainly take care of myself. Don't worry. Have a good time. Goodbye."

Lee blew her a kiss and walked out of the room.

"Mom's really uptight lately," she heard Sara say as she

started down the hall. "Acting totally weird. Who knows? Maybe it's that change-of-life thing. Doesn't that happen around forty?"

"You said this takes place up in the mountains? Where exactly are we going?" Lee asked as she fastened her seat belt. "I have to admit I'm more than a little nervous."

Socorro gave her a reassuring look.

"I know. And I'm honored by your trust in coming with me tonight. It's not far. We go up Hyde Park Road toward the ski basin, then take a dirt road for about three miles. Dream Singer bought a few acres up there years ago and built a little house. Of course his land is worth a fortune now. Some developer just made him an incredible offer, but he wasn't interested. In fact, he told the guy to get off his property or he'd sic Howler on him." She grinned. "I'll bet that was a hasty exit. Howler is ninety percent timber wolf."

"We're going to be sweating with wolves? Socorro, I…"

"Don't worry. Howler won't hurt you. He's an excellent judge of character. He's also a real addition to the ceremony. Sits guard outside the lodge while it's happening."

"Wonderful." Lee closed her eyes. Her empty stomach rumbled, and her head was starting to throb. "I'm starving," she said. "Why did you tell me not to eat anything today?"

"Because an *inipi* is a spiritual rite of purification, it's traditional to fast for at least a day beforehand. Besides, the heat is easier to take on an empty stomach."

"Does it really get that hot?"

"You bet. Dream Singer has been heating lava rocks all day in a ritual fire. The rocks will be brought in one at a time and placed in a pit in the center of the lodge. Be prepared to endure some serious heat. It's not for sissies, but my take is that you have a strength you're not in touch with."

"Oh, God, Socorro. I'm suddenly in touch with the fact that this sounds dangerous."

"It can be—but not as dangerous as this web you're caught in with Mascareñas. You must understand: A sweat isn't a sauna. It's a very serious and sacred ceremony. To participate in one is a gift. It builds endurance and strength. Like many things in life from which we benefit, it's not easy. That reminds me, did you bring tobacco for your Give-Away?"

"Yes. I ran out and bought a pack. I felt like a kid, sneaking it into my shopping basket along with low-fat yogurt, rice cakes and mineral water. But the checkout clerk didn't bat an eye."

"Why should he? Tobacco has been used ceremonially by Native Americans since prehistoric times."

"Why? I mean, why tobacco?"

"Because it has an affinity for spirit stronger than any other herb. The tobacco plant is awake in more worlds than one."

Weirder and weirder. "I really don't understand that."

"Because of its multi-dimensional nature, tobacco is able to translate what's in your heart and communicate that to the Spirit World. Dream Singer says it's like a telephone line to God."

"But you don't smoke, do you?"

"Only during ceremonies. That reminds me, did you drink plenty of fluids this afternoon?"

"I slosh when I walk," Lee assured her.

"Good. I don't want you to get too dehydrated."

Socorro turned off the pavement onto an unmarked dirt road. Expertly navigating the sharp curves with one hand, she reached under the seat and pulled out a large bottle of spring water.

"Here, drink some more while I give you a little background on what you're about to experience."

Lee forced down half the bottle while Socorro continued.

"The sweat lodge ceremony is an ancient method of cleansing both the body and the mind. It's been practiced by Native Americans—from the Eskimos to the Maya—for thousands of years. According to Lakota tradition, the sweat lodge and instructions for using it were brought to the people of *Pte Ska Win*, the Sacred White Buffalo Calf Maiden. The ceremony varies only slightly from tribe to tribe. Actually, the Lakota, or Sioux, language was adopted by the Indian Unity Movement in the early 1970s to be used during prayer and inter-tribal ceremonies, so most of the Indian words you'll hear tonight will be Lakota."

"Do I have to say anything?"

"You will be asked to state your reason for participating, or what you hope to gain from the experience. You can say as little or as much as you wish. Remember that the entire ceremony is a prayer. Anything divulged by participants within the lodge is held in strictest confidence. Anyway, it's pitch black inside, which provides a feeling of anonymity. It's a symbolic return to the safety of the womb. You don't suffer from claustrophobia, do you?"

"Not ordinarily. How long does it last?"

"Usually a couple of hours."

Lee turned her head to stare at Socorro. "A couple of hours? You've got to be kidding!"

"I've done sweats that have lasted up to three and a half hours. It depends on how many people attend and how many rocks are brought in."

Lee took several more swallows of water and leaned her head back against the seat. She closed her eyes and tried to ignore the queasy feeling in her stomach. *All of this because of Juan Mascareñas. Damn him!* She could see his face, the intensity of his smoldering eyes as he pulled her close...the feel of his bare skin against hers.

She jerked her head up and opened her eyes. Bring on the heat, she thought. *If the only way to get that bastard out of my system is to sweat him out, then I guess that's what I have to do.*

14

"Looks like a good crowd," Socorro said, pulling the Jeep up beside a dozen or so randomly parked cars and pickups. "I see that Crow Dog is here. He's an Apache silversmith and a cousin of mine by marriage. And that BMW belongs to Emma Feldman. You know Emma, don't you? She owns Santa Fe Gourmet."

"I don't really know her, although we've met a couple of times. She's on the Board of the Santa Fe Symphony. I'm surprised that she'd be here."

"Emma's a regular at Dream Singer's sweats. She's been one of his followers for years. A funny, warm-hearted woman. She describes herself as a Jewish princess who moved to Santa Fe and became an Indian."

Socorro opened the Jeep door and slid out. "Leave your purse here," she said. "You won't need it. Just bring your tobacco. If you'll help me get some things out of the back, I'll lock up."

Lee stuck the packet of tobacco in her jacket pocket and got out, feeling like she'd landed on an alien planet and was leaving the safety of the spaceship. Socorro handed her a large paper sack.

"Here, you carry the food, and I'll get the other sack."

"Food?"

"I brought a couple dozen burritos and some apple cider. Oh, can you grab those paper plates? It's traditional to have a potlatch, or 'feast of giving', after an *inipi*."

"What's in the other sack?"

"Our sweat dresses and some towels. All-women or all-men ceremonies are usually performed in the nude, but this is a mixed lodge. Dream Singer insists on modesty."

"Good."

"There's a tipi by the lodge where we can change. Come on, it's about a quarter of a mile up that path."

They walked a short distance and paused at the top of a hill. Below them was a panoramic view of Santa Fe, the Española Valley and, far to the west, the ancient Jémez Mountains.

"Look at that sunset," Lee said. "It looks like a painted backdrop. The colors are so incredible."

"The sun rises and sets in beauty," Socorro said softly. "I think of it as a daily reminder of how we should fill the hours in between."

Lee felt deeply touched. She nodded her head, not trusting herself to speak. The two women stood shoulder-to-shoulder for several moments, watching the crimson sky fade into a brilliant golden glow.

When Socorro continued down the path, she moved at a surprising pace. Lee, doing her best to keep up, was short of breath when they finally came to a clearing in the trees.

At least twenty people were standing around an open fire. Although most were Native American, Lee saw Emma Feldman talking to another Anglo woman who looked vaguely familiar. Both women wore sleeveless dresses. In spite of the cool evening air, the men were clad only in shorts or swimming trunks. A short distance away was a blanket-covered dome about ten feet in diameter and four feet high. That must be the sweat lodge, Lee realized with a growing feeling of dread. *How are all these people going to fit into that tiny space?*

Her eye was drawn to an elderly man kneeling in front of a rock-rimmed mound of dirt about two feet away from the opening to the lodge. He was dressed in faded blue jeans, cut off several inches above his bony knees. Thin white braids hung halfway down his back. Lee watched as, lips moving silently, he plugged small bundles of what looked like sage into the eye-sockets of a buffalo skull. Then he unwrapped a carved red stone pipe from a length of buckskin and propped it up against one of the horns.

"Dream Singer is preparing the altar," Socorro said. "We must dress. Hurry." She headed toward a tipi perched on the top of a nearby knoll. Lee hurried after her, lugging the sack.

"Take off your underwear, too," Socorro instructed as they ducked through the flap of the tipi. "You don't want to wear any more than you have to. And I brought some rubber thongs for you. It's too dark to walk around outside barefooted."

The only light in the tipi came from a kerosene lantern on a narrow table that was laden with an assortment of covered dishes and bottles of water and juice. The floor was covered with old blankets.

As Socorro unpacked the burritos and cider, Lee pulled two rumpled cotton knit sundresses from the sack. She undressed quickly and pulled one of the dresses over her head. When she turned, Socorro was nude, braiding her long black hair into a single braid. Lee couldn't help but envy her friend's full-breasted, slender figure. *Fabulous muscle tone.* Socorro was one of those women who looked as good undressed as dressed.

Out of the corner of her eye, Lee saw something large and

grey bound through the opening into the tipi. Before she could move, the wolf was upon her, its nose pressed into her crotch. She gasped. Socorro laughed.

"Hello, Howler," she said. "I was wondering where you were. This is my friend, Lee. She has a good heart, although it's not very strong tonight. I'm afraid you haven't helped. Come here."

The wolf raised its head and studied Lee with intelligent yellow eyes before turning to Socorro, who bent to press her cheek against his powerful muzzle. Howler opened his mouth and gently took the lower part of Socorro's face between his jaws, making a soft whining sound in the back of his throat. After a moment, he released her. Moving toward the tipi opening, the wolf yapped several times, the last yap ending in a melodious howl. Then he was gone.

"That's an impressive animal," Lee said weakly.

"He was telling us to hurry," Socorro said, reaching for her dress. "Wolves don't often bark. But they love to talk. Do you have your tobacco? Good. Now, drink some more water while you have the chance."

"I don't suppose there's a ladies room around here."

Socorro snorted. "We'll stop behind a bush on the way back to the lodge. At least that way we don't have to worry about your urine falling into the wrong hands!"

They were almost at the lodge when the drumming started.

"It's beginning," Socorro said. "Stay close and enter the lodge behind me. Remember that I am right beside you. When the heat becomes too much, cup your hands around your mouth and nose and put your face down close to the earth. The air will be a little cooler there."

"Oh, God…"

"There's a reason why this ceremony is considered sacred, Lee. Just as there's a reason for you to be here tonight. It's a profound experience. You'll be fine. Have faith. I'm psychic, remember?"

"You'd better be. Oh, no. I have to pee again."

"Squat right here. No one can see you. But hurry."

Moments later, Lee stood between Socorro and a heavyset Indian woman outside the lodge as, one by one, the group placed their Give-Aways—packets of tobacco, several crystals, beaded medicine pouches and small pieces of decorated pottery—around the buffalo skull on the earthen altar. They formed a semi-circle around the dying fire.

After a few moments, Dream Singer signaled for the drumming to stop. He stood still, gazing into the glowing embers that covered red-hot volcanic rocks. Although his face and neck were etched in deep lines, he appeared at least twenty years younger than his eighty-six years. He looked up with kind eyes.

"We have gathered here to perform an *inipi*, a sacred rite of purification," he said in a strong, clear voice. "We ask *Wakan Tanka*, Great Spirit and Source of All, to strengthen and purify us in body, mind and spirit. We thank Father Sky and Mother Earth for our many blessings. We pray for all forms of life—the plant people, the winged people, the four-legged people, the six-legged, and last of all, we pray for us two-legged people. Give us the courage, strength and wisdom, *Wakan Tanka*, to endure the unendurable. We ask the hot steam, which is the breath of *Tunkashila*, our Grandfather, to cleanse us of all sorrow, resentment and fear. We come ready to receive the gifts offered by this sacred ceremony. We come ready to learn whatever we need to know. *Hetch etu aloh*. It is so."

An enthusiastic response of "*Ho, hetch etu aloh*," sounded

from the group. Lee saw Emma break out of the circle and move to the entrance of the lodge. She carried an abalone shell, which contained a smoking smudge stick. At least that's familiar, Lee thought, remembering that Socorro had "smudged" them both with sage smoke when she'd come to the house last week.

The women lined up first. One by one, they turned in a slow circle, pausing to acknowledge the four directions, as Emma waved the smudge stick from their heads to their feet. Lee noted that the women all bent to kiss the ground, before disappearing through the small opening of the sweat lodge. Heart pounding, she fell into line behind Socorro.

"Crawl into the lodge clockwise," Socorro whispered. "Keep coming until you bump into me." A moment later she was out of sight.

Lee met Emma's eyes and tried to return her encouraging smile before turning in a slow circle. Taking a final deep breath of cool, pine-scented air, she dropped to her knees, kissed the earth and crawled into the lodge.

The first thing that hit Lee was the absolute blackness. She paused for a moment, feeling disoriented. The space seemed airless. There was a gritty taste of dust in her mouth. It was like being buried alive. She instantly thrust the thought away. *Back to the womb. Isn't that what Socorro said? Mother Earth.* Yanking on her skirt to clear her knees she felt her way along the blanket-covered floor.

"Socorro?" Her voice was a choked whisper.

"Right here."

Lee felt a hand on her shoulder, guiding her forward. She reached out, felt Socorro's bare thigh and scrambled close to her. Hiking her dress up, she arranged herself in a cross-legged position.

"You okay?"

"I don't know. It's pitch black in here."

"The darkness is a necessary part of this ceremony. It represents our ignorance. Also, being deprived of the sense of sight sharpens our ability to hear whatever messages Spirit may send to us."

The only message I'm getting is that I'm nuts to be doing this, Lee thought as someone brushed against her right knee and settled close beside her. She felt penned in, trapped in the suffocating darkness. And more than half of the people were still outside, waiting to come in. *How can they all fit?*

"There's not enough air in here," she whispered frantically. "I already feel like I can't breathe."

"That's just anxiety." Socorro's soft voice was calm and reassuring. "Take long, slow breaths."

"What if I can't do this? What if I have to get out of here?"

"You just say *mitakuye oyas'in*, which literally means 'all my relations', and the flap will be opened to let you out."

"Me-tah-ka-way what?"

"Just remember 'all my relations'. Calm yourself. I'm right here. I will get you out if necessary."

Lee closed her eyes and took a long deep breath. When she opened her eyes, she was relieved to see a few stars shining through the open flap about eight feet to her left. The view was soon blocked by another dark silhouette crawling through the small opening. There were soft sounds of movement. Someone cleared his throat.

She leaned toward Socorro. "When do they bring in the rocks?"

"The fire tender will bring them to the entrance of the lodge after everyone is inside. Dream Singer will then use a pair of deer antlers to place them in the pit."

"Where's the pit?"

"Right in front of us, in the center of the lodge."

Lee was alarmed to hear that the steaming rocks would be so close. She tried to scoot farther back, but was already up against a willow support of the structure. At that moment, she heard Dream Singer's voice from inside the lodge.

"Crow Dog honors us by serving as fire tender tonight. May his benefits from the ceremony be many. Ho, Crow Dog."

The medicine man was answered by a chorus of "Ho!"

"Bring the first seven rocks, Crow Dog," he yelled cheerfully. "We have work to do."

A glowing football-sized rock appeared at the entrance to the lodge. Lee could faintly make out Dream Singer's slender frame as he transferred the rock, which made a slight crackling sound, into the center of the pit—only a couple of feet from her knees. That rock was joined by six others and reverently sprinkled with sage. More red-hot rocks then joined the first seven. When the pit was more than half filled, the door flap was closed.

Oh, Yikes! Lee hugged her knees, pulling as far away from the heat as possible. The rocks provided a dim light, just enough for her to see how tightly packed the lodge was. Women crowded together on the north-facing side. The men, having entered last, took up the remaining space. *If anyone faints in here, they won't have enough room to fall over, unless they pitch face-forward into the pit.*

"The fire pit represents the sun, the great giver of life and energy," Dream Singer said, interrupting her thoughts. "The *inipi*, the lodge, stands for *Unchi*, Grandmother Earth, the Turtle Island we live on. In our ceremony tonight we utilize the Four Great Powers—Earth, Water, Fire and Air. We sit on the Earth, our Mother, who sustains and nourishes us. These ancient rocks, *Tunkayatakapaka*, honor us tonight by joining with Fire and Water in a Trinity of Power." He sprinkled another handful of herbs over the glowing rocks, filling the already steaming lodge with a sharp, pungent fragrance.

There was a low murmur of approval and shouts of "Ho to the Earth!" "Ho to our Mother!" "Ho to our brothers, the rocks!"

Lee swallowed several times, trying not to choke on the smell.

"We use water to call forth the Thunderbeings," Dream Singer continued, as he poured a ladle of water from a large bucket onto the hissing rocks. "Ho to the Thunderbeings!"

A cloud of searing steam exploded through the lodge. Lee gasped and turned her head away, but there was no escaping the brutal heat that seared her nostrils and lungs. Even her nipples were stinging.

She felt her pores open and sweat begin to run down her face, chest and back.

Dream Singer's "Ho" was answered by a chorus of voices, including Socorro's. How can they speak, Lee wondered as she buried her head between her arms. *It's all I can do to keep breathing.*

"We welcome the steam," continued Dream Singer, "as a gift from the rocks heated in *peta owihankeshni*, the fire with no end. We ask it to purify us so that we may live as *Waken Tanka* wills." He poured another ladle of water on the rocks. "There will be four rounds of prayers," Dream Singer said, "honoring the four directions. At the end of the rounds we will pass the *chanunpa*, the sacred pipe. But first we sing to welcome the spirits and announce our intentions."

Someone in the lodge began to beat a drum and the singing started, a haunting, chant-like melody in what Lee assumed to be the Lakota tongue. She could pick out Socorro's clear strong voice. Beautiful, she thought, hugging her knees to her chest and swaying slightly to the sound. For some reason, the song made her want to cry. She found herself wishing she knew the words so she could join in.

When the drumming and the singing died down, Dream Singer asked the participants to state their intentions or what they were "sweating for." One by one, prayers were voiced, each prayer ending in a fresh wave of steam. Lee tried to ignore the increasing heat by concentrating on what was being said. One man prayed for a son in prison, another man asked for strength to control his alcoholism. A woman prayed for wisdom and patience in dealing with her children. The next voice, a woman's, asked that a terminally ill friend be granted an "easy passing." The prayers went on and on.

Someone—the voice sounded like that of a young girl—delivered a tearful plea for an end of pollution and the survival of the rain forests. Lee found herself dreading the end of each prayer, knowing that it meant Dream Singer pouring another ladle of water on the hissing rocks.

By the time it was Lee's turn to speak, she wasn't sure that she could. Sweat was cascading down her forehead and into her eyes; her tongue felt as if it filled her entire mouth. Socorro patted her leg encouragingly.

"I'm here tonight…" She paused and tried to swallow.

"Louder," someone said. "I can't hear you."

"I came to this sweat tonight to ask for strength," she said. "I had an experience…. I've been going through a very difficult time." Suddenly, to her surprise, Lee began to cry. She felt Socorro's arm around her shaking shoulders. "I'm sorry," she said, "I can't…"

"Take your time, sister," Dream Singer said. "We are here with you, to add our prayers to yours."

Sobbing, Lee wiped at her face. Tears and sweat flowed together down her cheeks and dripped onto her chest. "Thank you," she was able to say. "I need your prayers. I'm going through a very frightening thing. I feel weak, out of control—unable to trust myself." She took a deep shuttering breath. "I feel very confused. I ask for clarity. And courage. Thank you for letting me join you tonight."

"Ho!" Dream Singer honored Lee's prayer with another ladle of water. This time Lee welcomed the wave of heat that enveloped her. She felt light-headed and weak, but somehow stronger.

After Socorro's prayers, which included one for a friend in trouble, Lee added her own "Ho!" to the group chorus and just barely noticed the blast of steam that followed.

Soon the round of individual prayers was completed. Dream Singer opened the flap and Lee felt a welcome rush of cool night air hit her wet skin.

"I'm proud of you, my friend," whispered Socorro.

"Is it over?"

"No. There's still quite a ways to go. Each of the four directions must be honored. But after each round the door flap is opened for a few minutes."

"I didn't know it was possible to sweat like this."

"You're doing fine. As Dream Singer says, anything worth wanting is worth sweating for."

"Can I have a drink of water?"

"A water bottle will be passed around halfway through the ceremony."

The flap closed and the drumming started. Several ladles of water were splashed onto the rocks, which responded each time with an explosion of steam.

"The rocks sing," said Dream Singer. "Let us join them."

Another Lakota song filled the lodge. This time, Lee found herself humming along.

"The East is the place of illumination," Dream Singer said, sprinkling sage and water on the still-glowing rocks. It seemed to Lee that the resulting heat was even more intense than it had been before. Her entire body was drenched in sweat.

"It is from the Medicine Power of the East that we seek wisdom and spiritual vision," Dream Singer continued. "The season of the East is spring, a time of rebirth and new beginnings. The animal of the East is the eagle, bringer of visions."

Time became distorted for Lee as the prayers and songs honoring the East continued. Disconnecting from the discomfort of her body, she began sinking deep within herself. Soon she was only vaguely aware of what was going on in the lodge. At one point, she was surprised to find herself singing aloud, chanting the ancient words.

How can I be singing with them? These are Lakota words. But, somehow, that doesn't seem to matter.

Waves of endless heat. Endless ceremony. Now honoring the South. She suddenly remembered Juan questioning her about the direction of her door that led to the spirit world. She had told him that it faced south. "The South corresponds to fire and strong emotions," he had replied, "as well as to innocence and trust." *He took advantage of my innocence and trust. Drugged me...seduced me...*

Then an inner voice spoke up. *Oh, come clean, Lindsay—that's what you're doing here! You know it wasn't that simple. You wanted Juan as much as he wanted you.*

Wiping at the steady stream of sweat from her forehead, she stared into the glowing pit. It seemed as though she saw a face in one of the rocks. She closed her eyes for a moment, then opened them. The face was still there. *A thunderbeing? No, that was the steam. My brain is cooked. I'm seeing things. I must be completely dehydrated....* She dropped her head and bent toward her lap.

She felt Socorro grab her left hand and force it under the blankets they were sitting on. Suddenly she felt the coolness of dirt. *Ah,* she thought, *wonderful. Mother Earth.* She stuck her other hand under the blanket and pressed them both flat against the bare ground. Then she pressed her cooled hands to her face.

"Put your face down," Socorro whispered. "Cup your hands over your face and breathe slowly through your mouth."

Lee bent down farther, twisting in her cramped space to do as Socorro suggested. The air was cooler there. She pressed her lips against the cold hard earth.

Mercifully, the door flap was opened. Cool, fresh air washed over her like a wave of happiness. The woman to her right handed her a large plastic bottle filled with water. Lee drank deeply, greedily, letting the water run down her chin.

"Not too much," Socorro warned. "You might get sick." She took the bottle and a couple of swallows, then passed it on.

Lee groaned aloud as fresh glowing rocks were added to those already in the pit. God help us, she thought, as the door flap was pulled down, we're being roasted alive.

For a moment she thought of Sara, at home alone, and of Nick, thousands of miles and another world away from this sweat lodge. *If they could see me now...sealed inside this sweltering hut... If Annabel could see me...* Her thoughts blurred in the onslaught of heat, distracted by remotely familiar songs and chants.

Dream Singer's voice, as strong as it was when the ceremony first started, broke through the wet haze that enveloped Lee.

"The Medicine Power of the West is that of introspection, of knowing yourself," she heard him say. "It corresponds to the autumn, to the middle years of our lives when we assimilate those lessons learned in our youth. The color of the West is black. The animal of this direction is the bear. Bear goes within, to the dream lodge, in deep hibernation. But when she or her loved ones are threatened, she rises up and walks like a two-legged being. There are times in our lives when we, like our sister the bear, must stand tall and be willing to fight."

Lee heard a loud ringing in her ears. The glow of the fire pit receded, becoming smaller and smaller until it was gone.

She was waist-deep in a gently flowing stream. Long black strands of freshly washed hair clung to her bare shoulders and breasts. She could see her tanned doeskin garments where she had left them, draped over a sourberry bush on the nearby bank.

Bending her knees, she lowered herself into the cool water. She watched her hair float out on each side of her face, as the soft current tried to take it downstream. Birds were singing in the nearby trees. The sun felt hot on her face. All was in harmony.

Suddenly, she heard a commotion on the bank—branches breaking and a frantic snuffling, growling sound. The birds stopped singing and took to the air. She froze, every sense alert.

A bear cub broke through the brush and splashed into the water, not twenty feet away. Close on its heels was a pack of six adult wolves. They stopped at the water's edge.

Without hesitation she rose up out of the water and scrambled onto the bank. "Scatter!" she yelled at the surprised hunting party. "Go from here!"

The wolves studied her for a moment. They began to growl and whine. She knew that they were waiting for a signal from their pack leader, a huge black beast. His mind was easy to read as he decided to challenge her. He would not be cheated. The bear cub was his.

Placing herself between the pack and the terrified cub, she gathered her Power. At that moment, she heard a loud crashing through the bushes. Seconds later an enormous brown bear charged into view. With a furious roar, the mother grizzly rose on her hind legs.

In moments the wolves were gone. The bear started toward her. She stood very still. I am friend! *She formed the thought and hurled in into the bear's mind. The bear continued to come.* I wish your cub no harm. I am friend! *She repeated the message with all the force of her will, staring up at the towering beast now less than ten feet away. She tried to ignore the four-inch teeth and deadly claws.*

The bear stopped. It studied her for a moment before dropping to all fours. Turning its massive head, the mother grizzly growled instructions to her cub and lumbered back into the bushes. The cub went splashing out of the water. Giving her a curious sideways look, it scampered after its mother. She stood alone and naked on the bank. For the first time since emerging from the stream, she felt the chill morning air on her wet skin. She began to shiver.

"Lee? How are you doing?" The whispered voice seemed to be coming from far away. Someone was shaking her arm.

Must get my garment from the bush, she thought. *Must wrap my hair in a drying fur ....*

"Lee!"

"What?" Lee was shocked to find herself in darkness. She was wet, dripping wet. And cold. Her mind seemed to be in some sort of whirlpool. Finally, it broke free. *The sweat lodge!* I'm still here, she realized. *But how can that be? I was somewhere else. In a river. Facing a bear—an unbelievably huge, brown bear. Was it a dream? No, not a dream. It was like the others. A memory. God help me! They've all been memories.*

"Are you all right?" Socorro's voice sounded alarmed.

Lee noticed that the entrance flap was open. Cool incoming air caressed her drenched skin.

"I...I don't know. I guess so. Is it over?"

"Almost. Just the round to the North. And the passing of the pipe. Sure you're okay?"

The flap dropped. Any reply Lee might have made would have been drowned out in the drumming and singing that honored the direction of the North.

"After the springtime of the East, the summer of the South, and the autumn of the West, we arrive on the sacred wheel of life, at the winter season of the North." Dream Singer doused the still glowing rocks with water.

Lee felt her pores open again as hot steam filled the lodge. How long can a person continue to sweat like this, she wondered, hugging her slick arms. *There can't be a single drop of water left in my body.*

"The Medicine Power of the North is wisdom," Dream Singer's voice continued. "Throughout nature it is a time for rest and renewal in preparation for rebirth, the next turn of the wheel of life. The color of the North is white, and its medicine animal is the buffalo."

Lee worked her hands under the blankets to cool them. *I can't take much more of this. It's got to end soon or they're going to be carrying me out of here.* She pressed her hands against her face, trying to wipe away the sweat.

As though she'd read her mind, Socorro felt for Lee's arm, then grabbed her hand.

"Hang on," she whispered, giving it an encouraging squeeze. "We're almost there."

Sometime later—ten minutes? An hour? Lee had lost all sense of time—Dream Singer passed the pipe.

"As we smoke the pipe let us remember all that exists is alive and related," he said. "We all share a common source, a common breath. The sacred tobacco smoke is breath made visible. White Buffalo Calf Maiden gave the gift of the pipe to our forefathers so that we might never forget our connection to all forms of life, to all our relations. As we dedicate our prayers and actions to the good of all, we ask the smoke to carry our prayers to all realms of the Spirit World."

The remaining water in the pail was poured on the rocks as the pipe was passed clockwise around the lodge. Through the steam, Lee could see a quick flare as it was frequently relighted.

"How do I do this?" she whispered to Socorro, pushing her dripping hair away from her face.

"When it comes to you, grasp the stem with your right hand and the bowl with your left. They are also passing a cigarette lighter. I will help you light it if the pipe has gone out. It's hard to keep it lit at this altitude."

When the two-foot-long pipe was passed to her, Lee held it gingerly and tentatively inhaled. Thick sweet smoke filled her mouth. She exhaled and passed it, along with the lighter, to Socorro.

After the pipe had made the complete round, Dream Singer's voice again filled the lodge.

"We have been purified," he said. "This sacred ceremony teaches that hardship and discomfort are only obstacles to be overcome on the spiritual path. Now, giving thanks for that lesson, let us go forth and live as *Wakan Tanka* wills."

The flap was opened. One after another, the participants began to crawl from the lodge and into the cool night air. Lee's hands and feet were tingling and felt slightly numb. Her dress was plastered to her body. Surprised that she had the strength to move, she followed close behind Socorro, pulling herself toward the opening. Finally, her head was free, and she was outside. Socorro helped her to her feet and gave her a hug before turning to Dream Singer.

"It was a good sweat," she said to the medicine man.

Dream Singer nodded. "A good hot lodge." His intense gaze fell on Lee. "Your first?" he asked.

"Yes." In spite of her exhaustion, Lee was experiencing a strange exhilaration. She felt refreshed, lighter in spirit as well as body. "It was…quite an experience."

"Take her to the tipi," Dream Singer instructed Socorro. "She needs fluids. First a glass of water, then juice and some food." He turned to Lee. "The weakness will pass. Honor and bless your body for the hardship it has endured. Treat yourself gently. Go now, and walk your path in life with firm steps."

"Thank you," Lee murmured.

With a sense of relief, she felt Socorro's arm slip around her waist. Walking together wordlessly, the two women headed up the hill.

After she had toweled off, dressed, and gulped down a large glass of water, Lee was surprised to find that she was a little hungry.

"When do we eat?" she asked Socorro, who was unwrapping food and setting out paper plates.

"As soon as Dream Singer prepares the spirit plate."

"What's that?"

"An offering of food to the spirits that aided us in the lodge," Socorro said, removing the plastic wrap from a large fruit salad. "Here he is now."

Dream Singer and the other men joined the women in the tipi. The group stood in silence as the medicine man placed a small portion of each available food on a paper plate. "We share our food with the Grandmothers and Grandfathers who shared their energies with us tonight. After they have partaken of its essence, may it be enjoyed by our brothers and sisters, the animals of this forest. *Wash Tay*. It is good." The medicine man left the tipi.

"Where's he going?" Lee whispered to Socorro.

"To put the plate outside, as an offering. Let's get in line. I want a piece of Emma's spinach quiche before it's all gone."

Lee suddenly felt famished. She loaded her plate with a large serving of tamale pie, a rolled chicken taco and a hunk of fried bread.

Socorro grinned, watching her. "You have proven yourself tonight" she said, filling her own plate. "Now, if ever your courage waivers, you will remember what you endured in the *inipi*. That will remind you of your strength."

"Speaking of courage, I had a strange experience in there. It was sort of like a dream, but different. I could have sworn that I was living it."

"Tell me about it." Socorro guided them to a small army cot where they sat down.

"Well, I was standing up to both a pack of wolves and a grizzly bear. It was as though I could communicate with them telepathically." She stared down at her plate. "I must have dozed off. I mean, that's the only rational explanation."

Socorro shook her head. "It's not unusual to receive a vision in the lodge. The experience is, in many ways, a descent into the subconscious. It can reveal things we need to know about ourselves.

"How long were we in there? I lost all concept of time."

"Over two and a half hours," Socorro said, glancing at her watch. "It's almost ten o'clock."

"You're kidding. No wonder I was seeing things." She ate a large bite of the spicy tamale pie. "I'm curious about something. We entered the lodge in a clockwise direction, and the entire ceremony followed that pattern: starting with the round dedicated to the East, moving to the South, the West, and finally, to the North."

"That's right. Ceremonies are usually conducted in a clockwise —or sunwise—direction, following the natural order of things."

"Juan invoked the spirits of the four directions during his

Awakening Ceremony. But as I think about it, he did everything in a counterclockwise motion."

Socorro lowered the bite of quiche she was about to put into her mouth.

"Well, that removes any doubts about his intentions," she said. "Moving counterclockwise, or against the turning of the earth, is a traditional occult method of summoning negative energies."

"Negative energies?

"Black magic, Lee. Juan was working black magic."

Sara's bedroom light was still on when Lee got home. She hurried down the hall, hoping to avoid Sara seeing her, knowing she must look a wreck.

"I'm home, honey," she called, and headed for the bathroom.

Moments later, Sara was knocking at the bathroom door. Lee came out, dressed in a robe with a towel hastily wrapped around her head. "What are you doing up?" she asked her daughter. "You need to get to sleep."

Sara stared at Lee. "Geez, what happened to you?"

"What do you mean?"

"Your face. You have mud on your face! Mom, where have you been?"

Lee ran her hands over her face, feeling the grit that was stuck on her cheeks.

"We were outside, sitting around a campfire. The wind came up. I guess…"

"You even have dirt under your fingernails," Sara interrupted. "And you look all flushed or something."

"I told you, I was sitting on the ground around a hot campfire. Now, back to bed so I can get cleaned up. You have school tomorrow." Lee blew her a kiss and closed the bathroom door.

A close-up look in the bathroom mirror explained Sara's shocked reaction to her appearance. Lee's face was streaked with mud, a result, she realized, of pressing her damp hands against the cool earth and then wiping sweat from her face. When she removed the towel from her head, her hair was matted flat and stiff with sweat.

On her way to the shower, she stepped onto the bathroom scale. One hundred and sixteen. No wonder I feel so much lighter, she thought. *I sweated off close to six pounds of water. Talk about a quick weight loss treatment.* She stepped into the shower, marveling that she could look so soiled, yet feel so cleansed.

15

Lee awoke early the next morning, feeling rested and rejuvenated. She'd almost forgotten what a good night's sleep felt like. *It might take awhile to wrap my mind around last night's experience, but the immediate results are certainly impressive. Maybe I can get some work done today.*

While dressing for work, she found herself mentally outlining her upcoming editorial on the pros and cons of growth in Santa Fe. *Better add a quote from the mayor.* She'd give her a call this morning, right after the staff meeting. She hurried downstairs to join Sara for breakfast.

She was in her study writing when the phone rang at nine o'clock that night. Should she answer it? It might be Juan. But if it was, she certainly didn't want Sara to answer. She picked up the receiver.

"Lee? How're you doing, babe?"

"Oh, Nick. It's good to hear your voice. I'm doing fine. I've had a very productive day. In fact, I'm still working on an article to round out the December issue. One of our writers left town rather abruptly."

"Well, it's good to hear you sounding like yourself again." He hesitated. "Did Mister come home?"

"No. I'm afraid there's little hope now. I found his collar in the arroyo behind the house yesterday morning."

"Just his collar? That's odd."

"Yeah. Odd. It was scratched and torn through in one place." She took a deep breath. "It's so hard, missing him and not knowing what happened."

"Of course it is. But try not to dwell on it. It's good to keep busy." When Lee didn't respond, he changed the subject. "Did you have a good weekend?"

"I kept busy."

"Good. Sara okay?"

"Just fine."

"Well, give her my love. We're planning the final launch early Wednesday morning. Then I'll need a day to look at the data. I probably won't get a chance to call again. The next few days will be pretty hectic."

"When will you be home?"

"Friday night, around nine-thirty. If there's any delay, I'll have one of the secretaries in the office get word to you."

"Okay. Hope it goes well."

"Thanks, babe. Hold down the fort."

"I will. I've had plenty of practice." Instantly regretting her sarcasm, Lee tried to soften her tone. "Take care of yourself, Nick."

"You, too. See you Friday."

Lee hung up the phone and turned out the light. For once she was glad that Nick was so involved in his work. *I guess I should also* be grateful that he takes me so much for granted, she thought ruefully. *It makes deceit so much easier.*

On Tuesday, for the second morning in a row, Lee awoke feeling refreshed. She lay in bed for several moments, thinking about her sweat lodge experience. *I have to hand it to Socorro. The ceremony seems to have worked wonders for me. I feel much stronger, both emotionally and physically. No wonder Native Americans have been doing it for thousands of years. I wish I could discuss it with Nick, but that's out of the question. How could I explain my motivation?* She tossed the covers back and stood up, doing several minutes of slow yoga bends before taking a shower.

Lee was in the garage emptying trash into large plastic garbage bags when she heard the telephone ringing. By the time she got back in the house, the answering machine had picked it up. She froze when she heard Juan's deep voice leaving a taped message.

"Where are you, *querida*? I trust that you are on your way. I have a strong need to see you. I'll be waiting."

Lee felt stunned. How dare he leave such a message on her answering machine? Did he know that her husband was out of town? *No, of course not. How could he know that?* She hit the replay button.

The sound of his voice, intimate and seductive, went through her like an electric shock. "I'll be waiting." Her hand was shaking as she hit the replay button a third time.

She sat on a stool at the snack bar for a moment, her face buried in her hands.

"No!" she said out loud. "He can wait until hell freezes over." She erased the message and hurried upstairs to get her purse and coat. Just as she was leaving the house, the telephone rang again.

The answering machine picked it up on the fourth ring.

"Lee? It's me, Socorro."

Lee grabbed the receiver. "Hi. I'm here."

"What's wrong? You sound upset."

"Juan just called. I didn't talk to him, but he left a message on my machine that he was waiting for me to return to Cavado."

"I'm not surprised. *Brujos* don't give up easily. How have you felt since the sweat?"

"Much better. I've actually been able to concentrate on getting this issue of the magazine out on time."

"Good girl. Listen, we need to talk. Could you drop by the gallery sometime today?"

"I should be able to leave the office a little early today. How about four o'clock?"

"Great. See you then."

At ten minutes to four, Lee turned off Paseo de Peralta onto Canyon Road. Once a prehistoric Indian trail, the narrow picturesque street had evolved in recent years into a major art center. She drove slowly past the centuries-old adobe buildings, remembering when many were private residences. Now they were almost all converted to art galleries, boutiques or restaurants.

A red Mercedes drove out of the small parking lot in front of Socorro's gallery. Must be my lucky day, Lee thought, pulling into the empty space. Parking was always at a premium on Canyon Road. She walked through the antique wooden doors into a large, well-lit room. A small group of people were examining a display of pueblo pottery and Navajo rugs. In a far corner, Socorro was chatting with a man in buckskin who looked as though he'd just stepped out of an old Western movie. She waved Lee over.

"Let's go into my office, "Socorro said. She motioned to a

young girl behind the counter. "Hold down the fort, Marilyn. I'll be back in a few minutes. Buzz me if Mrs. Wyatt comes back. I think she's really interested in that McBride painting."

Lee followed her into a cozy room decorated with a beige leather sofa and a gorgeous antique oak desk. Colorful Navajo rugs hung on the walls and accented the ochre Saltillo tile floor. Red geraniums bloomed in a south-facing windowsill. "This is a beautiful place," Lee said, looking around.

"Doesn't it have a marvelous energy? It was originally part of a huge hacienda built by Don Pedro Gaspar y Romero in the mid-eighteenth century. We bought it from one of his descendants. Some of the original adobe walls are three feet thick." She perched on the edge of the desk. "Have a seat."

Lee sank into the sofa. "What's up? You said you had something to tell me."

"I had an interesting conversation with my uncle, Luis Tafoya, last night. He's a deputy sheriff with the Rio Arriba Sheriff's Department. Actually, he's retired, but he talked them into hiring him back part-time, to answer the phone and things like that. I asked him about Juan Mascareñas."

Lee tensed. "And?"

"The name rang a bell with Uncle Luis. He remembered an incident involving Juan many years ago, when Juan was a student at the University of New Mexico. Some investigation."

"What kind of investigation?"

"Uncle Luis couldn't remember the details. But he promised to look it up in the police files. Tomorrow's my day off. I'm going to meet him for lunch in Española." She paused for a minute. "You know, I just had an idea. Maybe after lunch, I'll drive on up to Cavado. I could find some excuse to talk to Juan and just check him out. See what kind of feeling I pick up. I'd sure like a clearer reading on him."

"But you've said that it would be dangerous to confront Juan."

"Yes, it certainly would be, for you. But Juan doesn't know me. And I'd be on guard. I know how to protect myself against his magic."

"But what excuse…?"

"I don't know. I could come up with something." She shrugged. "It's just a thought. I may not have time tomorrow. There are always a million things to do on my rare days off. For instance, I need to swing by the pueblo and check on my grandmother. She was fighting a cold last week and her aura looked a little dark." She studied Lee for a moment, a satisfied expression on her face. "Speaking of auras, yours looks a heck of a lot brighter. It has from the moment you crawled out of the sweat lodge."

"Well, I certainly feel better. Thank you so much. I think you Native Americans are really onto something. Have there been any medical studies about the benefits of sweats?"

"I doubt it. You palefaces are generally slow to learn. But, I'm beginning to think there's some hope for you."

Lee laughed and stood up. "Thanks again. I mean it, Socorro. I don't know what I would have done without your support the last couple of weeks. Now, I'll do you a favor and be on my way. I know what it's like to run a business."

Socorro walked her to the front door of the gallery. "I'll call you later this week. With any luck, I'll have something concrete on the *brujo*." Her expression turned serious. "Keep your psychic shield strong, my friend. I still sense great danger around you."

"But I feel…"

"I know that you're feeling better. But you're not out of the woods yet. You must continue to protect yourself. Burn your candle. And always guard…"

"I know." Lee smiled. "Guard my light." She gave Socorro a hug. "You do the same."

Lee walked past a boisterous group of tourists in the parking lot and got into her car. *I wonder what Socorro would say if she* knew I'd had sex with Juan, she thought. *And how great it was—how I keep reliving it over and over again in my mind. She'd probably have me sweating every night for a month. Actually, I wish I could tell her. Maybe someday I will. But right now, I don't want to admit to anyone how weak I was. Not until I've come to terms with it myself.*

Pulling out of the parking lot and heading toward town, Lee tried to refocus her thoughts. It's best not to think about Juan right now, she told herself. *That just messes up my head. I certainly have other things to concentrate on, like the editorial I need to write tonight. But first, I'd better stop by the grocery store and pick up some beer for Nick; he likes it on the weekends.* Her mind went instantly to Juan walking toward her, carrying two bottles of beer. His naked body...

"Stop it!" She startled herself by saying the words out loud. Consciously ignoring the flush she felt spreading across her chest, she forced her thoughts back to her grocery list.

Lee held her breath each time the telephone rang that night, but there was no further word from Juan. She told herself that she was relieved. Obviously, he'd gotten the message. What had happened between them could never happen again.

A few minutes before midnight on Thursday night, Lee awoke and sat up in bed, her heart pounding wildly. She turned on the light. Another nightmare. Something terrifying...horrible. But now it was gone. It had involved Juan. That was all she could remember.

She got up for a glass of water, trying not to cry. *Oh, God, the dreams are starting again. I was so hopeful that they were over, that the sweat lodge had put a stop to them. What if they never go away?*

What if... Hold it, she ordered herself. *Everyone has dreams. Calm down and go back to bed.*

Lee tossed and turned for over an hour, unable to relax enough to get back to sleep. Although her mind had blocked the content of the nightmare, her body couldn't forget it. Damn, she thought, finally throwing back the covers and getting out of bed. *I give up. I can lie here all night, or I can take a sleeping pill.* Reluctantly, she decided on the pill.

"Mom?" Sara gently shook Lee's shoulder, pulling her out of a drugged sleep. "Aren't you going to work? Kevin's picking me up for school any minute."

Lee forced her eyes to open. "What time is it?"

"Seven-thirty. Didn't your alarm go off?"

"I'm doing some writing here at home this morning, so I didn't set it. Thanks for waking me, though. I need to get up. Boy, I'm groggy. I had a rough night."

"How come?"

"Just bad dreams."

Sara frowned. "Like the one you had about Mister?"

"I can't remember. But I woke up and had a hard time getting back to sleep."

"Maybe you should be taking some extra vitamins or hormones or something."

"Hormones? Have you been talking to Annabel?"

"What?"

"Never mind. Don't worry, honey. I'm fine. Have a good day."

Lee lay in bed for a while after Sara left, feeling drugged and depressed. Finally she got up and splashed cold water on her face. Then she put on her robe and walked outside to get the morning paper.

The sky was overcast, with thick clouds rolling across the

mountains like dark smoke. The weather certainly suits my mood, she thought grimly, as she hurried back into the house. She turned on the burner under the teapot and removed the rubber band from the rolled newspaper. Sighing, she sat down at the kitchen table.

It took a moment for her mind to register what she was seeing. She blinked, then gasped as she stared at the front page of *The Santa Fe New Mexican*. The caption under a photo of a familiar face read: *Socorro Tafoya-Hall, Santa Fe Gallery Owner, Dead at 36. Story onPage B4*. She brought her hand up to cover her mouth, staring in disbelief, then quickly turned to the obituary section and read:

Socorro Tafoya-Hall, 36, prominent Santa Fean and co-owner of Galería on Canyon Road was pronounced dead at Saint Vincent Hospital at nine-thirty Wednesday night. Preliminary examination indicated cerebrovascular hemorrhage, according to hospital spokesman Dr. Joseph Romero. An autopsy is scheduled. Tafoya-Hall is survived by her husband, Howard J. Hall, stepson, Chad Hall, a grandmother, Yolanda Tafoya of Santa Clara Pueblo, an uncle, Luis Tafoya of Española, and cousins Lydia and Maria Trujillo of Santa Fe. Memorial services will be announced at a later date.

"No!" Lee's voice echoed in her ears. She reread the short announcement, and sat stunned at the kitchen table. Gradually, she became aware of the shrill whistle of the tea kettle and rose automatically to turn off the gas.

Shock gave way to sorrow and Lee began to sob. *Poor Socorro! She was so good-hearted and funny. So beautiful. How can she be dead? Cerebrovascular hemorrhage? That's a burst artery in the brain, a type of stroke. But how can that be? I was with her, day before yesterday. She was fine, talked about going...* Lee was washed by a fresh wave of horror. It was difficult to breathe.

Stop it, stop it, she ordered herself. *Don't think crazy thoughts. Socorro had a stroke. People die of strokes all the time. Juan didn't have anything to do with it.* She paced back and forth through the kitchen, her mind arguing with reality. *This just can't be true! Socorro was so young—only thirty-six! And she wasn't sick. She was so vibrant, so alive.*

Lee remembered the expression on Socorro's face the last time they met. She had looked so worried as she warned Lee of possible danger. *Danger from Juan. Now she's the one who's dead.*

"Oh, God," Lee moaned, tears flowing down her cheeks.

She ran down the hall to her study and grabbed the phone book. "Dr. Mallory," she whispered, frantically turning the pages. "Be there," she breathed as she punched in the number. "Please be there."

16

"Just take your time, Lee. Sit back and relax for a minute."

She took a deep breath and leaned back into the soft cushions of the sofa. "Thanks for working me in again, Dr. Mallory."

"No problem. I had a cancellation this morning." He sat quietly, watching her. "Now, are you ready to tell me what's going on? I'm assuming that this is related to your visit two weeks ago."

"Yes, I guess you know about Socorro."

Mallory nodded, his round face turning sad. "It was quite a shock. My wife is taking it hard."

"The newspaper said it appeared to be an aneurism, a brain hemorrhage. But I don't believe that. I saw her Tuesday morning, and she was just fine."

"Apparently it happened right out of the blue. Edie talked to Howard, Socorro's husband, this morning. He said they were having dinner with friends when she just collapsed. Absolutely no warning. Poor Howard." Mallory shook his head. "Terrible thing."

"She was only thirty-six years old."

"I know. Well, unfortunately these things do happen. Probably a congenital weakness in an artery. I guess the autopsy should give us the answer." He reached inside the candy dish on his desk. "Join me?"

Lee shook her head and watched him unwrap a piece of peppermint candy and put it in his mouth. He sucked on it for a moment, studying her.

"Obviously, you followed my suggestion and talked to Socorro about your experience in Cavado."

"Yes, I did. In fact, we spent quite a lot of time together in the last two weeks. We became good friends." Lee's voice broke. She grabbed a tissue from a box on the end table and wiped at tears that ran down her cheeks. When she was able to speak again, she continued. "Socorro was so supportive. She conducted a healing ritual for me at my house and even took me to a Native American sweat lodge ceremony. I visited her again at her gallery on Tuesday morning. Although I haven't known her very long, I feel a terrible sense of loss."

"Socorro was a warm, generous person, easy to like. I'm not surprised that you two hit it off. It's only natural that you would feel shocked and saddened at the news. I am, too." He studied her for a moment. "But, somehow, I don't think you're here just to discuss Socorro's death. Am I right?"

Lee put her head in her hands, too overcome by emotion to speak. "There's more," she finally said. "A lot more."

"Tell me about it."

"I'm not sure where to begin."

"Just take it from our last meeting." He reached for his notepad. "Let's see, that was on Friday, exactly two weeks ago."

She took a deep breath. "Everything feels all jumbled together in my mind. I'm having trouble keeping things in order. Let's see... Juan called me that Friday night, right after I saw you."

"How did he get your home phone number?"

"I don't know. That's a mystery, too. He said he called the office and told the receptionist he needed to reach me. But Julie denies every speaking to him."

"Okay, go on."

"Well, he said he wanted to see me again. It was eerie. He seemed to know that I was alone. And he knew that I'd been sick. He said it was from the Awakening Ceremony."

"Wait a minute. Did he mention your illness first, or did you?"

Lee frowned, trying to remember. "I don't know. Maybe I did. He said I would feel better after he shook my sweat blanket to the four directions or something like that. Something about scattering my fears."

"Did he say when he planned to do that?"

"Two days later, when the moon was full."

"Go on."

"He talked about the ceremony saying that it had been very powerful. He denied drugging me."

"You confronted him about that?"

"Yes. And he said something about it being my own Power that I had felt, not drugs."

"Interesting. Anything else?"

"He insisted that I return to Cavado. I told him I couldn't, that I didn't want to go through with the next ceremony."

"How'd he take that?"

"He let it drop, saying something about not wanting to rush me. But he kept insisting that he had to see me again...insisting we had unfinished business."

Mallory snorted. "Persistent, isn't he?"

"I went back," Lee said in a small voice. "That next Tuesday."

Mallory's eyebrows shot up. "You did?"

"First, let me explain why, if I can."

She spent the next fifteen minutes describing her lunch with Socorro and her strange experience while meditating with the candle.

Mallory sat quietly, nodding occasionally and taking notes on a yellow legal pad balanced in his lap.

"I decided the only way to get to the bottom of this past life thing, to put it to rest, was to talk to Juan again. So, I went back." She took a deep breath and forced herself to give a brief but truthful description of her return visit to Cavado.

Mallory looked grim by the time she finished.

"How did you feel afterward?" he asked. "After having had sex with Juan?"

"Confused. Guilty, of course. And frightened when he started talking about taking me to Mexico." She stared at her lap. "But before that, while we were…" She looked up at him with an expression of wonder. "I have to admit that it was fantastic. The most exciting sexual experience I've ever had."

"Okay, we'll come back to that later. Go on."

"Well, then Socorro called after I got home from Cavado, insisting that she had to see me the next morning. You see, she was trying so hard to help me…" Lee stopped, unable to go on.

"Just take your time," Mallory said. "I know this is difficult."

Lee blew her nose and swallowed hard. "Socorro had been to Santa Clara pueblo to visit her grandmother and had some news about Juan or, at least, about his mother." Lee paused. "Socorro's grandmother said that Juan's mother, Sinopa Mascareñas, was a *bruja*—one of the most notorious witches in local history. It had even been rumored that Sinopa had murdered Juan's father when he objected to her practicing black magic. Juan did tell me that his father died before he was born. And she was also supposed to have done away with some woman in Cavado after bewitching her husband. Nothing was ever proven, of course, but Socorro felt certain that Juan's mother had passed her powers on to him. Especially after I told her that Juan was wearing Sinopa's amulet. She warned me to stay away from Cavado. She was afraid that Juan might be a spirit-sucker."

"A what?"

"A spirit-sucker. A sorcerer or *brujo*, who can steal someone else's spirit or will."

"Suck it right out of them, huh? Not a pretty image. Go on."

"Well, actually, Socorro concluded that Juan wasn't after my spirit because apparently *brujos* use sex to work that particular bit of magic. And Socorro didn't know that I'd had sex with Juan. I...I didn't tell her that I'd been back to Cavado. Socorro spent most of the morning with me, constructing a medicine wheel around my house and instructing me on how to strengthen my psychic shield."

"Your psychic shield?"

"Socorro maintained that we have a spirit body, an energy field that surrounds our physical body. When it's strong and healthy, it acts as a shield to protect us from psychic attack."

Mallory smiled. "I see. Naturally one would need a spirit shield for protection against a spirit-sucker." He shook his head. "Socorro and her psychic realms. Go on."

"Last Sunday, Socorro took me to a sweat lodge ceremony. That was quite an experience—almost three hours of utter darkness and intense heat. But it seemed to work wonders. I felt much better for several days afterward."

"I've never tried that. I'm a little embarrassed to admit that I suffer from claustrophobia. I know, shrink, heal thyself." He shuddered. "Just the thought of being confined like that upsets me. But I have to say, I find the possible psychological benefits of the ceremony intriguing. As a matter of fact, I know a clinical psychologist in northern California who started attending sweat lodge ceremonies and was eventually so impressed by the emotional breakthroughs she witnessed that she gave up her conventional practice. Now she just takes patients to sweats. She maintains that two hours in a sweat lodge can accomplish more than two years of therapy." He shrugged. "I guess it's something you need to experience to really understand."

"I would say so."

"Well, so you sweated and felt better. Then what?"

"Juan called Tuesday morning and left a message on my answering machine wondering where I was. He wanted me to come back to Cavado."

"Did you go?"

"No."

"Did you want to?"

Lee was quiet for a minute. "Part of me did. As I said, the sex with Juan was incredible. I try not to remember how incredible."

"And the other part of you?"

"That part feels guilty as hell. And frightened. Very frightened." Lee shook her head. "There are so many loose ends, so much that I don't understand."

Mallory urged her to continue.

"Later that morning, Socorro called and asked me to drop by her gallery. When I got there, she said that her uncle, who's a deputy sheriff in Arriba County, thought he remembered an investigation years ago—something that involved Juan at UNM. He promised to check the records. Socorro was planning to meet him in Española for lunch the next day and get the story." She hesitated. "There's something else, something that's really making me crazy. Socorro mentioned that she might go to Cavado herself. To check Juan out."

"Did she?"

"I don't know. That was the last time we spoke." Lee paused for a moment. "I need help, Dr. Mallory. I feel like I'm losing my grip on reality. I'm weepy and absent-minded, even at work. Annabel, my partner, had a little talk with me last week, suggesting that I take some time off. But one of the worst things is the dreams. I've been having such terrible dreams."

Lee described her nightmare about the raven killing Mister.

"When I woke up I smelled the sweating oil again. But Sara didn't smell it. So, I convinced myself it was just my imagination. But that very night, Mister disappeared. He went out and never came home. I found his collar—slashed—in an arroyo, but no trace of him."

She rubbed at the tears that rolled down her cheeks. "That's quite a coincidence, don't you think?"

"This has been a very difficult time for you, Lee. You've been under a lot of stress. And stress can do all kinds of things. It can certainly cause olfactory illusions."

"Is that all you think the sweating oil odor was? An illusion?"

"Lee, you had just awakened from a nightmare...."

"My life is becoming a nightmare! Look what happened to Socorro!"

"Are you saying that you think there's some connection between Juan and Socorro's death?"

"Yes! I mean...oh, God...I keep trying to convince myself that there can't be a connection, that it's crazy to believe Juan killed Socorro or Mister. But, down deep..." She took a breath, trying to steady her voice before looking into Mallory's eyes. "All right. Let me describe the demented thoughts I've been having, and then you can just go ahead and fill out the papers to have me committed.

"What if Juan killed Mister, somehow to punish me for refusing to run away to Mexico with him? And then, realizing that Socorro was on to him, maybe he did away with her, too. What if Socorro was right? What if he really is a *brujo*?"

Her voice broke and fresh tears streamed down her face. "While I thought he was making love to me maybe he was just sucking out my spirit." Lee grabbed another tissue and wiped her eyes. "I'm really frightened, Dr. Mallory," she whispered. "What's happening to me? Am I going crazy?"

"I certainly don't think you're going crazy. You've been through some extremely stressful situations and they're taking their toll. Let's just backtrack and re-examine some of these things." He leaned back in his chair. "We'll start with your first meeting with Socorro. You said that she felt certain, even then, that Juan was a *brujo*."

"Yes, and she called Cavado a 'vortex of evil energy', or

something like that. She talked about wanting to consult with her spirit guides and advised me to keep candles burning in my room at night."

Mallory shook his head. "Well, I warned you that Socorro considers…" He stopped, then corrected himself, "…*considered* herself to be psychic. I expected you to take all that with a grain of salt. Was Juan's so-called Awakening Ceremony familiar to her?"

"No, she didn't have much to say about that. Except that his counterclockwise motions indicated he was working with negative energies. And I couldn't find anything like Juan's ceremony in any of the books I read at the library." She paused, trying to organize her thoughts.

"Anyway, Socorro called later to say that she was going to Santa Clara to visit her aunt. She suspected that if Juan was a *brujo*, her aunt would have heard of him. Then she asked me if I'd left anything, any clothing or personal item, in Cavado. She said that *brujos* need something belonging to a person in order to put a spell on them. She really sounded worried when I told her that I'd used Juan's portable toilet. She seemed to think that urine, in combination with my sweat on the blanket, would make for a first-class spell."

"Okay, let's stop right there for a minute. You have to see that Socorro, well-meaning though she was, planted the unsettling idea of a magic spell in your head the first time you met with her. Even though you rejected the idea on an intellectual level, it began to work on you emotionally. That led to your 'past life' experience while you were meditating. You were already pretty upset and susceptible to this reincarnation and witch-spell business. You were nicely set up to overreact to a particularly vivid dream."

"But I've had other incredible dreams since then—all of them as real as memories. I had one after returning to Cavado and another one during the sweat lodge ceremony."

"Such dreams are a common reaction to stress, the mind's way of letting off steam. Speaking of steam, how long did you say you were in that sweat lodge?"

"About two and a half hours."

"That long? Good grief, Lee," Mallory said gently. "At the very least, that would cause severe dehydration, not to mention exhaustion. You probably passed out at some point and began to dream."

"I know that's the logical explanation. But something tells me it's not that simple. Dr. Mallory, how can you be so certain that Juan doesn't have supernatural powers?"

"Lee, these guys—*brujos*, if you will—have power only over the people who believe in that power. Of course, that can be deadly. Tell a believer in voodoo that a death spell has been placed on him, or a Native American that his spirit has been stolen, and he's apt to lie down and die. But the whole thing relies on the power of suggestion, not the supernatural."

"I know that makes logical sense. But I just feel…"

"I know what you feel. Look at the facts about Socorro's death, at the medical evidence. That points to a stroke, doesn't it?"

Lee leaned her head back against the sofa pillow and closed her eyes. "I guess so," she replied in a tired voice.

"Okay, so Juan called you, insisting that you return to Cavado. And even though you hadn't originally planned to, you went back to see him. Let's talk about why."

"I told you, I wanted to question him about some of the things he'd said. About his claim to have known me in a past lifetime!"

"Were you aware then of how attracted you were to him?"

Lee frowned. "No. Well, at least I didn't admit it to myself at the time. I was outraged at the idea of having been drugged during the interview. I wanted to confront him about that. But I was also intrigued by his references to reincarnation. Especially after my meditation dream. I wanted him to tell me more about our possible past life together. Although I was frightened of him, I desperately wanted some answers."

"So you arrived loaded for bear." Mallory leaned forward in his chair. "And?"

"And it just happened. I walked in the door and he started kissing me." She hesitated. "One thing very quickly led to another. I don't understand it at all. He didn't really force me. He didn't have to. The truth is I wanted him more than I've ever wanted anyone. I've never felt that kind of passion before."

"You didn't eat or drink anything?"

"Not until afterward. After we'd rolled around on the buffalo fur a second time. Then we had a beer."

"A beer?"

"Yes."

"Ah," Mallory said with a raised eyebrow. "*Brujo* Brew?"

Lee managed a small smile. "Apparently. The point is, I wasn't drugged this time. And I don't think there was time for him to hypnotize me."

"It wouldn't take long. Especially if you'd been hypnotized once before." He reached for another mint. "Got to kick this nasty habit before all my teeth fall out." He unwrapped it and rolled it around in his mouth with a thoughtful expression on his face. "Well, did our medicine man offer any more karmic info?"

Lee ignored the sarcasm. "He did talk a little bit about a past life we'd shared—as prehistoric Native Americans living on a mesa near Los Alamos. According to Juan, I was a medicine woman. That would explain the dreams I've been having for decades."

"I can give you more rational explanations, Lee. What other details did he offer about this 'past life'?"

"Well, I think he implied that he had been my mentor as well as my lover. But maybe that's just my impression from my dreams."

"Anything more?"

"Let's see. He did say that I was rather amply built in those days—something else I'd noticed in my candle-meditation dream."

Mallory rolled his eyes. "Too many buffalo burgers?" He apologized immediately. "I'm sorry. Go on."

"He mostly talked about this lifetime, about helping me to

get in touch with my Medicine Power and with the earth. He said he would help me remember how to communicate with plants and animals."

"That fits in with the animistic American Indian belief system. Animism assumes that everything in nature has a soul as well as a physical nature. Plants, animals, rocks, wind, rain—everything has its own spirit. It's an ancient belief, perhaps the origin of all religion." Mallory frowned. "But wait. Didn't you tell me that the Mascareñases were Spanish? I'd expect Juan to be Roman Catholic."

"His mother was Native American. Juan said that he'd studied with her people in the mountains of northwestern Mexico."

"Do you remember what tribe? Were they Yaqui Indians?"

"Yes, Yaqui, I'm sure that's what he said. Why?"

He made a quick note on his pad. "The Yaquis are an interesting tribe, rumored to have strange powers. I suspect that many of their religious ceremonies involve mind-altering drugs. Remember the books by Carlos Castaneda that came out in the late '60s, early '70s?"

"Yes, but I didn't read them."

"Well, Castaneda was a graduate student in anthropology who spent more than five years with a Yaqui sorcerer. As a matter of fact, the sorcerer's name was Don Juan. Don Juan Matus. Anyway, this old Yaqui had some incredible powers, including the ability to switch to a completely different reality whenever the mood hit him. According to Castaneda, that is. I have to point out that many people believe Castaneda was actually writing fiction. Anyway, his books came out in the middle of the hippie era and were very popular with college students looking for an excuse to stay stoned. If Juan is half-Yaqui, that sheds another light on this." He made some more notes on the legal pad, then looked up at her. "What else did he say about his mother?"

"Just that she had been an exceptional woman. 'Powerful', was the word he used. She's been dead for a long time. He didn't volunteer anything about her being a sorceress who passed her powers onto him. But according to Socorro…"

"Well, let's keep in mind that Socorro was part of the Native American culture. And, being a psychic, she had her own particular view of reality." He paused. "Let's talk some more about your feelings after having had sex with Juan."

She looked down at her hands clutched together in her lap.

"I can't believe it happened. It's like some kind of erotic dream." She bit her lip to stop it from quivering, and then continued in a strained voice. "Nick and I have a long history of mutual trust in our marriage. We made a pact years ago to trust each other and not give in to jealous fantasies while we're apart. That was the only way we could survive his frequent traveling."

She blinked back tears before continuing. "I've never been unfaithful to Nick before. It just never seemed worth the guilt and risk." She shook her head. "And now, after eighteen years of marriage, it's finally happened. And with a *curandero*, or whatever the hell he is. I just hope he doesn't have any sexually transmitted diseases."

"That's certainly a concern these days. I would advise an AIDS test. And, of course, report any unusual physical symptoms to your gynecologist." He hesitated. "Is pregnancy a concern?"

"No, thank God. I had a hysterectomy after a miscarriage years ago."

"I take it you don't plan to tell Nick about any of this. Is he still out of town?"

Lee sighed. "He gets home tonight." She ran her fingers through her hair. "God, no, I'll never tell Nick. What could I possibly say? 'Welcome home, dear. Sit down, I have something to tell you. You know how you've always encouraged me to develop my own interests? Well, I'm having an interesting little affair with a *brujo*. I peed in his pot, he collected my sweat, said some magic words, and now I'm in his power. By the way, we were lovers in a past life, when I had long black hair and a weight problem. I'll be back whenever the spell wears off or I finish my graduate work in Mexico—Witchcraft 401. Don't try to stop me because I think he's already killed Mister and Socorro. You don't want to make him mad'." She grimaced. "I can just imagine how understanding Nick would be."

Mallory smiled. "At least you haven't lost your sense of humor. That's an encouraging sign." His expression became serious again. "I agree that there's nothing to be gained by discussing this affair with Nick. Assuming that you still value your marriage."

"Of course, I do! I love Nick. I have a very nice life. This thing—whatever it is—with Juan can't really be considered an affair. It's just a...I don't know what it is. Temporary insanity. It won't happen again, and it certainly is no reason to break up my marriage!"

"Okay, okay, calm down. I agree that it isn't. I just wanted you to verbalize that. You have to keep what's real and important straight in your mind. You don't have much time to pull yourself together, if Nick's returning tonight."

Lee groaned. "I know. I can't tell you how I dread seeing him." She turned her wedding ring on her finger and looked up, her expression almost hopeful. "But surely everything will get back to normal then? It'll have to. Nick wouldn't tolerate a disruptive spirit-sucker in his orderly world."

"I'm sure he wouldn't." Mallory looked at the clock on the wall above her head. "I'm afraid our time's up. I suggest that you go home and relax. Try not to dwell on upsetting thoughts. You're not going crazy. Some quality time with Nick this weekend would also be good medicine." He gave her shoulder a reassuring pat as he walked her to the door. "And remember, I'm just a phone call away."

17

It was raining when Lee left Mallory's office. She turned the collar up on her jacket and dashed to her car. Like most New Mexicans, she expected the sun to shine and rarely carried an umbrella.

She sat in the car, thinking. *It's ten-thirty. The morning is already shot. I'll have to work until six o'clock to get caught up. That will still give me a couple hours to pull myself together before Nick gets home. God knows, I'll need it.*

Lee talked sternly to herself as she drove to the office. *Mallory's right. I was in a vulnerable state of mind and simply overreacted to Socorro's death. That's certainly understandable. But enough is enough. It's time to get a grip on myself. I can't afford to dwell on what happened with Juan. It was just one of those things, a mistake I'll have to do my best to get over.*

She cringed, trying to imagine Annabel's reaction to her choice of Juan as a lover, at the same time knowing how much she would love it. "He's a what?" she would ask incredulously. "A *curandero?*

How kinky! I knew it. You're definitely menopausal." No, she could never discuss this with anyone but Mallory. She couldn't risk having it ever get back to Nick. Cold fear washed through her. *Dear God, he must never find out.*

Lee was sipping wine and watching flames dance in the kiva-styled fireplace in the living room when she heard the thump of the garage door closing. She stood, tucking her shirt into her slacks. *There. Everything's neatly in place. Almost everything.* Lee glanced at the empty chair where Mister should have been curled up by the fire and felt a familiar ache.

She heard the door burst open and Nick's footsteps in the hall.

"I'm home," he announced.

Lee took a deep breath and stood up to meet him.

"Hi, babe," he said, dropping his suitcases and holding out his arms.

She put on a welcoming smile and walked into his embrace. "How was your flight?"

"Too long," he said, kissing her forehead. "And there was a crying baby behind me all the way from Salt Lake City." He hugged her hard. "It's been a very long day."

"Leave your bags here and come sit down. How about a drink? Sara, Daddy's home," Lee called as she and Nick walked arm-in-arm down the hall.

"I could use a Wild Turkey. On the rocks. Well, there's my girl." Nick held out his arms to Sara who came down the stairs, dressed in sweats. "What? No date on a Friday night?"

"Kevin's sick," Sara said. "The doctor thinks it's strep. They did a throat culture this afternoon."

"See why you're not allowed to kiss boys?" Nick teased, hugging his daughter. "They carry germs."

The three of them went into the living room where Nick collapsed into his leather recliner.

"Well, everything went off on schedule," he said, stretching his legs out in front of him. "I think we got good data this time. Oh, thanks," he said to Lee as she handed him his drink.

"What kind of data?" Sara asked, making room for Lee to sit beside her on the sofa.

"We launched a rocket from Poker Flats, just north of Fairbanks. The payload on that rocket was an electron accelerator that I helped design."

"I don't understand," Sara said. "Why are you accelerating electrons?"

Nick savored a swallow of his drink before answering.

"Well, sweetheart, we're trying to understand more about auroral processes."

"Auroral processes?"

"You know, the aurora borealis. I've shown you pictures of it from other trips."

"Oh, yeah, the northern lights," Sara said, remembering the pictures of the beautiful curtains of color in the dark night sky.

"That's right. We're studying the aurora in order to understand how the sun interacts with the earth's magnetic field. Even small solar changes could influence the weather here on earth. If our technique works, it could help predict global weather change."

"You mean like the next ice age?"

"Or its opposite, the greenhouse effect. Either one could be catastrophic. Whatever the future holds for us on this poor mistreated planet, we need to be prepared."

"Your work is really important, isn't it, Dad?"

Nick smiled. "I believe that it is. Otherwise, I wouldn't work so hard at it. I really don't like being away from you and your mom so much, you know."

Sara jumped up and flung herself into Nick's arms. "I'm so

proud to have you for a dad," she said, burrowing her face into his shoulder. "Really, really proud."

Watching Nick over the edge of her wine glass, Lee was surprised to see his eyes fill with tears. He didn't often display his softer side.

"I'm proud of you, too, princess," he said in a husky voice.

Lee felt on the verge of tears, herself. She drained her wine glass and escaped into the kitchen to refill it. *You're doing fine, she told herself, leaning against the refrigerator. Relax. Just act normal. And for God's sake, stop sniveling*! She stayed in the kitchen as long as she felt she could without attracting attention.

"When are you taking us to Alaska?" Lee heard Sara ask as she returned to the sofa. "Mom and I are ready for one of those king crab pig-outs."

"Right," said Lee, chiming in. "We sure are."

"Well, one of these days we'll have to arrange that." Nick swirled his drink in the glass, looking at Lee. "So tell me, what went on here while I was slaving away in the frozen north?"

"Well, you know that Mister disappeared," Sara said with a worried glance at her mother. "It's been pretty depressing, especially for Mom. He was really her cat."

"I know. Well, we'll just have to get Mom a new kitten to cheer her up."

Lee forced herself to smile. "I think you'd better scoot off to bed, young lady. It's almost eleven o'clock and you're going shopping in Albuquerque with Wendy tomorrow."

"Yeah, I'm about ready to turn in myself," Nick said with a meaningful look at Lee. "How about you, babe?"

Nick enveloped her in an affectionate hug when she came to bed.

"It's good to be home," he said, reaching under her pajama top to fondle her breast.

Lee felt her body tense. I don't think I can pull this off, she thought. *But I have to. I have to act normal.* She turned her face toward his and dutifully returned his kiss. As Nick stroked her, Lee closed her eyes and allowed her mind to float.

Suddenly, she was back in Cavado, lying on the buffalo rug. Juan's face came into focus above her, his features shadowed by the flickering candlelight. His mouth claimed hers. It was his hands that moved over her breasts and down her body, his knee that deftly parted her thighs. She pressed against him, smelling the tantalizing warmth of his skin as his strong naked body covered hers.

Once again, Lee was gripped by an alien and overwhelming desire. She moaned, abandoning herself to the heat that raged through her. Her body seemed to have a will of its own, a raw, savage need. She dug her fingernails into his back, ignoring his startled cry. With a quick impatient thrust of her body she rolled him over, straddling him. Eyes still tightly closed, Lee rode her wild passion to its climax.

Nick lay stunned for several moments after she rolled off and away from him. When he finally spoke, he sounded dazed.

"Wow!" He took a long, deep breath. "You were—Jesus— incredible. What got into you? You've never responded like that before." He reached for her across the rumpled sheets. "Honey? It was great. Fantastic. Why are you crying?"

Nick still had his head partly buried under his pillow when Lee rolled out of bed early the next morning. She slipped into a jogging suit and tiptoed into the bathroom to brush her teeth and hair. Carrying her walking shoes and socks, she eased the bedroom door shut. Moments later she was walking down the dirt road, away from the house.

The sun was peeking over the Sangre de Cristos, bathing the foothills below in soft shafts of golden light. Lee zipped her parka all the way up and pushed her hands into the pockets. She was glad she'd forced herself up and out of doors. Maybe the exercise and brisk morning air would help to clear her head. Anyway, it was better than lying in bed staring at the ceiling. She stopped, startled, as a flock of birds rose in swirling unison from a gnarled piñon tree nearby.

Suddenly, Juan's voice echoed in her head. "I want to teach you to talk to the birds again, Lee." *Talk to the birds?* She frowned, remembering the dream she'd had after returning from Cavado. In that dream she had somehow communicated with an owl. She'd called the owl "Bright Eyes," when she sent it for help after her fall.

Lee began walking rapidly, lost in thought. Her passionate lovemaking last night had been as much of a surprise to her as it had been to Nick. Thank God he couldn't know what was going on in her head. Awake or asleep, her mind was never free of Juan. Last night was no exception. She tried to reconstruct the final dream that had jolted her awake, leaving her with a pounding heart and a body clammy with sweat. It involved Juan—that much she knew for sure. Her steps slowed as memories of the dream broke free and flooded her mind.

She had been in Juan's embrace, lying in a dark, shadowy place. She remembered his urgent half-Spanish whispers in her ear and the feel of his warm breath on her neck. Then someone had called her name. Socorro! It had been Socorro's voice, calling her from somewhere in the shadows. She tried to answer, but Juan's hand had clamped over her mouth, cutting her off. Juan had spoken in Spanish to Socorro, his voice a low, menacing snarl. Then they were flying, hurtling through black space. She had clung to Juan, burying her face in his shoulder.... The dream-memory drifted away like a ribbon of smoke.

What had Juan said to Socorro? *"Tu eres una,"* you are a... what was the word? *"Molestia"?* Something like that. You are a what?...to me. Then, *"Tu vas a morir."* The words seemed to echo in her mind. You're going.... *"Morir"*? The word sounded threatening, but she couldn't quite place it. She would have to look it up in her Spanish dictionary as soon as she got home.

Feeling uneasy, the peace of the still morning disturbed by the memory of her dream, she turned and started back at a trot.

As she jogged down a hill, Lee lost her balance, sliding on some loose rock. She landed on one knee, catching herself with her open hands. Rising to her feet, she felt a sharp pain in her right ankle. Cautiously, she put her weight on it. It was okay. Just twisted a little, not really sprained. A sand-colored lizard raised its head from a nearby rock. It raced toward her, not stopping until it was inches from her foot. Lee thought of the lizard on her pottery candle and recalled Socorro's words when she'd presented it to her. *The lizard is a survivor. We can all learn a lesson from her.*

Lee bent down and studied the lizard that rested near her foot. It seemed to be watching her, too. Finally, it blinked a tiny yellow eye and darted away. She stood and brushed herself off, then walking gingerly, she started home.

The smell of muffins baking greeted Lee when she opened the front door. She discovered Nick in the kitchen, dressed in jeans and his old grey sweatshirt with *University of Colorado* in faded letters across the back. Lee stood quietly in the doorway, watching him spoon dough into a muffin tin. She shook her head fondly. Nick loved that old sweatshirt. Several times over the years he had prevented her from turning it into a dust rag.

"I see the master chef is at work," she said.

He smiled at her over his shoulder. "Apple bran muffins. The first batch is almost ready. I'm about to scramble some eggs to go with them."

"I think I'll just stick with coffee, for now. Thanks, anyway."

He turned to look at her. "Eat something, babe. You've lost weight lately. I don't want you fading away on us."

"I just haven't had much of an appetite."

He grinned. "Maybe not for food. I have to say, you really knocked my socks off last night."

Lee felt herself flush but she smiled and said lightly, "As I remember, your socks were already off." She turned away from him to pour a cup of coffee, eager to change the subject. "Maybe I will have a muffin, they smell so good."

Nick watched her as she set the table for two. "How was your walk?" he asked. "I was surprised to find you gone when I got up."

"I woke up early and thought I might as well get some exercise. It's a beautiful morning."

"Oh... Julie, your receptionist...she called a few minutes ago and invited us to brunch tomorrow at her house. Is she still married to what's-his-name? The would-be playwright with the phony Russian accent?"

"Boris. They're in the process of divorce."

"That's too bad. I'll miss his verbal attacks on my work at social gatherings. What a pain in the ass. I remember your office Christmas party, when he ganged up on me with that little prick who always wears a beret..."

"Allen. Why can't you remember his name? He's been writing for us for three years. You've met him several times."

Nick shook his head. "Those free-lance writers all run together in my head. Can't keep them straight. They're self-centered underachievers who expect to be recognized as great talents someday."

She stopped what she was doing and just looked at him.

"You know I hate it when you make generalizations like that. I shouldn't have to remind you that I was once a free-lance writer." She took a deep breath. The last thing she wanted to do was start a fight, but Nick had an annoying tendency to assume that those who didn't work in specialized scientific fields weren't contributing anything important in the grand scheme of things. It had been something that rubbed her the wrong way the entire time she'd known him.

She sighed, and—not for the first time—said, "Look, let's make a deal. You don't make fun of my co-workers, and I won't make fun of yours—you know, those brilliant overachievers with Einstein hairdos whose idea of party conversation is a heated debate about the nature of quasi-stellar objects."

Nick grimaced. "Ouch. Okay." Then he smiled. "It's a deal."

When he returned to his culinary efforts she said, "Well, what did you tell Julie?"

"I told her you'd call her back." He poured milk into the bowl of eggs and beat the mixture with a fork. "I'd be happy to escort you if you want to go. I know you were disappointed about my missing the Buchanans' party. I don't want to be the bad guy again."

Lee was quiet for a moment, considering the invitation. It would probably be a good idea to go, to be with people. She didn't want to spend an entire weekend at home with Nick. Not yet. Not until she could come to terms with what had happened in Cavado. Unbidden, Juan's face, with his intense, brooding expression, his compelling eyes, leapt into her mind. And his body, his strong, hard body…

"Lee?"

She jumped at the sound of Nick's voice "What?"

"I said, do you want to go to the brunch?"

"I guess so. If you feel up to it. I know you're tired from your trip."

"It might be fun. Besides, I haven't had a date with my best girl in some time."

Lee had trouble meeting Nick's eyes. She unfolded the newspaper and pretended to be engrossed in the front page.

After breakfast, Lee hurried up the stairs and closed herself in her study. She took her Spanish-English dictionary off the shelf. "*Molestia.*" She was certain that was one of the words Juan had said to Socorro in her dream. "*Tu eres una molestia para mí.*"

She found it: *Molestia: a nuisance or annoyance.* So, *you are a nuisance to me.* And what was the rest of it? "*Tu vas a morir.*" You are going to...she looked up morir. *Die. You are going to die!*

Shocked, Lee dropped the dictionary. She sank into her chair and leaned over, holding her stomach. For a moment she thought she might be sick. Her mind raced. *How could I dream words I don't even know?* She had studied Spanish long ago, in high school, but hadn't retained very much. Of course, she heard a lot of Spanish spoken around town. *I must remember more than I think I do,* she tried to assure herself. *Those words were just buried in my subconscious. It's the only rational answer!*

Still, no matter how hard she tried to talk herself out of it as the day wore on, Lee couldn't shake a growing feeling of apprehension. Nick must have noticed her preoccupation. She caught him watching her out of the corner of his eye as she worked around the house, trying to keep busy.

They sat down to dinner alone that night. Sara wasn't due back from Albuquerque until nine o'clock. Lee looked up from her salad to find Nick watching her with a worried expression on his face. He put his fork down and leaned back in his chair, frowning.

"Okay, honey, what's going on? You haven't been yourself since I got back."

"Really? I'm sorry. I guess I have been a little stressed. But it's nothing to be concerned about. It'll pass."

"I know you're mourning for Mister. But I get the feeling that it's more than that." He sipped his wine, watching her. "You were upset when I left two weeks ago. Is it still that Cavado business?"

Lee looked down at her plate. The soggy alfalfa sprouts looked like little white worms. She felt a twinge of nausea.

"No. It's just a combination of things. I don't know. Maybe I'm pre-menopausal."

"Seriously? Are you having female problems?"

"No, I was joking. It's just that I've felt a little overwhelmed at work and in general." She took a sip of her wine, trying to swallow the lump that was forming in her throat. "But, as I said, it'll pass. Dr. Mallory said that…" She broke off as his fork stopped midway to his mouth.

"Mallory? You saw Mallory while I was gone?"

"Yes, I did. I just haven't gotten around to mentioning it." Her scalp prickled as she struggled to get on safer ground. "I felt I needed to touch base with him. I haven't seen him in a couple of years, you know. And, well, I was upset about that interview in Cavado. I couldn't understand how I had let it get so out of hand." She swallowed hard. "I decided to talk it over with Dr. Mallory. I thought he'd make me feel better, and he did."

"When did you see him?"

"Friday before last." She hesitated. "And again yesterday."

"You saw him twice while I was gone? It sounds to me like you were more than a little depressed."

"The second time I was really upset about Mister, and…"

"Pardon me, but I just don't buy this. I think there's something you aren't telling me. People don't normally go running off to a shrink just because their cat disappears."

Lee blinked back angry tears.

"This may be hard for you to understand, Nick, but some

perfectly normal people are really attached to their pets. Mister may have been just a cat to you, but, dammit, I loved him. At least he was here all the time."

"Unlike me, you mean." He studied her for a moment. "Look, I'm sorry about Mister. I know he was important to you." He reached across the table and covered her hand with his. "I don't mean to be insensitive about it." He patted her hand and then picked up his fork.

Lee watched him. It was so like Nick to dismiss her feelings with a few words meant to end the subject. Over and done and filed in one of his little mental compartments labeled "minor irritations."

"What did Mallory have to say about the Cavado creep?" he asked.

"Well," Lee hesitated, then took a deep breath and picked up her wine glass. "He thinks maybe Juan drugged and hypnotized me."

"WHAT?" Nick's outburst caused Lee to jerk and splash red wine into her salad bowl. "Drugged you? Did I hear you right?"

"You don't have to shout."

Nick made an obvious effort to adjust his tone, but his shock and outrage were apparent.

"Let me get this straight. Mallory thinks this weirdo drugged you? How? And what do you mean hypnotized?"

Lee explained Mallory's theory to Nick, wanting to kick herself for allowing the conversation to take this turn.

"He said it would have been very easy for Juan to put marijuana or something in my tea. And he said that it might have made me sick afterward. Remember? I thought I had the flu."

"Jesus Christ!" Nick snatched his napkin out of his lap and slapped it on the table. "You didn't call the police?"

"The police?" Lee looked at him, then took another bite of her salad, stalling for time and hoping desperately to diffuse the situation. "Are you serious?"

"You're damned right I'm serious!"

She put down her fork and took a deep breath.

"Nick, calm down," she said, trying her best to sound reasonable and in control. "Listen to me. I didn't consider calling the police because that would have blown it up into a big deal. It might have even gotten into the newspapers, which would have been very embarrassing. I don't want anyone else to know about this." She leveled her gaze at him. "Do you?"

He considered her question, and then sighed.

"No, I guess not. But if this guy really did that, he shouldn't be running around loose! He's dangerous. Anything could have happened to you!"

"Well, nothing terrible did. He didn't hurt me." She drained her wine glass.

"That's a matter of opinion. You've been moping around, depressed as hell. You've been to see a shrink. Twice. I would call that hurting you." Nick's face was still flushed with anger. He poured more wine into both their glasses and sat down. "I think I'll pay that sneaky bastard a visit. I'll show him what to do with his sweating oil."

"No!" She put her hand on his arm. "Don't do that. It would only make everything worse. I just want to put the whole thing behind me. I would like very much to forget it ever happened."

Nick stared into space, obviously unwilling to let it go.

"I knew it was completely unlike you to go along with that 'ceremony of awakening' or whatever bullshit it was, but it never occurred to me…"

"It's over now. Let's just forget it." Lee felt a wave of exhaustion. "Promise me?"

"Maybe I should discuss this with Dr. Mallory. See if he doesn't agree that this guy should be investigated."

"No! We don't know for sure that I was drugged. That's just Mallory's theory. And it doesn't really matter now because it's over, and we're going to forget it." Her own irritation was creeping into her voice. "Okay?" she said, rather more curtly than she meant to. Then softer, "Okay?"

JANN ARRINGTON - WOLCOTT

Nick just looked at her for a long moment, his face flushed with indignation.

"No, it's not okay with me. Not by a long shot. But I don't want to upset you any more than you already are. If you're sure you don't want me to..."

"I'm sure!"

"Then I guess I don't have any choice but to drop it. But it galls me to see that bastard go unpunished." He pushed his plate away. "I've lost my appetite. Come on, I'll help you straighten up the kitchen. Then I'm going upstairs. I need to spend a couple of hours on the computer."

"Tonight? Nick, it's Saturday night." Even as she said it, a wave of relief washed over her. She wanted to be alone.

"I have a lot of data to analyze before the Monday morning staff meeting." He stood and started clearing the table.

"Don't bother," she said. "I'll take care of this." She offered him a smile.

"Lee, I want to help...."

"Just go on and analyze your data."

Nick started to speak, then changed his mind and walked out of the room.

Lee cleared the table and started the kitchen clean up. As she worked she began to tear up. *You can't help, Nick. I'm not sure anyone can help me now.*

Later, in bed that night, Nick reached for Lee. "Don't pull away from me, babe," he said. "I didn't mean to make you angry tonight. It's just that I'm so worried about you. You're acting strange as hell. You're so strung out...."

"Please, Nick. I don't want to talk about it. I mean, there's really nothing to talk about and, frankly, I've had more than enough.

I'm not angry. I'm just tired. I'll feel better in the morning. Let's go to sleep."

He sighed. "Okay. Sleep well." He rolled onto his side and within minutes was dead to the world.

Lee lay stiffly on her side of the bed, far from Nick, staring at the ceiling. When she closed her eyes, erotic images of Juan invaded her mind. She shuddered with guilty desire and buried her face in her pillow.

18

Lee sat at her makeup table in her underwear the next morning, trying to pull herself together for Julie's brunch. Peering critically at her reflection in the magnifying side of the mirror, she was alarmed by what she saw. She looked pale and tired. And the skin under her eyes was unusually puffy. I've got to lay off the wine, she thought, reaching for a small jar of eye cream. As she patted the cream under her eyes, she tried to remember how many glasses she'd had last night. Two, maybe three. It was dangerous to use booze to escape from reality. Daddy the Drunk had certainly taught her that.

She was smoothing makeup under her eyes when Nick walked in, carrying a cup of coffee. He leaned against the wall, watching her.

"You are a veritable vision, Scarlett ma deah," he said, launching into his Rhett Butler while twirling an imaginary moustache.

Lee forced the expected response.

"Why, ah declare, sir, how you do go on." She felt a sharp stab of nostalgia. The corny Rhett and Scarlett exchange was a ritual that

remained from the early days of their marriage. Years ago, the game
would end with Nick sweeping her up in his arms and carrying her off
to bed. Now, they just stuck to the timeworn dialogue. She turned back
to the mirror, feeling depressed.

"May ah lace yore corset, mah lovely?"

"Oh, fiddledeedee," Lee said, struggling to play along. "I
burned that ol' thing along with mah bra." She smoothed blusher along
her cheekbones and stood up, walking past him and into her closet to
find something to wear.

Her eyes fell on the blouse she had worn to Cavado. Suddenly,
she was reliving the moment when Juan unbuttoned it, slipped it from
her shoulders and tossed it on the floor. She closed her eyes and felt
his warm lips on her neck and her shoulders, his hands cupping her
buttocks, pulling her closer. She shuddered, feeling her nipples grow
hard. Lost in the memory, she began to stroke her breasts.

"Babe?" Nick's voice shocked her back to the present. "What
are you doing in there? Get a move on. It's after eleven."

She snatched a denim dress off its hanger. Then she took
several deep breaths, fighting to regain some composure before
rejoining her unsuspecting husband.

"Hi, come in!" They were greeted at the door by Julie, dressed
in a long corduroy skirt and cowboy boots, her sweater covered with
strands of turquoise and coral beads. "I'm glad you could come on
such short notice. I just had this sudden urge to throw a party. I hope
you're hungry." She slipped her arm through Nick's and escorted
them inside.

Colorful rugs, both Native American and Mexican, as well as
a few good paintings mixed with art posters competed for wall space
in the cheerfully cluttered living room. Lee estimated at least twenty-
five guests were crammed into the small townhouse. Quite a spur-of-

the-moment Sunday brunch, she thought. A handsome young man sat by the fireplace, singing and strumming a guitar. His music was almost drowned out by the loud conversation and outbursts of laughter. Lee, scanning the crowd for familiar faces, stumbled over a stack of books protruding from under an end table.

"Oops, be careful," Julie said, grabbing Lee's arm. "You'll have to excuse the mess." She rolled her eyes and repositioned a silver comb into the side of her wild mane of salt and pepper hair. "My cleaning lady couldn't make it yesterday. She found her boyfriend drinking with another woman at The Bull Ring and took an ax to the hood of his car. Then she slugged a policeman who tried to interfere. Now she's in jail, can you believe it?" She laughed merrily. "Oh, excuse me, there's the doorbell. Help yourselves to margaritas in the kitchen."

"Julie can afford a cleaning lady?" Nick asked in a low voice. "How much are you paying her?"

"Not nearly as much as she's worth. Oh, there's Alessandro and P.J. waving to us. You remember them from the Garretts' Fourth of July barbecue? They own an antique shop on Canyon Road. P.J. used to be a female impersonator in San Francisco."

Nick groaned. "So now he's impersonating a male in Santa Fe?"

Lee shot him a warning look.

"I'm sorry. I'll behave myself. But I'm going to need several margaritas to get through this, I can tell. And a bowl of posole. Can I get a margarita for you?"

"No. But I'd like some mineral water, if she has it."

"Okay. Here goes. If I don't come back, you'll know that Allen has me cornered again, trying to save the world from science." He moved away through the crowd, toward the kitchen.

As she was maneuvering her way across the room, Lee stopped. Several women directly in front of her were discussing Socorro's death.

"According to Leona, Socorro collapsed right after dinner,"

one of them said. "They were still sitting at the table, drinking coffee, when the poor thing just keeled over. Like she'd been shot. Can you imagine? The last thing in the world you'd expect to happen. Why, I saw her in her gallery early last week, looking absolutely smashing...."

Lee turned, desperate to escape the upsetting narrative, only to run into Annabel.

"Hi," she said. "Some party, huh? I understand that Julie just came into some money. A grandmother or something. Let's hope it isn't enough for her to retire on. We'd have a hell of a time replacing her."

Lee nodded her agreement, thankful for a change of subject.

"I was just talking to Leona," Annabel continued. "She was with Socorro Tafoya-Hall, when she died last week. You know, the owner of Galería on Canyon Road? You've met her, haven't you? They started advertising with us about a year ago. Anyway, she was full-blooded Native American—high cheekbones, long black hair, and thin, to boot. Looked a little like Cher. And she was so young! I doubt she was even forty. Anyway, Leona was having dinner with Socorro and some friends when she just dropped dead. Right at the table." Annabel's voice dropped to a confidential tone. "I guess it was absolutely grisly. Leona said Socorro suddenly grabbed her head with both hands. Her mouth was moving but no words were coming out. Then the poor thing's eyes started to bulge and..."

"Stop it!" Lee's voice rose. "I can't listen to this! Dammit, Annie, I just can't listen...."

She had a glimpse of Annabel's shocked face just before she whirled and bumped into an aproned woman, causing her to drop a large tray of enchiladas. The noisy room hushed. Horrified, Lee ran through the staring crowd and out the front door. She was leaning against her car, shaking uncontrollably when Nick arrived running.

"Lee? Are you all right? What on earth happened? Annabel rushed up to me and said that you just suddenly went to pieces."

"Take me home, Nick. Please take me home."

There was silence in the car as Nick pulled out onto the highway but Lee could feel his confusion and irritation.

"Are you ready to tell me what that was all about?" he asked, obviously trying to control his voice.

Lee sighed. She had no intention of telling Nick about Juan, but suddenly realized that Socorro's death would excuse her behavior. And it *was* a major factor in this latest upset. *But if she hadn't been trying to help me she wouldn't be dead!* She took a deep breath.

"Just after you left, I got acquainted with one of our advertisers, the woman who owns Galería on Canyon Road. Socorro Tafoya-Hall. We got to talking and really hit it off. We had lunch a couple of times, I went with her one evening to meet some people she knows—I was excited about finding someone I really clicked with, and making a new friend." Her tears began to flow again and she took a tissue from her purse. "Soccoro was a remarkable woman."

"Was?" Nick said.

"She died last week. Suddenly. She and her husband were at dinner with friends and she suddenly collapsed. A brain hemorrhage, they think." Lee took another deep breath. *Poor Socorro! It's all my fault.* Those thoughts brought a new flood of tears.

"I'm sorry, honey," Nick said. "Why didn't you tell me?"

"No reason. You didn't know her and I was dealing with it, but everyone at the party was whispering about it and then Annie started in gleefully recounting the details and…it was just too much."

When they got home Lee went straight to their room and changed into some sweats. She just wanted to just lie down and find some way to pull herself together. Nick followed her upstairs.

"I'm sorry if I embarrassed you," she told Nick, rubbing her forehead, feeling the low thrum that signaled the start of a headache. "And I suppose I'll have to apologize to Annie, too." She went into the bathroom and took a couple of asprin.

When she came out, Nick smiled at her, then took her by the shoulders and kissed her cheek.

"I wouldn't worry about hurting Annabel's feelings. She's about as sensitive as a warthog."

Lee smiled weakly and tried to change the subject.

"Sara's spending the afternoon with Wendy. I don't expect her home before five. I imagine you can use some quiet time?"

"I do need to spend another hour or so on the Alaska data," he said. "But first, I want to put a fresh coat of wax on the Volvo. This weather can't last. It'll be snowing before we know it."

He left the room and moments later, Lee heard the door to the garage open and close.

I can't believe I went to pieces like that, she thought miserably. *And in front of all those people! I'll have to call Julie later and apologize. And hope Annabel will forgive me for screaming at her. Now she'll be convinced that I'm going bonkers.* She closed her eyes, but images of Socorro—of her last dreadful moments as described by Annabel—filled her mind.

That's probably Annabel, she thought, when the phone rang moments later. *I might as well get the apology over with. Blame it on a migraine. Or rampaging hormones.* She lifted the receiver. Before she could even say hello she froze at the sound of a familiar voice.

"Lee? I could wait no longer."

"Juan?" she said in a horrified whisper.

"I must see you. Trust me. It is important. Come tomorrow."

"No! No, I can't come. I can't talk. My husband is here. I have to hang up."

"Tomorrow. I will be waiting. Trust me!" The line went dead.

Lee banged the receiver down. *This is totally out of control! That he would dare call here on a Sunday afternoon. Nick could have picked up the phone! If he had heard...* She shuddered. *I have to put a stop to this once and for all. Juan has got to leave me alone!*

She curled up, clutching Nick's pillow. After a while, the headache began to fade and she drifted into a light sleep.

When she woke, she felt a little stronger. It's up to me, she told herself, to get out of this mess. *Somehow, I have to get it through Juan's thick head that it's over between us. I have to make him listen to reason. Obviously, that can't be done over the telephone. I guess I'm going to have to see him again. Just one last time...to make certain that he understands the situation. I'll scare him. I'll tell him that Nick's threatening to call the police.*

She forced herself up and into a hot shower. By the time she was dressed and downstairs preparing dinner, Lee had almost convinced herself that the nightmare would soon be over. Enough of this *brujo* nonsense, she thought, putting a pan of marinated chicken thighs into the oven. *Juan is just a man. I can handle him. I can make him accept the fact that it's over between us.* She repressed a warning stab of uncertainty and even managed a smile for Nick when he came into the kitchen a short time later.

"Ummm, something smells good. Did I hear Sara come home a few minutes ago?"

Lee nodded. "She's in her room. On the phone, I imagine."

"Of course." He leaned against the counter, watching her. "You look better. Headache gone?"

"Just about. My little nap did the trick. Sara," she called up the stairs. "Will you come down and make a salad, please?"

"Did you hurt yourself?" Nick asked. "You're limping a little, favoring your right leg."

"I am?" She frowned, then shrugged. "Oh, it's nothing. I just twisted my ankle on my walk yesterday morning." She executed a graceful pirouette on the smooth tile floor. "See, no harm done."

"I'm relieved to see you acting more like your old self," Nick said. "You've really had me worried."

"Well, stop worrying. I'm fine. End of discussion." She busied herself setting the table. "Have you unpacked from your trip?"

"Yeah. While you were napping. I have a couple of sweaters and a sports coat that need to go to the cleaners. Could you drop them off for me tomorrow?"

"Sure," she said. "I'm not going into the office. Things are under control there. The next issue of the magazine is ready to go to the printers. I think I'll give myself a day off. There's some personal business I need to take care of."

19

Slamming the car door behind her, Lee marched resolutely up the dirt path leading to the small adobe house. She squared her shoulders and rapped sharply on the front door.

"At last," Juan said, opening the door. His shirt was unbuttoned almost to the waist. "I have been expecting you." He pulled her inside the darkened room and closed the door. Lee stood still, feeling her courage waiver. Eerie shapes and shadows on the walls appeared to be moving, closing in. She straightened her shoulders, determined to maintain her composure.

"Juan," she began in a firm voice, "we have to talk." She stiffened as she felt him slide her woolen wrap off her shoulders. Then, before she could resist, he pulled her into his arms.

"Let me go! I can't..."

His lips closed on hers, cutting off her words and speaking directly to her body. She pushed against his chest with her palms.

"Listen to me! I came here to..."

"I know why you came. I feel your need." He pulled her buttocks to him, pressing her hard against his body. "And you can feel mine, can't you?"

She twisted frantically in his embrace, aware of his erection pushing against her stomach.

"Don't fight me, *querida*." He held her fast. "You're still trying to fight me."

Lee had an image of a fly ensnared in a spider's web, becoming more hopelessly trapped with each frantic movement. She made an anguished sound.

"Trust me," he said. His voice was soft but insistent. "And look at me. I want you to look at me."

She stared at the wooden floor instead, her heart hammering in her chest. His hands moving on her back seemed to burn through her blouse. Again, she tried to push him away, but his power was too great. Slowly, she lifted her head. Her eyes traveled up his partially exposed chest and lingered on the amulet that dangled from the chain around his neck. The red crystal eyes seemed to glow with a light of their own.

She heard Juan's voice as if from a distance. "Let go of your fears, Lee," he said. "Trust me. Let yourself come into your Power."

She tore her gaze from the amulet and met his eyes. The passion she saw there almost made her knees buckle.

"No!" she said, wrenching her eyes from his and turning her face toward the door. "Please, don't."

His grip tightened around her waist and his free hand gently clasped her chin, bringing her face toward his.

"Trust me," he whispered. His voice wrapped around her like soft cords. "What is happening is meant to be."

Lee stared up at him like a rabbit mesmerized by a bright light. She felt her strength and will drain away, exposing her raw physical need. Her body seemed to have a will of its own and, in spite of her fears, it ached to press against his.

"What have you done to me?" she moaned.

"Shhhhh. Later," he whispered. "Trust me. We will talk later." She felt his fingers at her chest, unbuttoning her blouse. "I can wait no longer to touch you."

Lee lay exhausted in Juan's arms on the buffalo hide. She felt the soft tickle of fur beneath her naked buttocks as she buried her face against his neck. She caressed his chest, gently trailing her fingers through the soft, dark hair. As she moved her hand toward his throat, her fingers touched the amulet. She jerked them away. The necklace felt hot, almost too hot to touch.

Juan turned and slid his leg over her hip, pinning her against him as he had done before. He kissed her forehead and stroked her back. Far removed from the outside world, Lee sighed and closed her eyes.

She awoke with a start, shocked by her surroundings. It hadn't been a dream. It had happened again! She bolted upright, finding that she was alone. The room felt stuffy and uncomfortably warm. Glancing at the wood-burning stove in the corner, Lee felt a wave of panic. *What if I'm trapped, locked inside this dark, suffocating place? No one knows I'm here. No one would know where to look for me!*

Suddenly, from the other room, she heard the soft creak of the front door. She rose to her feet, clutching a blanket around her. In a moment, Juan appeared in the doorway, fully dressed and wearing a sheepskin jacket.

"You are awake," he said, smiling at her.

"Yes." She was uncomfortably aware of her nakedness. "Where were you?"

"I stepped outside for a moment." He moved in close and stroked the side of her neck. "What's wrong, *querida?*" he asked gently. "You look upset."

"*Everything's* wrong. I feel so strange, so lost." She let him draw her into his arms and rested her cheek against his shoulder.

"You are not lost, *mi vida.* You are just beginning to find your true self."

"How did you get up and dress without waking me?"

He laughed softly. "I can be as quiet as a shadow when I wish."

She took a deep breath and raised her head to look at him.

"Juan," she blurted, "did you know that Socorro died last week?"

He seemed to freeze for an instant, before bending his head to kiss her shoulder.

"Who?" He continued to slide his lips up the side of her neck.

"Socorro Tafoya-Hall." Lee felt her stomach twist into a tight fist. "She was a friend of mine."

"I know little of life outside of Cavado," he said, releasing her. He took off his jacket and hung it on a wooden peg. "You sound as though I should know this woman."

"I thought you might have heard of her. She was from Santa Clara Pueblo." Lee shivered.

"You are cold. Come, wrap the blanket around you and sit by the stove." He led her to the sofa and sat close beside her, one arm around her shoulders. He slid his other hand beneath the blanket and began to caress her breast. Lee pulled back. *It's now or never.*

"Juan, I have to talk to you. I came here today to talk. Not to…" She squirmed as his hand moved down across her naked stomach. "Don't, please. I don't know what kind of power you have over me, but I can't…"

"Don't you?"

"What?"

"Don't you know what kind of power I have over you?" His finger traced slow circles around her navel.

She turned to look at his face. A smile played across his lips. A memory of Mister toying with a captured mouse sprang to Lee's mind.

"How can I get through to you, dammit?" she blurted. "I cannot continue to do this!"

Juan frowned and withdrew his hand from under the blanket.

"You are blocking your memory of what is between us." His voice was low, but the irritation evident. "When will you allow yourself to understand?"

"What *you* don't seem to understand is that I'm a married woman! My husband is already furious about my first visit here—about the Awakening Ceremony. He's threatened to go to the police."

A muscle near the corner of Juan's left eye twitched.

"The police? Why?"

"He thinks you drugged me during our interview." Lee could feel cold sweat on her palms. "I...I can't see you again. That's what I came here today to tell you."

"You think you can walk away from me so easily?"

His expression was one of amusement, but beneath it she could sense the unspoken threat.

"Why won't you face reality? Our relationship has no future. You must know that. I love my family, my daughter...and my husband."

His hands gripped her shoulders roughly, turning her to face him.

"Your love belongs to me! Trust me when I say you are mine. You have always been mine."

His eyes glittered with a dark intensity. They burned into hers, scattering her thoughts and forcing her compliance. With a sinking heart, Lee felt her resolve desert her once again. She didn't even protest when he yanked the blanket from her naked shoulders.

It was late afternoon when she pulled into the parking lot of the City Different Cleaning Company and reached into the back seat for the clothes she had collected early that morning. She stared, frowning at the small pile. What happened to Nick's navy sweater? She twisted around in her seat to search the floorboard, certain she'd put the sweater with the other items to be cleaned.

"It's not here," she mumbled to herself. "But I distinctly remember.... God, what's happening to me? Am I losing my mind?"

20

"Mom?" Sara stared at Lee in amazement. They were alone in the kitchen, cleaning up after dinner. Nick had excused himself immediately after eating to work on a report that was due in the morning. "Do you realize that you just put the saltshaker in the refrigerator? You've been totally spaced out all night. What's wrong?"

Abashed, Lee retrieved the saltshaker. "Nothing."

"I don't think you've heard a word I've said," Sara whined.

"What?"

"You weren't listening, were you?"

"I'm sorry. I guess my mind was wandering. What is it?"

"Oh, nothing important. Just that my entire life is coming apart, and my mother obviously doesn't give a shit!" Sara's eyes shone with angry tears.

"Watch your language, young lady! And don't speak to me in that tone of voice."

"I can't talk to you at all lately!" Sara wailed. "I can't trust Wendy. You don't listen…"

"What on earth are you talking about? Sara, stop crying and tell me what's going on."

"Do you even care?" Sara grabbed a paper napkin and wiped her eyes.

"Of course I care. What's wrong?"

"I just found out that my best friend in the whole world is trying to steal my boyfriend."

"Wendy? Wendy's interested in Kevin?"

"More than interested! She has a serious case of the hots for him! The mere fact that we've been best friends since the fourth grade doesn't count for anything. I'm so mad I could scratch her eyes out. I'll never, ever trust her again. And then, tonight, when I try to talk to you about it, you act like you were on Mars or something." Fresh tears started to flow.

"I'm sorry, Sara," Lee said wearily. "I know I've been preoccupied lately. But that doesn't mean I'm not interested in your problems. I'm always here for you."

"Not lately, you're not."

Lee sagged under a wave of exhaustion. "Look, honey, can we talk about this tomorrow? I really can't…"

"Just forget it! It's only my life!" Sara shouted then whirled and ran up the stairs. Lee heard her bedroom door slam. She sighed and finished clearing the kitchen counter. Leaving the dirty dishes in the sink, she went upstairs to her bathroom.

Sitting at her dressing table, she stared into space as the tub filled with hot water. She'd spend some time talking to Sara tomorrow. *Just not tonight. Dear God, not tonight.* She slipped out of her clothes and into her bath.

Eyes closed, she leaned her head back against an inflated pillow. The hours she'd spent with Juan began replaying in her mind. *I was a fool to think I could control the situation, that I could simply tell Juan goodbye and be done with it.* Brujo *or not, he has a fierce hold on me. Socorro hadn't been exaggerating when she said I was in "deep shit." And I have no idea how to climb out.*

It doesn't make sense, she thought, certainly not for the first time. *How can I be afraid of Juan and so attracted to him at the same time? What kind of power does he have over me? There's the sex, obviously. But is it more than that? Am I, as Socorro believed, under some kind of spell?* She dismissed the thought, determined not to think about Socorro. Then her thoughts returned, as they always did now, to Juan.

Is he really someone I knew and loved in a past lifetime? Is that the source of this obsession? Sinking deeper into the fragrant, steaming water, Lee admitted to herself that only one thing was certain. Whatever the truth of the situation, she was in way over her head.

Nick was sitting near the window, reading a thick report titled *Experimental Ionospheric Observations and Theory* when Lee came out of the bathroom in her nightgown.

"I was beginning to think you'd drowned in there," he said, glancing up.

"I was just draining off negative energy."

"What?" There was a hint of a smirk in his tone.

"Never mind." She turned down the bed and crawled in.

"Is your headache back?"

"I'm just tired."

"You were so distant during dinner."

"Nick, I said I'm just tired! Stop interrogating me!" The words came out more sharply than she intended.

"Interrogating you? Is that what you think I am doing? You're my wife, dammit. And I'm worried sick about you. What am I supposed to do? Just keep my mouth shut? Not ask questions?"

"Just let me sleep. Please. I'll feel better in the morning."

"That's what you keep saying." He sighed. "Okay, I'll drop it. I've got another hour or so of reading here. Will the light bother you?"

"No. I'll wear my mask. Goodnight." She inserted earplugs, adjusted her satin sleep mask and quickly fell asleep.

A freezing wind whistled and moaned beyond the blanket-covered doorway. She crouched closer to the warmth of the open fire, thankful for the round opening at the top of the cave, which pulled smoke up and out of the small space. Then she began spreading her sacred objects on the hard-packed dirt floor. Picking up the two clear crystals that symbolized light and truth, she put them inside her medicine bundle. They would strengthen her magic. And she would need prayer sticks, she remembered, reaching for two pieces of wood, carved from a tree struck by lightning and decorated with emblems of Father Sun and Mother Earth.

Her thunder-speaker. She mustn't forget that. Set with sacred blue stones and attached to a length of rope woven from the hair of ancient Holy Ones—it reproduced the sound of thunder when whirled above the head, driving away sickness. She added it to the other items in the bundle.

Sacred snakes, carefully carved from a river tree and painted in the colors of the four directions—Yellow, Red, Black, White—felt warm, almost alive, to her touch. She murmured with satisfaction. Their magic would be strong tonight. She laid them beside a delicate pink and white spirit shell from the endless waters that lay far to the West.

Finally, she selected the spear-shaped leaves and small red berries that would be boiled for tea and made into medicine paste. It was all assembled, everything needed for a curing chant. She stood slowly, painfully, supporting her weight on her left leg, and reached for her walking stick that leaned against the wall of the cave. It was time to dress.

She pulled a soft doeskin ceremonial garment over her head, adjusting the bear teeth that decorated the neckline. Then she tied skunk fur pelts over her moccasins for protection from any evil that might be released during the ceremony. For added strength, she positioned an eagle feather in the leather band around her forehead.

She spoke softly to a large black wolf that was sleeping close to the fire.

"Accompany me to the Great Cave, Wind Runner," she said, wrapping herself in a long fur cape. "I will need the medicine of your keen senses tonight." The wolf yawned and rose it its feet.

Carrying her medicine bundle, she stepped out into the cold night. Snowflakes hit her face as she slowly made her way, bent against the blowing wind, along the narrow path, the wolf following close behind. She could hear the soft beat of medicine drums as she approached the ceremonial cave. "Iatik, Great Mother of All, be with me tonight," she prayed. "Help me restore the son of Miwana to harmony with the earth and heavens," she whispered as she walked.

A small figure wrapped in white fur lay on a flat stone in the center of the cave. A whispering group of women gathered around him, one of them crying. They fell silent and drew back, heads lowered in respect, as she approached. A handful of men, faces blackened with ashes, sat around an open fire beating a soft rhythm on their drums.

The child opened his eyes and began to cry as she came near him. Then he started to cough, a dry, wheezing sound that wracked his thin frame. Drops of perspiration glistened on his flushed face. He has the coughing sickness, she realized with a sinking heart. She was going to need her strongest magic to save this little one. He was too young, and already very weak. It was going to be a long night. She gently touched her hand to his hot forehead, then blew three purifying breaths across his face to cleanse away all traces of evil winds. The child began a thin wailing. Chanting softly, she opened her medicine bundle.

Lee woke up, chilled and trembling. She ripped off her sleep mask and lay shivering in the darkness, her heart hammering in her chest. *Another dream! And the most realistic yet. A sick child, a cave, a huge black dog—or was it a wolf?*

She raised her head and looked at the clock. Twelve-fifteen. *Get a grip, Lindsay! This is affecting everyone around you! You simply cannot allow yourself to be completely undone by vivid dreams.* She pushed strands of sweat-damp hair back from her forehead, removed the earplugs, and tried to relax by matching Nick's slow, deep breathing. But when she closed her eyes, that high-pitched wailing cry echoed in her mind—accompanied by a soft, rhythmic sound like distant drumbeats.

Cold panic rose in Lee's chest. She moved close to Nick, trying to control her shivers by fitting her body against the curve of his comforting warmth.

Lee turned off the alarm and groaned. Morning already. She used to wake up eager to face the day. Now it was a real effort to drag herself to work. But she had to go in. She'd been out of the office too often lately. She automatically looked at the foot of the bed and felt a lump in her throat.

"I miss you so much, sweet Mister," she whispered, blinking back tears. "There'll never be another cat like you."

Sara's response to Lee's "Good morning" was frosty to say the least. When she apologized again and promised they'd talk that evening Sara wouldn't even meet her eyes. She just tossed a chilly "Whatever" in Lee's direction and was out the door.

"Oh, Julie," Lee said, stopping by the front desk. "I meant to call you yesterday. I owe you an apology for leaving your party on Sunday. Not to mention causing the mess with the enchiladas. I hope you had enough food. Please forgive me."

Julie looked uncomfortable. "Of course I forgive you, and we had plenty of food. But I was worried."

"Yes. It was just a migraine. Is Annabel in yet?"

"She's meeting with a new advertiser this morning, that Thai restaurant on Cerrillos Road. I expect her around nine-thirty."

"Okay. I need to talk to her when she comes in." She hurried into her office and closed the door.

As Lee sorted through the stack of memos and miscellaneous correspondence, her thoughts kept returning to the dream she'd had the night before. *Sitting in a small cave on a dirt floor, gathering a peculiar bundle of things—decorated sticks, crystals, and a seashell—and tying them into a leather pouch.*

She sat back in her chair, remembering the cold walk through wind and snow to a much larger fire-lit cave, and the expression of fear on a small face staring up at her from a mound of white fur. She could still hear the child's hacking cough and shrill, haunting cry.

Unbelievably realistic. So vivid and detailed. I'm really worried about myself, and I don't know what to do. Call Dr. Mallory again? He'd attribute my dreams to exhaustion and a creative impressionable mind. Mostly a reaction to Juan's reincarnation line of bull. No, she decided. No need to take up more of Mallory's time. He's done all he can for me.

Her thoughts turned to Socorro and their last meeting, even as she felt the tears starting to well up. *Did Socorro go to Cavado? Her husband might know. But I don't want bother the poor man with questions at a time like this. He must be devastated. Besides, what could she say without sounding like a lunatic? If I admitted my suspicions, he'd think I was deranged.*

But if Socorro did go to Cavado, then that meant Juan had lied about not knowing her. Lee stopped cold. *Wait a minute... Socorro's uncle...the deputy sheriff! He was going to do some checking on Juan, something about an investigation from years ago. With all that's happened, it completely went out of my head. I've got to talk to the uncle and find out what he discovered. And he might even know if Socorro went to Cavado. But what was his name?* She thought for a moment. *Leroy? No. Luis. Luis Tafoya.*

She grabbed the phone book and looked up the number of the Rio Arriba County Sheriff's Department.

After several frustrating transfers, she was connected to the correct office. "May I speak to Deputy Sheriff Tafoya, please?"

"Speaking." The voice was gruff.

"Deputy Tafoya, my name is Lee Lindsay. I was a friend of your niece, Socorro. The last time I talked to her, she said that you might have some information about a man I met in Cavado. Juan Mascareñas."

"You the one that owns that magazine? Santa Fe...?"

"*Santa Fe Today.* That's right. Did Socorro mention me?"

"She just said that you'd had a run-in with Mascareñas."

"I guess you could call it that." She hesitated, unwilling to volunteer any more information than she had to. "I interviewed Mr. Mascareñas for an article. Afterward, I had some questions about him." She cleared her throat. "First, let me say how sorry I am about Socorro. She was a wonderful person."

"Yes, she was. It was a terrible shock. Very unexpected."

"I saw her the day before she died. She said she was going to meet you for lunch, and that you were going to check the records. Something about an investigation years ago involving Mr. Mascareñas? I'm very curious. Did you find anything?"

"Just a minute. What did you say your name was?"

"Lee. Lee Lindsay."

"Okay, just checking. That is the name I'd written down. Have to be careful, giving out information over the phone. Yes, I located that file. Let me get it."

Lee was put on hold for several minutes.

"Sorry to keep you waiting. I had to take another call," he said when he returned.

"Then there was an investigation?"

"In 1962. But it didn't amount to much. Mascareñas was questioned in connection with a missing person. Let's see...it was a twenty-year-old woman from California. Her name was Susan Miller. She was a student at the University of New Mexico when Mascareñas was there and, from all accounts, she was his girlfriend. They both dropped out of school suddenly, in the middle of a semester. According to the girl's friends, they were headed for Mexico."

Lee's mouth went dry. "Mexico?"

"According to the report, the Miller woman told her roommate that she and Mascareñas were going to spend some time studying a tribe of Indians in the mountains near Chihuahua. She was never heard from again. Her family alerted the Mexican police, hired a private investigator, and did everything possible."

"She was never found?"

"Not as far as I know."

"But Juan came back."

"Yes, he did, two years later. But the girl wasn't with him. Mascareñas claimed to have no idea where she was. His story was that she had jilted him for another man after they arrived in Chihuahua. But he stayed on in Mexico, traveling alone, until he learned that his mother was sick."

"Sinopa Mascareñas?"

"That's right. She died shortly after he got home." There was a short pause. "Sinopa Mascareñas. Man, she was really something. I met her right after I joined the department, more than forty years ago. But that's another story."

"I'd like to hear it."

"Well, as I remember, several villagers from Cavado came in, insisting that Sinopa be arrested. Her husband, Don Gregorio, had died a few days before and they were convinced that she'd killed him. They still weren't satisfied, even after old Doc Lopez diagnosed the cause of death as natural—a stroke or something."

Lee swallowed hard. "Did you say a stroke?"

"I think so. If my memory serves me...it was a long time ago. Anyway, I went out to Cavado and talked to Sinopa. I'll never forget her. She was beautiful. Black eyes that looked right through you. And all that hair hanging down past her waist. But she was very—what is the word?—haughty. She was *very* haughty. Cold as ice. It was easy to see how the rumors got started."

"What rumors?" Lee asked, but she already knew.

"Well, the villagers in Cavado were apparently terrified of her. Several went on record, claiming that she had supernatural powers."

"You mean they thought she was a witch."

"I guess so," the deputy continued. "There's a lot of superstition in those little mountain villages. And they don't take easily to outsiders. If I remember correctly, Don Gregorio met Sinopa and married her in Mexico. The villagers were upset when he brought her home to Cavado. It had been assumed that he would marry one of the local girls. So, of course, there was a lot of jealousy and resentment. That's human nature."

"I suppose so." Lee suspected it was much more than human

nature that contributed to any mysterious events connected to Sinopa or Juan.

"It didn't end with Don Gregorio's death, though," he continued.

Deputy Tafoya told her he remembered there had been more trouble concerning Sinopa, several years after that. He remembered that the villagers were up in arms again over "some nonsense" about her having put a death hex on a woman whose husband she'd seduced.

Lee asked what had happened.

"Nothing that I know of," he said. "I don't know if that woman lived or died. There were no formal charges and no evidence. As I said, there's a lot of ignorance and superstition in Cavado. Those folks are still living in the Dark Ages.

"But back to Juan and the Miller woman. The file says Mascareñas swore that he had no idea where she was. Seemed genuinely shocked that she was missing. There was no solid reason not to believe him. A girl like that, one who would suddenly run off to Mexico—no telling what kind of trouble she got into. The investigation noted that young people got into drugs and disappeared all the time back then. Especially in Mexico, with the whole Timothy Leary/LSD thing. The investigators concluded anything could have happened to her down there after she left Mascareñas and they closed the file."

"So you think he was telling the truth?" Lee asked. "That she left him for another man?"

"As I said, there was nothing in the file to make them question his story."

"You told Socorro all this?"

"Yes. She had already heard the stories about Sinopa from my mother, her grandmother. And based on that, she was ready to believe the worst about Juan. Socorro was always quick to jump to conclusions. And—I'm not sure how to put this—but from the time she was a child she had some very strange ideas. Used to talk to invisible people. 'Spirit guides' she called them."

"Deputy Tafoya, do you know if Socorro drove up to Cavado after she left you?"

"No. Why would she do that?"

"Well, she mentioned to me that she might."

"I doubt it. She was in a rush to get on the road after lunch, saying she had a lot of things she wanted to do that afternoon. I do remember her saying that Howard was taking her to a dinner party that night." He paused. "That's where she…"

"I know. Again, I'm so sorry. I was just getting to know her and…well, I miss her." For a moment she didn't know what more she could say. She ended somewhat lamely with, "Well, thank you."

"You're welcome," he said kindly. "I hope I've been of some help. As I said, as far as I know, Mascareñas was innocent of any crime involving the missing girl. And I've never heard of any other problems concerning him. I asked around after Socorro contacted me. I did learn that he's a *curandero*—no doubt he learned some healing skills from his mother—and he apparently leads a quiet life in Cavado. The villagers seem to think highly of him. After all, the Mascareñases are an old and respected family in these parts." He hesitated. "But Socorro indicated that he'd given you some trouble. Do you want to file a complaint?"

"No. I was just curious about him. He's quite a character."

"Well, is there anything else I can do for you?"

"I guess not. Thank you for your time. Oh, if you remember anything else about this case, would you let me know? You can reach me at the magazine office."

"Okay, I'll make a note of it. As I said, I hadn't heard anything at all about Mascareñas for years, until Socorro brought his name up. Of course, that doesn't surprise me. Those villagers tend to keep to themselves. They don't like the law involved in their affairs."

"I see. Well, thanks again for your time. Goodbye." Lee replaced the receiver.

That's that, she thought. *A dead end. Tafoya obviously*

believes that Juan was innocent of any wrongdoing. But I doubt that he succeeded in convincing Socorro of that. Damn! I should have asked if he had the results of her autopsy. I don't want to bother him again. Maybe Dr. Mallory has some information by now.

She'd call Mallory later. Her thoughts returned to Juan. The more she learned, the more of a mystery he seemed to be. What was he doing at that very moment? Was he at home in his grandfather's *hacienda*? Or was he already in his "office," treating a villager with herbs and mumbo-jumbo? He had spoken so matter-of-factly about removing spells cast by those with the "evil eye."

Rising abruptly, Lee paced around her office.

"I can't let myself dwell on this," she scolded herself, speaking aloud. "Mallory is right. I have to keep a grip on reality. I don't believe in witchcraft, at least the rational part of my mind doesn't. Socorro died of a stroke. And what happened between Juan and me has nothing to do with the supernatural. Juan is an attractive, charismatic, and extremely sexy man. That's all. I can't excuse my infidelity with fanciful theories about witchcraft and reincarnation."

"Lee?"

She whirled around to see Annabel standing in the doorway.

"Damn! You scared me!"

"Sorry. What were you doing? Standing at the window mumbling to yourself?"

"You might have knocked," Lee said, more accusingly than she intended.

"Well, excuse me." Annabel's feelings were clearly hurt. "I knew you were alone. Julie said you wanted to see me."

"Oh, Annie. I'm sorry," she said, crossing the room to usher her friend in so she could close the door. "I did want to see you, to apologize for the way I acted at Julie's brunch. It was so embarrassing. And I didn't mean to snap at you just now." Lee's eyes filled with tears.

Annabel rushed to give Lee a hug. "It's okay," she said. "I know you're going through a rough time. I only wish you'd let me help."

"You can't. I'm just tired. I really haven't been sleeping well."

"Are you having night sweats?"

Lee moved out of Annabel's embrace, expecting a menopause lecture was on the way.

"No. Well, not exactly." She reached for a tissue and blew her nose. "Please, I'll be all right. Just bear with me."

"What else can I do? We're partners, remember? That reminds me, are you ready for the Writer's Group luncheon today?"

"Oh, God. No! That's today?"

"Lee, you're scheduled to give the pep talk."

"I completely forgot! I can't believe it. I...I've just lost track of the days. I haven't prepared anything to say. What time is it? Oh hell! It's only an hour away! What am I going to do?"

"You're going to go home."

"Go home?" Lee said. "What do you..."

"Lee, calm down. Listen to me. I want you to go home. Call your gynecologist and make an appointment for a checkup. Then go to bed and get some rest. I'll cover for you at the luncheon. I hate public speaking, but I can do it. I'll give them the old 'perseverance counts' lecture."

"Okay, thank you. I'm so sorry, Annie. I'm a real mess lately, aren't I?"

"It happens to the best of us," Annabel said, giving Lee another hug.

Lee was surprised to see Nick's car in the garage when she got home a short time later. She found him upstairs, lying in bed with a washcloth across his forehead.

"Nick? What's wrong?"

"I don't know." His voice sounded strained. "I just suddenly got sick. What are you doing home?"

"I decided to work here this afternoon. When did you get sick? You seemed fine when you left this morning."

"I know. But halfway through the division meeting I got dizzy. Felt so lightheaded I thought I was gonna keel over." He looked at her with glazed eyes. "Must be one of those viruses going around."

Lee sat on the bed beside him and felt his forehead.

"You're burning up," she said. "Let me get the thermometer."

"No, don't bother. I took some aspirin. I just want to sleep for a while. Close the drapes, will you?"

"Sure. I'll be back to check on you in a little while. Go to sleep." She drew the draperies and straightened the blankets around him. "I thought you were immune to flu bugs."

"Must be some Alaskan super-virus. Don't get too close to me. I'll be okay after a little rest."

She placed a cool, wet washcloth on his forehead and left the room, closing the door behind her. It was really unusual for Nick to be sick, she thought, as she went down the stairs. She couldn't remember the last time he had missed work because of illness.

Nick slept fitfully for several hours. Lee checked on him periodically, slipping quietly into the bedroom. She stood by the bed, watching as he tossed and turned, throwing back the blankets and winding himself up in the sheet.

Lee was in her study in the late afternoon when she heard Nick cry out. She rushed into the bedroom to find him half out of bed, his arms thrashing wildly through the air as though fending off an invisible attacker. His eyes were open and he was making loud incoherent noises.

"Nick! What is it?" As soon as she spoke the words she smelled it. *The sweating oil!* "Oh, my God," she whispered.

"No. Get away from me!" Nick's voice was high pitched and frantic.

She grabbed him by the shoulders.

"Nick! It's me! Wake up!" The odor made her want to gag.

He jerked away violently, banging his head against the headboard. His eyes were unfocused and wild with fright. A trickle of saliva ran down one side of his mouth, and his breath came in ragged gasps. He was shaking his head from side to side.

"Honey, wake up. Please. You're having a nightmare."

Lee stared at him in horror. She had never seen Nick frightened. The cringing, babbling man before her was a stranger. The odor grew stronger. Forcing herself to ignore it, she touched the back of her hand to his feverish forehead. Hot. So terribly hot.

"Nick! Please. Wake up!"

Gradually, his eyes focused on her. "Lee? What…?"

She put her arm beneath his neck, helping him to lie down.

"I'm here. It's all right. You're just feverish, and you were having a nightmare."

She pulled the blankets up around his shoulders.

"Let me re-wet this washcloth for you and bring you some more aspirin. Don't try to talk. Just relax. I'll be right back."

Lee ran down the the stairs and into the kitchen. She flipped through the Rolodex and dialed Dr. Zimmerman's office.

"I need to talk to the doctor," she said to his receptionist. "My husband is very sick."

She was transferred to a nurse, who promised to have the doctor return her call as soon as possible. Lee poured ice water into a glass, grabbed the aspirin bottle and rushed back to the bedroom. The odor was gone.

Dr. Zimmerman, who lived several houses down the road, agreed to stop by to see Nick on his way home after work. Lee was talking with Sara about Wendy's unforgivable betrayal when the doorbell rang at five-thirty.

Lee breathed a sigh of relief.

"That's the doctor," she said to Sara. "I'll get it."

The doctor was on the porch, little black bag in hand.

"Dr. Zimmerman, come in. Thank you for coming. I know you don't usually make house calls."

"No, I don't. No time for that these days, I'm afraid. But you convinced me this is a special circumstance. And it is on my way home. How's Nick?" he asked as he followed her upstairs.

"He's asleep again. He's been sleeping most of the day. I'm really worried. I've never seen him like this. You know Nick. He never allows himself to get sick."

"Your husband may have the constitution of an ox, but there are some formidable viruses going around. Has he been traveling?"

"Yes. He just got home Friday from Alaska. Do you think he might have been exposed to something there? Or on the plane?"

"Probably. Let's wake him and see what we're up against."

Nick looked startled to find Dr. Zimmerman sitting on the bed beside him. He lifted his head, then collapsed back onto the pillow.

"My head," he moaned.

"Okay, just relax," said the doctor. "Open up so we can take your temperature." He inserted a thermometer into Nick's mouth and took out his stethoscope. "Now let's see what's going on here."

Lee watched anxiously as Dr. Zimmerman listened to Nick's chest and heart, peered into the pupils of his eyes and prodded along his abdomen. He removed the thermometer and held it up to read. "Any vomiting or diarrhea?"

Nick shook his head.

"Well, you're playing host to a real doozie of a bug. I'm pretty sure it's a virus, in which case, all we can do is wait it out." He began gathering up his instruments. "Your lungs sound fine, but you're running a fever of almost 103. That's high for an adult, and accounts for that headache. I want to hear from you tomorrow. If you're any worse, I'll schedule some tests." He made some notes on a pad while he talked. "Chances are, though, this thing will run its course in a few days. Drink plenty of liquids, take aspirin for the fever, and plan on being out of commission for a while."

"Thanks for coming by, Doc." Nick's voice was a weak whisper.

Lee closed the bedroom door and walked the doctor to the front door.

"Maybe I overreacted this afternoon, but I was really frightened. He was having a terrible nightmare. In fact, I thought he was delirious. I had a hard time waking him up. He seemed to think he was being attacked by something."

"That was the fever," Dr. Zimmerman said as he struggled into his coat. "A high fever like that can be dangerous. Keep an eye on it. Give him aspirin until it breaks. And call me if it climbs any higher. Goodnight."

"Goodnight. And thanks again." She closed the door firmly against the chilly night air and went back upstairs. Sara was waiting in the doorway of her room, obviously alarmed.

"Mom, I thought I should just stay out of the way. What did the doctor say? Is Dad going to be okay?"

"Yes. Of course he is, honey." Lee drew her daughter into her arms and hugged her. "Of course he is."

Later that night, Lee was awakened by a hoarse cry and thrashing beside her in the darkness.

"Nick!" She sat up, reaching for the bedside light. "What...?"

She broke off when she smelled the odor of sweating oil again, stronger than ever. At the same time she heard Nick hit the floor with a loud thud. She scrambled across the bed and stared down in horror.

He was rolling back and forth on the carpet, partially wrapped in the sheet. His eyes were wide with fear, his face flushed and anguished.

"It's chasing me, coming closer," he whimpered. "Please, no."

She jumped out of the bed and knelt beside him. "Nick, wake up!" She shook his shoulder. "It's just a dream," she said, talking to herself as much as to her husband. "That's all it can be!"

He looked at her with unseeing eyes. "Wings," he whispered hoarsely. "Giant black wings."

Lee felt an icy splash of shock.

"What?" she whispered. "Nick, what did you say?"

His eyelids fluttered closed as he slipped into a deep sleep.

"Stop it!" she cried. "Don't hurt him. Please, don't hurt him." She knelt beside her husband, sobbing. After awhile, she became aware of a ringing in her ears, and a chilling cold spreading through her body. The odor was gone. Lee forced herself to rise. Realizing that she couldn't get Nick back into bed by herself, she decided to make him as comfortable as possible on the floor. She slipped a pillow under his head and covered him with blankets before turning out the light.

She sat beside him in the darkness for a moment. Then, with sudden inspiration, she scrambled to her feet.

"Candlelight," she murmured to herself. "We need candlelight." She hit the light switch, then fumbled through her nightstand drawer for the book of matches Socorro had left with her. Finally, she managed to light the blue stoneware lizard candle that was sitting on her nightstand.

"Oh, Socorro," she whispered. "I hope you were right about the power of this candle. We need all the protection we can get."

She pushed a bedroom chair close to the side of the bed, turned off the light and sat down, wrapping the comforter around her.

Hours later, she was still huddled in the chair, listening to night noises and watching the candlelight dance across her sleeping husband's face.

She had just dozed off near dawn when she heard Nick struggling to sit up on the floor. He needed her help to get to the bathroom and then back into bed. She gave him three more aspirins and wiped his face with a fresh, cool washcloth, before getting into bed beside him. She curled up against his broad back and slipped an arm around his waist. Then, hugging his feverish body, she drifted into a light sleep.

Nick's condition seemed to be the same when he awoke several hours later. Although his temperature continued to hover near 103 degrees, it didn't rise any higher. He slept through the morning, waking at noon to sip orange juice and swallow a little chicken broth.

"You look pretty beat yourself, babe," he said, squeezing her hand. "Don't worry, I'm going to be fine."

"I know you are. Dr. Zimmerman said it will just take a few days. In the meantime, you're to rest and let me pamper you. I'm taking time off from work until you're well."

"Really? Are you sure you can do that? I know how hard…"

"I can do it. We have a very competent staff. The magazine is in good hands." She brushed a strand of hair back from his damp forehead. "And so are you."

He smiled weakly and nodded. Then he turned bloodshot eyes toward her nightstand.

"The candle," he whispered. "Why is it burning in the daytime?"

"It…it was a gift from Socorro. The woman I told you about who recently died. I thought it might improve the atmosphere in here a little. You know, create a nice, restful mood. Besides, you know I look younger in candlelight. Now go back to sleep."

"Yes, nurse," he whispered, closing his eyes.

Lee sat on the bed beside him, watching him sleep. She bit her lower lip, trying to hold back tears. Nick's getting better, she told herself. *He's going to be all right. The odor was just in my mind. That's what Dr. Mallory would say. Another after-effect of the Awakening Ceremony. Surely that's all it is….*

Lee realized she was in no condition to confront her suspicions about Nick's illness. She hid behind a detached routine that afternoon, keeping too busy to think. Mechanically, she straightened her closet. Something kept nagging at her as she worked, circling in the back of her consciousness but keeping just out of reach. She was on her way into the bedroom to check on Nick when it hit her. In a flash she realized what had been playing hide-and-seek in her mind.

Nick's sweater! His missing sweater. I put it in the back seat of the car along with the rest of his things to go to the cleaners. I know I did! Early Monday morning, before I went to Cavado. Before I had sex with Juan again. And then went to sleep.

She remembered waking alone in the dark room before Juan had come in from outside. *What had he been doing out there? Oh, dear God, what was Juan doing while I slept? Did he take Nick's sweater from the car?*

At that moment, she recalled Socorro's voice, confirming her worst fears: *"Brujos need something belonging to a person in order to cast a spell on them. A personal object, an article of clothing…"*

274

"No," she whispered to herself. "No, it can't be. It's the flu—just a virus. I have to stop giving in to crazy thoughts." She leaned against the wall for support as Nick's choked voice echoed in her mind. *"Wings...giant black wings!"*

Rushing back into her study, she closed the door and quickly dialed Mallory's number.

"I'm sorry," his secretary said. "He's with a patient."

"This is Lee Lindsay. I really need to talk to him. As soon as possible. Please. Tell him that it's urgent."

"Your phone number?"

Lee gave it to her. "It's my home number."

"I'll give him the message."

Lee hung up and paced around the room. She wasn't sure why she was calling Mallory. He didn't believe in witchcraft. Did she? Was she finally convinced? Nick describing the giant black wings had removed most, if not all, of her doubts. *That's just too damn much of a coincidence. Nothing makes sense anymore. I have to talk to someone. And now that Socorro is gone, Mallory is the only one I can trust.*

Less than an hour later, the phone rang. "Lee? What's up?"

"Dr. Mallory, I have to talk to you."

"Okay. I have a few minutes until my next patient. What's going on?"

"It's Nick. He's very sick. He's feverish and having nightmares about some kind of bird. With giant, black wings! Like the one in my dreams. And I smelled the sweating oil again. I know you think I'm imagining that, but I'm telling you, it was there! I lit Socorro's candle, and I think he's a little better now, but I'm terrified that..."

"Hold on a minute. Just slow down. Nick is ill? Has he seen a doctor?"

"Yes. Dr. Zimmerman was here last night. He thinks it's just a virus. But he's wrong. There's more to it than that."

"Why?"

"I went back to Cavado. The day before yesterday. I went to

tell Juan to stop calling me, to let him know that Nick was threatening to go to the police."

"Nick knows what's going on?"

"Oh, God, no. Only that I saw you while he was in Alaska. And that you think Juan drugged and hypnotized me. He really hit the roof over that."

"But he doesn't know that you've seen Juan again? I mean, after the so-called 'awakening ceremony'?"

"Of course not! I haven't gone that crazy."

"Okay, so you went back to Cavado. Did you convince Juan to leave you alone?"

Lee hesitated, feeling hot shame wash over her. "No."

"What does this have to do with Nick being ill?

"I think Juan stole one of Nick's sweaters out of my car while I was there." She fought to keep her voice steady. "And now he's using it to cause illness. Remember, Socorro said…"

"Okay, then listen to me. Nick is going to be fine. If Frank Zimmerman said it was just a virus, that's all it is. Now what were you saying about a candle?"

"Socorro gave me one that she had blessed by a medicine man to weaken Juan's magic. It's been burning since last night."

"I'm going to be frank with you, Lee. I'm more concerned about you than I am about Nick. Have you been getting enough sleep?"

"No, of course not! How could I? Can you prescribe something for me? I took my last sleeping pill a few nights ago. I don't like to take them, but I'm desperate. I keep having these dreams…" Her voice broke.

"All right. I'll call something in to the drugstore in De Vargas Mall for you. But I don't want you to start relying on pills to sleep. They can exacerbate depression and seriously impair your judgment."

"I'll be careful. I know I must sound deranged, calling you like this. I just…"

"Lee, listen to me. You're exhausted. It's easy to overreact when you're under a lot of stress. Just don't let your imagination run away with you. You've been doing a lot of that lately."

"You really think that's all it is?"

"I'm sure of it."

"Oh, before you hang up, what about Socorro's autopsy report? Do they know yet what killed her?"

"Still no word. I'll see what I can find out and get back to you. I looked for you yesterday at her memorial service."

"It was yesterday?"

"Yes. It was announced in Monday's paper."

"I didn't read the paper on Monday. There's been too much going on. Oh, hell! I should have been at the service."

"Don't, Lee. No guilt trips. You don't need any more burdens. You've got your hands full. Socorro would understand."

"I guess you're right. If anyone could understand, it would be Socorro. But I wish I'd..."

"You've got to try to take it easy," he interrupted, "or you're going to get sick, too. Keep things in perspective, and stop dwelling on this witchcraft business."

"I'll try."

"Nick's going to be fine. Believe it."

"You always manage to make me feel sane again. At least while I'm talking to you."

"You are sane. But you're on serious overload. I have to go now, but I want to talk to you again soon. Take care of yourself."

"Goodbye, Dr. Mallory." Lee hung up the phone and rested her head in her arms on top of the desk. She was unable to control the tears that dripped onto the polished wood.

Before long, she sat up and reached for a tissue. Enough of this, she thought, wiping her eyes and blowing her nose. *I have to do my best to stay in control, keep a cool head. Otherwise—Mallory's right—I'm going to make myself sick. And what would happen then? Who would keep the candle burning?*

21

By Thursday morning, Nick's temperature was almost normal and he was hungry. Lee put orange juice and two bran muffins on a wooden tray and carried it into the bedroom. She fluffed pillows behind his head and helped him sit up in bed.

"Sure sign of recovery," she said, placing a tray on his lap. "You can't keep a good appetite down for long."

Nick gave her a weak smile. Lee was struck by how much older he looked. The skin on his face was pale and slack, his three-day-old beard sprinkled with grey. When had his face started to sag? She felt a rush of affection for him and bent to kiss his cheek.

"Well, well," he said, raising one eyebrow. "I really like all of this attention. Maybe I should get sick more often."

"Don't you dare. Now eat your breakfast." She pulled the chair closer to the bed and sat down, facing him. "Nick?"

"Hmmm?" He drained the glass of juice and bit into a muffin.

"You've been having nightmares. Do you remember them?"

"Nightmares?" He stopped chewing and frowned.

"Yes, when you were running a high fever. They seemed pretty bad. I was wondering if you remembered what they were about."

Nick shook his head. "You know I hardly ever remember dreams."

"Don't you remember waking up on the floor night before last? I had to leave you there for part of the night, because you fell out of bed during a bad dream."

"No kidding?" He shook his head and took another bite of muffin. "I have no memory of it."

"I was just curious, that's all." She pointed to his empty glass. "How about more juice?"

"Later. Thanks, babe. I've got to call the office." He took his last bite of muffin and reached for the phone. "What is today? Thursday? God, I've lost most of a week." He punched in numbers and, cradling the phone under his chin, pointed to his briefcase on the desk. "Would you hand that to me? Diane? Hi, it's me. Back from the dead. Well, almost, anyway." He pursed his lips in an air-kiss at Lee as she lifted the tray from his lap. "What went on in the division meeting yesterday?"

Lee returned the gesture and left the room. As she walked down the hall, she could hear Nick giving his secretary brisk instructions. Nice try, Juan, she thought grimly, but no cigar.

The phone rang while Lee was fixing Nick's lunch. She heard him answer it in the bedroom. "Hello?" Hello? Is anyone there?"

Moments later, she walked in, carrying a tray. "Here you are, tuna salad with lettuce." She waited for him to clear newspapers to one side before placing the tray on his lap. "Who was on the phone?"

Nick shrugged. "I don't know." Must have been a wrong number. They hung up without saying anything."

Lee felt a chill. "That's annoying," she said, doing her best to sound nonchalant. I'm brewing some herbal tea for you."

"I'd rather have a beer. Do you have any in the fridge?"

"I do. You're really are feeling better, aren't you?"

"Still a little weak when I stand up. But definitely on the mend. I'll be able to go into work tomorrow." He took a bite of his sandwich.

"I don't think you should," she said. "You've really been sick. Don't rush it. You don't want a relapse."

"I'll be fine. There's an important meeting scheduled for tomorrow morning. And Tom Loree—I've told you about him, he's with the Department of Energy in Washington—is arriving to talk about next month's experiment. I need to be there. Don't worry, I'll take it easy."

"Sure you will. You're a workaholic, Dr. Lindsay."

"It runs in the family. Now, how about that beer?"

The phone rang again as Lee was walking into the kitchen. She heard Nick's annoyed demand, "Hello? Who is this, dammit! Hello?" She stopped in her tracks. *That's Juan. I know it is! He's hoping I'll answer the phone.*

She opened the refrigerator door and grabbed a beer for Nick. This can't go on, she thought. *I'll call that crazy bastard and tell him never to call here again. I'll threaten him.... Where did I put his number? I guess I could always try the yellow pages. Under "B" for* brujo. *Damn him!* She took a deep breath and tried to compose herself. Then she hurried down the hall, carrying Nick's beer.

Half an hour later, Lee peeked in at the sprawled figure in the bed. Nick was sleeping on his stomach, snoring loudly. She closed the bedroom door, went into her study and flipped through her notebook until she found Juan's number. Taking a deep breath to steady herself, she dialed.

He answered on the third ring.

"Juan! Now listen here…"

"Lee." His voice was soft and intimate. "How are you, *querida*? I've missed you. Do you know how much I've missed you?"

She felt her knees go weak. "How dare you call here? I've told you…"

"I wanted to hear your voice."

"God damn you! That was my husband who answered the phone!"

"Ah, yes. Your husband. How is he?"

She hesitated. "He's been sick."

"He is recovering?"

"Yes, he's recovering." She spoke rapidly, keeping her voice low. "Listen, I can't talk. But I'm warning you, don't ever call here again. I mean it! I don't know what Nick would do if…"

"I must see you. Trust me. You must come to me tomorrow."

"No!" She exhaled a soft, exasperated breath. "I absolutely can't do that!"

"You must trust me, *mi vida*."

"I don't know what to do about you, Juan, about this whole crazy situation. I know it has to end. I promise myself I'll never see you again, but then I hear your voice, and I can't think straight."

"You don't need to think, my love. Trust me. We both know what you need. I'll expect you in the morning."

"I said no! I can't." She pressed her forehead against the cool wall, forcing herself to think about Nick's missing sweater and his sudden illness. And Susan Miller. She wanted to ask Juan about the disappearance of his old girlfriend and to judge his reaction for herself. "But I do have to talk to you," she heard herself say. "For my sanity's sake, I need answers. About a lot of things. Will you come here, to Santa Fe? I could meet you somewhere—for coffee."

"Coffee?" He laughed softly. "You are afraid to return to Cavado? You are afraid of me, Lee?"

"Yes, I'm afraid of you! I'm afraid of what happens to me when I'm with you. You keep telling me to trust you. How can I do that when I can't even trust myself? I can't seem to stop myself...."

"That's because you don't want to stop yourself. What is between us is too strong. Don't fight it. Trust me. I will be waiting here for you tomorrow. *Hasta luego, mi vida.*" The line went dead.

Sara rushed into the kitchen a few minutes after four o'clock, her face flushed with excitement.

"Hi, Mom," she said, jolting Lee out of her reverie. "I'm home. But I've gotta hurry and get dressed. Wendy's having everyone over at her house for hamburgers before the dance." She paused. "That's okay, isn't it? Please say yes! I can't let Kevin go without me!"

"Wait a minute," Lee said, trying to cover her confusion. She glanced at the clock on the wall, shocked to realize that she'd been sitting at the kitchen table, staring into space, for over an hour. She felt like she'd been asleep. "Slow down. Now, what's going on?"

"The dance is tonight! The Halloween dance." Sara looked at her mother in amazement. "Don't tell you me forgot that tonight is Halloween?"

"It is?" Lee groaned. "Oh, no. I don't have any candy for trick-or-treaters. I'll have to run to the store." She stood, wincing as a sharp pain shot through her right ankle.

"What's the matter?"

"I hurt my ankle a few days ago. It still bothers me, off and on. Now, let me get this straight. You're planning to have dinner at Wendy's, then go on to the dance with Kevin from there?"

"Yeah. Is it okay?"

"Sure, that's fine. Does this mean that you've worked things out with Wendy?"

"I guess so. She swore to God that she's not after Kevin. I'm keeping a close eye on her though."

"I'm glad you talked it through with her, honey. Girlfriends are very important."

Lee started down the hall, limping slightly. That's strange, she thought, my ankle felt fine this morning. She grabbed her purse off the kitchen counter and a jacket from the hall closet.

"I won't be gone long. Go ahead and get dressed. But don't play your stereo. Dad's asleep."

"Oh, wow. I've been so excited about tonight I forgot to ask about Dad. Is he any better?"

"Yes, much better. But don't wake him up. I'll be back in a few minutes."

"Buy lots of Reese's peanut butter cups. And chocolate kisses." Sara shook her head, giving Lee a strange look. "I can't believe you spaced out Halloween!"

"Well, honey," Lee said, "I've had a lot on my mind."

Sara knocked on the bedroom door. "Mom? Dad? Are you two decent?"

Lee was sitting in the chair beside the bed, watching the early news on television with Nick.

"I'm afraid so," she called. "Come on in. We're just..." she broke off as a wild-haired apparition waltzed into the room.

"Well, what do you think?" Sara struck a dramatic pose in the doorway. "Is this a killer outfit, or what?"

Lee stared, not trusting herself to speak. Sara's brown curls had been transformed into long spikes that stuck out from her head like spokes on a broken wheel. Her eyes were outlined with thick black eyeliner and her mouth glistened with purple lipstick. She was dressed in a black denim mini-skirt and an off-the-shoulder blouse.

She wove toward them in high-heeled boots, carrying a black leather jacket over one shoulder.

Nick gasped. "What the hell..." He started to cough, "... do you think you're doing, dressing like that?" he finally managed to finish.

Sara looked at him, an exasperated expression on her face.

"Dad, I'm a punker."

"What the hell is a punker?"

"Oh, never mind. But isn't my costume just too wild?"

"You almost gave me a relapse, young lady," Nick said. "You certainly aren't going out of the house like that! Throw that outfit in the trash!"

"Dad!" screeched Sara.

"Nick," Lee explained, "it's Halloween."

"Oh, for heaven's sake." Nick leaned back against his pillow. "What a relief." He chuckled. "Halloween. I completely forgot. But I still don't approve of that getup!"

"Dad, please! Give me a break!"

Lee chimed in. "Yes, Nick. Give your daughter a break."

"I guess I don't have a choice. I'm out-voted." He paused, obviously trying to change his attitude. "Where are you going, sweetheart?"

"Over to Wendy's for dinner. Then to the Halloween dance at school."

"Well, okay. But be in by eleven. And be careful." Nick spoke in an eerie voice. "Remember, goblins are on the prowl tonight. And witches. Don't let them catch you, little girl." He gave her a witchy cackle.

Lee's throat tightened. "No," she echoed in a small hollow voice. "Don't ever let that happen."

Sara laughed and kissed them goodbye, leaving purple smears on both their cheeks.

It was a quiet Halloween night. The Lindsay house was too isolated to attract random trick-or-treaters. The only visitors were several groups of small neighborhood children who arrived early, escorted by their parents. Nick, still looking pale and drawn, went to bed before nine. Lee settled herself in the family room to wait up for Sara.

She spread a woolen throw over her legs and glanced at a stack of magazines on the coffee table. Picking up the latest issue of *Writer's Digest*, she turned to an article titled "The Effective Interview." *I could offer some advice on that subject*, she thought ruefully. *Don't drink any funny tea, and keep your clothes on.* She yawned. Halfway through the article, her eyes began to close and she fell into a deep sleep.

He lay with his back to her, his naked shoulder silhouetted against the glowing fire. She pressed against him under the soft furs, running her hand down his naked hip, caressing the hard muscled flesh of his thigh. He awoke and turned toward her with a soft, welcoming murmur. Her heart swelled with pride. He had chosen her. He had elevated her above the others. She ran her finger over the sacred red sign on his cheek. He was a child of the gods. They had marked him as one of their own.

He buried his face in her neck and began to gently massage her buttocks. She clung to him, flushed with sweet, hot pleasure. He moved on top of her, his long hair falling like a black curtain around her face.

"Mom? Mom, wake up. I'm back."

Lee jerked awake and stared at her daughter with uncomprehending eyes.

"What...? Sara. You frightened me. Did you just get home?"

Sara sat down beside Lee on the sofa.

"Yup. You must really be pooped to fall asleep in here. Why didn't you go on to bed?"

"Dad went to sleep early and I didn't want to disturb him. So I thought I'd wait up for you in here. How was the dance?"

"It was a total blast. And guess what? I won a prize for my costume." She held up a stuffed, black corduroy owl. "I think I'll call him 'Spooky'. Isn't he a hoot?"

Lee closed her eyes. "He sure is, honey," she said, suppressing a faint shudder. "A real hoot."

22

"Nick, I really don't think you should go into work today." Lee studied his face as he spread jam on a piece of toast. "You're still a little pale"

"I'm okay," he said, reaching for a napkin. "Can't miss the meeting." He bit into the toast, scanning the front page of the newspaper. "Those damned politicians are at it again, trying to cut our research budget."

"Here, take these," Lee said, handing him an assortment of vitamin pills. "You need extra vitamin C now." She refilled his juice glass. "And wear your heavy jacket. The newspaper forecast possible snow showers today."

"Yes, dear. Zimmerman is right. You make an exceptional nurse."

"And you make an impossible patient. More toast?"

"No time. Gotta run." He emptied his glass and leaned over to kiss her cheek. "I'll try to get home a little early tonight."

Sara came rushing into the kitchen, dropping a stack of books onto the snack bar. She poured a glass of orange juice and looked at Nick in surprise.

"What are you doing out of bed, Dad?"

"He's going back to work," Lee said. "I tried to talk him out of it, but he thinks he's irreplaceable."

"I am. Nice to see your hair back to normal, Sara," Nick said, waving at them as he left the kitchen. "I'll see you two mother hens tonight."

After Sara left for school, Lee walked into the family room and opened the draperies on the sliding patio doors. Dark clouds stretched across the horizon to the west and obscured the distant hills to the north. There was no doubt about it; winter was on its way. Sighing, she rested her forehead against the cold glass. She had half-hoped Nick would change his mind about working today, so she would be unable to go to Cavado. Now she had to make the decision. *What in hell is wrong with me? Why am I even considering seeing Juan again? I should go to the office. Annabel must be buried in paperwork by now.*

She climbed the stairs and walked down the hall to her bedroom, arguing with herself. *This whole situation is beyond insane. It's dangerous, and it's wrong. How can I do this to Nick? How can I do it to myself? I must be crazy. I'm obviously crazy because I know I'm going back to Cavado. I have to see Juan again. Just one more time, to get some answers and finally find a way to free myself from him!*

Lee walked into the bathroom and turned on the shower. Stripping off her robe and nightgown, she stood motionless under the hot water, letting it beat on the top of her head and cascade down her face and body. She didn't even think about envisioning the golden light.

Dressed in a sweater, a skirt and boots, Lee hesitated in her entryway. I can still change my mind, she thought, continuing to fight with herself. *I don't have to go.* She opened the coat closet and put on her fleece-lined leather jacket. *But I am going. God help me—I can't seem to stop myself.* She grabbed a pair of gloves and, remembering the forecast for snow, wrapped a red woolen scarf around her neck.

Occasional snowflakes swirled against the windshield as she pulled into Juan's barren front yard, parking her car beside his pickup. *I should turn around and drive away, while there's still time. Why don't I? Why can't I?* She was still sitting in the car staring miserably at the small adobe house when the front door opened, and Juan stepped out.

He stood shirtless in the doorway, his arms folded across his bare chest, and watched her get out of the car. His amulet flashed silver against his dark skin. Lee saw a slight smile play across his lips. He's making me do this, she thought as she walked toward him. *Somehow he's making me do this.*

He ushered her into the house without speaking and closed he door. As always, the only light came from candles flickering in the corners of the rooms. Juan unwound the scarf from her neck and tossed it onto a nearby chair. Then he removed her jacket. She turned her back to him. When he slid his hands under her sweater, she jerked away.

"Don't touch me!"

He ignored her words, resting his hands on her stomach, then sliding them up to cup her breasts.

"I mean it!" She pushed his hands away. "I didn't come here for...that. There are things we have to talk about."

"Later," he said, holding her face in his large brown hands and kissing her lips. "Trust me. There will be time for that later." Before she could reply, he was kissing her again.

With an effort, she pulled her mouth from his.

"I don't want you to…"

Her words trailed off as his lips grazed her temple, and his warm tongue began tracing the curve of her ear. Once again, his hands were beneath her sweater, sliding under her bra, gently squeezing an erect nipple. She felt warm wetness between her legs as her traitorous body responded to his touch. Socorro's expression, "spirit-sucker," echoed in her mind. That's what he is, she thought frantically. *He's stolen my spirit! His black magic has destroyed my will.*

He pulled her tightly against him, the hand under her sweater pressing hard against the small of her back. His other hand slid up the side of her throat to lightly caress her cheek. Suddenly, his strong fingers gripped her chin, tipping her head back so that his merciless gaze again ensnared her. She stared up at him, unable to speak. Candlelight played across his face, accenting the sharp hollows under his cheekbones and the inviting curves of his lips.

A feeling of detachment enveloped Lee, like a warm, thick fog. Her ears began to ring. As she closed her eyes, she wondered if she was dreaming. Could she make herself wake up? She jerked, blinking her eyes and trying to twist her chin out of his grasp.

"No," she pleaded. "Please. Let me go. Let me think. I…I can't do this."

"Don't fight me, *querida*," he said, tightening his grip on her chin. "You must trust me." His thumb pressed hard into her cheek. "It's not wise to fight me. Didn't your husband's sickness teach you that?"

Lee's blood turned to ice as his words registered in her mind.

"What?" she whispered. "What did you say?"

"I said that you should know better than to fight me." Juan's mouth curled into a cruel smile. "Your scientist has apparently recovered. The next time he may not be so fortunate."

Lee stared at him, momentarily stunned. Then an image of Nick's feverish face flashed through her mind, and she wrenched her face free, pushing against his chest with all her strength.

"You sonofabitch!" she screamed. "Let me go!"

"Never, *mi vida*." Juan roughly yanked her back into his embrace. "Never."

Lee sank her teeth into his bare shoulder. When he pulled back in surprise, she slapped him hard across the cheek.

"Take your hands off me," she warned, drawing her arm back to hit him again.

He grabbed her arm, bending it behind her back. With her free hand, she struck at his face, raking her fingernails across his cheek. Half-lifting her off her feet, he forced her backward until she was pinned against the closed door. He held her arms in a viselike grip.

"You were always a fighter," he said, bending his head toward hers. This time his mouth was not gentle.

Lee bit his bottom lip, tasting blood, then twisted her head to one side against the rough wooden door. She heard him chuckle, deep in his throat.

"Yes, yes," he whispered, his voice muffled in her hair. "It was often like this with us. Biting and scratching. You remember, don't you? You made love like a mountain lion."

She felt the hardness of his erection and squirmed frantically.

"You crazy..."

Her words were cut short by the pain of his sharp slap.

"You will remember," he said as he picked her up and carried her, yelling and pounding on his chest with her fists, into the other room. "I will make you remember."

He flung himself on top of her, on the buffalo rug. The weight of his body knocked the breath from Lee, turning her scream into a gasp.

"The memories are coming back," he said. "I can feel it in your body." His mouth moved across her neck and still-stinging cheek. Then he began to chant in her ear—the same harsh, guttural sounds he had spoken during the Awakening Ceremony.

"No! Damn you! No!" She twisted beneath him, pulling his hair and beating on his shoulders.

Juan's chanting continued, changing in pitch as his breath came faster. At some point she realized that her skirt was up around her waist. Then she felt her panties being yanked down. As his hand moved between her legs, she cried out, uncertain as to whether the sound sprang from the fear and outrage she felt—or from her sudden and shocking desire. He unbuttoned his Levi's with one hand and thrust into her.

The sounds she made in the moments that followed sounded completely alien to Lee's ears. And her cry when she climaxed—high-pitched and savage—seemed to rise from somewhere in the very depths of her soul.

Afterward, Juan held her close, stroking her hair and face.

"*Te amo*, Tarena," he whispered, "I love you."

Rigid and numb with shock, Lee could not reply. She felt divorced from time—torn between two realities and disconnected from her body. When he held a cup of sweet-tasting liquid to her lips, she swallowed it mindlessly. Sometime later, she was vaguely aware of Juan undressing her—tugging off her boots, removing her sweater, bra and skirt. Then he covered her with a blanket.

She awoke to a sensation of warm fur beneath her naked body. Her eyes opened with a start, scattering dream images of unknown, but somehow familiar scenes and faces.

She sat up in a panic. *I'm back here in Cavado! And Juan... Oh, God, he forced me.... Where is he? I've got to get away from here!* She threw off the blanket and stood up, looking frantically for her clothes. Then she saw them, lying under her purse in a neat pile on the sofa.

Shivering, she hastily stepped into her panties and skirt. She had just fastened the front clasp of her bra and pulled her sweater on when something caught her eye on the shelf above the sofa. Something sitting there, beside green and yellow gourds and tied stalks of dried purple flowers. Resting on top of a grey and white pelt was a small animal's head, with white bone showing through patches of torn fur. One pointed grey ear hung loosely, peeled almost off the skull. Lee moved closer. She stood on tiptoe and stretched up to take the terrible object off the shelf.

She knew, even before she touched the soft, familiar fur beneath the skull. Her mind reeled as she felt the poor torn ear and touched the grey and white whiskers still clinging to the muzzle above the small, sharp teeth, now exposed in a silent scream. *Mister!*

Lee clutched the mutilated head to her chest as she sank to her knees, her anguished wail echoing in her ears. Nightmare visions filled her mind. Mister running for his life while relentless dark wings and sharp talons drew steadily closer. Then ripping pain and gradual oblivion.

"No, no," she cried aloud, rocking back and forth on her knees.

The door burst open and Juan came in, wearing his sheepskin jacket. Lee caught a glimpse of his badly scratched cheek, as he stared down at her. Her grief-stricken wail turned into a scream of rage as she scrambled to her feet. The small head fell to the floor.

"You!" she screamed. "You murdering bastard! Why? Why did you kill Mister?" She grabbed her purse, swinging it toward him by the straps. Her screams rang in her ears. "You killed Socorro, too, didn't you? What the hell kind of monster are you?"

Juan ducked, raising his arms to protect his head. "*Querida!* What...?"

Lee grabbed a heavy pottery jar from a nearby table. She crashed it down on his head and ran past him out the door.

She ran heedlessly, barefooted, over sharp, snow-covered rocks and locked herself in her car. The fact that it was snowing hard finally registered. How long had it been snowing like this? How long had she been in there?

Lee gasped with horror as Juan staggered through the open front door, his forehead smeared with blood. She searched her purse for what seemed like an eternity while he stumbled toward her. *Keys! Where are the damn car keys?* Everything seemed to be happening in nightmarish slow motion. Her fingers finally closed around the keys.

Juan pounded on the car window, yelling her name. Snowflakes coated his hair and mixed with the blood that trickled between his eyes. The key wouldn't turn. It was stuck in the ignition. Then, miraculously, it turned, and the engine started. Lee threw the car into reverse, knocking Juan off to the side. She slapped at the steering column, searching for the windshield wiper switch while the car careened down the dirt road through a thickening curtain of snow. Finally, she hit the right levers and the front and rear windshield wipers began to move.

In spite of them, it was hard to see. *How far have I driven? Must be almost to the main highway.* She brushed at her tears with the back of her hand. Then her heart almost stopped when she glanced in the rearview mirror. Juan's pickup was behind her—gaining fast.

She pressed the accelerator, speeding past the service station and sliding onto the paved highway. Her breath came in loud sobs as she fought to control the car on the icy road. Something metallic flashed through the snow ahead. She rubbed at the fogged windshield, clearing it enough to see a car stalled in the road, directly in her path. She screamed and jerked the wheel sharply to the right.

There was an unreal sensation of skidding, bumping, rolling, and then flying, while a blurred white world spun in slow motion beyond the windshield. This must be a dream, she assured herself. *Just a terrible dream. I'll wake up in a minute and be home in bed.* Then reality arrived in a bright red flash of pain and everything went black.

Lee floated through a silent darkness, safe and peaceful. She tried to think, to understand where she was, but her thoughts kept sliding away. It didn't matter. Nothing really mattered....

A voice floated toward her from a great distance. Someone was calling her name. The voice was familiar. Growing louder. But whose? She tried to answer but was unable to make a sound. The voice was closer. "It's all right, *mi vida.* I'm here. I'm here with you."

The darkness lifted and she saw him, striding toward her through swirling grey mists. She felt a flash of recognition. He was here. He was here with her.... *Juan. But that isn't really his name. He has another name. Why can't I remember?*

Black hair hung over his shoulders and down his bare chest as he approached. Then his arms were around her, his breath warm against her cheek.

"Take strength from me," he whispered in her ear. "Don't let go. Don't leave me, Tarena. Don't leave me."

Tarena? Who is he talking to? Her scattered thoughts were interrupted by chanting. Sounds and words that were unfamiliar, yet some part of her knew their meaning—and their power. She almost remembered...something. Something important. But the memory melted away as shadowy forms appeared, whirling through the darkness around her. His voice broke once more through the dark fog. She strained to hear, to follow the words that faded in and out.

"Hear me, Raven, messenger to the Spirit World. Enter the great void. Implore the Guardians to spare this woman…for the sake of your brother who loves her…." More words, growing fainter.

She tried to move, to turn her head. A sharp pain shot through the left side of her chest.

"No," she tried to say. "You're hurting me. Please, don't… hurt me."

For an instant she remembered his real name and tried to speak it. Then it slipped away, and she felt herself being lifted, floating higher and higher, as the black fog receded and she spiraled upward toward the light.

23

Pain pulsed through her head, forcing her awake. Lee opened her eyes and found herself in a strange room. Nick was at her side, his eyes bloodshot and full of concern.

"Where am I?" Her voice was little more than a hoarse whisper.

"Just lie still, babe. You're okay. You're in the hospital."

"Hospital?" She moaned from the pain of jerking her head. "How did I get here?"

"Don't you remember the accident?" Nick stroked her right arm. Her left hand felt heavy, as if it were weighted down.

Lee's puzzled frown turned to an expression of horror as her memory began to return. *I was in Cavado with Juan. He was so brutal. He forced me—raped me! And Mister...Oh, God, what he did to Mister!* She groaned, squeezing her eyes shut at the thought of her shocking discovery.

"It's true! Oh, no! It's really true!"

"Lie still, honey. What's true?"

Nick's voice was blotted out by the memories that flooded Lee's mind. *Running through falling snow to her car...sliding along the winding dirt road...Juan's black pickup truck in the rearview mirror, coming closer and closer...the terrifying sight of a vehicle blocking the road ahead and then...nothing.*

"He was after me. Coming closer and closer..."

"Who? Who was after you?"

"Oh, Nick. It's horrible! He killed Mister. And Socorro, I'm sure he killed her, too. And he made you sick. He..."

"Lee, who on earth are you talking about?"

"Juan Mascareñas. He's a *brujo*, Nick, a witch! Socorro was right. I didn't want to believe it. I tried not to believe it, but it's true. The raven—my nightmare about the raven..." She tried to raise her head and groaned in pain. "My head hurts."

"Lie still." Nick leaned over her to ring for the nurse. "Don't talk," he said. "The nurse will be here in a minute. You hit your head. But you're going to be fine. Just fine. Hold on."

"You have to believe me, Nick. Someone has to believe me! He used black magic." She broke off, as pain jolted through her head followed by a wave of nausea.

Nick rang the buzzer again. Moments later, she heard murmured voices and felt the effect of the sedative inserted into her IV. The last thing she heard was Nick's voice speaking urgently.

"Nurse, she's saying crazy things. Where's Dr. Zimmerman? Get him in here!"

The room came slowly into focus. Nick was sitting in a chair across from her bed, his eyes closed. When she made a hoarse moaning sound, he was instantly at her side.

"Honey? I'm right here."

"I'm in the…hospital?"

"You were in an accident. Don't you remember?"

Helpless tears spilled out of the corners of her eyes and ran along the sides of her ears.

"Yes," she whispered. "I remember." She raised her right hand and touched something smooth where her hair should have been. "What's on my head?" she asked in alarm.

"Bandages. You hit your head pretty hard." Nick reached for a tissue and blotted her tears. "But you're going to be fine."

"What time is it? How long have I been here?"

"It's a little after eight. You've been here about five hours."

The door opened and Sara came in. She tried to smile when she saw Lee.

"Mom, you're awake. Are you gonna be okay?" She began to sob. "I've been so scared."

"Oh, baby. Don't cry." Pain vibrated through Lee's head with each word.

Nick moved in close and put his arm protectively around Sara. "The truth now," he said. "How do you feel?"

"My head hurts. And my arm. What's wrong with my arm?"

"You broke your wrist," he explained. "And you got a nasty knock on the head. But you're going to be okay."

"It hurts when I breathe."

"You also have a cracked rib. But, thank God, none of your injuries are life-threatening. You were incredibly lucky, babe. The car rolled several times."

The door opened and a no-nonsense nurse entered the room. "I'm glad to see you're awake, Mrs. Lindsay." She wrote something on a chart, which she attached to the foot of the bed. "Dr. Zimmerman will be in shortly. Any pain?"

"Lots. My head," Lee whispered.

The nurse nodded. "The doctor will order something for that." She stuck a thermometer in Lee's mouth and glanced at Nick and Sara, standing together by the bed. "No more talking, now. Just lie quietly until the doctor gets here. I'll be back soon." She left, leaving the door open.

Lee wiggled the thermometer around between her dry lips. Her mind was racing, trying to remember what she'd said to Nick earlier. Her efforts were interrupted when Dr. Zimmerman walked through the door.

"Well, hello, Lee. Welcome back. I have to say, you are one lucky lady. You gave us quite a scare." He walked over to Lee's bed, picked up her chart and bent to peer into her eyes. "Pupils back to normal. That's good." He removed the thermometer and glanced at it. "Does your head hurt?"

"Does it ever," she whispered.

He wrote something on her chart. Sticking his pen in the top pocket of his white coat, he looked down at her. "That's to be expected. You have a concussion and a somewhat serious cut above your left temple. Your left wrist is broken and you also have a cracked rib. Not to mention a minor cut on your chin and numerous contusions. Do you remember the accident?"

"It was snowing. There was a car stalled in the road. I tried to miss it. That's all I remember."

"You don't remember being in the ambulance, or in the emergency room? Dr. Gonzales said you were semi-conscious but disoriented."

"No," she said, closing her eyes. "I don't remember anything after seeing that car in the road." She felt exhausted. If only the pain in her head would let up.

"Any more nausea? You vomited in the ambulance and again in the emergency room."

"No," Lee whispered.

"What's today's date?"

"Friday. The first of November."

"What's your phone number, including area code?"

Lee repeated her number then stared at Zimmerman in alarm. "Am I going to be okay?"

"You're going to be fine. Your head injury isn't as serious as we feared it might be. Still, I'd like to keep you here for a few days, just to be on the safe side. I'm afraid you'll have a lot of soreness and pain around that cracked rib for several weeks. As I said, you also have extensive bruising over most of your body. It'll look worse before it looks better, but don't be alarmed." He smiled down at her. "You're going to be good as new."

"What about my wrist?"

"A simple fracture. It should heal nicely in five to six weeks. Now, I'm going to give you something to help you sleep and send your cheering section home. They can come back to see you tomorrow."

Nick and Sara took turns kissing her cheek.

"Sleep tight, Mom," Sara whispered. "You're going to be okay. The doctor said so. See you tomorrow."

Nick touched Lee's shoulder. "See you first thing in the morning."

She lay very still after they left, trying not to cry from the pain in her head. After a moment, the nurse reappeared and inserted another sedative into Lee's IV.

"Now then," the nurse said, "you'll be feeling better in no time. Take a few deep breaths for me. That's right. I know it hurts, but you don't want pneumonia setting in. Just a couple more real deep ones. Good. We'll be checking on you often through the night. But don't hesitate to push the buzzer by your right arm, if you need anything." She left the room.

A wave of drug-induced relaxation washed over Lee, dulling her pain, as she sank gratefully into a soft, black cushion of sleep.

Another nurse came into the room early the next morning to take her temperature and blood pressure. Lee groaned when she tried to lift her head. The left side of her ribcage throbbed and her body felt like one giant bruise.

"Can I go to the bathroom?" Lee asked as the nurse cranked her bed into a semi-sitting position.

"No need. You have a catheter inserted. Dr. Zimmerman wants you to stay in bed until he examines you later this morning."

"I'd like to brush my teeth."

"I'll bring you a basin and toothbrush."

"My purse. Is it here?"

"Let me check." She opened the door to the small closet by the bathroom. "Yes, here it is, right beside your coat."

Lee started as she saw a heavy sheepskin jacket hanging beside her blood-splattered sweater and skirt. She immediately recognized it as Juan's. She had an image of him standing in the doorway after she had discovered Mister's head. He had been wearing a sheepskin jacket. She remembered how he had looked as he pulled at the locked car door and pounded on the car window. Yes, she was certain. He had been wearing that jacket yesterday afternoon.

"Here you are." The nurse handed Lee her purse. "I'll be right back." She walked out, closing the door behind her.

Lee's mind raced. *I don't think I had my own jacket when I ran away from Juan. Or even my boots.* She remembered stepping on sharp stones as she ran barefoot through the snow to her car. *But what's Juan's jacket doing here?*

Blocked memories rose to the surface again. Lee suddenly remembered Juan's pickup following closely behind her through the snow, just before she saw the car blocking the road ahead. She squeezed her eyes shut, trying to think. *Juan must have been there with me, after the accident.*

More memories broke through. *I remember jerking the steering wheel and skidding off the road. But nothing else. Except...a dream.*

A dream about flying or floating. And Juan. Yes, Juan was in that dream. He was talking to me, holding me. And he was chanting. And praying. Praying to...a raven? There was something about a raven.

She pressed her palm to her forehead. *If that was just a dream, what about that jacket? Was I wearing it when I was admitted to the hospital?* Lee closed her eyes. *How can I possibly explain all this to Nick?*

The door swung open. "Now you're back in business, Mrs. Lindsay," the nurse announced cheerfully. "Here's a basin, fresh water, toothbrush, and even a mirror."

"Thank you." Lee fought to keep her voice steady. "Oh, Nurse? That jacket in the closet isn't mine. I would appreciate it if you'd take it out of here."

Nick arrived sometime later. He bent to kiss her cheek.

"Hi, babe. How're you feeling? You sure look better than you did last night."

"I must have really been a sight then. The nurse brought me a mirror a little while ago. I look like the bride of Frankenstein with this bandage around my head. And my eyes look like I got into Sara's Halloween makeup."

Nick gently touched her left upper arm. "You have some pretty fancy bruises there. And on your other arm, too, as a matter of fact." He frowned. "They almost look like thumb marks."

An image of Juan, dragging her across the room and shoving her against the door flashed through Lee's mind. She pushed it away.

"I must have bruises all over my body. You said the car rolled several times."

"At least three times. That must have been terrifying. Do you remember it at all?

"Not really. Just blurred impressions."

"How's your head?"

"It still hurts. But it's better. Where's Sara?"

"I left her sleeping. She's just wiped out, poor kid. Went to pieces when I phoned her yesterday. She had Kevin drive her here to the hospital." He hesitated. "I have to admit I was pretty shook up myself."

Lee reached out with her right hand to touch his cheek. "I'm sorry," she whispered. "You look so tired."

"I didn't get much sleep last night. I finally took one of those pills of yours around two this morning."

Lee braced herself. She'd decided to tell Nick that she'd returned to Cavado to interview someone else for another article. It was a weak story, but the only one she could think of. She prayed that he would buy it, that he would never learn the truth about her relationship with Juan. The truth would end their marriage. Nick would never understand or forgive her.

"Nick," she began, "I know you must have some questions…."

"Well, I think I have some idea now what happened."

Her heart almost stopped. "You do?"

He pulled a chair up beside the bed and sat down.

"You said some really strange things when you came to after the accident. About Juan Mascareñas being a witch and killing Mister and your friend Socorro. You even said that he'd made me sick. I didn't know what to make of it. I assumed you were just out of your head." He paused. "But then Jim Mallory called this morning. He wanted to talk to you about Socorro's autopsy report. I told Mallory about your accident. Then I said I wanted to know what the hell was going on. We had quite a conversation."

Lee held her breath, feeling cold dread seep through her body.

"Initially, Mallory wouldn't tell me much of anything. Professional ethics and all that. But, after I told him what you said about Juan being a witch who killed Mister and Socorro, he opened up a little. He admitted that he was worried about you, that you'd been under a lot of stress. I got the impression that he's already aware of your theory about Mascareñas."

"Oh, Nick. I know how crazy it sounds."

"I just don't understand. Why didn't you talk to me about it?"

"I couldn't. Because it does sound so crazy. I didn't want to upset you. I don't know, I just thought…"

"You just thought you'd go back out there and poke around. See if you could gather some evidence. Isn't that right?"

Lee swallowed hard. She reached for a tissue, stalling for time to assimilate what Nick had just said.

"That's what happened, isn't it? You were going to do a little investigative reporting."

"Well, I…" She stopped as tears of relief filled her eyes. Not trusting herself to speak, she nodded her head.

Nick sighed. "I guess I don't have to tell you how foolish that was. Not that I believe that charlatan was responsible for anything but upsetting the hell out of you. But he certainly did that. You haven't been yourself since you went to Cavado weeks ago. I just had no idea how much that idiotic ceremony had affected you. Where did Socorro fit into all of this?

"She was a friend of the Mallorys and he suggested that I talk to her about that Awakening Ceremony. Because she was Native American, Dr. Mallory thought she might be familiar with it. She was also psychic." She hesitated and Nick's eyebrow shot up. "And she was convinced that Juan was a *brujo*, a sorcerer."

Nick shook his head. "Mallory doesn't believe in any of that psychic crap, does he?"

"No, of course not. He just thought…"

"I'm surprised that he'd get you mixed up with someone like Socorro Hall. He knew you were already upset about the witch doctor. Christ, he should have known better than to involve you with another weirdo."

"Nick, please," Lee said with a tired sigh. "Socorro was a wonderful person. In fact, she was one of the most caring..." Her voice broke.

"Okay, okay." He patted her leg. "I don't want to upset you. I'm just trying to understand what happened. So you went back to Cavado yesterday. Did you confront Mascareñas with any of this?"

"Not exactly. I...I got scared and ran out. I even left my jacket there. By then it was snowing hard. The road is quite narrow and winding up there. And a car was stalled right in the middle—I tried to miss it. Apparently, I did, but I ran off the road. That's all I remember."

"I understand that the man whose car had stalled ran to a nearby filling station and called the police. You were lucky. If it had happened farther down that godforsaken road, there's no telling how long it would have been before someone came along."

"Yes, I was lucky."

"By the time the ambulance arrived, a passer-by had gotten you out of the car. Good thing you didn't have a spinal injury. He could have made it worse. Anyway, he disappeared before they could get his name."

Lee closed her eyes.

"You're too tired to talk anymore," Nick said. "I'd better go and let you get some rest." He stood up. "Honey, Mallory said that he felt he should see you again. I think so, too. In fact, I asked if he could come by here for a little session, as soon as you're feeling up to it. Is that okay?"

She nodded.

"I'll give him a call. Now, you take it easy. I'm going in to work for a while, catch up on a few things. It shouldn't take too long. I won't have the usual interruptions because it's Saturday." He bent to kiss her cheek. "We'll have to replace your car. You might give some thought to what you want."

"I loved my Subaru. We should probably get another one. Can we talk about it later?"

"Sure. I'll be back with Sara this afternoon. You'll be feeling better then."

"I hope so. One more thing before you go. I want an alarm system installed at the house. I'm worried about Sara staying there alone while I'm here."

He nodded. "That's something we should have done before now. I'll make the arrangements this afternoon. Oh, I almost forgot," he said, reaching into his pocket and removing a small envelope. "The nurse gave me your jewelry last night. They took it off when you came in." He spilled the contents into his hand. "Earrings, watch, wedding ring..." He stopped, frowning. "Where on earth did you get this thing?"

Lee's heart sank as Nick held up Juan's amulet, its crystal eyes glowing red as blood.

24

Lee was lying propped up after a lunch of soup and crackers, watching snowflakes hit the second-story window of her hospital room. She turned her head at the sound of a soft knock. The door opened slightly, revealing a familiar round face.

"Hi. Feel up to a visitor?"

"Hello, Dr. Mallory." She pulled a sheet up to cover her wrinkled hospital gown. "Come in."

"I've been quite worried about you." He stood beside her bed, arms folded across his chest. "How are you feeling?"

"Not as bad as I look. And a lot better than I did when they brought me in here."

"No roommate?" he asked, indicating the empty bed beside hers.

"Not so far, thank goodness. I'm in no mood for small talk with a sickly stranger. But I am glad to see you. Nick said you might be coming by."

"Yes, your husband and I have had several conversations." He pulled a chair close to the bed and sat down, crossing his short legs. "Nick answered when I called your house yesterday morning to give you the results of Socorro's autopsy. Actually, I had tried to call you on Friday."

Lee laughed, a short, bitter sound. "Well, I was a little out of touch on Friday."

"Do you want to talk about it?"

"You don't usually make house—or rather, hospital—calls, do you? Especially not on a Sunday afternoon."

"Not usually. But, I actually was, as they say, 'in the neighborhood.' Another patient of mine was admitted a couple of hours ago. Besides, under the circumstances, I felt you and I should talk as soon as possible."

"I appreciate you coming." She took a deep breath, then grimaced as pain shot through the left side of her chest. "I really need to talk to you. But first, tell me about Socorro. What did the autopsy report show?"

"She had a stroke. A massive cerebral hemorrhage caused by an aneurysm, a weak spot in an artery." He shook his head, looking sad. "It was a congenital time bomb just waiting to go off."

"That's all they know? An artery just happened to blow, for no apparent reason?"

"It happens. A defect like that can go completely undetected for years and then, with no warning—boom."

"That's not what happened to Socorro."

"Lee, I know you've had trouble accepting…"

"I'm totally convinced that her artery had some outside encouragement."

"You still suspect Juan of using witchcraft?"

"It's more than a suspicion! He as good as admitted that he caused Nick's illness. He was gloating over it. And he killed my cat." Lee began to cry. "That *brujo* bastard killed poor Mister."

"You'd better tell me exactly…"

"And that's not all! He raped me. He held me down on that damned buffalo rug and raped me. I fought him, Dr. Mallory. I really did. I tried to get away. But he just picked me up and..." She broke off, unable to finish the sentence.

Mallory's expression was grim. "My God, Lee. I'm so sorry." He was quiet for a moment, waiting for her sobs to subside. "Have you told anyone else about this?"

"No. Of course not. How could I?"

"I see your point. But you need to talk about it now. Do you feel like doing that?"

Lee nodded and blew her nose.

"I want you to tell me everything that happened in Cavado on Friday. Just take your time, and go through all the events that led to your accident."

Mallory sat riveted in his chair as Lee recounted Juan's comments about Nick's illness, the ensuing struggle, and their violent sexual encounter on the buffalo skin rug. She broke down, choking with the horror of the memory, as she described her grisly discovery of Mister's head.

"It was just sitting there, on the shelf. All mangled and torn. And his fur was rolled up in a neat little bundle." Taking several deep breaths, she forced herself to continue. "Then Juan came bursting in. He'd been outside, doing God-knows-what. I hit him over the head with something heavy, a pot of some kind, and ran to the car. I didn't even stop to get my boots or jacket."

Mallory nodded, encouraging her to continue.

"Before I could get the car started, Juan came after me. His head was bleeding. I remember blood running down his forehead. He was yelling and pounding on the car door—thank God it was locked—and snow was coming down—I couldn't find my car keys...."

"Slow down, Lee. You're doing fine. Just take your time."

Lee closed her eyes and tried to relax against the pillow. Her heart was pounding. After a moment, she continued.

"I finally got the car started and took off down the dirt road. I thought I'd gotten away. But just before I got on the highway, I saw Juan's pickup in the rearview mirror. I stepped on the gas. That's when I saw the car stalled in the road. I swerved to miss it—it all happened so fast—the next thing I knew, my car was sliding over to the shoulder of the road. And then it was rolling, over and over."

Mallory stood up and poured Lee a glass of water. She took a long swallow and handed it back to him with her good hand. "Thanks."

"Okay," he said returning to his chair. "If you're up to it, I want to go back over this, one piece at a time."

Lee nodded.

"Juan implied that he'd caused Nick's illness. Do you remember his exact words?"

"He said, 'It's not wise to fight me. Didn't your husband's illness teach you that?' Then he said, 'He got well, but next time he may not be so lucky.' Or something very close to that."

"Is there any way he could have found out that Nick had been sick?"

Lee hesitated. "Yes, I told him, on the phone, the day before."

"So, all he did was try to take the credit for it. That doesn't take any supernatural abilities."

"I...I suppose you're right. But he was so threatening, so convincing."

"He's a con artist, Lee. And a very good one. Now, you said that you struggled with him."

"I went berserk after he said that about Nick. I started screaming, hitting him. He grabbed me and I tried to get away. I remember biting his shoulder and scratching his face."

"Go on."

"He dragged me across the floor and slammed me up against the door. I know at one point he slapped me. Then he picked me up and took me into the other room—where he pinned me down on that damned buffalo rug and…" Her voice broke. "I can't talk about that any more right now."

"That's okay. You're doing fine. Let's go on to your discovery of the cat."

"Mister."

"Isn't it possible that you were mistaken about that? I mean, didn't you tell me that Juan has that place of his filled with animal skulls and bones? Can you really be sure that what you found was Mister? Couldn't it have been another cat that had been run over on a road somewhere?"

Lee shook her head, then groaned and shut her eyes, dizzy with a burst of pain.

"No! I'm telling you, it was Mister."

"But, he's been missing for how long? Close to three weeks? And you said yourself the remains were in bad shape." He hesitated. "Lee, this situation is traumatic enough, without your jumping to erroneous conclusions."

"I'm not jumping…"

"Now Lee, just let me finish. Juan had just attacked you. You were undoubtedly in shock. Isn't it just possible that you jumped to the wrong conclusion? That you mistook another dead cat for Mister?"

"When you put it like that, I have to admit it is possible. But I'm telling you, down in my gut, I know it was Mister."

"Juan knew that you were coming to see him Friday, didn't he? You said you called him the night before. Do you really think he would have carelessly left the carcass of your pet cat lying around for you to find?"

"Who knows what a *brujo* might do? I think he's capable of anything. And he's made me crazy." Her shoulders shook with sobs.

"Lee, let me assure you again, you aren't crazy."

"You don't know, Dr. Mallory. There's something you don't know. And I…I don't know how to talk about it."

"Try."

"It's about the rape. I guess I'm not even sure if I should be calling it a rape."

"What do you mean?"

"I mean, what exactly is the definition of a rape?"

"Did Juan force you to have sexual intercourse?"

"Yes."

"That's rape."

"Even if I ended up responding to him?"

"Technically, that doesn't make any difference. But emotionally, it's a loaded issue. And one that can cause you a lot of problems if we don't work it through." He was quiet for a moment, obviously deep in thought. "Before we tackle that, though, I'd like to go back and sort through your earlier feelings about Juan."

She looked down at her clenched hands.

"I've spent sleepless nights trying to do just that. I don't understand what happened between us. But I do know that I've been absolutely obsessed by him. Whether it's witchcraft or just a powerful sexual attraction, I've certainly been under his spell."

She met Mallory's concerned eyes.

"Can you explain it to me? Can you tell me how I could have been so terrified of Juan and yet so attracted to him at the same time? I mean, for weeks now, I've suspected this man of having supernatural powers, of being some sort of character out of a horror story. I've even gone back to meet him and, despite my best intentions, I've had sex with him, repeatedly. You can't tell me that's not crazy behavior!"

"Well, it's certainly ill-advised. I'll admit that. But I wouldn't go so far as to call it crazy." He pulled out a package of mints. "Care for one?"

Lee shook her head no.

"Let me tell you how I see your attraction to Juan," Mallory continued, unwrapping the mint and popping it into his mouth. "He's obviously a strong, charismatic personality. And from what you've said, I gather that he's not bad looking. There's something dark and dangerous about him, with his shaman mystique. And a dangerous aura, for some reason, is sometimes very sexy."

He sucked thoughtfully on the mint. "Now, let's combine those qualities with the fact that he managed to break down your normal barriers and establish a high degree of intimacy with you within minutes of your first meeting. As I told you weeks ago, the man is obviously a first-rate and utterly unscrupulous manipulator. He drugged and no doubt hypnotized you right off the bat. Then he played on your belief in reincarnation, setting you up for the seduction." He leaned forward in his chair. "Don't you see? That's a terrific line. 'Hey, we were lovers before. This can't be wrong. It's just history repeating itself'."

"That makes me sound so gullible."

"Not really." Mallory studied her for a moment. "I want you to try to look at yourself objectively for a minute. You're, what, forty years old? And because you grew up in a chaotic, dysfunctional home, you trained yourself early to keep a tight rein on your emotions. Watching your father's alcoholic rages taught you to equate passion with danger. Am I right?"

Lee shrugged, not saying anything.

"So you put a lid on those normally powerful teenage sexual impulses. You pushed them down somewhere deep inside. But suppressing feelings doesn't make them go away. They just simmer in the subconscious until someday, when conditions are right, they explode to the surface. That's what happened when you met Juan."

"But why? Why with him?"

"Because he's passionate and unpredictable, qualities that would appeal strongly to you on an unconscious level. Look, I remember you telling me once that you were still a virgin when you met Nick. Isn't that right?"

She nodded.

"So he was the first and has been, until lately, your only lover. After you were married, you threw yourself into a busy, productive, well-ordered life. Now, eighteen years later, here you are, married to an exceptionally intelligent but—by your own description—not especially passionate man. Add to that the fact that he's an admitted workaholic who's out of town half the time. That must get lonely. Frankly, I think you were ripe for an affair. Enter Juan—sexy, domineering, and more than a little mysterious. He's clever enough to sense your suppressed sexuality. And he manages to blow your caution all to hell.

"The fact that he comes from a completely different culture just works in his favor. The whole thing is so bizarre, so off-the-wall, it seems more like a fantasy than an affair. Your relationship doesn't seem *real* enough to be wrong. After all, you aren't meeting some ordinary man in a Holiday Inn. You're meeting a mystery man in an isolated hideaway and making passionate love by candlelight on a buffalo rug! Wow, Lee, that's straight out of every woman's secret fantasy."

Lee stared into space, a slight frown on her face. "What are you saying?"

"I'm just saying that it isn't difficult to understand. You don't have to convince yourself that supernatural spells are involved in order to justify your attraction to Juan."

"And that's what you think I've been doing—convincing myself that Juan is some kind of sorcerer, in order to give myself permission to have an affair with him?"

"Doesn't it make sense?"

"Yes, dammit, it makes perfectly logical sense. But I know there's more to it than that." She hesitated. "Something very strange happened while Juan was forcing himself on me. I...I don't know if I can explain it to you."

"Give it a try."

"While we were struggling, he kept saying things like, 'Yes, that's how it often was with us, biting and scratching.' I remember that he said that I 'made love like a mountain lion.' Dr. Mallory, he certainly wasn't talking about this lifetime. I hate to admit this, but by the time he threw me down on the buffalo rug, I was excited—sexually I mean. And during the act itself, which was fast and brutal, I truly felt like I was someone else. Like my body didn't even belong to me. Juan was whispering strange words in my ear—some kind of chant—and I just went wild. I had the most incredible orgasm of my life." She took a long, shuddering breath. "Afterward, I felt the most terrible emptiness. I was numb, literally unable to speak or move."

"You were in shock."

"I have a vague memory of Juan undressing me and giving me something to drink. Then I slept. When I woke up, I don't know how much later, I felt more like myself again. Juan was gone, outside, I guess. I was terrified, afraid he would never let me leave. As I was frantically putting my clothes on, I looked up and saw Mister's head."

"Lee, he drugged you after the rape. You must have been disoriented when you woke up. That's another argument against its having been Mister's head."

When she didn't respond, he continued.

"Let me just say that, given the strength and complexity of your attraction to Juan, I'm not at all surprised that you responded sexually to him."

"Even when he was forcing me?"

"As I said earlier, he lifted the lid on your suppressed sexuality. And he used those romantic past life references to fan the fire."

"What about my feeling like I was no longer myself?"

"It's called dissociation. And it's a common defense mechanism during a traumatic occurrence. After all, Lee, you were raped." He paused for a moment. "Have you considered bringing charges against him?"

"No! I couldn't do that. The most important thing right now is to protect Nick from all this. How could I accuse Juan of raping me without everything being revealed? I mean, what the hell was I doing there in the first place?"

"Okay, I agree that it wouldn't be in your best interest. But

Juan has proven now that he's more than just a backwoods con artist. He's dangerous. You can't afford to let him confuse you with any more supernatural or past life nonsense."

"But that's just it, Dr. Mallory. I'm not convinced that it is just nonsense. What about my dreams? They're so realistic, like I'm really living them. And I'm someone else in those dreams! There's something else I haven't told you, something that's really been haunting me."

"Don't hold anything back, Lee. Let's hear it."

"I remembered a dream, or what I assumed was a dream, when I woke up here in the hospital. I must have had it after the accident, while I was unconscious. Juan was holding me, chanting and praying, calling on a raven spirit for help. Asking the Great Spirit to spare me. And we weren't alone. I saw shadowy forms moving all around us."

Mallory watched her intently. "Go on."

"Only it wasn't a dream, I know that now. Because when I arrived here at the hospital, I was wearing Juan's amulet." She opened her nightstand drawer and handed the tissue-wrapped necklace to Mallory. "He must have put it around my neck after the accident."

"Interesting piece of jewelry," he said, examining it. "Quite old from the looks of it. This is an antique chain."

"Look at the stones. Juan said that they were a rare crystal, found only in the mountains of northern Mexico. When I repeated that to Socorro, she said that her grandmother used to talk about a legendary red crystal that had miraculous healing qualities. There was something about Aztec priests using it."

"Socorro knew all of those old stories. I'm surprised that she took that one seriously."

"She said she wasn't sure the healing stones even existed. She was just curious about this amulet. But she never saw it. At least, not as far as I know. Unless…"

"Unless?"

"I guess we'll never know whether or not Socorro went to Cavado the afternoon before she died."

"But you think maybe she did?"

"I'm afraid that she did."

"Lee, even if Socorro saw Juan, even if she confronted him— the fact remains that she was killed by an aneurysm. Not by the Cavado con man." He handed the amulet back to her.

"But how can you be so sure that Juan is just a con man? I was wrapped in his sheepskin jacket when they brought me here. And I was wearing his amulet."

"What does any of that prove?"

"I think it proves that Juan is sincere in his beliefs. Don't you see? There was no reason for him to be doing all that chanting and praying, unless he believed he was helping me. It couldn't have been some sort of show for my benefit. After all, I was unconscious, or almost, anyway."

She held the amulet in her palm, staring at it.

"Who knows? Maybe the crystals worked. Dr. Zimmerman told me he was amazed that the impact I suffered to my head didn't have more serious consequences. Apparently, the cut on my temple was an impact split—the kind you get when you hit your head really hard. Everyone agrees it was a miracle I escaped with such comparatively minor injuries. I wasn't even wearing my seatbelt, and the car rolled several times." She re-wrapped the amulet, returned it to the nightstand drawer and closed it. "Maybe my injuries were actually much worse and Juan healed them before the ambulance arrived."

Mallory shook his head. "You don't really believe that, do you?" he asked.

She didn't answer for a long moment. "I don't know what to believe anymore."

"What about Nick?" Mallory asked, changing the subject. "You haven't told me how you handled this with him."

"Fortunately, he'd already jumped to the conclusion that I went back to Cavado to gather evidence against Juan. I was more than happy to go along with that. The only thing I had to lie about was the amulet. I said I had no idea where it came from." She looked away.

"So everything is okay between the two of you?"

"I think so, as far as Nick's concerned. He's upset with me for being foolhardy, but the truth would never occur to him. And I certainly don't intend to try to ease my conscience—or end my marriage—by confessing it. I just want to put this behind me and get on with my life. Do you think I'll ever be able to do that?"

"Yes. But it's going to take some time. And it's going to take all the strength you can muster where Juan is concerned."

"What do you mean?"

"I suspect you'll be hearing from him any day now. He won't want to give you up."

"He doesn't have a choice. It's over!"

"I certainly hope you mean that."

"I've never meant anything more."

25

Bloody, mutilated cats were everywhere—littering the floor, sprawled in tortured positions on chairs and tabletops, stacked like firewood against the wall. Lee pushed the furry bodies aside with her feet in her frantic scramble for the door. It was locked. She rushed to the window. It wouldn't budge. Pounding on the glass, she yelled for help. A familiar shape materialized out of the darkness beyond the window. She stood frozen as he moved closer, his feet seeming not to touch the ground. When he was inches from her, his grinning face pressed against the glass, she began to scream.

The ring of the telephone jarred Lee awake. She rolled over in the hospital bed, hurting her cracked rib and knocking a box of tissues to the floor. She fumbled for the telephone and finally succeeded in pulling it onto her chest.

"Yes? Hello?" She was answered by a faint hum of silence at the other end of the line. "Hello?" She was about to hang up when she heard Juan's voice.

"Are you alone? Can we talk?"

Lee's chest constricted. "No! Never…"

"Don't hang up. Please. Tell me how you are. It has been so hard, *querida*. So hard to be separated from you."

Lee squeezed her eyes closed. "Stop…just stop it."

"Stop what? You sound so strange." There was a pause. "Is there much pain?"

"Yes," she angrily spat the word into the receiver. "There is much pain. There has been much pain since the day I met you. Now leave me alone. Get the hell out of my life. I don't ever want to see or hear from you again!"

"Why are you angry with me?" His voice sounded genuinely puzzled. "You must explain your anger."

"You really are crazy. I don't have to explain anything to you!"

"You still don't understand…?"

"You're the one who doesn't understand," she interrupted, her voice shaking. "It's completely and forever over between us!" She slammed the receiver onto the bed beside her leg. Then she pulled it back by the cord and replaced it on its cradle. She lay exhausted, staring at the white ceiling, as tears ran down the sides of her face and made small stains on the pillow.

A short time later, Lee heard the muffled squeak of the door and opened her eyes to see Nick peeking into the room.

"Hi," he said. "I thought you were asleep." He stood above her for a moment, staring down with a concerned frown on his face before he bent to give her a quick kiss.

"I napped earlier, but I woke up a little while ago. I was just resting." She licked her lower lip. Her cheeks felt hot and tight with dried tears.

"Would you hand me my makeup kit? Sara brought it last night. I think she put it in my purse. She obviously thought I needed it. I must be quite a sight."

"You're a sight for sore eyes to me," Nick said in a tender voice. He opened the bottom door of the nightstand and fished a small leather case from her purse. "I guess this is it." When she nodded, he handed it to her. "Are you still in pain?"

"No, not really," she said, avoiding his eyes. "Only when I move. " Or think or remember, she silently added. She flipped open the clasp and looked into the mirror. Her eyes were red and swollen, and the skin under her right eye was a colorful mix of blue and purple. Her entire face looked blotchy and bruised. "Lipstick certainly wouldn't improve this situation," she said, snapping the case shut.

"You've been crying, haven't you?"

She nodded, her eyes blurring with fresh tears.

"I can't seem to stop blubbering. Do you see a box of tissues on the floor?"

Nick bent to retrieve it, pulling one out for her before sitting in the chair beside the bed. He sat silently as she wiped at her eyes and blew her nose. When he spoke, his voice was hesitant.

"Honey, I don't know if this is a good time to bring this up or not. But I've been thinking about something."

She dropped the damp tissue into a wastebasket by the side of the bed.

"What?"

"Well, you know that I'm several years overdue for a sabbatical." He shifted in his chair. "Remember how we've talked about both of us taking a year off and going someplace where I could teach physics? Somewhere away from Los Alamos and Santa Fe. A complete change of scene."

"Yes, of course. But I thought that's all it was, just talk."

"Well, I think we ought to do it. George Washington University has an opening for a guest professor in my field. I talked to them this afternoon."

"George Washington? As in Washington, D.C.?"

He nodded. "I think it might be a good thing for all of us. It would be broadening for Sara, a real change from Santa Fe High. You could take a well-earned break from the magazine to concentrate on your writing, or even finish your master's degree at GWU. You used to talk about going back to school. Annabel and the staff could get along without you for a year. What do you think?"

"I think this is very sudden. I don't see how I could just leave the magazine for that long. And what about your experiments?"

"Larry Morrison can keep them going. He's been my right hand for years. And I can always fly back for a day or two if there's an emergency. The truth is, I could use some time off from the program. I'm beginning to feel a little burned out. I think you are, too."

"I admit that the idea is tempting. Actually, very exciting. But I just don't see how I could leave."

"Sure you could, babe. That's one of the advantages of owning your own business. You can't be fired."

"But what about Sara? She won't want to leave her friends, especially Kevin."

"I think she'd adjust quickly. Besides, it would only be for two semesters. She'd be back in the middle of her junior year."

"Wait a minute. You're talking about making this move right away? Couldn't we at least wait until next summer?"

"GWU needs someone next semester. One of their physics professors had a heart attack last week and took a year's leave of absence. It's great timing for us. Sara could begin school there the first part of January. Kids do that sort of thing all the time. For Sara, with her outgoing personality, it'd be a breeze."

"I don't think it'd be quite that easy for her." Lee's mind was filling with thoughts of what it would take to accomplish a move on such short notice. "Then there's the house. We couldn't just go off and leave it empty."

"We'd rent it, and rent a place there. You know, one of those fancy apartments."

"I don't know what to say. I'm…"

"I think it might be just what you need," he said, leaning forward in his chair to stroke her arm. "Mallory said…"

"Mallory? You've talked to Dr. Mallory about this?"

"Well, yes I did. We just…"

"Wait a minute. Why would you talk to him about this before you mentioned it to me?"

"I called him this morning, and it came up. We're both concerned about you. You've been going through such a rough time lately." He paused, staring down at the floor for a moment, before looking up again to meet her eyes. "I hope you know how proud I am of what you've done with your magazine. You've worked your butt off for years, running a business and a home—not to mention raising a great daughter. And I know it hasn't been easy. Especially with me traveling so much. Mallory suggested that a rest and change of scenery might be just what you need right now."

"Let me get this straight. You talked to Mallory, then called GWU and they just happened to have an immediate opening?"

"That's how things happen in this business. I don't have to remind you that I spend a lot of time in Washington. I have contacts at the University. Morrie Pongratz—he's head of the physics department—is willing to pull the necessary strings. They've been looking for someone with my experimental background."

"Nick, you love your work here. Teaching would be a big change for you."

"It would be good for me. Good for all of us." He reached for her hand. "It's true that my work is important to me. But you've always been more important. You and Sara. I just assumed that you knew that.

Your accident has shown me how much I've taken for granted."

Lee turned to face him, looking into his anxious blue eyes. She was again struck by how tired he looked. Deep lines creased his forehead and slashed vertically between his brows. Puffy bags lay under his eyes. She pulled his head toward hers and kissed him lightly on the lips.

"I love you," she whispered. "I really do."

Nick's grin erased years from his face. "And I love you. Promise you'll think about Washington. Just imagine. The Kennedy Center. Long afternoons wandering through the Smithsonian." He wiggled his eyebrows. "Eating soft-shelled crabs in one of those ritzy Georgetown restaurants."

"You silver-tongued devil."

"I think it's time for you to get some rest now." He stood up, pushing the chair back. "Besides, I have a date. I promised Sara I'd get home early and take her to the Zia Diner for dinner. We'll both be back to see you tonight. Now, no more tears. Deal?"

"Deal."

He blew her a kiss and left, closing the door behind him.

Lee spent the rest of the afternoon carefully weighing the pros and cons of spending a year far from Santa Fe. There was no contest. The pros won. She reached for the phone and dialed Annabel's private number.

Lee could tell from Sara's face when she walked through the door several hours later that Nick had tried to enlist her support for the proposed move. It was also obvious that he hadn't succeeded. Sara's eyes were red and swollen, her expression guarded.

"I have some good news," Lee said, striving for an upbeat tone. "Dr. Zimmerman said I can go home tomorrow."

"Hey, that's terrific," Nick said, putting his arm around Sara's shoulder and hugging her close. "Isn't it, princess?"

"Yeah." Sara touched the cast on her mother's wrist. "How long do you have to wear the cast and bandages and all?"

"Well, the cast stays on for five to six weeks. Zimmerman says the rib will be painful for a while, but as long as I don't take up bungee jumping, I should be okay. You guys will have to put up with me looking like this until the bruises fade. The stitches come out next week."

"That'll be tough, Mom," Sara teased, making an obvious effort. "We'll have to keep you locked in the guest room. Leave food outside your door."

They all laughed, breaking the tension. Lee looked at her husband and daughter, noting the strong family resemblance. Although everyone remarked on Sara's resemblance to Lee, she definitely had her father's nose and smile. Lee felt a surge of love for them. Her family, the center of her world. She took a deep breath. The craziness with Juan was finally over. It was all behind her.

"Sara and I have been talking about me taking a sabbatical," Nick said, interrupting her thoughts. "She was a little upset at first, but I think she understands that it would be a good experience for all of us. Probably our last chance to do something like this as a family. Before we know it, our baby girl will be off to college."

"Now, let's not rush that," Lee said, watching Sara. "Honey, how do you really feel about the idea?"

"Well, I don't know. It scares me. I mean, I don't want to leave my friends and all." She glanced at Nick, then looked down at the floor. "But I guess it wouldn't be so bad. After all, we'd be coming back."

"Sure, we would," Nick interjected.

"But I'll just bet Wendy will try to snatch Kevin up the minute I leave."

"Hey, you'd have so many new boyfriends you wouldn't have

time to worry about Kevin." Nick looked at Lee. "Well, babe. What's your vote?"

"I talked to Annabel this afternoon. She encouraged me to go, reminding me that she had taken off for nine months when Milt had his heart attack. She even had the nerve to say that they could manage fine without me." She paused. "I had the definite feeling that you had already talked to her, Nick."

"Guilty as charged." He grinned. "So, is it settled then?"

"It really does sound wonderful...."

"Great! I'll call GWU in the morning. And I'd better contact a realtor about renting our house. We could rent it furnished. Just store the valuables, take a few essentials: clothes, computers, books."

"My TV, stereo, and posters," Sara added.

Nick laughed. "Well, maybe just a few posters. We'll want to travel light and rent something furnished in Washington. After all, this is going to be an adventure. Let's keep it as simple as possible. Tell you what: I'm going back there for a meeting next week. I can find us an apartment then. And check into the schools." He smiled, looking from Lee to Sara. "Now, let me see some real enthusiasm."

They glanced at each other in silent agreement before bravely returning Nick's smile.

The telephone rang as Lee was finishing her breakfast the next morning. She stopped, a spoonful of cereal halfway to her mouth, and let the phone ring twice more before reaching for the receiver.

"Hello?"

"Don't hang up, *querida*. You must speak to me."

Lee pushed the tray away, feeling her last bite stick in her throat.

"You still don't get it, do you? How many times do I have to say it? I refuse to have any further contact with you—ever again!"

"Then just listen. Let me tell you how it is with me. I don't eat, I don't sleep. I think only of you. Trust me. This is the truth."

"Stop it! I don't want to hear it. I told you…"

"I know what you told me. But you're wrong. You can't end it between us. You belong to me."

"No, I don't belong to you. Look, I don't know what kind of power you've had over me. But it's over. It ended last Friday."

"I can't lose you. Trust me when I tell you I can't let that happen again. I won't let that happen." His voice grew harder. "*¿Comprendes?* Do you understand?"

"You're the one who doesn't understand! I'm leaving. My family and I are moving away."

"Moving away?" He sounded stunned. "What do you mean, moving away? Where do you think you're going?"

"That's none of your business."

There was another long silence. She was about to hang up when she heard his voice, so thick with anger that she almost didn't recognize it.

"Understand this, Lee. You aren't going anywhere. I won't let you go."

"You can't stop me. You can't…"

He laughed, a mirthless, vicious sound that sent chills through Lee's body.

"You think not? You think I can't stop you? Then you are very mistaken. Do you think I saved you—brought you back—only to let you leave me?"

"What do you mean, you 'saved' me?"

"It's not over," he said, ignoring her question. "You'll see, *querida.* It will never be over between you and me. Ever." The line went dead.

Lee replaced the receiver, trembling with shock and fear. Mallory was right. Juan wasn't going to give up easily. Still, she hadn't anticipated the extent of his fury or his threats. *How does he plan to stop me from leaving? Will he tell Nick about our affair?* She tried to imagine the scene between the two men—Juan insisting on a prior, past life claim to Lee and her husband's outraged reaction. *When angry, Nick can be pretty formidable himself. And even if Juan told Nick he'd slept with his wife, Nick wouldn't believe him.*

Her thoughts were interrupted by Dr. Zimmerman's striding through the door.

"Hi there. How're we doing this morning?"

"I'm ready to go home. The nurse said you had to give the final okay."

"Let's change that bandage on your head." He cut away the tape and peered at the stitches above her temple. "Looks good" he assured her. "You'll only have a thin scar. And that'll be hidden by your hair when it grows out. The cut on your chin was superficial. No stitches. The bruises are still pretty colorful, but they'll fade soon. Still having headaches?"

"A slight one yesterday. But it's gone this morning."

"How's the rib?"

"Still really sore," she admitted "But I'm learning to be cautious in my movements."

"Good. No belly dancing for a few weeks."

"Oh, well, there goes my new career," she said, trying to appear cheerful.

He smiled. "I want to see you in my office early next week. I'll remove the stitches then." He taped another bandage on her head. "You can take shallow baths. Just be careful not to get the tape or the cast on your arm wet. I'm afraid you're going to have to live with that cast for a while longer. It's going to cramp your style at work, isn't it?"

"It'll give me an excuse to sit back and play boss."

"Okay. I'll sign the papers springing you from this joint. Is Nick picking you up?"

She nodded. "He went into work early this morning. But he's planning to take off as soon as I call him."

"Good enough. Remember to call my office and schedule an appointment for Monday or Tuesday."

"I will. Thanks so much for everything."

Nick had left instructions to be called out of his meeting when Lee called, and his secretary put her through immediately.

"I'll wind things up here and hit the road," he said. "Be there in about an hour."

"Don't forget to stop by the house and grab something for me to wear home. Just a jacket, panties, sweats." She hesitated. "And bring my old brown boots. Somehow, the emergency room staff managed to misplace my new ones."

She hung up the phone, realizing that she was fast becoming a pretty smooth liar. No wonder, she thought bitterly. *As Mother always said, practice makes perfect.*

26

"Yes, Annie, I'm taking it easy. But it sure feels strange to be sitting around the house instead of coming into the office. I'll try to enjoy it. Thanks for dropping the packet off. This issue looks great. Nice cover. How many subscribers did you pick up this month?" Annie started in on one of her long stories and Lee interrupted her. "Oh, good. Listen, I've got to go. There's a man here installing a burglar alarm, and he needs to talk to me. Thanks for calling. I'll get back to you later."

She hung up the receiver and turned off the telephone ringer. *Better let the answering machine screen messages in case Juan tries to call. Of course, he might leave a message, one that Nick could overhear. That bastard called before when Nick was at home. And now that he's so crazy mad, there's no telling what he might do. Well, I'll just have to take that chance. No way in hell am I going to leave myself open to another conversation with him.*

Lee was resting on her bed and looking through magazines when Sara came home from school.

"Hi. Aren't we burglar alarmed yet? No sirens went off when I unlocked the front door."

"Not yet. This is a big house. It'll take a couple of days to get the system installed. How was school?"

"The usual. Everyone is really knocked out that we're leaving. I think Kevin is super sad." She grinned. "He said he'd write to me every night. Oh, here, I picked up the mail." She tossed a pile of envelopes and fliers on the bed and left the room.

Lee shuffled through assorted bills and advertisements. She opened a large manila envelope from the office, stuffed with correspondence Julie thought Lee should see. One return address immediately caught her eye. Luis Tafoya, Rio Arriba County Sheriff's Department, Española, New Mexico.

She ripped the envelope open and removed a Xerox copy of a newspaper clipping from the *Albuquerque Journal*, dated June 18, 1962. Attached was a one-sentence note:

"Mrs. Lindsay—Thought you might be interested in this old clipping re: Juan Mascareñas. Regards, L. Tafoya."

Lee stared at the picture of a pretty, smiling young woman. Underneath was the caption: *Susan Michelle Miller, age 19, reported missing in Mexico.*

The story was brief:

> *A missing persons report has been filed on Susan M. Miller, sophomore anthropology major at the University of New Mexico. When last seen the California native was reportedly en route to Chihuahua, Mexico, in the company of another UNM*

student, Juan Mascareñas of Cavado, New Mexico. Neither Miller nor Mascareñas has been heard from since April 13.

Miss Miller is described as five feet, seven inches tall, 118 pounds, with long blond hair and blue eyes. Her sudden departure has baffled family and friends.

"Susan said they were leaving for a week to ten days," said the missing woman's roommate and long-time friend, Jessica Manning. "I was surprised because it was the middle of the semester. Susan has always been a serious student and very reliable person. It's not like her to just take off and disappear like this. Everyone is terribly worried."

Mascareñas, a sophomore psychology major, is described as six feet tall, 170 pounds, dark hair and brown eyes.

Anyone with information concerning the whereabouts of Miller or Mascareñas is asked to contact the Albuquerque Police Department.

After rereading the article, Lee took a moment to study the young woman's picture. Although it was a photocopy of a black and white photo, there was no denying the obvious: Large eyes, small upturned nose, oval face with a slightly squared jawline—*A blond with blue eyes.* Even the height and weight matched.

Lee replaced the article in the envelope and slipped it into her nightstand drawer. Her hands were shaking. The resemblance was remarkable. Twenty years ago, Susan Miller could have been her twin.

Nick came home from work Friday night with a wide smile and a surprise for Lee. Parked in the driveway with a huge pink bow on the windshield was a new cream-colored Subaru station wagon.

"I didn't know when you'd feel up to shopping for a new car, so I decided to spare you the hassle," he said. "A station wagon will come in handy for the trek to Washington. Well, what's the verdict? Did I do good?"

Lee put her arms around his neck and hugged him as hard as her sore rib would allow.

"You did just great." She gave him a long kiss. "I love you. I hope you know how much."

Nick beamed down at her. Then his expression grew serious.

"I've never doubted your love, honey. We've been through a few rough patches in the last eighteen years, but we've always been a team. And I wouldn't trade that for anything."

Her chest tightened and she buried her face in his shoulder.

"Neither would I," she said, trying to control the quiver in her voice. "Not for anything."

The weekend passed quickly. Nick was delighted with the intricate alarm system and patiently instructed Lee and Sara in its use.

"Remember," he repeated, "the police are automatically alerted when the alarm goes off."

"Geez," Sara sighed. "That thing's a computer. You need a Ph.D. to understand it."

"Or a father with a Ph.D. to explain it to you," Nick said.

"I hope the renters can figure it out," Lee said.

"I'll write out detailed instructions. By the way, have you heard anything from the realtor...what's her name?"

"Stephanie. She called yesterday to say that she's working

with a young couple who sound perfect. They're going to be in town in a couple of weeks. She'll bring them over then."

"Great. I'll see what I can find for us to rent in Washington next week."

"How long will you be gone?" Lee felt a pang of anxiety at the thought of Nick being out of town again.

"I leave on Tuesday and get back Saturday night. It'll be a busy trip. I've got back-to-back meetings scheduled for Wednesday, but that'll leave me Thursday and Friday to look for an apartment and find a school for Sara."

"I still can't believe we're going," Lee said.

"You're not having second thoughts, are you?"

"No. I'm really eager to go," she assured him.

"Good. I was thinking that we should plan to leave the Saturday before Christmas. Just as soon as school's out. Christmas in Washington. Doesn't that sound terrific? They go all out with decorations back there. You'll see. It's going to be great!"

Lee was standing in her closet early Monday morning, trying to decide what to wear. It had to be something that would fit over her cast. She had a list of errands to run that morning, before her appointment with Dr. Zimmerman. And she was determined to spend the afternoon at the office. There were a few problems to be ironed out. Her year in Washington would require a little reorganization. They'd have to hire another editor. She agreed with Annabel that Julie should be promoted to office manager. And that meant that they would have to find another receptionist.

She struggled to remove a loose-fitting blouse and slacks from their hangers with one arm. The rib was feeling a lot better, and today she would get the bothersome stitches removed from her head. Then she would just have the cast to cope with.

"Mom?" Sara called, running up the stairs. "I'm leaving for school now. Kevin just honked."

"Okay, honey. Have a good day. And wear your down jacket. It's chilly outside."

"I know. Oh, that reminds me. Have you seen my red scarf? I thought I left it in the downstairs coat closet, but I haven't been able to find it."

"Your scarf?" Lee froze, remembering. The last time she went to Cavado, the day of her accident, she had worn her heavy leather jacket. And because it was cold, getting ready to snow, she had wrapped that red scarf around her neck. Sara's scarf! She'd completely forgotten about it, had never given it another thought.

"Mom?" Sara was standing at the closet door, staring at her. "Are you okay?"

"What? Oh, yes, I was just thinking.... I borrowed your scarf the day of my accident. I'm sorry. I guess it got...lost."

"Don't worry about it. No big deal. I can wear my blue one." She gave Lee a quick kiss on the cheek. "Gotta run. See you after school."

Lee collapsed in the nearest chair after Sara left, feeling like she couldn't breathe. She'd left Sara's red woolen scarf, which was monogrammed with Sara's initials, along with her own jacket and boots, after that last, nightmarish visit to Cavado. Juan had the motivation and—thanks to her—the means for a terrible revenge.

27

"Lee?" Annabel's voice penetrated her frantic thoughts.

"I'm sorry. What?"

"I asked if you like the Glad Rags Boutique ad layout. Honestly, you act like you've already left us. You hardly said a word during the staff meeting. Are you all right? Did your visit to the doctor go okay this morning? You know, I still get chills when I think of you wrecking your car out on that road. It's an absolute miracle...."

Lee interrupted her. "I was very lucky. And the doctor said I'm doing fine now. I just have a lot on my mind."

"Well, of course. You must be running in circles, getting ready to spend a year in Washington! I'm green with envy. The shopping there! Kiddo, you're going to think you've died and gone to heaven. I spent six solid hours in Loehmann's when we went back to Washington for Milt's last high school reunion...."

Lee tuned her out, as she glanced up at the clock on the wall. *Sara should be home from school by now. I've got to make sure she's okay and remind her to never open the door to a stranger and to reset the alarm when she's there alone.* She reached for the telephone.

"Excuse me, Annie, I really need to call Sara."

The phone rang and rang. No answer. Close to panic, Lee sprang to her feet.

"I have to go! There's something I have to check on."

"What? Where?"

"At home. Listen, the layout looks great. I'll call you later." She grabbed her purse and ran out the door.

Lee pulled into the garage and jumped out of the car. When she opened the door to the house she noticed that the burglar alarm was off.

"Sara!" she screamed, running down the hall and up the stairs. "Sara, where are you?" She flung her daughter's bedroom door open.

Sara was lying across her bed, telephone in hand. She looked up at Lee with startled eyes.

"What is it, Mom? Why are you freaking out?"

Lee sagged against the door frame in relief. "I called you twenty minutes ago but you didn't answer. I knew the school bus should have come by then."

"I didn't ride the bus. Kevin brought me home and we stopped for a Coke. What's the matter? I thought you were going to be at work all afternoon."

Lee sat on the bed and put her arms around Sara. "Oh, baby," she said, "when I didn't know where you were, I just got scared. I don't know what I'd do if anything happened to you."

"Why should anything happen to me? I just stopped for a Coke. I've done that before, and you've never minded."

"I know. It's probably the accident...but from now on, let me know when you're going to be late. Okay?"

"Okay. Sure. Uh, I'm on the phone, Mom," she said with a nod toward the receiver pressed against her stomach.

"Oh...I'm sorry. Go ahead and finish your conversation. I think I'm going to lie down and rest for awhile." Lee walked into her room and collapsed on the bed. After a few seconds, she got up and reset the burglar alarm.

"So, Doc Zimmerman said you were healing nicely?" Nick had just gotten home from work and was laying out shirts, ties, and underwear, starting to pack for his trip to Washington.

Lee was sitting in her bedroom chair, watching him and determined to sound normal.

"I guess the rib will be sore for a while yet. But it's nothing I can't live with. Makeup covers the cut on my chin. And look, there's only a hairline scar at my temple."

He peered down at her. "I can't even see it."

"I combed my hair so that it doesn't show. Is there anything I can do to help you pack?"

"No, just sit there. You look bushed. Sara and I can fix sandwiches for dinner."

"I am tired. I guess I'm still not in shape for full-time work. I think I'll go to bed early. I could really use a good night's rest."

Lee awoke in the darkness, sweating and breathless. It was a familiar and terrifying dream. She had been falling from a great height, grabbing frantically at empty air. She'd managed to force herself awake just before smashing into the rocks below.

She shuddered. It was the first nightmare she'd had since she was in the hospital. *They're starting again!* She tried to calm her breathing, to force her muscles to relax. *The Native American man— the one with the birthmark like Juan's—was in the dream again. But this time our relationship was different. He was no longer my lover. Instead, he was an angry, threatening presence. Trying to force me into doing...something. Some ceremony I didn't want to perform?* The memory flitted across a dark corner of her mind and out, but the anxiety and adrenaline remained.

Lee threw the covers back and sat on the edge of the bed. *This has got to stop! Before I go completely nuts.* She just sat there for a moment, motionless, her mind struggling to find a solution to the turmoil the dream always triggered.

She got out of bed, careful not to disturb Nick, and walked into the bathroom. The shades were up on the bathroom window. After swallowing a sleeping pill and turning off the bathroom light, Lee paused to look outside. It was a bright night. The moon, only days away from being full, reflected off the light snow that had fallen earlier, casting an eerie luminescence across the midnight landscape. From the hills beyond the house came the lonely yipping cry of a coyote, answered by the barking of a neighbor's dog.

The sounds triggered thoughts of Mister, and brought a heavy sadness to Lee's heart. Maybe Nick was right. Maybe they should adopt another cat when they got to Washington. Mister could never be replaced, but a kitten might help fill the void he'd left in her life.

She was about to turn from the window when a slight movement caught her eye. Just beyond the house, beside a large piñon tree, something was moving. Lee leaned her face closer to the window, straining for a better look. What she saw caused her entire body to tighten in terror.

A man stepped away from the tree and stood clearly silhouetted in the moonlight. The set of his powerful shoulders, the arrogant angle of his head left no doubt as to his identity. For a long moment he seemed to gaze toward the darkened window where she stood, locked in fright. Then he moved back behind the tree.

Lee held her breath while her blood roared in her ears. For a moment she thought she might faint. What was Juan doing out there, skulking around in the middle of the night? Maybe she should wake Nick. Or set off the alarm to scare him away. Before she could decide what to do, Nick opened the bathroom door.

"Babe? Are you all right? I heard you get up."

Something inside Lee crumbled. It was time for the truth—at least part of it.

"There's a man out there," she whispered, almost choking on the words. "Hiding in the trees."

"What? Where?" Nick pressed his face against the window. "I don't see anyone." He turned away from the window and grabbed his robe off the hook on the bathroom door. "You stay here. I'm going out to have a look." He slipped loafers on his bare feet and hurried down the stairs. Lee was right behind him.

"Go back upstairs," he said over his shoulder.

"No!" She hesitated for only a moment. "Nick, I know who's out there."

He stopped at the bottom of the stairs, staring up at her. "Who?"

"Juan."

"The medicine man? What makes you think so?"

"I recognized him! Nick, he's dangerous! We have to call the police."

Nick quickly zipped a down jacket over his robe and turned off the alarm.

"No! Nick—please!" She grabbed his arm. "Please! Don't go out there!"

"Lee! Let go," he said, prying her hand loose and grabbing a heavy wrought iron fireplace poker. "I've had more than enough of this character. Stay here and lock the door behind me." He left through the sliding glass door that led to the patio. Lee locked the door and leaned against it, watching Nick move around the side of the house and disappear behind the piñon trees. Her heart was thundering in her chest as though it might burst. *Oh, dear God, what will Juan do to Nick? He's capable of anything!* She gripped the door handle as she stared through the glass.

Something moved behind one of the piñons. She drew back, holding her breath. Suddenly a huge raven flew out of the tree and over the top of the house. Lee heard a ringing in her ears, just before her knees buckled and she slumped to the floor.

A loud banging on the door yanked her back to awareness.

"Lee! Lee!"

Fighting a wave of nausea, she pulled herself to her knees and unlocked the door. In an instant Nick was beside her.

"Are you all right? What happened?"

"I…I guess I fainted. Oh, Nick, you're safe."

"Of course, I'm safe. I circled all around the house but didn't see anyone. What made you…"

Lee started to cry. "It sounds crazy. But I did see Juan, when we were upstairs. Then a big raven flew out of the tree."

"Are you saying that you fainted because you saw a bird?"

"You don't understand. The raven was in the tree! The same tree that Juan was hiding behind. The raven…"

"Honey, ravens are common around here. I see them all the time." He helped her to her feet and took a moment to reset the alarm. "Come on, let's go back to bed." With his jacket still on and his arm around her waist, he half-carried her up the stairs.

"Easy now," he said, pulling the covers over her. He peered down at her with a worried look. "Do you feel sick?"

"Yes."

"Let me get a wet cloth for your head," he said, going into the bathroom and turning on the light. He came out holding the bottle of sleeping pills. "How many of these did you take?"

"Just one. I had a bad dream and…"

"Are you sure you only took one? Maybe you took one and then forgot and took another one. That could easily happen. They're pretty strong."

"I only took one, dammit!"

"Well, it obviously hit you hard. You're still weak from your accident. It's going to take awhile for you to recover completely." He zipped the pills into his jacket pocket and tossed it, along with his robe, across a chair.

"No more of those pills while I'm gone," he said as he crawled into bed. "You clearly had some kind of reaction to them tonight. I'm just glad you didn't hurt yourself when you passed out." He yawned. "I've got to get some sleep, babe. Big travel day tomorrow." He kissed her cheek and rolled over. Before long he was snoring.

Lee lay awake, staring at the ceiling and trying to process what had happened. *No wonder Nick thought I was drugged out of my mind. I insisted that Juan was lurking outside, and then passed out cold at the sight of a raven. There is no way to make him understand. Any rational person knows that a man can't turn into a bird. I can't say anything about this to anyone, not even Dr. Mallory. Not if I want to be considered sane. But I know what I saw. Juan was out there. And he'll be back.*

28

Lee was in her study the next afternoon, staring at the newspaper picture of Susan Miller. She was haunted by the girl's face, so like her own. Luis Tafoya had said that she had never been heard from again after she went to Mexico with Juan.

Mexico! Juan wanted to take me to Mexico, too. Dear God, what happened to Susan Miller down there? Juan swore she'd left with another man. The police believed him. Is that the true story? I doubt it. Lee folded the piece of paper.

Glancing at the clock, Lee realized that it was almost time for Sara to get home from school. She disarmed the alarm system and hid the clipping in the back of her desk drawer.

She heard the front door open and Sara calling from downstairs.

"Mom? Where are you?"

"Up here."

Sara ran up the stairs and burst into the room. "Mom, it's the neatest thing!"

"What?"

"It must be someone's pet. It's totally tame."

"Sara, what are you talking about?"

"A colossal black bird—I guess it's a raven—but it's the most gigantic one I've ever seen! Perched on the courtyard wall, just sitting there as calm as anything. I opened the gate and walked right up to it and it still didn't fly away. It just cocked its head from side to side and went 'Kraaak Kraaak'—but kind of soft, like it was talking to me."

In a flash, Lee was out of the room and down the stairs. She ran through the family room and yanked open the front door. The courtyard wall was empty.

"Where?" Lee demanded urgently, as soon as Sara caught up with her. "Where is it? Where is the raven?" She grabbed Sara by the shoulders, ignoring a stab of pain in her side from her damaged rib. "Answer me!"

Sara stared at Lee, shocked.

"What's with you, Mom? Why are you freaking out? I mean, it was just a bird!"

Sara looked worried during dinner that night, watching her mother out of the corner of her eye. Lee did her best to make conversation and appear normal, but she knew Sara wasn't fooled.

At eight o'clock she rechecked the already locked doors and windows and activated the alarm system. *Command, Stay.* All set. Then she gave Sara a goodnight kiss and went straight to bed.

A deafening sound pierced the night, catapulting Lee out of bed and into the hall before she realized what she was doing. Sara ran out of her room to join her, face pale with fright.

"What's happening? What is it?"

"It's the burglar alarm!" Lee grabbed Sara's arm and pulled her into the master bedroom. Then she locked the door behind them and ran to examine the alarm control panel on the wall. Flashing red lights indicated that the downstairs sliding patio door had been opened. The high-pitched siren continued to scream.

"Mom? What should we do?"

"I don't know! Nothing. We're going to stay right here until the police arrive." The bedside clock told her that it was just after midnight. She hurried into the closet and felt behind Nick's ski boots. Sara gasped when she saw the pistol appear in Lee's hand.

"A gun? I didn't know we had a gun! Oh, Geez, are we going to have to shoot somebody?"

"I hope not. Maybe the siren scared them."

"The cops will be coming, won't they? Do you think they're already on their way?"

"They'd better be."

Within minutes a police car was pulling into the driveway. Sara cheered.

Lee put the gun in her nightstand drawer and slipped into her robe. "Now you stay here while I go downstairs and let them in."

"No way. I'm not staying up here by myself." Sara hurried down the stairs behind Lee.

A policeman was at the front door, his partner in the driveway, shining a flashlight into the darkness on the side of the house.

"Come in," she said, clutching Sara's hand. "It's the patio door that went off. Through there—through the kitchen. Shall I turn it off now?" She pointed toward the downstairs control panel. "The siren, I mean?"

"Yes, ma'am, please. Then I want you two to stay right here, by the door. Where are the light switches for the kitchen?"

"Right there on the wall. By the bookcase." She punched in the numbers to deactivate the system. The instant silence was almost shocking. She felt a draft of cold wind just before light from the family room flooded the foyer, exposing the open sliding patio door. Lee stared at it in horror. She knew she'd locked that door. In fact, she'd checked and rechecked all the doors in the house before going to bed.

"Looks like you forgot to lock up, and someone just slid it open," the second policeman said, coming in through the open patio door. He stayed with Lee and Sara while the other man went carefully from room to room, turning on lights and checking the house.

"But I didn't forget! I know that I locked it."

"There's no broken glass, or sign of forced entry."

"But, officer, I'm telling you, I locked that door!"

He shrugged. "Well, anyway, I'm sure whoever it was is long gone by now. Probably just a kid looking for quick drug money."

The second policeman reappeared and shook his head.

"There's no one in the house, ma'am. We'll check the grounds again before we leave. But I think you're safe now. Usually, all it takes to spook these characters is the sound of the alarm. Whoever tried to break in is probably halfway to Albuquerque by now." He gave Lee and Sara a reassuring smile. "That patio door is locked for sure now. And all the outside lights are on. I doubt that you'll be bothered again tonight. Just turn your alarm back on after we leave. Good night now."

"Good night. Thank you." Lee locked the front door behind them and reactivated the alarm system, then hurried upstairs with Sara.

"Can I sleep with you tonight, Mom?"

Lee looked at Sara, who looked very young and shaken.

"You bet, honey. To tell the truth, I'd appreciate some company, myself."

They got into bed and Lee turned out the light.

"Mom?" Sara's voice was a nervous whisper. "Who do you suppose was trying to burglarize us?"

"You heard the policeman. Probably just some kid with a drug habit planning to steal a television or a VCR."

"Do you really think you locked that patio door?"

Lee stared up into the darkness. "Well, I thought I did. But I must have been mistaken. Anyway, we're all locked up now. Sleep tight, sweetie."

Sara rolled over and was soon asleep. But Lee lay awake until dawn, staring at the red lights on the alarm control panel—her frantic thoughts swirling around a red woolen scarf, Sara's "colossal crow," and a locked patio door that had been opened without any sign of forced entry.

Lee returned from the grocery store the next morning to find a police car parked in front of her house. The burglar alarm was screeching, shattering the silence of the otherwise peaceful neighborhood. She pulled to a stop at the end of the driveway and bolted from the car. A young police officer was just coming around the north side of the house.

"What's going on?" Lee called, rushing up to him.

"Are you the owner? Mrs. Nicholas Lindsay?"

"Yes."

"We got a call from your alarm service that the system was triggered. I've checked all the doors and windows and everything is locked up tight. It's probably just a malfunction."

"The alarm went off last night," Lee said, shouting over the noise and doing her best to stay calm. "Someone opened the patio door after the alarm was set."

"An attempted break-in? In that case, I'd better do a thorough check of the inside of the house. I'll need the key to the front door."

"Just a minute." Lee ran to the car and got her keys out of the ignition. She handed them to the officer and started to follow him toward the house.

"Wait out here, ma'am," he said.

Moments later, he stuck his head out of the front door. "The downstairs seems secure. How do I disarm the system?"

Lee gave him the code. "Can I come in now?"

"No. Wait outside until I check upstairs."

Before long the officer was back. "No sign of forced entry," he said. "Everything's locked up tighter than a drum. Had to have been a malfunction. Is it a new system? Sometimes it takes awhile to get the bugs out."

"Officer, please...come with me to check all the rooms?"

"I just did that."

"Did you look under the beds and in all the closets?"

"Well, no. But I rechecked all the doors and windows. As I said, there's no sign of a break-in."

"Please."

"Of course. I won't leave until you feel safe."

"You might be here for a long time," she said, forcing a smile.

"Ma'am?"

"Never mind." Lee went in the front door and followed the man as he went from room to room, searching every possible hiding place.

"Do you notice anything missing or out of place?"

"No."

"Okay." He paused at the front door. "I think you can relax now, Mrs. Lindsay. There's no one in your house."

"If I seem unduly nervous it's because my husband is away and my daughter and I are alone this week," Lee explained. "And I did see a prowler several nights ago. Then last night, someone tried to break in."

"Would you feel better if we kept an eye on the property for the next few days? I can arrange to have one of the patrol cars drive by and check things out several times during the day and night. That's usually enough to discourage anyone who's watching the place."

"I'd really appreciate that."

"You won't know they're there unless there is a problem."

"Thank you." Lee closed the door behind him and locked it. Moments later, she remembered that the back seat of the car was filled with groceries and reluctantly went back outside. Not until the car was parked inside the garage, and the garage door closed and locked, was she able to breathe somewhat normally again.

Sara seemed unusually subdued when she returned from school that afternoon. She disappeared into her room and closed the door. Lee, noting the absence of the rock music that normally blared from behind her daughter's bedroom door, went to investigate. When she opened Sara's door, she found her lying on her bed, surrounded by her menagerie of stuffed animals. "What's the matter?" Lee asked, sitting on the edge of the bed.

"I don't know. I just don't feel so good. My head hurts, and I feel sort of...wobbly."

"Wobbly?" She felt Sara's forehead. It was warm and slightly damp.

"Yeah. You know, kind of weak. And a little dizzy when I climbed the stairs."

A bolt of icy terror shot through Lee.

"When did this start, honey?"

"Around noon. In fact, I only had a Pepsi for lunch. Everything in the cafeteria looked yucky to me."

"Are you hungry now? I could fix you some soup."

Sara wrinkled her nose. "No thanks. But would you get me something for my headache? It's really killing me."

Lee fought rising panic as she hurried into the bathroom. *Calm down. Sara caught one of the bugs that's going around. Please,*

God, let that be what it is. Her hand was shaking as she shook out two aspirins, filled a water glass and hurried back to Sara's room.

Sara napped on and off for the rest of the afternoon. She refused to eat, turning down even a bowl of her favorite ice cream. By eight o'clock she was in a deep sleep. Lee felt far too anxious to go to bed. She decided a hot bath might help her unwind a bit.

She submerged herself in the warm water, trying to relax her tight muscles. She decided to focus on a pleasant, happy memory, something far away from the chaos of her life. Allowing her mind to float, she visualized a beach in Hawaii, on the island of Kauai, that she had visited with her parents when she was a teenager. It was one of those great times when her father was on the wagon, and her parents seemed almost happy together. She remembered thinking Kauai must be the most beautiful place on earth. *Poipu. That was it. Poipu Beach.* She could see the white sand, warm turquoise water, palm trees, and red and purple bougainvillea clinging to a high lava rock wall.

Lee felt some of the tension seep from her body. She could almost smell the sweetness of plumeria blossoms and feel the warm humid air against her skin. Maybe Nick would take them back to that beach, as soon as his sabbatical was over. A real family vacation. Sara would love it. She smiled, visualizing the three of them walking together on the warm beach.

She got out of her bath and into a flannel nightgown, feeling almost drowsy. She checked on Sara, who seemed to be sleeping peacefully. Her forehead felt cooler. She told herself Sara would be better in the morning.

All the doors and windows were locked. The alarm was set. Lee did some neck rolls, trying to ease her still-knotted muscles. Bed's going to feel good, she thought, as she pulled the heavy quilted bedspread back.

Lee reeled back, staring at her pillow, not believing what she saw. She must be hallucinating! She closed her eyes, and opened them again. It was still there! The cat's skull she had found at Juan's, the skull that was unmistakably Mister's. Hand clamped over her mouth, she staggered into the bathroom—barely reaching the toilet before she vomited.

Frantic, she stood in the bathroom door, eyes fixed on the skull. *Sara! Sara could wake up and come looking for me. I have to make sure she doesn't see what's left of Mister. Oh, God! Juan will stop at absolutely nothing!* Lee remembered Socorro warning her not to underestimate Juan. *Well, I did. And it's cost me dearly. I'll never make that mistake again.*

She forced herself to face the truth. Juan must have left the skull there while she was at the store that morning. And, in doing so, he'd triggered the alarm. But how did he get in without breaking a window or forcing the lock on a door? Could he possibly have a key? *He could have made an imprint of my keys while I slept in Cavado.* Then an even worse thought gripped her. *Maybe he doesn't need a key. Maybe a brujo just uses magic to come and go as he wishes.*

Pushing that thought from her mind, she opened the cabinet under the sink and took out a small trash bag and then a second one. She slipped one inside the other and went back to the bed. Ignoring the strong odor, she picked up the partially fur-covered head, holding it to her chest, closing her eyes with a brief prayer for Mister's precious little soul before slipping it into the bags. Then she walked into her closet and gently placed the skull on the top shelf, behind her beige suede purse.

She removed the loaded pistol from her nightstand and, holding the gun in front of her, walked through the house, rechecking all the windows and doors. Satisfied that everything was as secure as she could possibly make it, she went into Sara's room.

Lee felt her daughter's forehead. *A little warm, maybe a slight fever. No way I am going to leave her side tonight.* She put the gun on the floor, just under Sara's bed. Then she got into the bed, inching close to Sara's slender body. Taking deep breaths, she stared into the darkness. Finally, her eyes began to close.

It was just past midnight when Sara started screaming. Lee jerked awake.

"What is it? Sara, what's wrong?" As she fumbled for the light on Sara's nightstand, she smelled it. Sweating oil!

Sara was sitting up in bed, staring blindly, her face twisted in terror. She screamed again. "No! Get away! Mommy! Mommy, help!"

The smell grew stronger. Frantic, Lee cradled her daughter's thin frame in her arms. Sara felt very hot.

"I'm right here, baby," she said. "Mommy's here." Was the smell real? Lee no longer had any doubt that it was.

"Save me! Don't let it bite me!"

"Honey, wake up. You're having a dream. Please, wake up!"

Sara twisted violently in Lee's arms. "The bird! It's after me!"

Lee's blood turned to ice. There could be no doubt. It *was* Juan. In some way—some impossible way—he was causing Sara's sickness. Just as he'd been responsible for every terrible thing that had happened in the past month—Socorro, Mister, Nick's illness, her accident, and now—now the ruthless sonofabitch was after Sara! Lee remembered his angry voice on the phone when she had spoken to him in the hospital. *"You think I can't stop you from leaving me? Then you are mistaken. You are very mistaken."*

"Mom?" Sara's eyes, wide and glassy, were now focused on Lee. "Why are you in here with me?"

"You were having a nightmare. It's all right. Let's get you into a different bed.

Lee helped Sara out of the tangle of sweaty sheets. The odor of the oil seemed to follow them as she led Sara into one of the guest rooms. Fighting to stay calm, she gave her two more aspirins and tucked her into the queen-sized bed.

Hurrying back down the hall, Lee grabbed the gun from under Sara's bed and went to her own room for the pottery candle Socorro had given her. When she returned, she locked the guest room door behind her, taking care to hide the gun in the folds of her nightgown. But there was no need for such caution. Sara's eyes were closed.

Setting the candle down, Lee quietly slipped the gun into the nghtstand drawer, within easy reach should she need it.

"Mom?" Sara's voice sounded weak and fretful.

"I'm here, honey," she said, as she lit the candle and got into bed. She slid close to Sara and gave her a hard hug. "Go back to sleep, darling. No more bad dreams. Nothing's going to hurt you." Anger flared into a red-hot rage inside Lee, overshadowing her fear. "I promise," she whispered fiercely into Sara's hair. *I'll do whatever it takes to keep you safe!*

After Sara had fallen into a fitful sleep, Lee lay staring at the candle flame. Then, figuring more must be better, she got up and gathered three more candles from her bathroom shelf. When the guest room was illuminated by the candlelight, the odor of the oil suddenly disappeared.

Lee climbed back into bed, her mind racing. *What can I do? Go to the police? But I have no evidence against Juan, no proof that he's done anything at all.* Bitter tears of helplessness rolled down her cheeks. *I am so alone. If only Socorro were here. She'd know how to fight back. But Socorro can't help me. Juan saw to that.*

Suddenly, Lee was hit with a terrifying realization. *Juan has been in this house! He could have stolen—and no doubt did—any number of our personal items. Now we are completely at his mercy, not that he has any.*

Sara's voice rang in Lee's head: *Save me, Mommy!* And then Socorro's words came back to Lee in a rush. *...only the death of a spirit-sucker can free those who have been bewitched....and spirit-suckers don't die easily.*

By dawn the wax candles had burned completely down, and Lee had come to terms with what she had to do.

Sara was still asleep when Lee dialed Juan's number. He answered on the third ring.

"Lee."

"All right, you ruthless bastard," Lee said in a toneless voice. "You win. I'll come back to Cavado. But stop what you're doing to Sara. Do you hear me? Stop it right now."

There was a short silence at the other end of the line. "I will be expecting you, and bring the amulet," he said softly. Lee imagined his smug smile. "Come alone. Don't try to trick me, *querida*." He paused. "Did you like my little surprise?"

She clutched the countertop with her free hand. "You're evil. Or crazy. I don't know which."

"There is much you don't know. But no matter. *Los ojos se abriran*, your eyes will be opened. I will be expecting you tomorrow. Come early."

Lee replaced the receiver, backing away from the phone as though it were Juan, himself. For a moment she thought she was going to be sick. She sat at the kitchen table, taking deep breaths until the nausea passed. He'd been waiting—like a spider in the dark, poised on his sticky web—confident that she would call, knowing that he had given her no choice. She forced herself to her feet and turned on the burner under the teakettle. *Juan is in for a surprise. Tomorrow, I'll be calling the shots. Literally.*

Filled with grim resolve, Lee stood in the kitchen, willing the water to boil.

Sara's temperature remained high. Then, in the late afternoon she awoke from a nap in her own clean bed, her condition dramatically improved. In fact, her fever was almost gone and she was hungry.

Relieved but still wary, Lee went to fix her a peanut butter sandwich and hot tea. She told herself she had succeeded, that Juan must be convinced that he'd won. But attacking her innocent daughter had been a mistake—a deadly mistake.

29

"Are you sure you're well enough to go to school?"

Sara nodded. "I have to, Mom. I have an exam on *Macbeth*." She gathered her hair into a ponytail and sighed. "Why couldn't Shakespeare have written in plain English? Without all that 'forsooth' and 'henceforth' business. I get a kick out of the witches though. They're cool. We had to memorize one of their scenes." She started to chant: *"Round about the caldron go. In the poisoned entrails throw. Toad that under cold stone..."*

"Terrific," Lee interrupted. "You'd better hurry. It's getting late. I called the school yesterday, so you shouldn't need a note."

Sara continued: *"Days and night has thirty-one; Sweltered venom sleeping got; Boil thou first in the charmed pot."*

"I hear Kevin honking outside. Wear your down jacket."

Sara gave her a quick kiss and started down the stairs, still chanting: *"Double, double toil and trouble; Fire burn and caldron bubble. Eye of newt and toe of frog..."*

"Goodbye! Good luck on the test." Lee hesitated, wanting to call

Sara back and hug her close, to tell her again how much she loved her. But she couldn't give in to fear, she had to let her daughter go.

"I love you, baby," she called out. "See you after school."

The front door closed, and Lee walked resolutely into the bathroom. She ran a brush through her hair and automatically applied a quick smear of lipstick. Then she stopped and stared at herself in the mirror. Grabbing a washcloth, she rubbed at her lips. No need for makeup this morning, she thought grimly. *This is no social call.*

She opened her closet door and collected what she needed, trying to block the thought of Mister's head, resting out of sight on the top shelf. Poor Mister was beyond her help. What mattered now were Sara and Nick. It was her fault that they were in danger, and she was the only one who could save them.

She dressed quickly in a pair of loose-fitting jeans, a flannel shirt and boots. When she opened her jewelry box to get her watch, she saw the amulet. Holding it for a moment, she wondered briefly about the role it might have played in her recovery. *Amulets are said to offer protection from harm. Could it have helped me?* She shook her head. *Well, I don't want any part of it, whether it has magical power or not. I want no reminders of Juan. He wants his family heirloom back. Fine, it can be buried with him!* She dropped the amulet into her shirt pocket and walked to her nightstand. Steeling herself, she reached inside and transferred the handgun to her purse.

Cold determination to protect her family blocked all other feelings, as Lee drove along the now-familiar road to Cavado. It was hard to imagine actually using the gun. But one thing was certain: Juan had to be stopped. He isn't going to hurt Sara or Nick again, she vowed, not while I have life in my body! A few short weeks ago, she wouldn't have believed that something like this could happen in her world. But she had been drawn into another world—a world of passion and danger—the first time she had looked into Juan Mascareñas' eyes.

Lee rounded a curve and saw the gas station ahead. The accident must have occurred right about there, she realized, looking across the narrow road at the rough terrain beyond. She imagined her car sliding off the road and rolling over and over, through piñon trees and over the rocks. *It's really a miracle that I wasn't...* She didn't let herself finish the thought.

Too soon, she was in front of Juan's shuttered adobe. Not allowing herself to hesitate, she got out of the car and marched up the dirt path, her purse, with the gun in it, slung over her shoulder.

The door opened before she could knock, and Juan materialized from the darkness within.

"So," he said. "The time has finally come." His eyes held no mercy as they locked onto hers.

Terror gripped her and Lee knew, too late, that she was the one who'd made the mistake. She had no defense against the sheer force of his personality and powerful will. As she turned to run, he seized her arm and pulled her inside.

A strong odor burned her eyes. Before she could react, Juan held a small smoking bundle of what smelled and looked like dried feces mixed with small leaves beneath her nose. She coughed and tried to pull away, but he held her in place. Smoke filled her lungs, choking her. Her eyes closed as the room began to spin. She felt her knees buckle and heard her purse hit the floor.

"No!" she screamed, the sound echoing in her head as everything went black.

At first she thought that she was dreaming again. The cave, lit by the soft glow of candles, had a surrealistic quality about it, which was somehow familiar. She was lying on soft fur, naked from the waist up. She lifted her left arm, and became aware of the weight of the cast as she touched soft suede covering her hips. Instantly she was wide awake, and the cave resolved itself into a room. Juan's sinister room. And she was lying on the buffalo rug, dressed only in the bottom half of the ceremonial outfit she'd worn before. She tried to sit up, gasping as pain shot through the left side of her ribcage. She fell back, dizzy and nauseated.

"Lie still." Juan's voice seemed to come from nowhere, startling her. "The sickness will soon pass." She raised her head and saw him sitting in a dark corner, his face hidden in shadows as he watched her. He appeared to be naked, except for the glint of silver around his neck.

"Thank you for returning my amulet," he said in a low voice. "It fell from your shirt pocket when I undressed you."

"What did you do to me?" Her voice sounded hoarse, and it hurt her throat to talk.

"I did what was necessary. To prepare you." When he stood and walked toward her she saw that he was wearing the loincloth he'd worn in the Awakening Ceremony. He dropped to one knee, looking down at her. Lee gasped when she saw that his face was painted with white streaks, in a distantly familiar zigzag pattern.

"It is time for the Final Ceremony," he said. "It is time for us to go through the Spirit Door together."

Lee screamed. Before she could make another sound, Juan's hand clamped over her mouth and nose, cutting off her cry and her breath.

"No more of that," he said. "Do you understand?"

She nodded, frantic for air. He removed his hand.

"Now it begins. Our journey into the Spirit World. There you will find your true identity. You will regain your lost Powers."

He stood and picked up his black gourd rattle from a nearby table. Shaking it, he moved counterclockwise around her. Lee tried to think, even as something deep within her knew the answer. Once through the "Spirit Door" with Juan, she wouldn't be coming back. At least not as she knew herself—as Lee Lindsay, Sara's mother and Nick's wife. She would be changed. Rejoined with the medicine woman Juan was determined to possess.

"The sacred circle is cast," he said, standing over her and stretching his arms toward the ceiling. "The space between the worlds has been created."

Overwhelmed by fear and the lingering smell of nauseating smoke, Lee fainted.

When she came to, she was lying on her side and Juan was kneeling beside her, fastening a necklace around her neck. It was a leather cord threaded through a small wooden bird-like figure, dressed in red and covered with tiny black feathers. The piece he had showed her that first day.

"*Ye-Na-Lo-He*," Juan whispered. "Guardian of Those Who Fly. Remember, I promised that she would accompany you into the Spirit World. Now, sit up!"

"No! You can't!"

"I know you're afraid." His voice was suddenly gentle. "That's why you must do it, *querida*. To regain your courage. There was a time when you knew no fear." His eyes shone with a distant memory. "You were a woman of strong medicine who feared no one, not even me, when…" He broke off, an expression of anguish on his face.

"Juan," she pleaded, "this is crazy. I know you believe I was someone else. But even if I was, I'm not now. I don't want to be that person. I want to be me. I want to live the life I have now." Tears ran down her cheeks. "Please, just let me go."

"Enough! No more talk."

She could see his anger. This wasn't going as he'd intended.

He held a bowl of hot liquid to her lips. "Drink!"

She turned her head to one side. "No! I won't! I won't!

He grabbed her hair and yanked her head back. Then he held the bowl to her mouth again.

"You will drink it," he hissed next to her ear. "Or I will pour it down your throat."

Lee choked down a small swallow. It was bitter with an almost sweet aftertaste, unlike anything she had ever tasted before.

"Drink it all." He gave her hair another blindingly painful yank.

When the bowl was empty, Juan released her hair.

"It pains me to hurt you," he said like a scolding parent. "But you leave me no choice."

"Is this what you did to Susan Miller? Did it 'pain you' to hurt her, too?"

A strange expression—part shock, part outrage—distorted Juan's face.

"What did you say?" He gripped her shoulders. "What do you know of that? Of Susan?"

"You took her to Mexico." Lee fought a wave of dizziness. "She…she never came back."

"It was a long time ago. I was young. My deep memories were still hazy, although I had seen you clearly in a vision—your blond hair and blue eyes—when you, as a young girl, first started having dream-memories of us. When I saw Susan, I mistook her for you. But I soon realized my mistake." He gazed past her, his eyes narrowed to slits.

"She had only wanted to use me, to research my people and their ways." He paused and his expression turned vicious. The next words sounded rehearsed. "We were in Hermosillo when she left our room one night. I found her later in a bar, dancing with another man, some *gringo*. I left her there. And I never saw her again."

Suddenly, he refocused on Lee.

"*Basta, ya no mas.* Enough about that. It is of no importance. Now, the time has come. Lie back down on the sacred buffalo. Don't be afraid. Trust me. I will be with you on the journey. But first we must purify ourselves with the sweating oil."

Lee closed her eyes as the room seemed to tilt. When she opened them again her vision was still blurry. A familiar sickening smell interrupted her fragmented thoughts. Then she felt him rub the sweating oil across her breasts and midriff and she flinched as he passed over her ribs, still sore from the accident. His hand moved up under her skirt and down her legs. She closed her eyes helplessly when he began to chant.

He held her tightly while they both sweated beneath a heavy blanket. Lee had snatches of dreams of a shadowy female figure with the face of a bird. She tried to force herself awake, to organize her mind. *Crazy. He's crazy....* Her thoughts trailed off and she drifted, carried by the soothing rhythm of Juan's chanting.

"Drink the Water of Remembrance," he said, propping her head up and putting another bowl to her lips.

Lee was so thirsty she drank it all before his words registered. Her queasy stomach forced her to lie back down.

Juan sat cross-legged beside her prone body. Beating on a small drum, he began singing repetitive lyrics. The sounds ricocheted through Lee's head, evoking emotions too complex for her to identify.

For a while, nothing happened. She strained to stay alert, to keep an eye on Juan, but something was wrong with her eyes. Everything was growing darker. She heard a ringing in her ears and felt a soft sensation of upward movement. Then she was floating, drifting through darkness into lighter swirling mists.

She raised herself into an upright position and found that she could walk. Not walk, exactly, but move as she wished, trailing a thin shining cord. She understood that the cord was connected to her body, which was still lying on the buffalo rug. *This is what I did as a child, I floated out of my body. But I never went this far.*

Lee stopped, realizing that she wasn't alone. Other shapes moved through the mists, hovering near her. *I know this place, I've been here before. After my accident. And he was here with me. Juan. No, not Juan. His name was...*

Then he was beside her, as he had been for so long in her dreams. His black hair hung down his chest and over his shoulders, and the medicine mark of the scarlet spider clung to his cheek. Recognition came to her in a rush.

"Kamulko." Her voice was a dry whisper. "Shape Changer."

He smiled. "My Tarena, She Who Talks To Animals."

At that moment a terrible memory burst into her mind—Kamulko's furious expression as he faced her on the edge of a high rocky precipice, and the horror of realizing what he planned to do.

"You killed me," she blurted. "You pushed me from the top of Sacred Mesa!"

"No, Tarena. It was an accident. You lost your balance and fell, don't you remember? I moved fast, but was unable to save you."

"Liar!"

"My grief was unbearable," he continued, as though she hadn't spoken. "I followed you into the Spirit World shortly after your passing. Ah, but none of that matters now. We are together again. At last. In new bodies. The sacred vows cannot be broken."

"You broke your vows when you perverted the Power, when you abandoned all that you had taught me about how it should be used. You used your magic against your own people. You betrayed us. And when I tried to stop you..."

"You pushed against me and slipped. Your crippled foot could not sustain you. I would never have harmed you."

"You cannot deceive me, Kamulko. I had become too great a threat for you. You had taught me too well and my Power was too strong. You could not allow me to live."

"No, no! It broke my heart to lose you...."

"You lost me long before I fell to my death. But you refused to accept it. It was not what you had planned. You always had to have your way, taking what you wanted, whatever the cost to others. You misused your gifts. And you continue to misuse them in this life. You work black magic against my family. I am Lee now."

"You are also Tarena, High Medicine Woman. She Who Talks to Animals."

His words released another flood of long-forgotten memories and emotions. She heard the voices and saw the faces of those she had loved in another lifetime. Those she had tried to protect from Kamulko's ruthlessness.

Something shifted and welled within her. Her two selves merged. Although she was still Lee, part of her was once again the medicine woman called Tarena. A woman of tremendous Power. The veil between lifetimes lifted and she saw her situation with stunning clarity. History was repeating itself. Once again, she must do battle with her ancient lover and enemy. She must fight for her identity in this present lifetime, and—even more important— she must fight for the lives of Sara and Nick. Kamulko meant to destroy them and reclaim her, body and soul. She must get back— return to Lee's body! He had seriously underestimated her. And this time, she would prevail!

As soon as she had willed it, she felt herself being sucked back through the mists and the darkness. Down...down...then a sensation of impact and heaviness. She was lying on the dark fur, shivering. Her body felt cold and weak. Juan was beside her, slumped over the drum with his eyes closed. In his open hand lay the small black figure of a raven.

A dizzying pain clutched at her head, but Lee forced her reluctant body into an upright position. There was no time to lose. Juan might return to his body at any time. She had to find her purse— and the gun.

Crawling to the sofa where her clothes lay in a pile, she dug through them frantically until her fingers touched the smooth leather of her purse. The gun was still there.

With a wary glance at Juan's motionless body, Lee got to her feet. The room tilted and whirled. Lee took a deep breath, fighting for equilibrium. Out of the corner of her eye, she saw Sara's scarf on top of a nearby table, coiled like a red woolen snake around a canine skull. She staggered forward and snatched it, knocking the skull to the floor. It rolled toward the center of the room, toward Juan.

He jerked violently and opened his eyes. Surprise flashed across his face when he saw her holding the pistol. He laughed.

"A gun? You brought a gun? You surprise me, Lee. There is more of Tarena in you than I suspected." He sat up and looked at her with an amused expression. "When will you learn, my love? You're no match for me. You never were."

"Don't be too sure of that. And don't call me your 'love.' You never loved me—in this life or any other. You have no idea what the word means."

"Ah, Tarena, you are lecturing me again. After all this time." He wiped at the white streaks on his cheeks, smearing them. Then he held out his hand. "Give me the gun."

She shook her head, steadied the gun with both hands, and pointed it at him. "No way in hell."

"What do you think you're going to do? Shoot me? I don't think so."

"You won't hurt my daughter again. Or my husband. I won't let you destroy my family."

His face twisted with an old bitterness.

"Your family?" he sneered. "I don't want to hear any more about your precious 'family.' You belong with me! Were your eyes not opened on our journey?"

"My eyes were opened, all right. I saw you for what you really are, the ruthless *brujo* that you've always been."

"Give me the gun." He held out his hand. *¡Damelo!* I said give it to me!" His eyes blazed with fury as he sprang to his feet and lunged toward her.

Lee jerked to one side, her scream lost in the sharp crack of the pistol discharging.

He was thrown backward, staggering. Lee saw a bright red bubble of blood burst from a small hole in the center of his chest just below the silver amulet. He covered it with his hand.

"No," he said in a shocked voice. "You can't have done this." His eyes fastened on hers with an expression of utter disbelief.

When he let out a roar and lunged toward her, she shot him again.

His expression turned to one of great sorrow. "Tarena," he whispered. "Tarena," he whispered. "My Tarena." Then he crumpled, face down on the buffalo hide.

Lee sank to the floor, the gun in her hand. She had no idea how long she sat there before she heard Tarena's voice in her head issuing orders.

"Go! Run from this place! Now!"

Scrambling to her feet, she dropped the pistol back into her purse. She shoved her bare feet into her boots, pulled on her coat, grabbed her clothes and Sara's scarf, and started toward the door.

Wait! Nick's sweater! I shouldn't leave it here. She whirled and ran into the small room containing the portable toilet.

The sweater was there, splattered with a dark, dried substance and nailed outstretched to the wall. A part of her mind noted that it was a north-facing wall. *"North,"* Tarena's voice whispered, *"the direction of winter. The direction of death."*

Lee ripped the sweater off the wall and ran from the room. She averted her eyes from Juan's body as she headed for the front door, but not before she saw a pool of blood, seeping into the dark fur and spreading slowly across the wooden floor.

30

Lee clutched the steering wheel and raced along the narrow, twisting road. All that mattered was getting back to Santa Fe. Home to Sara and sanity. After what seemed like an eternity, she was finally in her own driveway. She parked the car in the garage and stumbled into the house.

Not until she removed her coat and saw that she was still wearing only the leather ceremonial skirt, did the terrible reality of what had happened hit her. She recoiled at her reflection in the bathroom mirror—oily, disheveled hair, wide staring eyes in a shockingly pale face. And around her neck, hanging between her naked breasts, was the feathered fetish. She yanked it off and worked furiously to untie the knot in the leather cords that held the skirt around her waist. When it fell to the floor, she sank to her knees on the bathroom floor and let the tears come.

Lee's hysterical sobs were soon replaced by feelings of panic. *I killed Juan. My God, I could go to prison!* A band tightened across

Lee's chest at the realization of what that would do to Sara and to Nick. She scrambled to her feet, fighting for breath.

I can't deal with this, she thought. *You can and you will!* said Tarena's voice, echoing in her mind. *Burn them! Burn the skirt and fetish—destroy anything that carries his evil energy!*

Suddenly Lee felt calmer, as if something or someone was lending her strength. She gathered up the leather garment and necklace and went downstairs. She got lighter fluid from under the sink and went out onto the patio, where a small fire pit lay in the center of a sunken seating area. She tossed a few pieces of kindling into the pit, before throwing the leather and necklace on top. Then she doused them with the lighter fluid, lit a match, and threw it in. She stood back, as the small pile burst into flame.

Cleansing fire, she thought, and then wondered where those words had come from. She tossed a little more kindling on top and replaced the screen cover before going back into the house.

Lee went upstairs and into her bathroom where she swallowed half a Valium. Then, for good measure, she gulped down the other half before taking a long hot shower. This time she used the healing golden light exercise Socorro had taught her.

By the time Sara got home from school several hours later, Lee was in bed and under chemical control. The draperies were closed and a cloth lay across her swollen eyes.

"Mom? What's wrong?"

"I guess I caught your bug. Don't turn on the light, honey. I have a terrible headache. How are you feeling?"

"Fine. I feel great, completely well. But now you've got it. Bummer. You've sure been sick a lot lately. Can I get you anything?"

"No. I just need to lie here for a while. Are you sure you're feeling okay?"

"Yeah. I had this really killer headache until third period. Then—it was weird—all of a sudden, right in the middle of the English exam, the headache just disappeared and I felt fine." She hesitated. "I think I screwed up the last question on the test, though. We had to discuss the use of imagery in *Macbeth*. We were supposed to list three main images—blood, water, and darkness. But the only one I could remember was blood—"

"Sara," Lee said, cutting her off. "Don't worry about it. You're well again. That's all that matters." She paused, fighting to steady her voice. "That's absolutely all that matters."

Lee forced herself to watch the early local news on television that night. But there was no mention of Juan's death. They haven't found him yet, she told herself, pacing back and forth in her bedroom. The tranquilizer had worn off and panic was starting to rise again.

What should I do? Who can help me? If I tell Dr. Mallory what happened, he'll insist that I turn myself over to the police. Then there would be an investigation. A trial! I can't let that happen. I have to keep my wits about me until I can decide what to do.

She swallowed another pill.

In bed, two hours later, Lee was still wide awake. She spent most of the night tossing and turning, reliving those hideous hours in Cavado. *I really did it. I killed Juan. But if I hadn't, would he have ever let me go?* Alone in the darkness, Lee knew the answer. *Not a chance.*

She woke suddenly. It was still early and the house was quiet. The horror of the previous day rushed at her. With great effort, Lee changed her focus. There was something she had to do, something that couldn't wait any longer. She pushed herself out of bed, opened the closet door, reached behind her purse, and felt the plastic bag.

Stifling a sob, Lee wrapped Mister's head in her favorite silk scarf. Then she emptied a shoebox, lined it with a white hand towel and placed the precious bundle inside. As an afterthought, she added Mister's collar and his catnip-filled cloth mouse, which had been hidden out of sight in her dresser drawer. She dressed hurriedly in heavy sweats and tennis shoes. A peek into Sara's darkened room satisfied Lee that her daughter was still asleep.

She crept down the stairs and disarmed the alarm system. Carrying the small makeshift coffin and a shovel, she climbed the hill behind her house. It took longer than she'd anticipated to dig a hole in the frozen ground. When it was deep enough, Lee knelt and gently lowered the shoebox into it.

"Goodbye, little buddy," she whispered, her voice choked with tears. "I'm sorry, so terribly sorry that you had to pay for my weakness. Both you and Socorro. But the *brujo* didn't get away with it, Mister. And he'll never hurt anyone again."

Using her hands, Lee gently filled the hole with dirt. She placed three large rocks over the slight mound, the only marker she dared to leave. Neither Sara nor Nick must ever know about the little grave—or its heart-breaking contents. That would raise too many questions, questions she could never answer. Weak with grief and exhaustion, Lee made her way back to the house.

There was nothing about Juan in the morning's paper. Nor on the Saturday night local news. Waiting for Nick to get home, Lee felt physically sick with apprehension. Why hadn't Juan's death been reported? He was, after all, a well-known person around Cavado. On the other hand, an unexplained shooting in a remote mountain village might not make the Santa Fe paper. Cavado probably didn't see a policeman for weeks at a time. And it was common knowledge that the residents of those little mountain villages took care of their own problems, avoiding the police whenever possible. But if the local *curandero* was found murdered, especially if he owned most of the town, surely the authorities would be notified. It would probably be in tomorrow's paper.

She went into the bathroom, intending to take another Valium. Nick mustn't see her in this condition. But as she opened the medicine cabinet, an inner voice told her to stop. *No more pills.*

Lee closed the cabinet door. Glancing into the mirror, she almost screamed. Staring back at her was a dark-skinned woman's face, her strong features framed by long, straight black hair. An instant later, the image faded and was gone. Lee stepped closer to the mirror, raising a hand to her pale cheek. I must be seeing things, she thought, her heart pounding in her chest. *Probably the pills. Or lack of sleep.*

But deep inside, Lee knew better. As she stood there, time seemed somehow to be suspended and she became aware of a profound shift in her consciousness. Hallucination or not, the image of Tarena had given her an unexpected surge of strength.

I can get through this without pills, she realized. *I must. What did Socorro say about drugs separating us from our inner knowing? She was right. I have to remember that. I have to stay connected to myself—whoever that really is.*

Lee forced herself to do some yoga exercises, while concentrating on deep breathing. After a few minutes she felt much calmer. No one can connect me to Juan's death, she thought, standing at the sink. She ran cold water and splashed it on her face. *No one even knows that I saw him yesterday.*

Unless...unless the guys at the gas station saw me drive by! Her stomach knotted at the thought until she realized they wouldn't recognize her new car. *Only Dr. Mallory and Nick know I had a connection to Juan. And neither of them would ever believe I could be capable of shooting him.* Suddenly, she thought of Socorro's uncle, the deputy sheriff. *If Juan's body was found, he would certainly remember my call and all my questions about the Mascareñases.*

After a few breaths, Lee told herself Tafoya only knew she'd had a little run-in with Juan. Hardly a motive for murder. And the deputy might be more inclined to call her, just to let her know Juan was dead.

Several more deep breaths helped to assure her that she was safe. Sara and Nick were safe, too. Her family was still together. Lee closed her eyes and buried her face in her hands. Then, after a moment, she lifted her head and squared her shoulders. *I did what I had to do, under the circumstances. Now I'll have to learn to live with it.*

She brushed her hair back. Nick would be home soon. She frowned at her reflection in the mirror and opened her makeup drawer, wishing that the circles under her eyes were all she had to conceal.

"I'm back!" Nick came up the stairs, lugging his suitcase. Lee flew into his arms.

"Let me put this down," he said, laughing. Then he gave her a long kiss. "Boy, am I glad to be home."

"I'm glad to have you home." She kissed him again.

"If I'd known I was going to get such a great reception, I'd have hopped an earlier flight."

"How was it?"

"Not bad. No crying babies this time, believe it or not. I had my laptop computer with me and actually got some work done."

"Do I hear Dad?" Sara came out of her room and down the hall to give Nick a hug. "Well, did you find us a neat apartment?"

"I sure did. Better than neat. Large rooms and a great view of the Potomac River. Plus, it's in a very good school district. Come on," he said, with an arm around both Lee and Sara. "Let's go downstairs. I'll fix myself a drink and tell you all about it."

That night in bed, Lee put her arms around Nick. Pleading the effects of a twenty-four-hour virus, she resisted his sexual advance.

"I just want to be held," she said.

"Happy to oblige," Nick said, holding her close. Within moments, Lee was fast asleep.

Socorro's face, serene and smiling, looked even more beautiful than Lee remembered. Her voice was gentle and comforting.

"Be at peace, Lee," she said. "All is exactly as it should be."

"Socorro! Is it really you? I thought you were dead."

"My earth walk has ended," Socorro replied. "But let that be no cause for grief. Death is only an illusion, a transition. Trees do not grieve that they must drop their leaves and rest through the winter. They know that spring will soon return and with it another season in which to grow. So it is for all of us."

"He killed you, didn't he? Juan killed you. And he was going to kill Sara and Nick. I had to stop him, Socorro. I had to shoot him. He was a spirit-sucker and you tried to warn me...." She broke off, sobbing.

Socorro nodded. "Don't you see, Lee? It is all part of the dance."

"What dance? I don't understand."

"The dance between you and Juan began long, long ago. It has played out in different ways, many different times. All earthwalks are a circle. It is all a learning."

"But how do I live with what happened, with what I've done?"

"I will help you. Close your eyes."

Lee heard the sound of drumming. Then Socorro was singing in her sweet, soft voice. At first the words sounded strange, although the melody was familiar. As Socorro sang, the sounds washed through Lee like warm, soothing water.

"Your spirit knows the song," Socorro whispered. *"Let it come back to you. Rise above your pain and sing your healing with me."*

Lee began to sing, hesitantly at first, stumbling over the words. Gradually, her voice grew stronger and her tongue slipped easily around the strange sounds. For what seemed like hours, she sang with Socorro, their voices blending together in a song as old as time. Lee felt her grief begin to release, and to be replaced with a feeling of great peace and love.

The drumming died away. *"I must leave you now,"* Socorro said.

"No. Please, don't go. I need you...."

"My work here is finished. Yours is not. You still have much to learn. And much to teach. My arms are always around you, my sister."

Lee felt the touch of a warm hand on her forehead. She watched as Socorro's face faded into a soft, golden light. Slowly, the light disappeared.

Lee opened her eyes. Her cheeks were wet with tears. "Socorro," she whispered.

Nick rolled over to face her. "You okay, babe?"

"Yes. I'm fine."

"You were making a humming sound in your sleep. Having another dream?"

"No," Lee said, smiling in the darkness. "I don't believe that was a dream."

31

"Lee? Hi, it's Jim Mallory."

"Dr. Mallory. Just a moment." Lee put her hand over the telephone receiver. "Thanks, Julie. Just leave those articles on my desk. I'll get to them sometime this morning." She waited until Julie left her office and then closed the door.

She sat back down at her desk. "Hi," she said, hoping she didn't sound as guarded as she felt.

"I had a few minutes between appointments and thought I'd check up on you. I see you're well enough to be hard at work."

"This is my first week back. It's been quite an adjustment after being out of the office for so long."

"I'll bet. How's it going?"

"Very busy. I have a lot of loose ends to tie up before we leave for Washington.

"When's that?"

"In two weeks."

"That soon? You really must be busy. Well, you're obviously on the mend physically. How are you doing otherwise?"

She hesitated for just a moment. *It would be such a relief to go into Mallory's office and tell him everything, to share the horror of that last trip to Cavado. But...*

"I have my ups and downs," she said. "But I'm doing pretty well, all things considered."

"Is Juan giving you any trouble?"

"No," she answered truthfully. "I haven't heard from him in some time."

"That surprises me. But I'm very glad to hear it. Well, if I don't see you before you go, have a great year in Washington. I think the change will be good for you."

"I'm counting on that. Thank you for calling. And for all the support you've given me," she said sincerely.

"You bet. Be good to yourself, Lee. It's time to put all of this behind you."

"That's what I'm trying to do. I really am."

As Lee hung up, she closed her eyes, fighting for composure. Hearing Mallory's voice cracked the fragile wall of control she had managed to erect during the past three weeks. *Put it all behind me? Will I ever be able to do that?"*

There were so many unanswered questions. She still waited and watched for some word about Juan in the newspaper or on television. But there had been nothing. Not a single word. Sometimes she found herself wondering if it had really happened. She had certainly been drugged, both by that terrible smoke and by whatever he'd forced her to drink. *Could it be that the entire ceremony—my journey to the spirit world, my fusion with Tarena—and even the shooting had just been a drug and hypnotically-induced hallucination?*

As much as Lee wanted to believe that, she couldn't. Nick's sweater and Sara's scarf had provided tangible evidence of her last moments in Cavado. They had remained hidden in the back of her closet for almost a week until a strong impulse made her burn them, just as she had the bird fetish necklace and ceremonial skirt, in the patio fire pit. Immediately after she scattered the ashes behind the house, a wind had come up and blown them away.

I can't afford to kid myself, Lee thought. *The unbelievable did happen in Cavado. Several times.*

But why didn't Juan's death make the news? Could it be that I only wounded him? He was wearing his amulet when I shot him. Maybe the healing crystals.... Is it possible? Is he recovering in Cavado and plotting some diabolical revenge? I have to know!

Before she could stop herself, Lee picked up the phone and dialed Juan's number. As the phone rang, she held her breath, half expecting to hear his voice. She let it ring for almost a full minute. No answer. Trembling, she replaced the receiver.

Of course he's not there. I killed him. I shot him in the chest. Twice. Dear God, there was so much blood. Suddenly, sick to her stomach, she bolted out of her office and down the short hall to the bathroom. She locked the door and turned on the water in the sink to cover the sound of her vomiting.

Afterward, she splashed water on her face, and smoothed her hair back from her forehead. As she looked into the mirror above the small sink, Lee remembered the image she had seen in her bathroom mirror, the night after the shooting. *An image of Tarena.* The memory soothed her and gave her strength.

I need to guard my light, she thought, returning to the privacy of her office. Sitting at her desk, she closed her eyes and envisioned her spirit body, as Socorro had taught her to do. She soon found herself humming a strange, soothing tune.

For just an instant, she could have sworn she heard Socorro's voice, singing along.

32

"Grab your parasol, Scarlett darlin'," Nick said as he rinsed his coffee cup in the kitchen sink. "The wagons are loaded and ready to roll."

Lee managed to return his smile as he headed for the garage. The time had come. A truck carrying the items they would need during their stay in Washington had just left. They were going to follow in the two family cars.

She hoped the renters would take good care of everything. They had impressed her as a trustworthy young couple, eager to lease the furnished home while they were designing and building their own dream house.

Walking into the family room, Lee was torn by conflicting emotions. It was hard to leave the magazine she had spent so many years establishing, even though it was in good hands. She planned to stay in close touch with Annabel and be involved in any major decisions. Still, she knew she would miss the daily interaction, the frustrations, and the excitement. Just as she would miss the beauty and special charm of Santa Fe. But she was ready to go.

"Mom, I can't possibly live for a whole year without my posters," Sara said, bursting into the room. "Can I put them in the back of your car?"

"Sure. Oh, and don't forget your hairdryer. I saw it on the counter in your bathroom."

"Oh, geez—Kevin's picture! I almost forgot Kevin's picture!" Sara ran back up the stairs.

Lee smiled. *Kevin will soon be out of sight and out of mind.* She put on her jacket and took a final walk through the house and out onto the master bedroom balcony. The sun had risen just above the mountains, warming the early morning sky to a delicate salmon hue. It promised to be a beautiful day. She leaned against the west-facing wall, trying to memorize the snow-spotted landscape that stretched to the Old Taos Highway. Her eyes lingered on the hills and shadowed arroyos where Mister used to hunt and play. She bid him a silent goodbye, feeling sure that his spirit still happily roamed the area.

Her thoughts turned to the medicine rocks that Socorro had placed around the house. It would be a comfort knowing that they were here, guarding the property while she was gone.

Just then, a lizard with a ragged stump where its tail used to be darted up the wall, close to Lee. She observed the tiny reptile, damaged but undefeated, carrying on in spite of its injuries. *A courageous spirit.* I'll remember the lesson, Socorro, she silently pledged. I'll remember everything you taught me.

"We'd better get going," Nick said, walking up behind her. "It's almost seven o'clock. We really lucked out with this good weather. Let's hope it holds." He put his arms around her. "You doing okay?"

She nodded. "I'm just saying my private goodbyes. Did you leave instructions for the renters about the alarm system?"

"Everything's taken care of. Sara's already in my car. I told her she can drive to Albuquerque. Then when we head east on I-40, she can ride with you, if you want company. Now that she has her learner's permit, she needs to get in some practice on the road."

"I agree," she said. "But I'd rather you drove through town. Let her practice on that nice straight stretch to Albuquerque."

"Okay, babe. Let's get started. We have a long day's drive ahead of us." He took her hand. "Take it easy on your wrist. You just got the cast off last week."

"It's feeling stronger all the time. I'll manage fine."

"We'll meet you in Albuquerque for breakfast." They walked through the bedroom and down the stairs. "How about the Marriott? It has a nice coffee shop and it's right next to the freeway."

"Fine. I'll meet you two there." Lee walked out the front door, and turned to watch Nick lock it behind them. She got into her car and waved to Nick and Sara as they pulled out of the driveway. Then, after a long last look at the house, she fastened her seatbelt and drove down the dirt road into town.

Lee turned off the radio, wanting to be alone with her thoughts as she drove south. Soon she was out of the city limits and Santa Fe was receding into the distance through the rearview mirror. As she neared the top of the long slope of La Bajada Hill, Lee impulsively pulled over to the side of the road. She turned off the ignition and got out of the car, walking around the rocky shoulder of the highway.

She stood motionless, captivated by the panoramic view. Squinting against the early morning brightness, she scanned the Sangre de Cristo mountain range that stretched far into the distance. Santa Fe shimmered below, nestled in the foothills and bathed in cool pure light.

I'll be back, she pledged. *Santa Fe will always be home to my heart.*

Her eyes were drawn farther north, to where Cavado lay hidden. An image leapt, unwelcome, into her mind. She saw Juan's face bending toward her, his dark eyes smoldering with passion. Then it was replaced by another, even more vivid image—Juan lying motionless on a bloody buffalo hide. She shut her eyes tightly, forcing the memories away.

When she opened them moments later, Lee saw an enormous raven circling above her. She watched it glide gracefully through the air, sleek black wings parallel to the ground. In the next instant, the bird turned and landed on a branch of a piñon tree not ten feet away. Stretching on its perch, it screeched—a hoarse, croaking "Kraaak!"— and beat the air furiously with powerful wings.

The hair rose on the back of Lee's neck as her rationality was invaded by something far older, a mindless primordial terror.

"Juan?" she whispered. "Is that you?"

The raven fixed her with a fierce, unblinking gaze.

"No, it can't be! This is crazy. You're just a bird. Juan's dead!"

Suddenly she heard Socorro's voice warning. "Never underestimate a spirit-sucker, Lee. They don't die easily."

At that moment, Lee's reality seemed to shift. The thought of her brave, dead friend ignited an ancient anger. Fed by long-buried memories of injustice and betrayal, it blazed into a powerful rage that dissolved her fear.

"Keep your distance, Shape Changer," she heard herself warn in a strong voice that no longer sounded like her own. "Or I will use the Power against you. I will call on the Grandmothers to curse you, to trap you in that black shape."

The raven shrank back. It cawed once more—a terrible anguished sound—and flew into the air.

She watched the bird fly northward until it dwindled to an insignificant dot in the clear morning sky. For a long moment Lee stood there, her heart pounding. She felt confused, like a visitor in her own body. Finally, she made her way back to her car and locked herself inside.

Her thoughts were confused. *Oh, my God! What just*

happened? She turned the key in the ignition, shifted into forward and, after a quick backward glance, sped over the hill.

A few miles down the road, Lee began to feel more like herself—except better than she could remember ever feeling, centered deep within and lighter, as though a heavy darkness had finally lifted.

Of course it's possible that my imagination just ran wild back there, she told herself. *Maybe that was only a raven. A common raven.*

Lee found herself smiling, and then she laughed out loud. *But then again, maybe not. Maybe She who Talks to Animals just worked a little magic of her own.*

JANN ARRINGTON - WOLCOTT

ABOUT THIS BOOK

BRUJO was originally published internationally in 1998, and filmed as a TV movie titled, *Seduced by Evil.* This is a revised version of that book, re-titled *BRUJO: Eye of the Raven,* and the first in a proposed trilogy.

JANN ARRINGTON - WOLCOTT

ACKNOWLEDGMENTS

I am indebted to the following people who encouraged the original version of BRUJO, subtitled after the movie, Seduced by Evil.

First of all I must acknowledge Dr. Tom Loree and his wife, my cherished long-time friend, Bliss Kelly-Loree, both of whom believed in this story and edited, edited, edited.

Dr. Stephen Blumberg, treasured friend and eagle-eyed professor/proofreader, and his wife, Wendy Wolf Bloomberg, award-winning poet and one of the most loving, spiritual people I've ever met.

My wise, loyal, and beloved soul-sister, Arlena Markinson, for always giving me valuable advice and for helping me to understand, on a soul level, the stories that come through me.

Bobette Perrone, who has my love, admiration, and respect for the integrity of her approach to research, writing, and life. You are one of the great loves of my life, dear heart.

Jim Gautier, photographer/philosopher and trusted confidant.

Dan McBride, beyond-talented artist/singer/songwriter, who has long been my soul-brother.

David Salk, artist, mystic and ever-supportive teacher, in good times and the very worst.

Last, but never least, all my writing buddies who were part of the talented and supportive group, known as Writers at Elaines.

It's been quite a journey to revisit and revise this book—my first attempt at fiction two decades ago. I feel that age and experience have given my characters a new depth, and I am grateful for the opportunity to slide back into the story.

Kudos to my talented, beautiful and brave daughter, Janna Szalay Bunnell, for her careful and insightful editing. Thank you for sharing this amazing earthwalk with me, my darling.

Thank you to Barbara Bloomberg, a most literary, talented, and valued friend for her keen eye and support of my work.

Grande gratitude to Lucy Moore—author, environmental mediator, facilitator, scholar, editor *extraordinaire*, and bright light on this planet. *Muchas gracias y amor siempre, mi amiga!*

And hugs to Kimerick F. Hayner, my adored, multi-talented, life-long friend for his brilliant editing, encouragement and for never letting me down. Words are inadequate.

Special thanks goes to Annette Chaudet of Pronghorn Press, a world-class story editor and one of the most artistic people I know, for wanting to publish this revised version of Brujo, and for her right-on contributions, including the designing of this awesome cover. Once again, Annette, I am a Lucky Girl to be connected to you, on so many levels.

About the Author

Jann Arrington-Wolcott is a third-generation New Mexican, raised on a cattle ranch near the Mexican border. This background exposed her to the legends and traditions of New Mexico, which she put to excellent use in BRUJO, her first novel. She has published both fiction and nonfiction, in addition to more than 100 magazine articles. "I feel as though I've lived many different lifetimes in this one body," she says with a laugh.

"I've been a fashion model, professional actor, high school teacher, spiritual seeker and world traveler. I'd always wanted, however, to focus on writing. The desire continued to grow, and so on my fortieth birthday, I decided I'd better get going. I finally discovered what I wanted to be when I grew up, and I've never looked back.

"I've seen and experienced so much throughout my interesting and often challenging life. At the center of it all, however, has long been my roles as wife, mother, grandmother, and friend to some of the most amazing people on the planet."

Arrington-Wolcott lives in Santa Fe, NM, with her retired

physicist husband, John Wolcott, and her two angel doggies, Lola Bella and Frederico Mateo (also known as Rico the Tongue).

You can connect with Jann through her website at:
JannArringtonWolcott.com

She's also on Facebook and on Twitter @ JannAWolcott.

Watch for Jann's blogs and feel free to comment. She's always anxious to connect with her readers!

DISCUSSION QUESTIONS

1.   BRUJO, Eye of the Raven is the story of a successful but ordinary woman who finds herself in an extraordinary situation. Was her story believable to you? Did the plot draw you in?

2. Arguments are made for Lee's obsession with Juan having a metaphysical cause or for it being just the result of a mid-life crisis. Which do you believe and why?

3. Arrington-Wolcott describes Lee as a woman in transition. Discuss the various transitions you have passed through in your own life. Do you feel they strengthened you, and how?

4.   Did the author succeed in bringing the character of Lee to life?

5.   What about Juan? Did you believe he was on the level? Did you feel any sympathy for him?

6.   Socorro played an important role in the story, emphasizing the importance of friendship between women. How important have same-sex relationships been in your life?

7. Lee's love and fear for her family finally pushed her over the edge. What do you think you would have done in her place?

8.   Dr. Mallory plays "the voice of reason" in this story. Do you think he did a convincing job?

9.   Did you find Nick a believable character? Discuss his emotional growth throughout the story.

10.   The theme of this story is that we are stronger and more complex than we think we are. Do you agree?

BRUJO   EYE OF THE RAVEN

CPSIA information can be obtained
at www.ICGtesting.com
Printed in the USA
FSOW02n0258130915
10933FS